TORTURED JUSTICE

GUANTANAMO BAY

Richard Kammen

the Peppertree Press
www.peppertreepublishing.com

Dedication

This book is dedicated to the men and women of the Military Commissions Defense Organization and the men and women who have selflessly defended those who have been and are confined at Guantanamo Bay. They, more than most, have done what lawyers should do, stand up and speak out for those who cannot stand or cannot be heard.

In many cases these men and women sacrificed their careers and endured great personal and financial hardship. It is tragic that their achievements have gone largely unrecognized.

But those who know, know,

They did not let the bastards grind them down.

As Victoria Hancock walked out of the Guantanamo courtroom, I, for perhaps the thousandth time asked myself, Mendelson, *Why did you ever get involved in this mess?* And for the thousandth time I still had no good answer.

CHAPTER 1

Nearly two years earlier, I'd returned from court to my office on the thirtieth floor to find a voice message from Jennifer LaGrange of the ACLU. "Are you interested in working on a Guantanamo Bay case?" I was in such a hurry to return her call that I misdialed a couple of times.

When we connected, Jennifer said the ACLU was looking for a death penalty lawyer to lead a team in defense of Hussain Al-Yemeni, supposedly the mastermind of an al-Qaeda attack on a US airbase in Kuwait in which over sixty airmen and women were killed. Through a Military Commission, the government wanted to execute him after a military trial at Guantanamo Bay.

"We need you," Jennifer said with New York brusqueness. "You're used to traveling, working in new environments, and you win."

I am, I now recognize, a fool for flattery. Then, I did not recognize the real criteria they sought was an attorney so egotistical and ambitious that he would not appreciate the tar pit he was being offered. Egotistical and ambitious. That's me.

Jennifer also described the Military Commissions as "a goat rodeo," much like handling a death penalty case in Texas, Alabama and Mississippi combined.

"No law, no precedent," she said." Connor, this may be a no-win deal."

"I'm in." As I said, egotistical and ambitious. Also, perhaps dim.

Soon after my conversation with Jennifer, I met the team of military and civilian lawyers I would lead. The meeting took place in Crystal City, Virginia, across the Potomac and three Metro stops from the heart of Washington, D.C.

The setting was gray on gray, the twenty-foot conference table, the carpet, the painted walls. A large video screen dominated one end of the room. The only wall decoration was a poster of Aldrich Ames, warning against discussing classified material and threatening a life sentence. Four people, three military and one civilian, sat together at one end of the table. Another woman, with shiny skin like melted dark chocolate, wearing a Marine Corps uniform, sat a noticeable distance from the others.

One white man wore the dull green of the Army. A black woman wore the Navy's tan fall uniform and sat next to a white man in Air Force blue. The civilian wore a well-tailored blue suit. In contrast to the crisp uniforms, I'd, perhaps stupidly, decided that my uniform that day would be a red and blue checked, long-sleeved shirt, blue jeans, and running shoes.

It felt that there was some tension within the group. Everyone was stone-faced and not looking at each other. I thanked them all for rearranging their schedules and was beginning to go into the introduction I had prepared when the dark woman seated away from the others interrupted.

"Sir, may I speak freely?" I nodded.

"Some of us don't think we need you. I've read your resume, and okay, you've done a lot of death penalty cases, but we've been working on this for a while, and frankly, I don't think we need civilian help." Before I could respond, she continued on a monologue about how civilians just did not understand the military. In the end, from what she had heard, "civilians bailed when things get rough."

I interrupted her rant by holding up a hand, palm out, and with a smile that I hoped masked my anger at her assumptions, asked, "Excuse me, you are?"

"Major Fredricks, United States Marine Corps, Sir."

"Major Fredricks, I'm curious how many death penalty cases have you tried?"

"None, but we can do this. I don't think we need you. It's just a murder case. More serious penalty, but still, it is just a murder case."

The man in the blue tailored suit, a dark tan, muscular, maybe 5'10". Buzz cut. Said softly with a lilt that reminded me of time I spent vacationing in Mexico turned and looked at Fredricks.

"Major, you're wrong. Huge difference between a life sentence and the client getting killed. If you've seen an execution, you'd know that. "

I asked him his name.

"King Reyes, Sir. I'm an investigator." Reyes went on to tell the group how he had witnessed the execution of Freddy Young, a drug dealer who was a client of a lawyer he'd worked for. He described Young as "a good guy who grew up hard and drifted into drug trafficking and killed a couple of guys in a drug war." He told the group how the trial was in a small town: vindictive prosecutor, white jury.

"The trial was a joke. Appeal was worse. No one but his lawyers gave a shit."

Freddy had wanted Reyes to be there when they killed him. He looked at Fredricks.

"You just don't get it. You build a relationship with a client, and then they fucking kill him." His head went down. He rubbed his eyes.

There was no sound but Reyes' hard breathing. Everyone was looking at Reyes or looking down. Reyes looked up, looked at Fredricks, and said, gesturing at me, "I think we do need him,"

A slight woman with short black hair wearing the tan uniform of the Navy raised her hand.

"Sir, I'm LN1 Roseborough, a paralegal. I, maybe all of us, don't know much, anything really, about death penalty cases. Can you give us an overview?"

I nodded, thanked her, and, looking at Fredricks, began explaining how a death penalty case is not a murder case with a harsher penalty. It is a different kind of case. For example, in a murder case, if your client is convicted, you lose. But if the government seeks to kill your client, if the client gets anything other than a death sentence, you win. So the calculus is different.

I told them how the preparation is different and how there are two lines of investigation. The first is, can they prove the client committed the crime? In this case, was the client really the mastermind or even involved in the Kuwait attack? The second investigation is what is called the mitigation investigation. Mitigation is the explanation for his involvement, not an excuse, but rather an understanding of the client's life that explains why, to him at that time, attacking a US air base would make sense. But it is bigger than that because mitigation involves anything that can lead a juror to believe a sentence less than death is appropriate.

There was an interruption as a woman in a blue Air Force uniform poked her head in the door and said, "Mr. Mendelson, General Ward asked that you see him at your convenience."

"Thanks, Tell the General I'm meeting with the team, and I'll be along after I finish up here."

She looked at me with quizzical eyes and shook her head slightly. There was a brief pause then she smiled.

"I'll deliver that message."

Turning back to the team, I continued about death penalty cases.

"Where was I? Oh. Mitigation."

The paralegal, Roseborough, asked, "Would torture be mitigating? The CIA tortured our client."

"Yes. Exactly." I continued to explain how the concept of mitigation is very broad. Anything that would make one juror think that killing him was not necessary is mitigating.

"We'll be hiring a mitigation specialist to lead that investigation. One of the best, Jill Hanson, is willing to work on the case with us."

I continued to tell them how important it was for the lawyers to have credibility. Because if the client is convicted, the penalty phase begins shortly afterward before the same jury. So any guilt defense must be congruent with the theory of mitigation. I concluded, "So, in my mind, these cases are about the truth—the truth of the crime. The truth of the client and this, too, makes it harder. The truth of the pain felt by victims and survivors. The pain and anger of the victims are a big part of death penalty cases. Maybe the biggest part. And these cases take a lot longer."

I told them how the typical federal capital case takes three-four years. Also, these cases are stressful as hell for the lawyers, for everyone involved. Really hard.

"They can ruin relationships. Maybe ruined my marriage. I'm separated from my wife."

Fredricks's look suggested that she remained unconvinced that I should be part of the team.

But then the large, balding white man dressed in the green and black of the Army looked at Fredricks and then the others.

"I'm the senior officer, and I'm making the call."

He looked at me.

"I think we need him. So, Mr. Mendelson, you are now our death penalty expert. And Major Fredricks, you will," and will was emphasized, "Work with Mr. Mendelson. Understood." Not a question.

Fredricks just glared, and there was a slight nod of agreement.

I looked back at the balding Major. Major Jack Carter. I asked him to tell me about himself and his skills. He was from Oklahoma City and had been in the Army for fifteen years. JAG Corps. Twelve years. Because he'd had some conflicts with senior leaders, he was sure he was never getting promoted. He thought he was "an okay trial lawyer."

"Maj. Carter, were you in Oklahoma City when the bombing happened?"

He looked down.

"Yes."

"Friends killed?"

"Yes."

"Look, I'll just say this. These cases are not for everyone. If you." and here I looked at all of them, "If any of you feel at any time it hits too close or is screwing up your life, we can talk it out. Figure out what is best. Is that fair?"

"'Preciate it, Sir."

"Please. Stop the sir stuff."

Carter laughed.

"Probably not gonna happen, Sir."

As I turned, I heard, "Maj. Fredricks. Sir." Her voice was still hard. She explained this was her first defense assignment and her skill was working with evidence. In fact, that was all she'd done as a prosecutor.

"Okay, and how do you feel about defending a terrorist who supposedly killed a bunch of US military?"

"It's my job, sir. "

Something about her tone, her vibe, felt off. *Need to have a one-on-one with her. Something is wrong here.*

Fredricks then said the government was talking about a trial within eighteen months. I responded that that was unrealistic, given the logistics. Client thousands of miles away, the investigations mainly in other countries.

"That is another definition of fat chance. At least if there is any interest in it being fair."

Carter said, "They don't have much interest in being fair. At least, that is my opinion.

He paused.

"Are you sure you don't want to meet with the General?"

"No, I'm good. I want to finish here first."

The two paralegals explained their roles within the military structure. They focused on case organization and dealing with the military bureaucracy. Roseborough explained,

"For example, getting permission to travel and booking flights and hotels can take two or three days."

Collectively they had no experience in big document cases. When I said I'd heard there might be maybe two hundred, three hundred thousand pages of material, possibly more, Roseborough looked with wide eyes at the tall black man in a dark blue Air Force Uniform, their heads shaking back and forth. They seemed to be silently saying, "Holy shit."

I turned back to the group.

"What can you tell me about the case?"

Reyes explained that the team did not know much other than the newspaper accounts and the Air Force inquiry, where they tried to decide who was at fault for allowing the attack.

He explained that two trucks with explosives drove onto the base without being stopped by the guards. The trucks were painted to look like the trucks that routinely delivered supplies. One drove into the dining hall, the other the fuel dump. Carnage. Over sixty were killed.

"Lot's of wounded. The military is angry," Reyes said. "Wants revenge."

"What links al-Yemeni to this?"

They looked at each other, and Reyes said, "Who knows?"

Fredricks added that because no case had been filed, the defense had no information from the prosecution. That would come in a few months after the case was formally filed.

She explained that the Convening Authority, the bureaucrat who runs the legal proceedings, will have to review that and agree that the case should be prosecuted and it should be a death penalty case. That's a formality. We've been told that will happen in a few months.

"And the client? What's he like?"

Carter smiled.

"He's a piece of work."

He described how the team met with him for six hours a day for four days. And al-Yemeni had "maybe told us fifteen minutes of useful stuff." He described how al-Yemeni was volatile.

"His personality can change in seconds. He can be quite nice for a few minutes, and then boom, everything changes."

Reyes added that al-Yemeni would go into a rant about where they are holding him, how they transport him, what 'fucking animals the Americans are and how he could not trust American lawyers.'

I smiled.

"To sum up, we have a case where the client won't talk with us, and we have no information about the crime. It sounds like we have them where we want them. Easy peasy." That merited a couple of weak smiles.

"Now, what can you tell me about the Military Commissions?

Carter and Fredricks looked at each other, trying to figure out who would answer.

Carter spoke.

"Sir, do you know FUBAR?"

I shook my head, "No."

"Military phrase: Fucked Up Beyond All Recognition. And from what I can see, the Military Commissions are FUBAR."

Fredricks interrupted and continued telling me that, in her view, the Department of Defense took the worst parts of the federal court and court-martials and combined them into a system designed to screw the defendant. One example she gave was that the defense can't subpoena witnesses – we have to ask the prosecutor for his approval. And she went on about other ways the system was designed to hamper the defense. She concluded with, "Definitely FUBAR."

"So I have this question. How do you guys feel about working in this system? I know you're assigned here, but if you really wanted out, I'm sure you could get out. So why do this?"

Carter answered.

"This may sound corny. But, if I'm here, I want to do it right. If these guys have their way, this will be a show trial. That's not right."

I nodded.

"Hope you all feel that way. We'll just have to try to throw some wrenches into their plan. Here is my attitude. I can't promise we'll win. It sounds like a very uphill climb, but pardon my language, we're gonna make these fuckers know they are in a war. You guys okay with that?"

Some nods.

"Thanks for meeting with me. I'm looking forward to working with all of you. Major Fredricks, I hope you'll come to the view that I can help."

She looked at me but said nothing. And we all stood.

"I guess I ought to go see General Ward."

Carter smiled.

"Yes, I think you probably should. Please come see me after you meet. I'll be interested to hear how it went."

Outside Ward's office sitting at a dark, faux oak desk, was the same Air Force Sergeant who had summoned me. Young, pretty,dark blue uniform with lots of ribbons on her chest. Her black name tag identified her as "Lopez." On her desk were photographs of a child.

"Is this a convenient time?"

She looked up, appraisingly giving me a clear once over. Seemed to find me wanting. It could have been my informal clothes. It could have been my smug attitude.

She shrugged, "I'll check."

She knocked on the dark wood door with a black plaque telling the world that this was the office of Brig. Gen. Charles Ward, Chief Defense Counsel.

"Sir, lawyer Mendelson is here to see you."

I heard an exasperated, "Finally," then, "Send him in."

She nodded her head toward the door and said, "Please."

Ward's office was large. I estimated 30 feet by 30 feet. Dark blue carpet, white curtains, many plaques, and photographs on the walls. Mementos from prior assignments. Plaques given at departure from one unit or another. To Chuck Ward, Leader, Friend. That sort of thing. His career on the wall telling everyone who entered, I've been a military success. Behind him was memorabilia from the Indianapolis Colts. A framed Peyton Manning Jersey. A football with signatures and a Colts horseshoe.

Ward was seated behind a large desk that had surprisingly few papers on it. There were a couple of books—no family photos. His green Army uniform jacket was hung on a tall brass hat rack. His light green uniform shirt did not hide a middle age paunch.

I stood at the desk and stuck out my hand.

"Good morning, sir. I'm Connor Mendelson."

Ward did not stand and gave me the most perfunctory handshake I'd ever received. The air kiss of handshakes.

"You wanted to meet?"

"Yes." He looked at his watch. "Yes, some time ago."

I raised both hands slightly.

"I apologize. I can come back if this is not convenient now."

His hand slammed the desk.

"At this command, at your convenience, means now. It means at my convenience. If you arrive at 7:59 for an 8:00 meeting, you're ten minutes late. Am I clear?"

"Yes, sir," I said. *What a piece of work.*

"Mendelson, I want to be clear. If I had my way, we'd have the trial this year, but I understand that is not likely. But I want it as soon as possible. Do your job for sure, but no bullshit delays. That's how I see this." No response was sought.

I was still standing. He had not asked me to sit.

I said, "I hope you appreciate the reality that this is a death penalty case, which certainly will move slower than the typical case and much slower than the typical military case."

Ward looked at me with hard eyes.

"Mr. Mendelson, I don't know anything about the death penalty. And, frankly, I don't see why that should make a huge difference. If your client is a terrorist and killed a bunch of Americans, of course, he should get death. I don't see a problem with that. I can't see why you would care, either."

"But that is beside the point. The head of the Army JAG Corps has made it clear to me that SECDEF has made it clear to him that he wants a trial as soon as possible. The SECDEF is taking orders from the President. So even if I was sympathetic to your case, which I'm not, you are going to trial as soon as is realistically possible. I have my orders, so you have yours. There will be trials, and those trials will be in eighteen months or sooner. Am I clear?"

"Sir," I tried to inject an air of calm.

"That's just not the way it works."

I explained, "To be professionally competent, the defense has to do a thorough investigation into both guilt and innocence and mitigation. The team's job is to find out if he's guilty or innocent and find whatever mitigation exists. In this case, that will almost certainly include finding out the details of torture. It takes time to find evidence in any case, which will be especially true here, where a lot of it is in other countries. So it's just going to take time, probably a lot more time than you or the SECDEF or the President want. And I'm gonna need more resources."

Ward shook his head violently, jowls jiggling.

"You are not listening. This case is going to be on a fast track."

Have I made a mistake? A huge mistake? I told Ward that I would need a mitigation specialist; who might need an assistant; and at least one more trial lawyer, preferably an experienced civilian, someone else who has done murder or capital cases.

"Plus, I'm certain we'll need several expert witnesses."

Ward responded that I needed to get him estimates, and he would get us what we needed. Within reason.

"But do it quickly."

He continued.

"My mission, which I WILL fulfill, is to ensure this process works quickly."

Ward raised his voice to nearly a shout.

"No one in the command is going to undermine my mission. I did not become a general by failing, and I'm not going to start now. Am I clear, Mr. Mendelson?"

I shrugged. *I should just tell this guy to go fuck himself.*

"Within my ethical obligations, I'll do my best, sir."

He looked at me hard and stood.

"Good meeting you, Mendelson." No hand offered.

As I left, Sgt. Lopez said, "Have a nice day, sir."

I poked my head into Carter's office. Fredricks was sitting there. They looked up, their eyes twinkling.

"How'd that go?"

I laughed.

"So apparently, generals don't like to be kept waiting. Thanks for letting me know. "

Carter smiled back.

"We tried to tell you. We asked if you wanted to go see him." And he laughed. "You were on a roll. Plus, the bad part of me wanted you to see the real General Ward."

Fredricks said, "I'd have loved to hear what he was saying and doing while you kept him waiting. Just imagining his head exploding makes my day."

They both laughed.

"No one who knows anything about defending a capital case would focus on having this done in eighteen months. His attitude is so legally backward that it is ridiculous."

In a fake deep voice, Carter said, "Welcome to the war, son, welcome to the war."

CHAPTER 2

For three months, the FBI interviewed countless people who'd spent time with me during the past twenty years. They contacted every school I attended, reviewed my finances, and even called a couple of golf buddies to ask about my morals. Of course, my family and I were questioned too. All this to ensure that I was what they described as a loyal, impervious to blackmail American. The culmination was a Pentagon briefing conducted by a functionary who was more bored than I was. Basically, I was told that whatever our client told us, especially about any torture inflicted on him, was the equivalent of nuclear secrets.

I was assigned to a small office in the al-Yemeni section of the defense building. Ten by ten, with a cheap brown desk and credenza on the left side and a government-issued computer. Two vinyl visitor chairs complimented the black chair behind the desk. A gray steel bookcase rested on the back wall next to the door. To the desk's right was a gray two-drawer safe with a large black combination dial to store classified documents. At this juncture, I had no classified documents and had not been trusted with the combination.

The only information I had about the bombing was from news accounts and an Air Force inquiry into the attack. Photos displayed wrecked buildings and carnage. The attack had been on the dining facility during the height of the breakfast hour—graphic photographs of dead and injured. A second suicide attack hit the fuel depot, destroying jets, equipment, and more people. When the fuel depot exploded, a fireball rocketed two hundred feet in the air. Several airmen died fighting the fire, which took eighteen hours to extinguish. The blaze spread to jets and vehicles parked nearby.

Osama Bin Laden issued a statement praising the attack's success and the bomber's courage and demanded the US leave the Middle East.

I was reviewing the Air Force report when a brief knock on the door interrupted me, and a red-haired woman poked in her head.

"Mr. Mendelson, got a minute?"

"It's Connor," I said. "Come in. "

She was tall and very thin, dressed in a straight dark blue skirt, white blouse, and black low-heeled shoes. A single pearl on a delicate gold chain was around her neck, a small diamond engagement and wedding ring the only other jewelry.

"Hi, I wanted to introduce myself. I'm Linda Mann." Mann told me that she was a researcher and analyst assigned to assemble as much information as possible about the torture the CIA had inflicted on al-Yemeni and others now held at Guantanamo. She said she had over a thousand pages of material.

"I am your resource for all things torture."

Linda gave me a detailed description of al Yemeni's initial detention in Dubai in late 2002. First, she told me how al-Yemeni was questioned by the Emirati security organization, adding that it was common for the Emirati to beat prisoners. Her opinion was that, most likely, the CIA was helping the Emiratis both with the questioning and the beatings. Then al-Yemeni was turned over to the CIA, which held him in a series of torture centers, "black sites," for four years. The CIA admits to waterboarding him three times, but her research indicated that it was more likely that he was waterboarded eight times. She also told me that some of the reports noted that part of the torture involved sexual humiliation and rape.

Mann concluded, "Surprisingly, the lead interrogator may have been a woman. Cables are kind of vague, but there are hints. And her code name was Hermione."

My response was, "Sounds like we know most of it."

Mann shook her head.

"When I began this, a former CIA guy told me, 'If they admit waterboarding your client, that is what they are comfortable with you knowing. Your job is to find the stuff they don't want you to know." So that's what I've been looking for. That is what you'll have to present in trial."

"When can I see the reports?"

She said, "Fredricks has the copies in her safe, and they must be stored in a safe when you are not using them. Can't leave them lying around because they are classified."

Mann stood.

"I'm a resource. I'm down the hall. Anything you need relating to the CIA and the torture program, see me first. Save you a lot of time as I may already have it. I've been living with this for nine months."

"Sounds really hard."

She looked at the floor, shaking her head from side to side, eyes misty, "It's so bad." Softly, "It's so bad."

"Thanks. Is it tough to live with this?"

"I'm okay."

She said softly.

"Hard not being able to talk to my husband or anyone about it because it is classified." And here she bowed her head, and I noticed her eyes were still misting.

After Mann left, I poked my head into Fredricks' office to ask her for the classified cables Mann had described. A few minutes later, she brought me a thick blue notebook with a cover page announcing in large red letters that the contents were classified. She opened the safe quickly, and I noted that she had memorized the combination.

"Sir, when you have finished, just put them back in the safe, close the drawer, and spin the lock. You want the combination?"

"Can I write it down?"

She looked shocked. The question was apparently quite stupid.

"No, sir."

"Then you'll be my memory because there's no way I will remember this kind of stuff."

She dismissively shook her head and scowled.

"Anything else, sir?"

Remembering my concerns when we first met, I waived to the chair, "Please sit down. Let's chat."

I closed the door.

She recoiled trying to shrink back in her chair when I sat in the chair next to hers. Her eyes darted. Arms went across her chest left over right. Hands clenched. What seemed like a sharp intake of breath. *She'll relax in a minute.*

"I'd like to get to know the team members a little better. Other than the big meeting, we've never really talked. So, please tell me about yourself?"

She said she joined the Marines after college because it was a family tradition.

"Father and uncles were all Marines. So it seemed like a good idea at the time."

Said as though it was no longer a good idea. The Marines paid for her law school in exchange for a five-year post-law school commitment. She'd then been sent on a series of assignments, including Camp Pendleton, Lajune, and then "The Suck."

"The suck? What is the suck?"

"Afghanistan, sir. I was an SJA to a battalion commander."

"Excuse me; I'm just learning the language. What is an SJA?"

"Staff judge advocate, Sir. I'd advise the commander. Kept him from doing really stupid stuff. Also, I paid bribes to tribal leaders and paid off families when we killed their kids."

Her hands had become fists again. Knuckles showed white.

"I'm curious. Why did you come here after that assignment?"

Her eyes darted left and right like she was looking for a place to hide. Arms wrapped tighter, giving herself a fierce hug. Then she stood.

"Sir, I have a lot of stuff to do. May we continue this later?"

This is strange. I gestured for her to sit, but she remained standing.

"Major, this will only take a few more minutes."

She shook her head.

"I'm sorry, sir, but I really need to get back to my duties. Please excuse me."

Said in a rushed voice, and before I could respond, she turned and was out the door.

I sat for several seconds. From what I knew about life and the military culture, this was strange, almost insulting behavior. I replayed the meeting, wondering if I'd somehow said or done something inappropriate. I concluded I had not.

Fredricks' door was closed, and she did not immediately respond when I knocked. But after a few beats longer than necessary, I was told to come in. She looked up. Said nothing.

"Major Fredricks, I need to know the details of your assignments to figure out how best to use your skills."

She glared. Then rifled through some files and handed me a folder. She told me this was her military file and would have everything I needed.

"Major, do you want to be here?"

She looked at the door behind me. It seemed she was trying to will me out the door. Then in a clipped voice said, "Sir, I have three more years before I can leave the Marines."

She looked away.

"Where I am, what my duties are, this is as good a place as any."

She turned and looked at her computer. Clearly, I was expected to leave. And taking the hint, I did.

CHAPTER 3

Before my first trip to Guantanamo, a little research told me that our base at Guantanamo Bay was ceded to the US after the Spanish-American war. But the government that gave it to the US was a government we installed, so the transaction was phony. We still pay Cuba $4085 per year for Guantanamo. But out of pride, Cuba will not cash the check.

I learned that before 9/11, the Clinton and Bush administrations were considering closing Guantanamo. But a desire to detain Muslims free of US law after 9/11 made Guantanamo useful as a detention facility as well as a small naval base.

Maj. Carter briefed me about the process of traveling to Guantanamo. I would need my passport and a military-issued country clearance allowing us to go to Guantanamo. We were to leave Sunday and return on Friday. Military flights were the only way to get to and from Guantanamo.

He laughed, "The government tries to preserve the fiction that Guantanamo is a foreign location even though the United States completely controls it."

Carter, Fredricks, an interpreter, Mohammed, and I were on my first trip. I was told to arrive at Andrews at 6:30 am for a 10:30 flight. At about 9:00, there was an announcement that "The Guantanamo flight will now depart at noon." There were none of the expected groans from those who were waiting. Carter observed, "Hurry up and wait; that is how military flights are."

The flight to Guantanamo, on a large Delta plane chartered by the military, was about a quarter full. Everyone had their own row.

The flight took three and a half hours. As the plane banked sharply to land, my forehead was against the window. There were multiple shades of blue ocean crashing against sharp cliffs. The landscape was much browner, and more arid than I expected. As things became more distinct, I saw armies of cacti light green against the brownish landscape. After landing and having our documents checked multiple times, we took a bus from the airstrip to a ferry and then across Guantanamo Bay to a check-in facility for the military commissions, where we were given housing assignments, and each of us was issued a large white Ford truck.

Carter and Fredricks drove me around the base. They pointed out the NEX, a combined grocery, clothing, hardware, sporting goods, and jewelry store. They also showed me McDonald's and other places to eat. We went into the well-equipped Dench gym. We drove over a hill, past the ratty golf course, which Carter called "al-Qaeda National," then through a checkpoint to the prison complex.

There are multiple prisons at Guantanamo. As we drove around, Carter pointed to a large complex.

"That is Delta, As many as 600 prisoners were here, but now there are only around hundred and fifty." A few miles later, he pointed out Echo, a smaller complex where we would meet with al-Yemeni.

Carter explained that al-Yemeni is what the CIA calls a High-Value Detainee. All of the people with this designation are held in Camp Seven. Camp Seven is not part of the main prison complex and is in a different location on the base, so he will be brought to us at Echo. Carter smiled.

"Now we have to get you badged, and we can show you the ELC."

"What is the ELC?"

Carter told me ELC stands for expeditionary legal complex. An homage to the fiction that this is a temporary facility in a foreign country.

After being photographed and issued the multiple badges necessary to function at Guantanamo, Carter and Fredricks took me into the ELC through a checkpoint manned by four guards. Another two guards were assigned to protect the courtroom from unauthorized intruders. After touring the cavernous courtroom, we went to see the team's Guantanamo office space, which was in a compound next to the courtroom surrounded by a chain link fence topped by razor wire. Access to this compound was controlled by a gate programmed to read the blue badge.

Our office was in a long metal building that looked like someone had taken the plans to a mobile home and doubled the size.

Carter explained all the security was because the entire building was called a SCIF, a secure facility where we could discuss classified information. Our office was about thirty feet long and twelve feet wide with light yellow walls and brownish carpet. Both the walls and the rug had splotches of black.

Fredricks shook her head as she pointed to the Rorschach-like black patterns, "These are bigger than when we were here last. Whatever it is, I hope it doesn't grow into another life form."

Several desks with multiple computers for the classified and unclassified system, numerous printers for each system, and a safe to hold classified information ringed three sides of the room. A large whiteboard on one wall and a couple of brown, faux wood bookshelves completed the ensemble. A long brown table with folding legs served as a conference table.

I was shivering.

"Why is it so cold in here?"

"They say it is to keep the critters out. You'll see large rodents from time to time around here. Banana Rats. Some are as big as small dogs. They supposedly don't like cold. Even during the summer, you'll need a winter suit or a heavy sweater to work here."

Leaving the building to use the portable restroom brought relief, rapid warming, and sweat because of the Cuban humidity. But, of course, when I used the blue badge to swipe myself back into the office, I became even more chilled as the sweat accelerated the cooling process.

Later, Carter, Fredricks Mohammed, and I went for drinks and dinner at Kelly's bar, a fake Irish Pub where Guinness, Harp Lager, and Jameson Whiskey signs competed with the several televisions showing the games that were on that night.

Carter smiled ruefully.

"This is one of the few places that feels normal, or GTMO normal. You'll know the menu by heart as we'll be here a lot." The menu - fried bar food, hamburgers, grilled chicken sandwiches, one steak option, and salads.

Sitting in one of the booths across from the wooden bar, Fredricks told me that when President Obama was inaugurated, he issued an executive order closing Guantanamo. But Congress resisted the closure. The story was it had to stay open because Guantanamo was necessary to the war on terror.

She frowned as she said that.

"More likely, the real reason is that contractors make millions of dollars a year out of this place, and I'm cynical, but I bet some of those dollars, a lot of those dollars, flow to campaign contributions,"

Fredricks continued that the cost of running the prison at Guantanamo is 400 million dollars a year. The cost of the Military Commissions is around 600 million dollars. The cost to house a prisoner at Guantanamo is 10 million per prisoner per year. She shook her head,

"Money down a fucking rat hole."

I noticed that Fredricks' eyes kept darting around the room. Always looking, checking things out. Seemed weird. As we walked the half mile back to our quarters, she wouldn't walk with Carter and me. She went almost at a trot and got back to our housing at least five minutes before us. When she was out of earshot, I asked Carter if he knew why Fredricks acted as she did.

He turned as we walked.

"Got no idea. She certainly does keep to herself. But I'm the wrong guy to ask. I just keep my head down. Try to stay out of people's shit."

The next day, Carter, Fredricks, Mohammed, and I went to see Hussain. On the way, they reminded me that al-Yemeni spoke little English and that I should be prepared to speak slowly to let Mohammed translate. Arriving at what was called Echo II, we went through more oppressive and pointless security. Two searches and an examination of the blank papers we were taking in. Cups of coffee and individual packages of sugar or Splenda were counted and logged. Stirrers were taken away as "they might be weapons."

I had a spiral notebook full of empty pages. My practice was to use this to keep everything in a case together. But Carter had reminded me that everything Hussain said was classified. So I would have to pull the notes from the notebook and put them in an envelope, which would be sealed before we could leave the facility. When I showed the notebook to the guard, a young soldier with three stripes, he looked up and said, "Sorry, sir, spiral notebooks are prohibited."

"I've taken a notebook like this to some of the most fierce prisons in the US. Supermax, Leavenworth, Attica."

"Sir, the spiral can be grabbed by the detainee and used as a garrote. Sorry, Sir."

I began to argue that the notion someone could take the notebook from me and remove the spiral wire was "just ridiculous" when Carter touched me on the arm and shrugged. A silent, "Drop it."

As the guard took my notebook, Carter whispered, "FUBAR. You'll get used to it."

The room where we met al-Yemenni was dull white with a gray floor. On the far end was an air conditioner set to frigid, the room was meat locker cold. Below the air conditioner were five white plastic chairs surrounding a white table. There were brown and black stains on the walls and some on the gray floor.

Seated at the table was a slight man who appeared about thirty. Dark black hair, caramel skin, and blazing eyes. Dressed in a white jail uniform. He was not handcuffed, but heavy leather cuffs circled each of his ankles. A heavy chain ran between the cuffs through an eyebolt cemented into the floor. I guessed that he could walk about two steps in any direction.

Carter and Fredricks wore fatigues. Earlier, Carter laughed as he told me that if they'd worn more formal uniforms, they'd have had to remove the metal insignia lest Hussain grab them and try to use the quarter-inch pins as weapons.

Fredricks and Carter greeted Hussain warmly. Al-Yemeni only said hello. He did not seem particularly glad to see them. Carter said, and Mohammed translated, "Hussain, this is Connor Mendelson. He is the expert lawyer we told you about."

I put out my hand and said, "Connor Mendelson. I'm a lawyer. Because the government has announced it will charge you with being the mastermind of the Kuwaiti bombing and is asking for the death penalty, I have been asked to help the team. I am an expert in defending death penalty cases."

Al-Yemeni rapidly spoke in Arabic, with Mohammed translating. Rapid arm movements punctuated his high pressured monologue.

"This is bullshit. If they wanted to kill me, they'd just kill me. It is a trick. I don't believe you are a lawyer. If you are really a lawyer, can you get them to let me be able to walk around this room like a human being? Can you get them not to move me blindfolded like a cow being led to the butcher? A lawyer can do that. If you can't do that, I don't want to talk to you."

Fredricks reminded me that this is not where he is housed, and when he is transported here from Camp Seven, they put on blindfolds and big ear muffs. He does not like that. He really hates it.

Carter turned to Hussain, put up his hands, and smiled, "Can we slow down a little bit? I think I understand your concerns, but…"

As al-Yemeni spoke, Mohammed tried to match his rapid speech.

"You don't understand anything. I've been treated like a dog for years, and you say lawyers help people. So if you're really lawyers, help me. Get me out of the chains and blindfolds. Otherwise, go away."

I said, and Mohammed translated, "You're right; we don't understand. We need your help to help us understand. So what do you think would help us understand your situation?"

Al Yemeni slammed his fists down so hard the table jumped.

"Do you think I am too stupid to see that this is a trick? This is all a game, and I'm not going to play your games." He then crossed his arms and stared at us.

After several seconds I said, "Okay, will you be willing to listen to what we have to say?"

"I don't care."

"I'm a lawyer. I work in trying to save people from the death penalty. And I've volunteered to help Carter and Fredricks.

"We know you were in CIA black sites, torture centers. Don't know much about what happened to you there. I don't know if we can change things quickly, but we will try. What is it you want us to try to change?"

Al-Yemeni glared, then in even faster Arabic, said, "I told them again and again about the hood and the blindfold, the muffs, the cuffs, the truck with no windows. I told them I needed that to be fixed. I talked about that a lot, yet nothing happens. Real lawyers could fix this."

Carter stood.

"Maybe we can get things changed, and maybe we can't. We can't make promises and won't lie to you. There are no guarantees."

"Well, if you can't do anything, just leave, just fucking leave."

Again we sat in silence.

I coughed, "Is there anything you'd like to ask us? Anything at all?"

He looked at me.

"You, you married? Children?"

"Separated, still friends with my wife, two daughters. Wife is named Molly. Daughters are Emily and Anabel."

He turned, "Carter?" "Married, twenty-two years, three kids. Two boys, one girl. Wife is Susan; children are Jack junior, Samuel, and Lucy."

Mohammed told Hussain he was married to Esmir. No kids.

Her turn, Fredricks brusquely answered, "Not married, no kids."

Al-Yemeni looked at the three lawyers, "Any of you a Jew?"

I should have known that was coming, but I was still surprised by it. I thought about lying, defusing a possible issue. *How would he find out?*

"I am. I'm not particularly religious, but I am Jewish. Is that a problem?"

He glared and raised his hand palms up. Forcefully said, "How can I trust you? You're American; you're Israeli."

"I don't know what you mean by Israeli. I'm American. I'm a non-religious Jew. If that is a problem, then that is a problem."

I paused and decided *why not,* "And Mr. al-Yemeni here is the cold reality. The Government of the United States wants to have a trial and then kill you. I'm an expert in defending these kinds of cases. If you don't want help because I'm Jewish, American, or both, that is your decision. Perhaps we can find another lawyer who's willing to help you, but probably not. I understand you have no reason to trust me. I hope, in time, I'll earn your trust. I hope I will. But right now, we are all you have."

We looked at each other.

"I need to think about this."

"We understand. Let's stop for the day, and we'll come back tomorrow. That okay?"

I expected more of a fight. But he said, "Okay. Come back tomorrow."

As we were driving away from the meeting, Mohammed turned to us, "I told him he should work with you. That I think you do not lie and are good people."

We then talked about how his mood so abruptly changed and his reaction to my religion. I observed that such rapid mood changes could be symptomatic of severe PTSD and that we'd need to consult a physician who treated a lot of PTSD. I also thought he'd be sufficiently put off by a Jewish lawyer that he would ask for someone else.

Mohammed said, "No, he'll stew and say you're okay. For all his bluster, he's scared."

I said, "You know, if I put myself in his place, I don't know what I'd do. Americans, military, a Jewish guy. I'm not sure I'd trust us or trust me."

Mohammed looked at me.

"He really has no choice. He knows Carter and Fredricks. You're here. He says no to you, and then what? Would you say no to a Saudi lawyer if you were arrested? Would you say go away; I'll fight this on my own? No way. Not ideal, but you'd have no choice."

Later that evening, over fried pickles and drinks at Kelly's, Carter, Fredricks, and I sat quietly.

Fredricks said, "If you don't mind me asking, what was your reaction to the whole Jewish thing?"

I shrugged.

"Honestly, in my practice, it's only come up a couple of times. Normally when some fool wants a 'good Jew lawyer,' I double the fee and take the money." I paused and took a drink. "But I'm being glib. Truthfully, I don't know how I feel. It's complicated. When I spoke with Jennifer LaGrange about becoming involved, I told her that she might want to find someone else just because I'm Jewish. She reminded me I'd defended guys in the Aryan Brotherhood and asked what was the difference?"

"And?"

I sighed, "To me, it feels a little different, maybe the Arab thing, maybe I just wanted to avoid this situation. I guess I just did not, do not, want the drama. I'm not religious. I am conscious of being Jewish, but I'd rather not have it be an issue."

I shook my head and shrugged.

Fredricks took a sip of her drink and nibbled a fried pickle chip.

"You asked us how we feel about defending a terrorist. How did you resolve that issue?"

I explained that somewhere, sometime I decided that if I was going to be a criminal defense lawyer, I could not pick and choose crimes. Right or wrong, My attitude is if I take the case, I'll defend them as best as I can. Not all lawyers agree with this.

"Maybe I'm a moral leper, but that's how I see things. So to me, a terrorist is no different. But so far, I'm not in love with Mr. al-Yemeni."

I took a pull of bourbon and felt the warmth.

"Here, more than anything I've done, I, we, all of us, really, are defending the Constitution. If they can do this to non-citizens, they can do it to citizens. Molly, my wife, says we're defending the soul and the honor of the nation."

We all sat in comfortable silence for a minute. Pulls of whiskey and dips of pickles in the little black plastic cups of ranch dressing.

"So, what do you guys know about the prosecutors?"

Carter described the Chief Prosecutor Robert E Lee Lawson as 'a pompous asshole.' He knows he's the smartest guy in the room and wants to make sure you know it too. Officious. And he'll cheat.

"Lawson has no use for me. We were together in Iraq, and I called him out on some stuff. He did not like that. Or me."

He then spoke of the others.

"Tom Willis. By reputation, he's a Lawson clone and a suck ass. Not a star lawyer. I've met him a couple of times at conferences. He wants to talk about how he played football at Michigan State. Says he might have gone pro but hurt his knee. It's bullshit. I checked. He was on the roster for two years but never played.

"Major Jennifer Sanders is supposed to be good. She is attractive. Her Army JAG reputation is as a straight shooter. But if she's working for Lawson, in my mind, that's a question."

He continued, "Lawson is the most ambitious guy I have ever met. He'll cheat to win. Trust me on this."

I asked, "And the Judge, Colonel James Pierce?"

Carter described Pierce as a complete pimp for the prosecution, and in this case the Air Force JAG Corps chief has probably told him how to rule. Everyone is under pressure to make this trial happen. And they really want our guy to be sentenced to death.

I nodded at him and then at the menu.

"You want dinner, or are we going just to drink and eat this shit?"

Fredricks smiled, "You know, if there is a trial here, if we're here for months, I'll weigh two hundred pounds. Nothing really fresh to eat, too much drinking, too much fried food."

We all laughed when Carter said, "Ahh, but the pay is good."

After ordering another drink, I asked, "Lots of times in a death penalty case, the prosecution is willing to drop death for a life sentence. Any chance of that here?"

Carter took a long pull on his drink. Shook his head with a big smile.

"They could hold Hussain forever since they claim he is a prisoner of war. In their minds, they don't need a trial to get a life sentence. With politics being what they are, no way do they drop the request for death. There will be a trial. Lawson wants a trial. Ward wants a trial. The judge wants a trial. There will be a trial."

Fredricks shook her head.

"I wonder how I'll look and feel when I'm a blob?"

I stood, stuck out my stomach, jiggled my belly, and grinned, "You'll look like this. Not so bad."

Fredricks looked up but did not smile.

"You mean I'll be fat, white, and balding? Fuck that." And she held a finger to her head like a gun and pulled the trigger as we all laughed.

Fredricks pursed her lips, "Can I ask you something personal?"

"Sure."

"You said you're separated. What happened? Will you get back together?"

I sat back down, wondering why she was asking such a personal question. Fredricks seemed so closed. I shrugged.

"Don't know if we'll get back together. I want to. We still talk. I value her counsel and," I paused, "But I was gone so much, and she says I'm so intense and focused that she needed a break. She says my ambition and ego screwed up a good thing."

"Yet you are here? That can't help."

I laughed softly.

"Yes, I am here. Apparently, my ambition and ego drives me to want to hang out with you rascals here in this wonderful place, eating this wonderful food while defending a terrorist who hates Americans, especially me."

I held my drink up in a mock toast.

"To ambition and ego."

Another basket of pickles and a drink later, we went to our quarters. Tomorrow we would see Hussain again and deal with the issue of my religion.

CHAPTER 4

As we walked into the meeting room, Hussein's anger was a toxic presence. He was sitting, arms folded across his chest, his right leg pumping up and down so rapidly that the chain between his ankles made a loud clanking sound. He didn't stand. No handshakes. No greetings. I sat across from Hussain, Mohammed to my right, and Carter to my left. Fredricks next to Carter. Hussain glared.

I nodded. Asked, "Did you sleep well?"

"What do you care?"

Angry rabic with a rapid translation. But the attitude was so obvious no translation was necessary.

"If we work together, we need to care about and for each other."

After Mohammed translated this, there was a rapid response to Mohammed, and the conversation in Arabic continued for a couple of minutes. Mohammed turned to me and said, "He does have some questions, but he says he does not believe you will tell him the truth. So he says if you are going to lie, why ask?

I looked at Hussain.

"What are your questions?"

More back and forth in Arabic.

"How can you as a Jew defend me, a freedom fighter against the US and Israeli incursions into our lives?"

I tried to look directly into his eyes. I told him that I was not religious, although I am proud that I am Jewish, and I don't know if you are a terrorist. That is what the government of the United States says. But the government often lies.

He responded, "Suppose I did much of what they say I did. Suppose I helped with the attack? What then?"

I tried to explain that in our system, the prosecution had to prove his guilt. If they could not do that, then he should go free. And if he did lead the attack, we would try to understand why he did that. To try to save his life. I was unsure if he understood, and I was becoming increasingly annoyed with him.

He stood and took a step back, which was all the chains around his ankles would allow. The clanking of the heavy chains rattled and changed the room.

"I just don't know if I can trust a Jew."

Fuck this. "Would you like me to leave?"

Before he could answer, Mohammed began speaking with him in hurried Arabic. After a few minutes of back and forth, Mohammed said, "I've told him he should ask you some more questions before he rejects you. That he is being unfair."

More back and forth. Mohammed turned.

"Is your wife Jewish?"

"My wife is not Jewish."

More chatter, and then, "What religion is she?"

"Christian. Although she is also not observant."

He sat silently and then resumed with Mohammed. Finally, another question, "Do you have Muslim friends?"

"No. Not a lot of Muslims in my town."

"Do you know the Koran?"

"Only what I learned preparing to meet you. I generally know the five pillars of Islam. I know the American notion of Jihad is incorrect. I know many Americans' opinions of Islam are wrong."

"How can you say that?"

"Well, Islam is not about violence or killing; it is about grace and love. Some believe that proper support of Islam is violent, but that is like some Christians think killing is proper to support Christianity."

"But," He shook his head. "Perhaps I am a freedom fighter. I am Muslim. How can you, as a Jew, defend me? Understand my concerns?"

I shrugged.

"My ability to understand your concerns has nothing to do with my religion. I need you to teach me about your concerns and why you fought. If we understand, we can do our best to explain your concerns to the court. But you will have to teach all of us, and we will do our best to learn from you."

"And do you know what the US did to me?"

"Not any details. When you are comfortable, we'll talk about that."

He and Mohammed then had a long conversation. I assumed they were talking about me and my religion by the way they glanced at me and used what I assumed to be the Arabic word for Jew. But the longer it went on, the more the thought crystalized - *If you don't want me as his lawyer, your loss.*

Mohammed said, "We should go now."

"Why?" I asked. "We've not been here long."

Mohammed smiled.

"Trust me."

We stood, and Husain stood.

"I need to think about things. Will I see you tomorrow?

Then, "If you wish, you can come back."

He looked at us.

"Inshallah."

As we drove away, Mohammed said, "I think this problem is over."

Fredricks asked, "Why do you say that?"

"Well, I told him Mr. Connor is one of the best lawyers I've seen, and he should be grateful you are willing to work on his case."

I laughed, "You don't even know me."

"Ah, but Mr. Connor, we are a team."

And while I doubted that al-Yemeni had any real trust in us, for the first time since I'd met these lawyers, I thought we might become a team. But even as I felt that I noticed Fredricks looking out the window with blank eyes and a scowl.

For the next several months, we went to see Hussain once a month for three or four days at a time. He continued to be volatile, although the outbursts were less frequent.

Somehow, Carter and Fredricks worked some magic and got the prison to transport him without being blindfolded. They were pretty vague about how they got it done.

Fredricks only said, "Sometimes you have to ask in the right way."

There were rumors about a case of scotch, but I'd learned a long time ago that often it's best not to ask. But after he was no longer blindfolded, al Yemeni sometime smiled when he came into the meeting room. And in time, he occasionally greeted us with handshakes and hugs.

CHAPTER 5

I reviewed the notebook of classified cables that Fredricks had delivered. The cables spanned close to four years.

The first cable generated in November 2002 suggested that with the assistance of a CIA operative, code-named HERMIONE, the Emiratis had seized al-Yemeni in Dubai outside the bar in the Marriott at the Marina. He was taken to some facility maintained by the Emirati authorities, where for about a month, he was periodically questioned USING TECHNIQUES LAWFUL IN THE EMIRATES. I made a note to find out what that meant.

At the end of 2002, al-Yemeni was TAKEN INTO CIA CUSTODY and was in a series of different locations over the next four years. The locations were never directly referred to by country, only by color, Red, Green, Cobalt, and several other colors. Throughout the cables, there were references to STRESS POSITIONS, CHAINED STRESS POSITIONS, SENSORY DEPRIVATION, THE WATER TREATMENT, WATERBOARDING, WALLING, THE BIG BOX, THE SMALL BOX.

The cables demonstrated that Hermione followed al-Yemeni from place to place. Confirming that HERMIONE was a woman was an entry from site YELLOW that when she had insulted his manhood and grabbed his genitals, he had SAID IN ARABIC, I'LL SHOW YOU WHAT KIND OF MAN I AM, AND GRABBED THE AGENTS RIGHT BREAST. The response by HERMIONE was to have other agents, SUBDUE AL-YEMENI, USING EXTREME AND OVERWHELMING FORCE.

I assumed all this meant that she'd ridiculed him, and in response, he'd lashed out and, for his efforts, got the shit beat out of him.

As best as I could tell, when al-Yemeni got to a new site, they would question him and subject him to increasingly brutal treatment when he did not comply with what they wanted. It was disturbing how they documented the abuse. At one site, he'd been put in:

THE LARGE BOX FOR FORTY HOURS AND WHEN HE WAS REMOVED HE WAS SMELLY AND FILTHY, AS HE HAD SOILED HIMSELF. SUBJECT WAS CLEANED WITH HIGH-PRESSURE HOSE WHILE BLINDFOLDED. PARTICULAR ATTENTION WITH THE HOSE WAS SPENT ON SUBJECTS RECTUM AS THERE APPEARED TO BE BLOOD. SUBJECT WAS ALSO SCRUBBED WITH THE WIRE BRUSH.

The blood on his rectum perhaps came from an earlier episode of ANAL HYDRATION.

In that same location, they found his weakness; they told him his mother was in custody and that multiple men were prepared to rape her FRONT, BACK, AND MOUTH if he did not tell them what they wanted to hear. So AL-YEMENI'S KNEES BUCKLED, AND HE BEGGED TO TELL US WHATEVER WE WANTED, JUST PLEASE RELEASE MY MOTHER.

There were references to WATER TREATMENT as well as WATERBOARDING. I did not know if this was the same or different forms of abuse, but after one episode, there was a reference that MEDICS WERE IMMEDIATELY SUMMONED, AND THE DETAINEE WAS REVIVED WITH NO PERMANENT HARM.

Two cables were especially perplexing.

TO: HQCIA, DODJSOC, OVP, SSECDEF, AG, NATSEC

FROM: SITE ORANGE, 12 SEP 2004 1200 GMT

QUESTIONING OF CIADET 037 (AL-YEMENI)

CIADET 037 (AL-YEMENI) IS COMPLIANT UNDER QUESTIONING BUT IS INCREASINGLY RESISTANT TO HIS SURROUNDINGS. HE HAS BEEN DISCIPLINED TWICE, INCLUDING ONE INSTANCE OF RECTAL FEEDING. HE INSISTS HE HAS NO MORE INFORMATION, AND GIVEN THE PASSAGE OF TIME, THAT IS ALMOST CERTAINLY TRUE.

Rectal feeding? Rectal Hydration? What is this craziness?

The response was absurd.

YOU ARE INSTRUCTED TO CONTINUE INTERROGATIONS AS BEFORE WITH INCREASED, REPEAT INCREASED PRESSURE. DAILY REPORTS ARE MANDATORY.

The final cable was chilling.

REQUEST FOR GUIDANCE

CIADET 037(AL-YEMENI) HAS BEEN REPEATEDLY QUESTIONED USING BOTH NORMAL AND EXTREMELY AGGRESSIVE TECHNIQUES. HE IS COMPLIANT. HE IS NOT PROVIDING NEW INFORMATION BECAUSE HE HAS NO NEW INFORMATION.

QUESTION: WHAT IS ENDGAME? DO WE CONTINUE TO HOUSE-FEED AND GUARD HIM? THERE ARE OTHER OBVIOUS OPTIONS

REQUEST OPINION OF SENIOR LEADERSHIP.

The response:

TO STATION HEAD SITE PURPLE

PLEASE RETURN BY CIVILIAN AIR TO CIA/HQ FOR CONSULTATION. ADVISE ARRIVAL DATE AND TIME. DCI REQUESTS MEETING SHORTLY AFTER ARRIVAL.

Jesus fucking Christ. I shook my head as Mann's guidance came back to me.

"This is what they are comfortable putting on paper."

I took the notebook of cables down to Carter's office.

"Have you read this?"

"Yeah."

And he tossed his pen on the desk, so it skittered to the floor.

"Makes me fucking proud of my country."

"I don't even know where to begin with this. I'm just stunned."

Carter shook his head.

"Some of this stuff keeps me awake, and I was in Iraq. Saw some shit we did when we were questioning guys. This is way worse. The whole episode where they kept Hussain, bent over in his own shit really got to me. Can't believe we'd do that kind of stuff."

I wandered down to Mann's office.

"I guess I need to meet with you. Get an overview of all this. Now that I've read the cables."

Her desk was piled high with books, notebooks, and loose papers. She waved me into an empty chair. Next to her computer was a four-inch thick, black notebook, which she held up.

"This is what I've put together about the RDI program."

I must have looked blank.

She explained that the CIA ran the RDI program. That stands for Rendition, Detention and Interrogation. CIA would grab guys take them to black sites, torture centers, really, question them, and hold them. It lasted four years till they were taken to Guantanamo. Although, we suspect that Guantanamo was, for a time, a black site.

"Do we know what all this means, stress positions, big box, small box, walling?"

"Generally, the CIA had certain so-called Enhanced Techniques. Torture really. There are several approved stress positions. The big box is like a coffin; the small box is about the size of a floor safe. Waterboarding is waterboarding. It's a war crime, but we did it. Japanese generals were executed after World War II for waterboarding US prisoners, but now the Attorney General says it's okay. What crap."

We both sat in silence. She seemed to be waiting on the next question. I could not find words.

I was directed to cables that suggested that people on the scene were saying he knows nothing more, and headquarters said to keep going.

She nodded. Shook her head.

"This keeps me awake. It really gets to me. It was torture for the sake of torture."

She shook her head and frowned.

"Imagine being told to give us more, and you have nothing to give." Her voice seemed to break as she softly acknowledged the obvious. Anyone would lie, would have said anything to stop what the US was doing. Again we sat in an uncomfortable silence dealing with our thoughts or perhaps our fears.

I asked if she had any idea who Hermione was.

"No. That is the Holy Grail of your case. If you can find out who she is, subpoena her; who knows what will happen? They will do almost anything to protect agents' identities, and she seems despicable. She seemed to get off on the sexual stuff. We see it over and over with her. She described it in one cable as 'a job, a job I've come to like.'"

We looked at each other.

"This is just fucked up shit."

She smiled.

"Welcome to 'Merica. I was in the Army for twenty years. I really believe in what we are supposed to stand for. And it wasn't this, not at all. Makes me sad, ashamed."

As I walked back to my office, I suddenly felt my chest tighten and my belly clench. I stopped and stood in the hallway, looking at nothing. I realized, *"Fuck, you have to expose this."*

And when I got to my desk, I sat and tried to come to terms with overwhelming feelings of responsibility. A sense of responsibility that I'd not felt so strongly since the day my oldest daughter was born.

CHAPTER 6

After being approved for work in Guantanamo, the first person I called was Jill Hanson. Jill is a mitigation specialist. She looks for evidence that explains a crime. She tries to answer the question: 'How did the accused go from being a baby in his mother's arms to the person in the courtroom on trial for his life? What was the journey? Where did the rot set in, and who or what caused it?'

Jill is mid-forties, five-foot-seven, not thin, but not heavy. Solid, muscular. Works out a lot. Dark black skin is highlighted by the small gold and ruby piercings in her nose. She sports dangling earrings that might be gold, red, orange, or whatever suits her fancy that day. She's unmarried but says with some glee, "There have been men, lots of men."

Jill grew up in New York City, went to public schools, and then Princeton. She got her masters in social work at NYU. Social work led her to the Bronx Public Defender's Office, where she spent a few years helping white lawyers from privileged backgrounds understand and explain to prosecutors and judges their poor Black or Hispanic clients' lives.

Seven years after joining Bronx Defenders, she "took a sabbatical" to work on a death penalty case in Alabama. There she helped save her first life. After that, she left the Bronx Defenders because "Capital defense work is my calling." Within a year, she was working on cases in five different states.

Ultimately she landed in the college town of Ripon, an hour north of Madison. In Ripon, which she calls her refuge, she lives in a three-bedroom, multi-story house two blocks from the twelve-hundred-student college. She calls herself "the black dot over the I in Wisconsin."

In time she became JILL HANSON. When death penalty lawyers sit around over drinks, they often talk about the Jill Hanson stories they heard about or were, if they were lucky, a part of. She is a legend in the community.

I was fortunate to have worked with Jill on several cases. Because al-Yemeni was so complicated and damaged, I felt Jill could help breakthrough with him. I'd seen her do it with other clients.

Tony Spinelli was accused of organizing a series of murders inside the Montana prison system. The US Attorney was "cracking down on white nationalists" and was seeking the death penalty against Tony. To say Tony was initially uncomfortable being defended by a team that included a Jewish guy and a Black woman is an understatement. He was outraged. When we first met, he called me "the little fucking Jew lawyer who's gonna get me killed."

When I introduced him to Jill, he looked up and said, "No sir, no fucking way," and launched into a stream of invective in which n**er was among the least of the insults. Jill just sat there and listened. As his rant wound down, she gave him a long look and said, "I'm curious. You're supposed to be so fucking tough. Do you want to die on the execution table in Terre Haute? Do you really want to go out with them putting poison in your arms? Is that how you want to go? Lying down?"

The tattoos on his neck pulsed, "No, I don't want to die, but no fucking Jigaboo is going to save me. They might as well just kill me now. Jesus, a Jew, and a Jig. I'm so fucked."

Jill sat, smiled, and looked at him, "Sorry, dude. This fucking Jigaboo, and the Jew over there are the only ones that can save you. So cut the shit, and let's get to work."

Tony sat silent, and she continued.

"So, tell me about your family." A few months later, I watched as Tony told her through shoulder-shaking sobs how he kept his younger brother and sister safe by submitting to the sexual abuse of his uncle and then his uncle's friends.

When the jury rejected a death sentence and sentenced Tony to life–he turned first, with tears streaming, to Jill. He was, by then, calling her "my real mother." I was still "the fucking Jew lawyer," but the tone was much more playful.

I called Jill, explained what I knew of Hussain's case, and asked, really begged her, to sign on.

"Only if Grace is part of the team," she said.

Grace Atwater was Jill's assistant. Grace was white, blonde, thin, very cute, early thirties. She lives in Madison, Wisconsin. Close enough to Jill to be efficient, far enough that she can have her own life. And, in her words, "It's easier to cut one out of the herd in Madison."

Grace can find any record that exists or ever existed. In-person or on her computer, she can work magic. In Tony's case, she located school records long buried in a warehouse. She combed thousands of dusty, moldy pages to find the records of little Tony Spenelli's visits to the school nurse because his "butt was bleeding." The school nurse did nothing other than put some Neosporin on the anal tears and remain silent.

"Of course, Grace is part of the deal."

Her reply, "What do we know about this guy?

I sighed,"Not much."

She sighed, "Sounds like there'll be lots of travel."

I allowed as that was correct. Guantanamo, DC, Europe, the Middle East, and who knows where else.

"This is kind of a homewrecker."

Laughter.

"Speaking of wrecked homes, I heard you're separated. Your choice or hers? "

"Hers, I pretty much screwed things up."

"Care to talk about it?"

"I was doing a trial in Detroit. I only came home once and didn't ask her to come up. That seems to have been the thing that finally caused her to throw me out. But it was probably a lot of things. I don't know. But for sure, it's my fault."

"Any chance you guys will work things out?"

"Hard to say. No one has filed for divorce. We talk a couple of times a week. We're friends and have the occasional meal, but so far, she has no interest in getting back together." So, I put on a begging voice,

"Could I interest you in an older white guy?"

She laughed across the country, "No problem with the white part, and you're not all that old, but the married part stops me.

The banter continued, "For you, I can fix the married part."

She said wisely, "No, you can't; I know you. You care for Molly too much."

I responded, "Ah well, none of the important women in my life will sleep with me. So I'm just resigned to a life of desperation."

Mutual laughter.

"OK, Grace and I are in. When do we start?"

CHAPTER 7

Kristina Moretti is 5'5" tall. Her muscular frame is perfect for the four or five marathons she runs each year. She has jet-black hair, cut to about shoulder length that, she tells us, becomes impossibly curly in humidity. She is the color of coffee, diluted with a lot of cream. When she smiles, which is often, her slightly crooked teeth enhance her look.

Moretti comes for the interview in a narrow black sheath dress showing a slight hint of cleavage. A small dainty cross on a delicate gold chain is in the center of her chest, barely visible against her skin. She smells of Chanel 5 with a hint of garlic.

She tells us she grew up in Brooklyn "before Brooklyn became what it is today." When asked what that is, she smiles.

"It's become a hipster hell hole. The real people, the working people, are being driven out as all the small Manhattan money moves there. No one but the insanely rich can afford Manhattan."

After high school, she went to NYU with the goal of a degree in theater.

"But that was too much self-indulgent bullshit. So I changed to Economics and Political Science. Ended up at Brooklyn Law."

"Law Review?"

"Yes, but honestly, that was just checking a box. I discovered midway through law school that I was drawn to trial work, and the criminal courts were the only way to do that."
Fredricks asked, "Were you a prosecutor?"

"Yes, briefly, but then a PD job came open. Moved up to murders in three years. I've tried four murder cases. About twenty jury trials."

"Death penalty?"

"No, New York has no death penalty."

Reyes asked her. "How do you feel about the death penalty? For it? Against it?"

She looked at him, then all of us.

"I guess I'm reflexively opposed, but honestly, that's just political correctness. I don't know too much about how the system works. My suspicion and my reading indicate that it's a function of prejudice and poverty."

Fredricks again, "Why do you want this job, representing an accused terrorist in Guantanamo?"

"Seems interesting. I want to get out of New York. I need a change."

Fredricks persisted, "Why leave NY? Lots of jobs there. You can make more money in private practice. Why move to DC?"

"Yes," but then she paused and looked down. "Honestly, I need to move. I made a mistake. I slept with a married guy—a judge. I want to be clear. I pursued him. If anyone was a victim, it was him. Long story. My doing. Predictably, things turned to shit. His wife is angry at him and, of course, me. I'm pretty much untouchable in the legal community right now. I figure you know about it or will learn about it, so there it is—no way to sugarcoat it. I messed up. Big time."

Carter now, "Running away? How do we know you'll stay?"

She looked right at him, then all of us.

"You don't. I can promise I'll stay, but we all know that's not how it works. If you like my work, and I like the work, there is no reason to leave. But I did some homework. People leave these teams from time to time. Military gets transferred, and things happen. So all I can say is I'll see it through from what I know."

I said, "That's honest."

"I've got faults, but I don't sling BS. I'll tell you straight.

Fredricks, "Ever served in the military? Know anything about the military?"

"No, just men and women in uniforms to me. I am not being critical. I'm sure that it is a different life. But I don't know much about it."

Fredricks glared at her but said nothing.

I said, "Anything else you want us to know?"

She seemed to grow taller.

"Yes, and obviously, you can take this for what it's worth—meeting you guys and getting a sense of the vibe here. I really want the job. Obviously, I have personal reasons, but this seems important and interesting. In my mind, that makes up for the money. I'm smart and hard-working. Final selling point. I make the best lasagna you'll ever, ever have."

Carter turned to me.

"Lasagna is a deal breaker. I'm a meatballs guy," and smiled. Then he looked at her, "What about your meatballs?"

She smiled, "It's trite. I use my Grandma's recipe. Combine veal, pork, and beef, shredded, not ground. Eggs, garlic, and lightly toasted breadcrumbs, got to be toasted—next, parsley. You have to chill them after they're formed. Then bake. Might not be as good as my lasagna, but they'll do."

Carter's response, signaling to all of us she had his vote.

"Veal. Hmm, Interesting."

Finally, one of the paralegals spoke up.

"One final thing, this is a pretty free-flowing atmosphere. Lots of dirty talk and not too many secrets. You okay in that environment?"

Moretti smiled ruefully.

"I just told you I slept with, no, let me be more specific, I chased and fucked a married guy. Created a huge shit-storm for myself. Plus, I go to jails, and you know how that is. Hear all kinds of stuff there. I'd like to think that question has been answered." She paused. "You know, I think that sounded a lot more bitchy than I meant it. If so, I apologize. I'm just trying to say that that kind of stuff doesn't bother me, and I think I'll fit in."

And she turned and looked at Carter and me and then the others.

"Not sure who the decision makers are, but please, give me this opportunity. You won't regret it.

After she left, we all discussed her.

"Well, what do we think?"

Carter smiled, "Do you think we should have told her it was okay to sleep with the married guys?"

"Seriously," I asked, "Is she the one? We've interviewed five people. She seems like the best, but what do you all think? It's a group decision."

Nods all around the table.

Moretti uprooted from Brooklyn and moved to Alexandria, Virginia. After that, she received her clearance and met Hussain.

CHAPTER 8

We had made arrangements for the team to see Hussain. Carter, Fredricks, Moretti, Jill, Mohammed, and I made the trip to Guantanamo. There was a little pushback from the prison about the number of visitors, but we pointed out that we all had security clearances, and did they think we would try to organize some kind of escape? Get serious.

Before we sat down, Hussain exploded.

"Why do you insist that we meet in this room?"

We looked at each other. A silent, 'What is this about?'

Carter sat next to him.

"Hussain, what is the problem?"

"I do not want to meet in this room anymore, and if you cannot get them to change it, then I will not meet with you. In fact, please leave."

Jill sat on the other side and gently touched his arm below the elbow. When he did not jerk away, she slid her hand down to his wrist and gently covered his hand.

She whispered, "Can you explain why you hate this room?"

Mohammed translated his halting response.

"I think this is where the CIA held me and hurt me when I was here before. I was kept here for several months the first time I was here at Guantanamo. I was always in either the cage," He pointed at the area with a cement bed covered by a thin blue foam mattress and a stainless steel commode, all behind heavy gray steel mesh that took up about a third of the room, "or where we are now, they would question me." Softly, "And hurt me."

"Why do you think this is the same place?" Jill asked

Hussain's eyes darted. There was a dark spot on the wall. He looked at it but could not talk. His mouth just moved, and he put his head in his hands. A minute later, he looked up and shook his head, side to side.

Jill said, and Mohammed translated using the same soft tone.

"I understand. They did something to you here."

A silent nod.

She moved closer. Softly, "We'd like to talk about your time with the CIA."

"No, I don't want to talk about that."

"Please, will you try?"

"No, You know what they did. I don't need to talk about it."

"But we don't know."

"You are lying. All Americans lie. They told me they had my mother and that she would be raped. That was a lie. You are just like the others. Worse," He looked at me. "You are a Jew. Fuck you, leave. Leave now! "

Hussain was standing, shaking. He kicked the small stool on which his green prayer rug and papers lay. They all flew. He waved at the video camera signaling the guards to come and make us leave. He was shaking and sweating and breathing very hard. And he let out an anguished Arabic moan which Mohammed translated; "I hate this place."

Seeing how upset Hussain was, I wanted to try to defuse the situation and still make some progress. As one of my mentors often said: "No Balls, No Babies."

"Hussain, I'd like to try something. It's a kind of play called a psychodrama. You don't have to do anything. You are the director. Would you mind doing that?"

"This is a trick."

"Pick one of us to play you. Who would you pick?"

He glared at me for several seconds.

"I pick you."

"Okay. Now, in the black site, pick a day you recall. How am I, and I'm playing you, being held? Tell me, and I'll get in that position."

"Get on the floor, on your knees. Lean back so the back of your legs touch your calves. Knees are touching the wall. Now put your head on the wall."

I do that as best as I can, which is not well. Hussain looked at Moretti and told her, "Push his head against the wall."

Moretti does that with some force.

"Jeez, that hurts. Okay, how long will I have to stay like this?"

Hussain seems calmer.

"Sometimes for hours, maybe a day, maybe more."

"Blindfolded?"

"Yes, there is a hood."

Jill puts a sweatshirt over my head. The darkness adds a new dimension. I feel disoriented.

"Go hit him." Moretti gave me a tap, and Hussain shouted in Arabic, which Mohammed mimics in tone, "HIT HIM," and she did, knocking me sideways. She hit me harder from the other side, and I fell over. Not being able to see when or from where the blows were coming was frightening. No way to prepare, no way to protect.

Fredricks made a sound that was half sob, half moan.

"What next?"

"Stand him up."

Jill and Moretti grabbed me and pulled me up.

"Put him against the wall and put his arms up."

"Chained up?" One of them asked.

"Yes, arms up."

"Clothed?"

"No, naked."

Jill said softly to Fredricks, "We do not want to see his little white dick and his scrawny ass," and they laughed softly.

"Food?"

"Stuff from a plastic bottle. Chalky stuff. Makes you shit."

"Where is the toilet?"

"In the bucket between your legs."

A book became the bucket.

"And ..."

"The woman would come."

"What woman?"

"The woman who followed me from place to place. She led them."

"Pick someone."

"I pick Miss Jill."

"And?"

"She was horrible."

Jill comes up to me as I'm standing, blindfolded with arms raised as though chained, and hits me, grabs me, grabs my neck, my face, says, shouts, "Tell me what you are planning?" '

And then slaps me, three times, hard. Then she takes the sweatshirt, wraps it around my neck, and slams my head against the wall.

"Is that how it was?"

Reyes asks.

"Yes," Hussain says.

"But hit my head many times. Hit me many times, made me stand for hours, and loud music. She told me that men were going to rape my mother."

His voice broke. Crying.

"She told me that here, in this room."

We sat in silence. Reyes softly whispered ,"Those motherfuckers." Fredricks looked at him and shook her head and then looked at the floor.

Hussain broke the silence and our despair. He looked at us and said, "and then she would put me in the box."

Jill asked, "Put you in the box? What is the box?"

Hussain looks around and points at the small footstool. Moretti took it and put it by me. Hussain gestured for her to turn it upside down and said, "Get in and kneel down."

I step in the stool and get down about halfway.

"This is as far as I can."

And Hussain says, "No."

He waved me aside, pulled the stool next to him, stood in it, bent down, and hitting himself on the back; he compressed his body until he was folded within the four corners of the two-by-two-by-three stool. Seeing this, *'those fucking monsters.'*

In a shaking voice, Jill asked, "How long?"

"Hours. Once, I think, a whole day."

We are silent. The only noise was the rattling of the air conditioner and breathing. The smell was sweat and fear. And perhaps shame.

Jill stands and waves at the camera to call the guards. She says, "I have to leave; I'm going to be sick."

She is crying.

She does not wait for the guard, a massive breach of the rules, but she gets out the door and vomits onto the rocky pathway.

"Oh, God," she moans. I look up and see Fredricks is crying. I have a sense of pride. *I finally got him to open up.*

The guard watched disdainfully as Jill collected herself and, holding her elbow, escorted her back into the room. He then shrugs and hands her a bottle of water. She takes a big swallow, smiles wanly, and sits. We all sit silently, looking at each other. Kristina looked softer, different. She is wiping her eyes.

I touch Hussain on the shoulder and look at him.

"I don't know what to say. I am so sorry. I am ashamed. Ashamed to be an American right now."

"Shukran." Thank you.

We sat in silence. Jill is sucking on her fist and drinking water. Fredricks wiped her cheeks with her palms. Carter's head was down. I feel like an invisible wall has come down, protecting me from all this pain.

After a few minutes, Jill moved her chair next to him.

"Thank you, that was very brave of you to share that. I am sorry that I became ill. This makes me," and she waved at us, "it makes all of us so sad."

And Carter added, "It makes me angry. Hussain, I understand now why this room makes you angry. We will try to get them to change it. I don't know if that will be successful or not. But I promise we will try."

Hussain nods.

"Mr. Connor, I am very tired. Can we quit?"

"Of course, we, too, need to think about this. Do you want us to come back tomorrow? We will have to meet here, in this room."

Hussain looks different. Less angry.

"Yes, please come back tomorrow. We have much to discuss."

Driving away from the meeting, the team considered dinner.

"Connor, at which of our indifferent choices would you like to eat?"

"You know, I'm pretty tired. That was intense. I think I'll skip dinner. Just chill. I've got some frozen stuff in my room. I'll use the kitchenette or the microwave."

Jill looked at me. Looked at my belly.

"Not like you not to eat. You okay?"

"Just drained. Tired."

Four hours later, I was sitting on the living room couch. The room was lit only by a small desk light. The TV was off; the computer closed. I still had not eaten. I had tried to nap, but I could not get the image of Hussain squatting within the four legs of the stool out of my mind. So, I turned to whiskey. A water glass of Maker's and ice was three fingers short of full. It was my second.

There was a soft knock. It was Jill.

"Came by to check on you. Are you okay? That was pretty intense in there today.

"Yes, it was. But we got him to open up."

"Connor, I've seen some awful stuff in my life. We've seen awful stuff. Remember Tony telling us about the things his uncle did to him? That rolled off us. But I was throwing up today. Everyone else was upset. You seemed detached. Removed. That troubles me."

"Why? Just because I wasn't crying like you guys? I got him to reveal the stuff. That should count for something. The day would have been a waste without that. Made huge strides."

I felt myself getting defensive and angry.

"I'm not criticizing. Of course, the work you did was important. But if you get too numb to the pain, it's not healthy. Not good for you or the team or Hussain. And there is a cost to this, a cost to you. Honestly, I'm kind of worried."

I took a drink. Looked at the glass. Looked at Jill.

"I'm fine."

"Connor, you know I drink. But if the whiskey is to numb you, that's not good. Somehow you have to scrape the callous from your heart so you can feel the pain. That is better than being numb. I don't know how you'll do that, but that is my advice."

"I'm not sure what you mean."

She looked at me. Her eyes glistened.

"I think you know exactly what I mean. But, assuming I'm wrong, If you think about it, you'll understand. Give it some thought."

She stood.

"I've said my piece. I need to get some sleep. We've got a big day tomorrow."

I stood; we looked at each other and hugged.

"Thanks, I know you mean well. I'm doing the best I can."

She smiled and hugged me again.

"My friend, you are believing your own bullshit. See you tomorrow."

I finished the glass, poured another, and called Molly.

"Got a question?"

"Are you drunk dialing?"

"A little. Perhaps a lot. But Jill said something, and I need your opinion. She said I needed to scrape the callous from my heart. I'm not sure what that means, but is that true?"

There was a long pause. I finally asked, "You there?"

"Just thinking how to answer."

More silence.

"Connor, you can be both the most empathetic person I know and the coldest. I get that you need both to do the work you do. But sometimes, it gets blurred. And I think what Jill is saying, and I'm guessing here, is that the cold part is taking up too much space."

She continued, "When was the last time you really cried?"

"I cry all the time. I cry at movies. I cry at coffee or McDonald's commercials. Things with kids. You know that."

"Yes, but when was the last time you really, really cried?

Silence. A long pause.

"When my father died."

"Connor, that was when we were dating. That was years ago. All the pain you see, All the misery. Sometimes, you can be too strong. So I think that is what Jill was saying. That is just my opinion. Of course, what do I, as a trained psychologist, know?"

I could see her smile over the phone.

"Thanks. I'll give it some thought."

"So, how are things going with the case?"

"Good. We got him to open up about the torture. It was pretty bad. Can't talk about it, but it was bad. Really bad. "

A long pause.

"Well, I'll let you get some sleep. Thanks, Molly."

"Hang in there. We'll talk when you get back."

I sat, looking at the phone. Poured the rest of my drink into the sink. I curled up in the empty queen-sized bed and considered the day; what we had seen, and the callous that was apparently on my heart. A couple of tears leaked from each eye. *Well, that's a start.* And I fell into a fitful sleep.

CHAPTER 9

The first public event in a criminal case is the arraignment, the proceeding where the accused enters a plea of guilty or not guilty. Hussain's arraignment, like his trial, was to be in Guantanamo.

As this was the first time Hussain would appear in court, it was a big media event. The diverse groups of people authorized to attend the hearing assembled for the flight to Guantanamo. The groups included media, prosecution and defense lawyers, the judge and his staff, as well as selected family members of those killed or survivors of the attack. As Fox News headlines rolled across multiple TV screens in the sterile waiting room, a recording warned us to "hide from, run from, or fight active shooters." The atmosphere in the waiting room was even more surreal as the potentially hostile groups tried not to mingle or even acknowledge each other.

Sitting, reading my email, I sensed a presence standing over me. It was a white black-haired, middle-aged woman in a long-sleeved shirt with a military logo over her left breast.

"Yes, can I help you?"

"Hi, I'm Samantha Brooks. I'm with the Los Angeles Times."

From the time I'd first heard of Guantanamo, I'd read Samantha Brooks' articles. She was the only reporter consistently covering GTMO. I told her that and also told her that I was honored to meet her; I felt I was in the presence of a journalistic star. She seemed unimpressed by the compliment. I invited her to sit, and we chatted for about an hour. The case, the judge, the prosecutor, the food at Guantanamo, and restaurants in DC. My history. Her history.

She had grown up in Bakersfield, California. 'Couldn't get out of there fast enough.' Then the University of Michigan and Columbia School of Journalism. We could have easily crossed paths if I had gone to Columbia a few years later. She first wrote for the Tampa Bay Times and now Los Angeles. She had been a big fan of the military since she embedded with the First Mountain Division during Desert Storm. She asked if I would mind if she called me occasionally.

"No problem. I think people should know what bullshit this all is."

"Funny, the prosecution says it's fair and great."

"Look, I'm a death penalty lawyer. I've seen a lot of stuff in a lot of states. If this works the way they want it to work, the situation is just fucked. Pardon my language."

"This on or off the record?"

"On, I don't care. On the record, unless I say off."

"So, I hear you claim your client was tortured. Is that true?"

"I don't just claim it. It happened. And Samantha, it is bad, real bad."

"You know, I keep hearing that, but I don't think it was the US. I suspect it was other countries."

"Sorry, you're wrong. I can't say too much, but I've seen the reports. It was the US."

She scowled. Shook her head.

"I'm just not buying it. I just don't think the US would do that."

"Okay. Hopefully, it will come out. You'll see."

We chatted a bit more and agreed to stay in touch. She said she was at Guantanamo every few weeks because that was her beat. She gave me her phone numbers in Guantanamo and LA. Said in Guantanamo, she was at Kelly's most evenings, so perhaps we could have an occasional drink. Not said as a come-on, just a reporter cultivating a source.

We boarded the flight to Guantanamo in groups. The status of least to most important as determined by the military. The most despised were the press, who were seated at the rear of the plane. Then, in order of dislike, the defense and the prosecutors. The judge and his staff, the Convening Authority staff were next, and family members and survivors were seated last.

I was on the aisle at the front of the defense section, and Carter was in the window seat. I'd put my papers on the middle seat to keep it free. But the plane was full, and Jennifer Sanders, one of the attorneys with the prosecution, was looking for a seat. I looked at Carter, and he shrugged, "Why the fuck not."

Sanders, who was about five-six, solid, white but tan, muscular, had short brown hair. She wore a tee shirt that said: Guantanamo, Pearl of the Antilles. *Irony is just lost on these people.* A tan backpack hung by one strap on her shoulder. I signaled her, and she walked up.

"Beggars can't be choosers," she said. "I'll sit in the center."

"No, I'll move. Keep you away from Carter. He's a rascal. Can't be trusted."

She smiled.

"That's what I hear about you."

"Nope. I'm harmless."

I moved, putting the papers in my brown leather briefcase, a relic of a trip with Molly, back when she would travel with me.

Sanders turned, "This is really weird. After the plane takes off, I'll see if one of the press or someone will change seats. You have to be uncomfortable. I am."

I smiled, "Really, not a big problem. But if you sleep, no head on my shoulder."

She smiled.

"Why? Afraid I'll drool and get spit on your raggedy shirt?" She glanced at my very worn denim shirt.

I held up a hand.

"Well, there's that, and of course, I might get aroused, and then we'd have a situation that would certainly make headlines."

A shake of her head.

"Only last a minute or less. No one would notice. Especially me."

"Geez, is it gonna be like this for three hours?"

Her eyes sparkled, "You wanna play in the big leagues? Bring your A game."

She then pulled out a computer and fired up a movie. I did the same. She watched some kind of action movie; I watched a Rom-Com. Carter slept.

As we neared Cuba, Sanders shut her computer down and turned to me, "Can I say something? I hear you think we're all assholes."

"No, only Lawson and, by reputation, Willis."

I gave her what I thought was a winning smile.

"The jury is out on you."

She shook her head.

"Well, I'm doing my job, but it's just a job. I want to try to get through this without unnecessary animosity. Too much conflict makes me crazy."

I shook my head in turn.

"Ahh, I'm sorry, but you're in the wrong business. You guys are trying to kill Hussain. I like Hussain. But whether I like him or not, his life is my responsibility. Hard to not have animosity toward people who want to take a life I'm responsible to protect."

She sat a minute as though it had never occurred to her that asking for the death penalty was trying to kill someone. I'd seen that before, prosecutors who never connected their request for capital punishment to the reality that they were trying to kill another human being, using the law as their weapon.

She looked sad, "That puts things in a harsh light."

She asked about the people who were impacted by the attack.

"Do you have any responsibility to them?"

I told her that I thought my responsibility was to represent Hussain to the best of my ability, which meant bringing out the truth. And that, hopefully, people could appreciate that.

She frowned.

"Well, I just want to keep the hostility to a minimum."

I shook my head.

"And I'd like a fucking pony."

My smile had no impact as she turned and said nothing for the rest of the flight.

Carter nudged me as we got off the plane and walked across the tarmac.

"Man, you are really smooth. That how come you're separated?"

I shook my head and laughed, "No, I was way worse to my wife."

"Seriously," he said, "Was that necessary? She was just trying to develop a professional relationship."

"Ahh," I shrugged. "I just never know what's going to come out of my mouth."

I thought about what Carter had said about Sanders. I decided I should try to mend the fence, so as we waited for the ferry that would take us across the bay to the main section of Guantanamo, I found a moment, pulled Sanders aside, and said, "Look, I was a bit harsh on the plane. I'm sorry if I was a dick. I apologize."

She looked directly at me.

"Yes, you were a dick, but honest, and I can respect that."

"Fair enough. We good?"

"Sure, we were never bad or good. "

For some reason, that stung more than it should have.

CHAPTER 10

Before the arraignment, we were given a set of instructions two pages long on how to access the courtroom. Drive this way, park here. Go in this door. Carter, Moretti, Fredricks, and I rode together in the four-door Ford truck that I had been issued upon our arrival. Carter also had a vehicle, but he preferred to ride with me, observing kindly,

"It's so rare to see a Jewish guy driving a truck that I want to etch this in my memory."

As we prepared for the arraignment, Carter kept telling me that I had to defer entering a plea. He explained that in the military, when the defendant enters a plea, the trial immediately begins. As we were nowhere near ready for trial, a plea of not guilty at this time would have been a disaster.

After his explanation, I smilingly asked, "So, do we plead not guilty at the beginning or the end of the hearing?" Catching the joke, he said,

"Some hotshot lawyer you are. Apparently dumb as a stump."

Approaching the court on the designated route, we came to a checkpoint where we were stopped and asked to show the badges we'd been issued to allow us access to the court area. As the badges were being reviewed, a young soldier scanned the bottom of the truck with a mirror, looking for, I guess, bombs.

Carter said, "Ahh, security theater."

"What do you mean?"

"Watch and learn, son, watch and learn."

As we left the checkpoint, we drove through a maze of bright orange plastic barriers. Of course, if we were hostile, the truck could have sped through the maze scattering the barriers and reaching whatever the target was.

"These people are idiots."

"This would explain why you're still a major," I observed.

"Bad attitude."

"You haven't begun to see my bad attitude." He said, smiling.

We drove to another checkpoint, where again, our badges were checked. Then we were routed to another maze that led to the parking lot, which was, of course, surrounded by even more orange barriers.

Fredricks asked, "I wonder whose brother-in-law supplied the orange barriers at, no doubt, double cost to the government? "

After parking the truck in the specially marked designated area, we walked to a brown, upside-down-U-shaped, semi-permanent building about forty yards long and fifteen paces wide. The tan door told us in big red letters that this was the Courtroom Access Point.

We entered a tangle of shiny posts and black belts taking us this way and that. A young female soldier wearing a flak jacket and a sidearm at the first station asked to see our badges. Then a right turn took us to a walk-through metal detector with green lights if you successfully passed and red flashing with a lot of air raid siren noise if you failed. My car keys set off the red lights, creating quite a stir. Mercifully no weapons were drawn, but hands went to hips.

The next left took us to another soldier, also in combat gear, who asked to see our badges which prompted a sarcastic, "Again, really?"

A second right turn took us to the soldier who asked, "Any cell phones or computers?"

And then, after another left turn to what appeared to be the final obstacle, yet another combat-ready female soldier asked again to see our badges and then asked about cell phones and computers.

At this final station, the guard observed the large, white, three-ring binders that Carter, Fredricks, Moretti, and I were carrying. She told us we could not take them into the courtroom.

"They might be weapons."

For Fuck's sake. I explained that we were the defense lawyers. We need these notebooks for the hearing. Please check with your superior. She did, and the superior confirmed that notebooks would not be allowed.

"Okay, here is what we'll do. I'm going to have my paralegal stay here with the notebooks. I trust you, but they contain sensitive information, and it's best for both of us. You good with that?"

"Sure."

"And tell me, who is your superior? "

"Major Robinson, sir."

"I suspect the judge will want to speak with Major Robinson, so please ask him to remain available."

From the checkpoint, we endured a fifty-yard walk through a corridor of chain link fencing topped with razor wire and covered with black netting, which I would learn was to protect us from nonexistent snipers. Then into a courtyard.

Entering the courtroom building, a large barn-like structure, we encountered yet another badge check in the anteroom. Then, after another well-armed young man hunched over a lock to hide the keypad and punched in a code, we were admitted into the courtroom. The room was about one hundred feet long and fifty feet wide. On each side of a center aisle were six rows of tables. The right side was for the prosecution, and the left side was for the defense. On the left side of the defense table, a large metal eye bolt was sticking out of the floor to help secure the defendant's chains. At the front, a large bench for the judge was raised three feet above the lawyers. On the wall behind the judge, in a neat row the symbols of all five armed forces: Army, Navy, Air Force, Marines, and Coast Guard.

I advised the court staff of the notebook issue. The judge's assistant, a Captain, probably a newly minted law school grad who had joined the Air Force JAG corps, looked at me as if I had three eyes.

"Really?"

"Hey, what can I tell you?"

"I'll let the judge know."

About ten minutes later, Roseborough came in, lugging the notebooks and a huge smile.

"What's so funny?"

"You should have heard Major Robinson trying to explain how a notebook could be dangerous. Judge just laughed at him. Reamed him a new one."

As we sat and waited for the guards to bring in Hussain, Carter observed, "That was a perfect metaphor for this place. A pointless maze leading nowhere, accomplishing nothing, all at an extraordinary cost."

CHAPTER 11

We sat at our table, watching the spectators enter the viewing room, separated from the court by thick glass. They would hear what was said on a forty-second delay to protect them from hearing any classified evidence. However, the only classified evidence was about the torture inflicted on Hussain, which was unlikely to be discussed in any detail today.

Then Hussain was brought in, escorted by four large guards, two on each arm walking slowly. I flashed on how stupid this was; he was 5'5", and 120 pounds. *Where the fuck was he going to go. Swim to Jamaica? This was all for show.*

As he sat down, Hussain turned and looked around the room and gestured with his right arm sweeping, "is this all for me?" with Mohammed translating.

"Yes."

"Oh. Who are those people at the back?"

I replied, "People who were in Kuwait, or their families and the press."

He looked down, "I am sorry for the pain the people feel. Can you tell them I am sorry?"

"Perhaps, you'll have the chance to tell them, but not today. Today you just sit quietly."

The judge, Colonel James Pierce, took the bench, and we were off. As part of the arraignment process in military courts, the defendant must formally accept representation by counsel. This officially commences the attorney-client relationship. This unique process was preserved when military commissions were created, even though our attorney-client relationship with Hussain had existed for months.

When Pierce got to that part of the arraignment process, all of us were stunned when Hussain told Pierce, "I would prefer that Mr. Mendelson not be my lawyer."

Pierce looked at me and glared, "Did you know this was coming?"

"No, Your Honor."

"Mr. al-Yemeni, you have a right to death penalty qualified counsel. There is unlikely to be another. So why don't you want Mr. Mendelson?"

"Because I cannot trust him. He is a Jew."

Pierce rocked back. The courtroom was hushed.

"Counsel, before I decide how to proceed, I am going to recess. I'd like you to go back to the cell behind the court and meet with Mr. al-Yemeni."

He turned, looked at Hussain.

"I'd advise you to reconsider. Mr. Mendelson's credentials are first-rate. This is a difficult situation for you, and you need his counsel."

The team huddled as we waited for Hussain to be escorted back to his cell.

I said, "I'm not going to go back to the cell. I don't really care how this plays out. You guys meet with him." *Fuck him.*

Carter left. I stared at the notebooks in front of me. I heard the hum of the air conditioning system that kept the room so cold that a winter suit was necessary. I realized that I was smiling. I felt different, lighter. I was relieved. The internal struggles I'd felt had perhaps been resolved. Of course, a public firing due to my heritage was not pleasant, but that would pass. I*'m glad to be out of this.*

Then Willis and Sanders came toward me from their side of the courtroom. Willis spoke first, "Did you see this coming?"

"No, it came up some time ago. I thought we'd diffused this nonsense."

"We've decided that Judge Pierce has the authority to appoint you no matter what al Yemeni wants. Jennifer felt we should tell you that that would be our position."

"But what if I say no? The client does not want me. No reason for me to be here."

Jennifer looked over.

"You entered your appearance. Only the chief defense counsel or the judge can excuse you. Doubt that would happen over this complaint."

"Look, it will be a mess if I'm forced on him. And I think on reflection that I'm not sure I'm the right lawyer for this. So you guys should just let him fire me if that's what he wants."

Jennifer laughed, "And I'd like a fucking pony. No chance." Then she winked at me. Friendly actually.

"I guess I earned that." And smiled back.

"But in the long run, this might be better with someone else."

Willis shook his head.

"Can't let the inmates run the asylum. Sorry, but if we let him fire you, there will be no end to it."

As Sanders and Willis walked back to their side of the room, Carter said that Hussain wanted to speak with me.

The cell was about ten by five. Made of metal. Yellow walls. Meat locker cold. Carter sat next to Moretti. I stood by the cell door with my arms crossed. Mohammed, the interpreter, stood next to Hussain, facing the bed. I nodded at Hussain.

"Mr. Connor. I am sorry. I just needed to tell the judge how I felt. I know you mean well, but I just cannot fully trust you. I am sorry."

"Hussain, I will not lie. I was angry. But perhaps now I am relieved. I don't want to be your lawyer if you don't want me. So if this is how you feel, I accept that and wish you good luck. I will try to honor your wishes."

I turned slightly and explained to Carter that the prosecution would insist that the judge keep me on the case no matter what Hussain wanted.

As I waved at the guard to let me out. Hussain asked, "Mr. Connor, will you do your best?"

Insulted by his question, I brusquely snarled, "Of course."

And I signaled again for the guard to let me out.

Ten minutes later, I sat at the long counsel table pretending I was reading. But, actually, I was just trying to calm down.

Carter bent down, "He wants you to promise the judge that you will do your best and that you harbor no ill will toward Muslims. Then he will agree that you can be his lawyer. For now."

I shook my head. Thought *Fuck him.* I nodded in agreement.

Everyone reassembled. Pierce looked down.

"Where are we?"

Carter stood.

"Your honor Mr. al-Yemeni wants Mr. Mendelson to assure him and you that he will do his best and that he harbors no ill will toward Muslims. Then he will accept Mr. Mendelson."

I stood and told Hussain in as monotone a voice as I could muster that I would do my best and that I had no ill will toward Muslims. That was translated. We looked at each other. He nodded. I was impassive. Hopefully, letting my anger show.

Pierce cleared his throat.

"Do you accept Mr. Mendelson as your death penalty counsel?"

"For now, I do."

Pierce looked at the lawyers, "Okay, let's move on to the voir dire."

In the military, both sides can question the judge about things that might make him partial to one side or the other. The questioning of the judge was straightforward; he said he had no conflicts, no opinion as to Hussein's guilt or innocence, and was "agnostic" as to the death penalty.

I asked, "Do you think torture is mitigating?"

"If someone was truly tortured, it's possibly entitled to some mitigating weight."

"Well, what does the phrase truly tortured mean to you?"

"The rack, medieval stuff."

"Is waterboarding torture? Is sleep deprivation torture?"

"I don't know," He didn't know what torture was and didn't know or seem to care if the process was fair. He said, "My job is to follow the law, and if it leads to" and he used finger quotes, "an unfair result, well, so be it. I just follow the rules."

"So, you are indifferent to the fairness of this proceeding?" I asked.

"Counselor, I follow the rules. I hope the rules provide fairness. But whether they do or not, my job is to follow the rules and to get this process concluded. That is best for the people in the back, the public, and your client."

The reference to the client was a clear afterthought.

When we'd exhausted all the subjects he didn't know or hadn't thought about; we had no further questions. *Hussain, you are so, so fucked.*

Pierce then followed the script and asked about a plea.

I looked at Carter and smiled.

"Your Honor, the defendant enters," and I paused. Carter looked ill, and I smiled more.

"He enters no plea."

Carter relaxed, and I sat down.

"Got you."

"You sure did. You buy dinner tonight."

The judge then turned to scheduling.

"Gentlemen, Ladies, I want motions for discovery filed in ninety days. I want motions to dismiss filed in one hundred and eighty days. I'm looking at a trial in thirteen months."

I stood.

"Your honor, that is not realistic."

"Mr. Mendelson, we in the military believe in swift but fair justice. I'm setting a trial in thirteen months. We'll work toward that trial date."

The judge brought up discovery. The prosecution is required to provide certain material in advance of trial. Here the material was expected to be voluminous. It was the prosecution's position that it would take "at least" six months to provide us thirty thousand pages of classified discovery and "about three or four months" to provide about three hundred thousand pages of unclassified discovery. I responded that this made a trial in thirteen months hopelessly unrealistic.

Pierce turned to Lawson, "General, you have two weeks to get them all the unclassified discovery."

"I don't think we can do that, your honor."

"General, this is an order; you fail to comply at your peril. Understood? "

"We'll do our best, your honor."

Said dismissively as in, 'I don't really care what a Colonel has to say. You don't give me orders.'

"Defense, does that solve your concerns?"

"No. thirteen months is just unrealistic if you want us to be prepared and provide proper counsel."

"Trial will be set in thirteen months. If there is a delay from that, it will be short, very, very short. These folks," and here he nodded at the survivors, "have been waiting years for justice, and I'm going to have a trial at the earliest possible time. Am I clear?"

All I could do was say, "Yes, sir."

Then Pierce stalked off the bench. As we were leaving, Sanders gave me a quiet nod and a smile.

CHAPTER 12

Two days after the arraignment hearing, the entire contingent returned to Andrews. I was standing next to Sanders, waiting for luggage.

She touched my arm, "I hope there are no hard feelings that we pushed to keep you in the case. And the pony thing. Got to admit I enjoyed that."

Without thinking, I asked if I could call her and have a drink.

"To keep lines of communication open."

Surprisingly she said, "I'll think about it." And gave me her email address.

A couple of weeks later, I reached out, and she replied, "Against my better judgment, I'll meet you. I can only stay an hour or so. How about the Board Room in Alexandria?"

Two days later, I was at a very public table in the middle of the central area of the Board Room. I'd arrived a few minutes early and was sitting, trying to figure out why I'd asked Jennifer to meet. It made no sense. She is a prosecutor in a capital case. I'm nominally married, hoping to become more, not less, married. *Connor, you idiot, no good will come of this.*

As I was thinking of canceling, she appeared, dressed in a pink oxford shirt and tan slacks, hair in a ponytail. I waved.

Before we could even exchange pleasantries, a perky waitress came and asked, "So what'll it be to get the juices flowing?"

Jennifer nodded, "You first."

I ordered a Makers Mark on the rocks, and she one-up'd me with "a Woodford Reserve with one big ice cube."

I smiled, "A whisky drinker, nice."

"I suppose you thought I was a Chardonnay girl."

"No, I figured you for White Zin."

A smile.

"Why the invite?"

I cupped my chin in my hand for a second:

"Good question. I've been asking myself that. I realized I was an asshole in GTMO. You were trying to do the right thing. And you got me back when Hussain was being stupid. And having someone on the prosecution, I can talk to might be helpful to both sides. But to be honest, I was thinking of canceling."

She shook her head, "Well, in the military, it's more collegial, so it's okay. Plus, I've thought about the things you said. What you said about responsibility makes sense. We are trying to have your client executed. That must weigh on you."

She took a drink, "So, what shall we talk about?"

"Tell me about yourself. Seems safe."

"Easy," she said. She grew up in Kansas City. Went to Missouri undergrad and law. Went into JAG to get out of Missouri. Married, three years, no kids. She'd served at Ft. Bragg. Iraq. Ft. Carson. She saw the Military Commissions as a good career move because General Lawson, the Chief Prosecutor, was well thought of and could open doors for her.

"How does your husband deal with the travel and hassle?"

"He's military, too. So we're separated a lot. In fact, he's away on temporary duty this week. Some kind of war games; infantry stuff." She gestured toward me.

"And you?"

"Columbia law, a long time ago. Always done defense work. Two kids, separated."

"If it's not too personal, what was the problem?"

"Travel. Gone too much. Too big an ego. Too often, I guess I was an asshole."

Sanders smiled.

"I can see that."

And we both chuckled, remembering the flight to Guantanamo. Sanders looked directly at me. "Other women?"

"Wow, that was quick. Not going there. You know how it is."

"No, actually, I don't."

"And will you get back together? Guessing this case doesn't help. All the travel."

"No, the case doesn't help at all."

"Why criminal defense?"

I explained that criminal defense was always what I wanted to do. When I was in law school, trials were the only thing that really interested me. I'd cut school and go downtown and watch trials. Learned more from the court watchers than I ever learned about trials at Columbia.

"What are court watchers?"

I explained that every courthouse had people who spent their time watching trials. I told her about a guy in New York, Leonardo DiSilva, who, while he was not a lawyer, took me under his wing. Taught me a lot.

"Sounds colorful."

I smiled at the memory. I'm watching the start of a murder trial. Waiting on jury selection to begin. Judge is messing with the defense lawyer, and wants to know if his client has an alibi. Lawyer is taking no guff. Now I'm a law student. I think judges are all scholars, all legal giants, and I am stunned that a lawyer would be so disrespectful. DiSilva leans over and, in a Brooklyn Italian accent, says. "Kid. Judge is fucking with the lawyer. He knows the client doesn't have an alibi because the odds are the client did it. But the lawyer, Winkler, knows the case is shitty because the cops are idiots who couldn't find a Jew in Tel Aviv. Or maybe he's hoping the case will turn to shit. Happens a lot with this prosecutor who could screw up a wet dream. Watch. The jury will be bored by the third witness. Actually, the judge and lawyer are friends. They both belong to the same Democrat club."

Jennifer laughed.

"DiSilva and the other court watchers would take me out. Tell me stories. Teach me. I learned a lot."

The hour passed smoothly, and we parted, agreeing to remain in contact.

CHAPTER 13

A few weeks later, the first tranche of discovery was delivered on a thumb drive. There were, as best we could tell, 220,000 documents. Hard to tell how many pages. There was no identifying information, just al-Yemeni 000001, 000002, and so on. Everyone was given a copy of the drive and an assignment to review a section of the documents cursorily so we could figure out what we had. By the end of the following week, we understood that there were a huge number of documents pertaining to the attack. These included photographs, FBI reports of the investigation, and witness statements. Also, records related to the autopsies of the airmen and women killed in the attack. Other sections dealt with al-Yemeni's treatment while at Guantanamo since 2006. There was nothing about his time in CIA custody.

The following Tuesday, Moretti came into my office with Carter and Fredricks in tow. She was holding several pages.

"We found his confession."

The pages she found revealed that in February of 2007, four months after al-Yemeni was brought to Guantanamo, he had been questioned by the FBI. Three FBI agents, two men and a woman, and an interpreter met with him over four days at Echo, where we met with him. Each day the FBI told him that they were not part of the same group that had questioned him in "other locations." They also said he could leave at any time, which was nonsense. Where was he going to go?

The FBI summary of his statement made several references to "what I told the people a long time ago" and nothing about any abuse.

The summary described the Kuwaiti attack and according to the FBI, al-Yemeni acknowledged being the leader of the planning and the execution of the attack. There were brief references to "Walid and Assad." In the statement,he talked about Bin Laden's desire for a big body count, which is why al-Yemeni claimed he selected the dining facility and the fuel dump. If this statement was true, it was damning.

As we sat in my office, Moretti and Fredricks in the chairs and Carter pacing back and forth, yellow pad in hand, Fredricks and Carter took turns criticizing the FBI and how the statement was taken. As one spoke, the other would scribble and then weigh in, the deficiencies becoming increasingly evident.

"No rights warning. No way for him to leave. No way for him to know what would happen if he refused. We don't know what he told the CIA; they won't give us that. So this is just nonsense."

Moretti chimed in. The reports were misleading because he seemed like a regular guy talking to his friends. But she pointed out that al-Yemeni is a mess and can't go ten minutes without showing symptoms of PTSD. He was probably more symptomatic then. But nothing is documented. And he's just parroting the story he told the CIA. The question is, is that story true or just what they wanted to hear?

We made some notes about what we needed, collectively drafted a letter to the prosecution outlining a series of demands for additional information, and sent it off by email. A few days later, we got a polite response "that additional classified and unclassified information would be coming in due course. "

By then, we had discovered even more objections and issues undermining his reliability by reviewing his medical records. Three days before the FBI questioning began, there was an entry in his records that began, 'Because the FBI is coming to question al-Yemeni, we have been instructed by the FBI to take him off the psychotropic medication which keeps him calm. The FBI does not want lawyers to claim he was on drugs when he was questioned.'

Simple Internet research told us that taking someone off this medication would leave them symptomatic and agitated, but the FBI did not document any agitation. So we made a note to find experts who could testify about this error.

Carter's analysis:

"This dog won't hunt. This is a farce. It's insulting. No responsible prosecutor would try to get this into evidence."

CHAPTER 14

I was walking into my office when Moretti stopped me.

"I was going through the victim's information. Senior Airman Darryl Decker was from your city. Do you recall anything about it when the attack occurred? Must have been in the papers."

"Yes, it was in the papers. I casually know his parents."

Moretti looked shocked.

"That going to be a problem?"

"I thought about it. I talked with my wife as well. But we were only nodding acquaintances with the parents, and Airman Decker is not central to the case. So, I don't see an issue."

"What did your wife say? Did she agree?"

"No, she didn't want me to take the case in the first place. Felt that with travel and everything else, it would be hard to address our problems. So in her mind, this was just another reason for me to say no."

"Have you spoken to the parents? Smooth things over?"

"Called once. I left a message, but they didn't return the call."

I shrugged.

"And if the parents testify? Which almost certainly will happen; what then?"

"We'll deal with it then. More important things to worry about right now. It's not a big deal."

Kristina looked at me with sad eyes and shook her head in little movements.

"I think you're wrong. I can see it being a big issue."

"Kristina, I don't know these people that well. But there are more important issues here than their feelings."

"Connor, I don't even know what to say. "

CHAPTER 15

I was in my room at Guantanamo, nursing a drink. The fluorescent light on the ceiling caused the yellow paint on the cinder block walls to glisten chartreuse. The brown couch in the living room sank a bit more than was comfortable. It was difficult to distinguish between the pattern on the tan carpet and the many stains of dubious origin. The bowl of Fritos I was snacking on left an odor of corn, grease, and chemicals. It went well with the smell of the whiskey.

We'd come down to see Hussain. We'd seen him for six hours a day for two days. And the visits had become productive. He'd even joked about trying to fire me. Tomorrow, we would see him again.

I'd called Molly, and my daughters. TV held little interest. I didn't feel like watching a movie. I was just sipping my whiskey and letting my mind focus on whatever thoughts wandered into my consciousness.

A light knock on the door interrupted my trance. Jennifer Sanders was at the door, dressed in a green army tee shirt, green running shorts, and Asics running shoes, smiling, holding a six-pack of Sam Adams Beer.

"Are you doing anything?"

"No, but I'm not going for a run if that's what you had in mind."

She smiled, "I was thinking of running but decided a chat with you would be more fun."

She walked in and looked at the brown grip on the dining table, socks and underwear off to the side.

"Travel light?"

"Hey, it's GTMO, no court, not much to do. My tux is at the cleaners. You bring a full wardrobe?"

"Well, Lawson makes us bring a lot of different uniforms. He assigns a uniform of the day at eight the night before. But it can change on his whim the next morning. So, we gotta be prepared. Want a beer?"

"I raised my glass; I'm having whiskey, thanks. You want some?"

"I'm good with beer tonight."

Sanders sat in the tan, deep back chair. The large arms on her chair protected her from flank assaults. Ninety degrees from the couch. '*I'm here to talk, nothing more.*'

Whiskey in hand, I sat at the end of the couch, farthest away from her. '*Message received.*'

"So what's going on? What brings you to the slums? Looking to see how the defense devils live? Where we hide our dead?"

Jennifer spent the next several minutes complaining about the petty intrusions, insults, and requirements that were wearing down the morale of Lawson's staff. After a bit, she had finished venting and had run out of invective.

"Are you sure you should be telling me this?"

Sanders launched into another series of complaints about Lawson ending with, "He treats us like fucking children. Or slaves or both. Plus, I don't trust him. I don't know why. How do you put up with the bullshit? The nonsense?"

I explained that it was different on the defense side. General Ward was pretty hands-off. He only cares about the case going to trial as soon as possible. And as a civilian, the military structure did not affect me as much. Finally, I told her that, for some reason, I could laugh at a lot of the stuff we had to deal with.

She looked at me strangely.

"No, really. That's the truth." I continued, "I just try to appreciate the insanity of all this. Laughter," and I raised my glass, "and whiskey helps."

The conversation became lighter, movies, law school comparisons, trial stories.

An hour had passed. Sanders was on her third beer. I was into my second Maker's. *Hard to see where this was headed.*

"I'd best be leaving, so you don't take advantage of me."

"No worries. I wouldn't do that unless you wanted me to take advantage of you." We looked at each other *Talk about a conflict of interest.*

Jennifer shook her head, "Nope, just came by for a chat."

Said firmly.

"Want me to check the hallway and make sure no one is around? Don't want your reputation sullied."

And then, by unspoken consent, a hug. Nothing more, just a long, firm hug.

She whispered, "Thanks for listening."

"You're always welcome to vent. Your secrets are safe."

"Thanks, I appreciate that. And the hug was nice too. I guess I needed that."

I went out the door, looked both ways, walked down the hall, came back, nodded my head, and she was gone. Only the empty bottles, the unfinished beers, the scent of her, and the questions remained.

CHAPTER 16

At a team meeting in DC, Fredricks and Jill were chatting.

"How do you even know where to begin your mitigation work?"

Jill smiled and said that mitigation, the search to explain a horrible crime, begins with the client but always extends quickly to his family. The family knows the history and knows what went wrong. But, getting the family to reveal the backstory that brought the client to the courtroom is often a considerable challenge. Family secrets are not easily revealed. Before learning the secrets, we must learn the family dynamics and obtain the family's trust.

Our team's problem was that Hussain did not know how to contact his family. When he last saw them about ten years ago, they'd lived in Mecca, the holy city of Saudi Arabia. But going to Saudi was difficult, and for non-Muslims, Mecca was out of reach. Hussain recalled that he had an uncle in Yemen, Ahmad, who kept in close contact with his family. So we decided that the best option was to go to Yemen to see if we could find Ahmad and perhaps find Hussain's family.

What gave us pause was that al-Qaeda dominated some areas of Yemen. There was little security, so the few tourists or foreign businessmen who went there risked being kidnapped for ransom. This is not a place where you'd choose to go.

As I often did when facing a dilemma, I spoke with Molly. When I told Molly we were thinking of going to Yemen, she reacted, "Are you serious? I know the girls are grown, but they still need their father."

"I understand," I said, "No other way to try to find his family."

"What about your family? I don't want you hurt or worse. Sometimes you have to walk away from stupid. I told you not to get involved in this case. Now Yemen? "

"It'll be okay. And you're still the beneficiary on my life insurance."

She did not find this funny.

Asking reporters and others who had been to Yemen, we were directed to Nabil, who lived in Sana'a, the capital of Yemen. We were told Nabil was the guy who could find anyone, find anything, and get you in to see anyone.

Jill and I e-mailed and then spoke with Nabil, who assured us he could find Ahmad, and that travel to Yemen was pretty safe unless you have to go to the tribal areas, which is more chancy. "But we'd probably be okay."

A couple of weeks later, Nabil said that he'd located Ahmad and that Ahmad would meet with us if we came to Yemen.

When we spoke to the Yemeni embassy, we found the officials happy to assist us.

"We don't have too many requests for travel to Yemen since the recent kidnappings."

Leaving the embassy, Carter said, "A country whose slogan could be: You Probably Won't Be Kidnapped, does not get a lot of visitors."

Weeks later, Jill and I hopscotched around the world from DC to Dubai and then to Sana'a. The flight to Sana'a was only about a quarter full. Mostly men dressed in white Yemeni robes. A few in business suits. The few women were in black robes, fully veiled with black Hajibs, showing only their eyes. The flight took us from the desert of the Emirates over the Indian Ocean and then into Yemen, which was quite mountainous and green.

Nabil was outside customs holding a small sign with our names: Mr. Connor, Ms. Jill.

Nabil was taller than most of the Yemeni men surrounding him—5'8", thin, dressed in a black robe with a colorful patterned border at the hem and around the cuffs. A thick woven belt of red, green, and white was cinched at the waist. The scabbard on his belt held a Jambiyh, a curved knife with a large brass handle, and he wore black wingtip shoes. This, we learned, was traditional Yemeni garb. Nabil's jet-black hair glistened with Brilliantine.

His first question, "Did you happen to bring some liquor? I can sell it for a lot because liquor is not allowed in Yemen."

While waiting for our luggage, a man in a business suit and wide colorful tie approached us and asked politely, "Why are you here?"

Nabil promptly moved us away and told us not to speak with him.

"PSO," he said.

"What is PSO?"

"Political Security Office. Secret Police. Keeping tabs on foreigners. We will possibly be followed."

Our hotel, the Burj al Salam, was in the Old City of Sana'a. To get there, we went from the "new city," reasonably modern looking with signs for Deloitte & Touché and KFC, through the Babb ali Yemen gate, which Nabil told us was around a thousand years old. Nabil, acting as tour guide, told us about the hundred mosques, the 6,500 homes, the souk, and the other wonders of the Old City.

He said, "The Old City, the central part of Sana'a, is a warren of random streets and alleyways; the shops are small, the houses are unique."

We could see that each house was two, three, or four stories high, topped with a flat roof. Throughout the old city, stained glass windows were everywhere, and their reflection left lovely green, red, blue, and yellow patterns on the streets and walls during the day. Nabil described the architecture as 'Fifteenth-century modern.'

After a meal at the hotel and sleep disturbed at five in the morning by the Muslim call to prayer booming from dozens of mosques near our hotel, Jill and I faced a day of waiting for Nabil to confirm our meeting with Ahmad.

Jill suggested, "Let's wander the Old City and get used to Yemen and let Yemen get used to us."

So, we wandered and ended up in the Suq al Milh, a marketplace where we bargained and bought spices and Yemeni Jambiya, the curved daggers unique to Yemen. People wanted to practice their English or get messages to their family members living in the US.

Several shopkeepers pointed out the two Yemeni men dressed in white robes, red and white checked scarves, and wide colorful belts holding the curved knives. "PSO" was routinely whispered.

That afternoon, Nabil advised that Ahmad said he would not come to Sana'a but would welcome us to his home.

"Why won't he come to us?"

"PSO, too many PSO. Too much hassle."

"Is this safe?" Jill asked.

"Yes, probably safe. Should be no problem."

Probably safe was hardly encouraging, but as Jill said, "It can hardly be more dangerous than South Central L.A., and we went there. We're here. Let's go."

She laughed lightly, "And if it becomes an issue, I'll tell them you're Jewish. No reason for both of us to get killed."

Nabil and a driver picked us up early the following day in a dark red Toyota SUV with a big tire attached to the back. As we left Sana'a, we came to a checkpoint manned by men in dark green Yemeni Army uniforms. Our passports were examined, and there was a lot of excited chatter in rapid Arabic among the soldiers. There was also a lot of pointing at us, followed by laughter among the soldiers and Nabil. As we left the checkpoint, Nabil told us there were many questions about why we were going to Ahmad's village. Jill laughingly suggested that the soldiers were probably making bets on our chances of getting back alive. She can be quite comforting when she puts her mind to it.

We drove up steep winding roads with no guardrails. The only rule of the road seemed to be that the largest vehicle always had the right-of-way. After an hour of climbing, we began our descent into a beautiful valley filled with large groves of vibrant green trees.

"The trees are Khat," said Nabil, referring to the national pastime of Yemeni men, chewing Khat. While walking in the old city, we'd observed that men would meet, chat and chew the stimulant from about two o'clock in the afternoon into the evening. Work pretty much stopped by mid-afternoon.

At the base of the valley, we came to a small village. The traffic on the narrow road was crawling as it was a market day, and stalls selling clothing, meat, spices, and household goods spilled into the street. Young men ambled through the market. They were dressed in robes, and Keffeyh, red and white checked headscarves, carrying Kalashnikovs, the Soviet-made automatic rifles with large curved magazines.

I asked, "So what do we do if they attack us?"

Nabil shrugged, "I guess we will be killed. They are not expecting us. They have no reason to attack us. It's unlikely to be an issue."

Despite his air of confidence, Nabil was noticeably calmer when we were out of the village and on a less congested road through groves of Khat trees and terraced fields cut into the sides of the mountains.

At the turnoff to Ahmad's village, Suq Althulatha, we began a very steep climb up a rutted dirt road. The driver stopped several miles up the dirt road and got out of the truck. He pointed to a trench about four feet deep and six feet wide that had been dug across the entire road. On the right side is an impassable mountain wall; on the left is a cliff. No way forward. Unconcerned, Nabil was on his phone and, after a couple of calls, said, "We walk around the cut. There is a small trail. A friend of mine, a guy, will come to get us. He'll drive the rest of the way. It'll cost $100 U.S." A fortune in Yemen.

A half-hour later, a Toyota Hilux arrived, and we clambered aboard for a long climb up an impossibly steep hill on a road that petered into non-existence; it was indistinguishable from the large rocks over which we were slowly driving.

As we crested the mountain, we were stopped by four young men carrying Kalashnikovs. They looked into the car and began yelling at Jill, who had a tiny amount of hair peeking out from her headscarf. Nabil apologized, Jill promptly covered the errant hair, and we were allowed to drive to the village.

Ahmad must have heard we'd made it up the mountain because he was waiting outside his home. A brick multi-story, stained-glass windowed, flat-roofed home similar to those in the old city of Sann'a. Ahmad was short, had smooth dark leather brown skin, and black hair fringed with hints of silver. His hands had calluses as thick as the soles of my shoes. He wore a white Thobe but, remarkably, no knife. Sandals protected dark-skinned feet from the sharp rocks and dirt that seemed to be the street to his home. Ahmad appeared to be around sixty, although his weathered look possibly disguised his age. He led us inside a large room with many stained-glass windows, gray cement floors covered with carpets, and many huge, embroidered pillows. The windows made kaleidoscope patterns on every surface. There were no chairs.

Yemeni custom dictates that guests must be treated warmly, which means a feast must occur. So a feast had to be prepared. We were left sitting for an hour to chat with Ahmad and some village elders.

We explained that Hussain sent his blessings and why we had come to meet with Ahmad. Ahmad apparently had consulted the elders and agreed that he would give us the telephone number for his brother, Hussain's father. We continued to chat with the group, with the Saudi sun pouring directly into the room. My blue button-down shirt was becoming increasingly soaked.

For dinner, we went to an even larger room where a large red rug was totally covered with various plates of food. Ahmad and the elders beckoned us to join them on the floor. There was a large plate for each of us, but no utensils as the food was to be scooped with flat unleavened bread similar to pita. Young women kept bringing plates of the bread, still very hot, from the wood oven. The bread alone made the adventure worthwhile.

The feast included many Yemeni delicacies, including roast baby lamb, saffron rice with raisins and nuts, a meat stew, and marinated thin chicken with curried rice. It was all spicy and delicious, and I ate heartily. We ended our feast with a gooey dessert with honey and nuts.

We spoke of Hussain, his father, his mother, and life in Yemen and Saudi Arabia, where Ahmad had lived for several years before returning to Yemen. After the meal, the men and I chewed khat, a post-dinner tradition in Yemen. Jill looked on doubtfully as we chewed boluses of green cud, spitting into cups. By this time, the necessary courtesies had been respected, and Ahmad and the elders were not paying too much attention to us, so they hopefully didn't notice me trying not to gag. Ultimately I discretely spit the ball into a cup, and Jill and I talked. Then lime water was passed, and I greedily drank in the heat, excitement, and tension. After the third cup of lime water, I smiled and looked at Nabil, "I'm guessing drinking this is not the best idea I've ever had?"

He nodded, "No, I live in Yemen, and I wouldn't drink that. But you got Hussain's family's phone number, so if it kills you, it was for a good cause."

At Jill's request, Ahmad called Hussain's father and introduced us. Using Nabil as an interpreter, we spoke with Hussain's father, who made it clear that there was no reason for us to come to Saudi Arabia as they would not meet with us.

Jill said later, "We'll keep calling them. They'll see us."

Night was approaching, and we pressed Nabil to make our exit. Refusing offers to spend the night, we said our goodbyes with kisses between the men. Ahmad profusely thanked us as he told us what a good son and nephew Hussain was.

When we got back down the mountain, we found one tire on our SUV slashed. The knife left in the tire. Clearly a warning.

The drive back to Sana'a was now in complete darkness. The driver, still chewing Khat, was slightly stoned. Jill allowed that this was worse than South Central. I nodded. For the most part, we were silent, worried that the driver would fall asleep and wander off a cliff or into an oncoming truck.

Arriving back at the hotel, a drink, several, would have been nice. But respecting Muslim tradition, alcohol was not available. So before we crashed into sleep, we toasted with orange juice.

Jill had a big smile, her eyes were twinkling.

"That was some trip. Hundred ways it could have gone bad. The road, the Khat, the Kalashnikovs, and who knows what else was going on. I've done some strange, dangerous stuff, but this is in the top two or three. But at least I did not drink lime water."

"So far, so good, maybe I'll be lucky, and I won't get sick."

My luck lasted long enough to fly to Dubai and check into the Jumeirah Beach Hotel. We were sitting in one of overly ornate bars decorated in modern Middle Eastern furniture, staffed by attractive women from eastern Europe. As we prepared to have the first post-survival alcoholic drink, the lime water kicked in. Jill looked at me strangely.

"You okay? You look pale."

"No, all of a sudden, I feel awful. Got to go to the restroom."

As I stood, I felt sweaty, queasy, and desperately explosive. Not so gently pushing aside old men and dodging around women and children, I ran down the wide hallways searching for a sign that would direct me to the nearest restroom, where I barely made it to a stall before the monstrous eruption. Returning shakily to the bar, I told Jill I would skip dinner - perhaps for the rest of my life. I made it back to my room before the next salvo. Morning found me drained from a night spent riding waves of nausea, vomiting, and epic diarrhea.

Jill called to say she was going to search for Natasha, a Ukrainian hooker who had been Hussain's 'friend" when he was in Dubai. My description of my symptoms merited no sympathy. She said, "The stupidest thing I ever saw. Drinking Yemeni lime water. What an idiot."

The "Yemeni crud" kept me in bed, on the toilet, or in the shower for the next two days. The room attendant thoughtfully asked, "Do you need anything, sir?" every couple of hours. But I suspect his thoughtfulness was because hotel management wanted to ensure that if I died, which at times I was hoping to do, they could remove my body quickly before it began to fester.

CHAPTER 17

Reyes poked his head into my office. He said he'd located a former CIA analyst who would speak off the record but only at her home in Iowa. She says she knows a lot about the CIA and the torture program. Her name is Connie Mathot. She'll only speak with you.

In a pleasant but firm voice, Mathot was quite clear. She would only speak in person. No notes or recordings; all conversation was off the record. She was not going to be a witness. And she would not reveal classified information. But if I wanted to make the trip to Grinnell, Iowa, she'd be happy to talk with me.

Two weeks later, I was greeted with barks, then licks and jumps, by her black Lab, Nikita, and more distantly by her at the door of her clapboard home on Broad Street, three blocks from Grinnell College.

She and Nikita led me to her living room, decorated with evidence of a life of travel. Turkish rugs, art from Mexico, Eastern Europe, and Asia. The furniture was worn and serviceable. The sun-bleached green couch on which I was seated was cushy. Nikita quickly put her nose in my lap, checking for other dogs and wanting ear scratches. Then she circled a bit and settled in a corner where she carefully watched me. The smell of mown grass and early summer floated through the open windows.

Mathot appeared to be in her early fifties. Not wrinkled, but weathered. Worry lines on the sides of eyes that perhaps had seen too much of life. She was athletic with a bit of a bulge at her waist. She had short brown hair with a hint of silver and wore distinctive round Ferrari red glasses.

We talked a bit about my career and how our paths might have crossed had I been slightly younger. She told me of her present position as an Assistant Professor of Political Science at Grinnell and that she did some "consulting" for some midsize companies that can't afford big names.

"So, you've come a long way for what might be a short conversation. You know the ground rules. I'll answer any questions within those rules, but you must understand one thing. I will report this conversation to my friends at the agency. "

"Why do you feel the need to do that?"

"When I left the agency, I promised there would be no more lies. So if I answer a question, it'll be the truth as I know it. But to me, it would be dishonest to meet with you and not tell them what your questions were. I probably should have clarified that before you came all this way."

Well Fuck. I said, "Well, let's see how it goes. I know so little now that my questions may not be too probing."

"Okay, ask away."

"Give me your overview of the CIA?"

"That, she said with a smile, "covers a lot of territory." Her monologue was that there are really two CIAs. The good and the bad. Both are staffed by patriots. The good part of the CIA behaves with honor, dignity, and respect. But when it goes off the rails, the bad traits of the CIA can take over. It can become too political and too focused on the end rather than the means. And because so much of what we do is secret, it becomes easy to hide things. Also, there can be a culture of deception because, in the end, the CIA is an intelligence agency that works clandestinely.

"What of your history can you share?"

She looked directly at me—no apology in her eye or tone.

"I began in clandestine services for a time. Posted to various countries posing as an economic assistant or some other cover."

She shook her head and smiled, "I guess I was bait. If some target hit on me, I was to report it, and a guy would take over and try to cultivate him or her as a source."

After a few years, she transferred to the analysis side and spent the rest of her career there.

"Why did you transfer?"

She thought for several beats. Wheels were turning.

"I think I was too squeamish for the position. While I was never ordered to sleep with any of the targets, I think they would have preferred that I did. And it's a pretty macho group of cowboys. So while I can be as frisky as the next girl, I was probably too discriminating."

An hour later, after conversation about being a spy, which she described as "generally boring with little James Bond stuff," I changed the topic.

"So, what can you tell me about the torture program?"

She shook her head.

"You must understand we missed the USS Cole and the Kuwait attacks. We were arrogant."

And, she thought the agents who had detected some of the 9/11 plotters probably thought they could catch them before they struck. She thought their ambition outweighed good judgment. And the CIA was humiliated. As individuals and as an agency. And, of course, as a country. Those who had tried to warn of possible attacks were frustrated and afraid of more attacks. So for a time, the focus became, do what you need to do to get information. But after a while, it just became getting even. Al-Queda had embarrassed the US and the CIA, so we beat the crap out of them. She concluded, "Then, I'm ashamed to say it became experimental. At least, that is my opinion." She scratched her head and told me that there was a time, within about three months after their capture, when we knew people had told us all they knew. But the interrogations continued, and the abuse became worse.

"It was shameful."

"I've seen a cable that suggests that there was a suggestion that the torture victims should be killed. You know anything about that?"

"That makes sense. We kept asking what is the end game? No one would confront it. Makes sense that on the collection side, it would be the same. The rumor was Hermione suggested to the director, George Tenant, that all the detainees be killed and that Tenant nearly soiled himself at the prospect."

By now, it was after 5. And she offered me a glass of wine. The wine was served. Nikita let out, fed, and scratched. We all resettled.

"Here is the sixty-four dollar question. What can you tell me about Hermione?"

Her eyes darted right and left, but she said nothing. *She knows who she is.*

"Will you tell me her name?"

"No." said firmly. "To do so would be a crime."

"I understand. Would you confirm if I got her name from another source?"

"As I said, there are no phone interviews. I probably could confirm something with a nod, which to me, does not violate the law. If you want to come back, we'll see. But again, I'm not keeping any meetings secret."

I don't know what to make of this. She is willing to speak with me but will tell the CIA what we discussed.

"What can you tell me about Hermione?"

"We started together. She was not as squeamish about the sexual stuff as I was and," a pause as she chose her words carefully, "she was more comfortable with the men on the clandestine side. They liked her too."

A wink conveyed a message.

"Do you know how she came to be in the torture program?"

"They were recruiting agency-wide. It was clear that torture was the place for advancement. But it was crap duty in crap locations."

Another pause.

"She told me, though, that she liked it."

"What is she doing now?"

She looked at me and smiled.

"Nice try. Not gonna answer that."

"When you tell her we're looking to identify her, what will her reaction be?"

"I don't want to be overly dramatic," she said with a big grin, "but every morning when you start your car, I'd check to see if someone is down the block with their fingers in their ears waiting for the explosion. Hermione is a very, very private person and will not want to be identified."

CHAPTER 18

Jill and I were to spend a few days meeting with Saudi expats and scholars in London. Then the rest of the team, a videographer and a Muslim psychologist would join us, and we would go on to Saudi Arabia to meet with Hussain's family.

On the plane to London, Jill and I reminisced about the hoops we had to jump through to get this organized. She recalled the hassle of dealing with the Saudi embassy, which claimed to support our trip to "help one of our citizens" but put several bureaucratic hurdles in the way. The Ministry of the Interior had to approve the trip because Hussain's family was "being monitored." We were told that his family would unlikely be allowed to travel to testify if there was a trial, so we needed a videographer to record interviews. But the MOI insisted that one or more of its operatives would have to be present during interviews, which made it unlikely that family members would be forthcoming.

Then there was Mecca. Non-Muslims could not go to Mecca, so Jill had to recruit a Muslim psychologist to come with us to go to Mecca to do interviews there. We laughed at the progression of our conversations with Hussain's family, a progression that morphed from "Don't come" to "When will you arrive?"

In London, we interviewed scholars who briefed us about the recent history of Saudi and how the Saudi government contributed to terrorism. As one historian told us, "In 1979, there was the attack on the Grand Mosque in Mecca. The very foundations of the monarchy were shaken. In an effort to shore up support from conservative clerics, the king struck a bargain. A very conservative strain of Islam, Wahhabism, would be imposed on the Kingdom."

"How does that factor into al-Qaeda?"

"During the Russian occupation of Afghanistan, the clerics encouraged young men to do Jihad, to support fellow Muslims. As a result, thousands of young men left with the blessing and support of the government. After the Russians left Afghanistan, the clerics continued to encourage young Muslims to help fellow Muslims in Chechnya, Bosnia, and South Asia. The government supported and encouraged this effort as the men who left were largely poorer men who had limited education and even more limited job prospects. The government's thinking: If they are gone, no problem. If they got killed, better yet. When the men tried to return, the government would not allow it, fearing they would become internal terrorists. So they went to Yemen, Somalia, and Sudan, and some coalesced around Bin Laden.

The historian then described the current atmosphere in Saudi Arabia. He explained how seemingly benign complaints could result in arrests. Protests met the strongest possible response, including arrest, torture, and execution by beheading or crucifixion. He told of a mass execution of young men and women killed for seeking a little more freedom.

As I was settling in and getting ready to sleep at the hotel, I heard a knock on the door. It was Jill.

"I know, this is weird. I just can't sleep. I keep having images of people being beheaded. I don't want to be alone. Okay, if I sleep here?"

"Ahh, sure. But won't this get complicated?"

"Connor. I just can't bear being alone right now. So shut up, and let's get into bed. We are going to talk and sleep. Nothing more."

The next day, over coffee, she said, "I know that was weird for you. But I just could not be alone last night. Thanks for respecting my boundaries. The whole beheading thing just weirded me out."

The team assembled at our London hotel the following day. We briefed them about what we'd learned and our plans for how we'd do our work.

The team was booked into the Marriott in Jeddah. The Ministry of the Interior, the Saudi secret police, is meeting us and transporting us there. The goal is to meet with family, get some people to Mecca to document "what we can," and locate any health or school records that may exist. We will meet with family members if they can come to Jeddah. Jill told us she wanted to know how the Saudis dealt with the accused terrorists who were returned to Saudi.

Carter said, "I assume with a sword." Slicing a finger across his throat.

Jill smiled, "Possibly, but they claim to have a care center where terrorists are rehabilitated. I'd like to see that."

The flight to Jeddah was filled with Saudis returning home and westerners who either worked in Saudi Arabia or were seeking business opportunities there. The men wore business suits, and the women dressed lavishly with lots of jewelry. About an hour before landing, there was a quiet migration to the restrooms. The men came out in white thobes, red and white checked head scarfs, and Igal, the black ring at the top of the scarf. The women wore black robes and hijabs, which covered their heads. Many women who had previously willingly showed their faces were now in Nqrob, only their eyes showing.

We landed, and while the others walked to busses to take them to customs, we were met at the plane's steps by MOI personnel who drove us to a separate lounge in a large Mercedes.

"We will collect your luggage and clear you through customs. Please wait here."

An hour later, we were escorted back to the cars. Driving to the hotel, we passed a lot of areas with small shops that looked like the shops in any big city, car repair, barbers, and restaurants. But despite the hour, one a.m., most were still open. Most businesses would close during the afternoon because three of the five prayers were within a few hours, so many small businesses would do the bulk of their work between six at night and two in the morning. Some ran multiple day and night shifts of foreign workers. I noticed a line out the door of a large AlBak chicken store, the Saudi KFC. Daphne, the psychologist who'd been to Saudi Arabia previously, said, "Best fried chicken you'll ever have."

The cars pulled up to a Crown Plaza hotel. I went to the leader with the translator, "I'm sorry, there must be a misunderstanding. We are booked at the Marriott."

The leader smiled, "Ahh, Mr. Connor. We canceled your reservation. You will stay here as guests of the Kingdom. The Kingdom will pay for all meals and amenities. You are our guests. You have complete freedom. We only ask that you tell us if you are leaving the hotel so that we can protect you. This is for your safety."

I began to protest, but he interrupted.

"It is late. Here are your keys."

He began handing out keys. He made a point of mentioning that Jill and I were assigned rooms next to each other.

On the elevator, she said, "Were we followed in London? This is weird."

I whispered back, "Yes. We should assume someone is listening and perhaps watching."

"Good night." No hugs.

The next morning, I noticed two men in white robes and headscarves sitting across from the elevator.

The rest of the team was in the restaurant, where an elaborate breakfast buffet was laid out. We could choose European, Asian, or Middle Eastern breakfast. Sitting over coffee, we laughingly discussed the changed hotel, the upcoming meeting, and the surveillance. Fredricks looked around the table, "I wonder if the rooms are bugged?"

"Probably," Carter said.

"But it's Saudi Arabia. The goal is to meet the family, get the information, and not get beheaded. Not getting beheaded is paramount."

Moretti nodded vigorously. Returning to my room, I noticed a second set of men had replaced the two who were there earlier. From their location, they could see the doors of our rooms—*clearly Ministry of Interior watchers.*

That afternoon, the team and several MOI members were in a darkly paneled hotel meeting room. An array of sweets and coffee was on a side table. The family came into the room, led by a wizened little man, who was Hussain's father, Mohammed—*got to keep this straight... another Mohammed.* Mohammed was wearing white robes and a headscarf that reached both shoulders. His skin was reddish tan with a scraggly beard colored orange with henna. His walk was unsteady, and he steadied himself with a shoulder-high wooden staff. Mohammed was followed by a group of men of various ages in white robes and red and white checked headscarves. Mohammed's sons, Hussain's brothers. Then a group of women, his mother, and three sisters, dressed in black, all veiled.

After everyone was seated and coffee was served, I rose. I spoke, and our Mohammed translated.

"I am Connor Mendelson. I am the lead lawyer for Hussain. Helping me in his case are Major Carter of the Army, Major Harriet Fredricks, Ms.Jill Hanson, her assistant Grace Atwater, and Kristina Moretti."

I introduced them and the rest of our entourage.

"Our goal in defending Hussain is to prove to the United States and the world that he is innocent of the claim that he was the leader of the attack on Kuwait. If Hussain is convicted, our goal is to save his life because the US is seeking to kill him if he is convicted."

With that, the older woman began shrieking in Arabic. Mohammed, the interpreter, said, "That is his mother, and she is begging you to save her son."

I turned to her and then to Hussain's father and said, "I, the team, will treat your son like our own children. We will continue to treat him with humility, honesty, and passion."

I could see their eyes fill with tears, and his father and I had a moment. In that moment, with nothing more being said, there was a bond.

Without prompting or planning, the men went to the table. The women moved to another corner of the room and sat in a circle.

I found myself with Hussain's father. We spoke quietly. Facing each other, Mohammed between us, translating.

"How is my son?"

"He is well. He sends his blessings and his love."

"Is my son healthy?"

"Yes, but the US treated him badly, very badly, and that still affects him."

"Can you arrange a telephone call with my son? His mother is ill. I am old. We would like to speak with him."

I grimaced.

"We are trying to arrange that. I cannot promise we will be successful, but I will promise we will continue to try."

He sighed and took my hand between both of his heavily calloused hands.

"Mr. Connor, I am an old man. Hussain's mother will die soon, and I will die soon. I will make you a promise. If you make it possible for us to speak with our son before we die, I will make sure that when you pass on, there is a place for you in heaven."

We looked at each other and embraced. He kissed me on each cheek, a sign I would learn of exceedingly high regard in this culture, and whispered, "Our son, my son, is in your hands. Be good to him."

Over the next several days, we did video interviews with family and friends. As always, the men from the MOI hovered, but culture and a bluff kept them at bay. In Saudi culture, men cannot be with women who are not family unless the women are covered. So when Jill interviewed Hussain's mother, aunts, and sisters, the MOI operatives were effectively excluded from the room.

When Carter or I began interviews of Hussain's father, brothers, or friends, the MOI sought to sit quietly and watch.

I told the leader, "That is, of course, fine, but we will need your names."

"Why? That is a problem."

"Well, under US law, every witness to the conversation may have to testify, so we will need all your names to bring you to Guantanamo for the trial."

Of course, this was complete bullshit. No Balls, No Babies.

After several consultations, it was agreed the MOI operatives would sit outside the door and listen. Naturally, we hoped that they would become bored and quit paying attention. But their absence from the room made a huge difference. The men were noticeably more relaxed.

After the interviews were finished, Jill and I compared notes. Collectively we pieced together the basics of Hussain's story.

Jill gave the team the summary:

Hussain was born the second of nine children. His father was from Yemen and could not obtain Saudi citizenship. His mother, a Saudi, was from a poor Saudi family. After they married, they lived in Mecca, where the father was a skilled tile installer creating beautiful tile floors, walls, and ceilings throughout Mecca. His work was in the homes of wealthy Saudis, businesses, and mosques. The family was not wealthy by Saudi standards but lived comfortably.

Hussain was not a good student and struggled in school. At nineteen, he tried to join the Saudi military, but because his father was not a Saudi citizen, he was not allowed to join. At loose ends and embittered, he was drawn to the clerics suggesting young men should go to help fellow Muslims who were under attack. He went to Chechnya. From there, the family lost touch with him and assumed he had been killed after several years.

The women had told Jill that when Hussain was seized in Dubai, the family was arrested by the MOI, allegedly to obtain DNA samples. But the entire family was held in a Saudi prison for several months. They were reluctant to speak of their time while incarcerated.

I was met with moody silence when I raised it with the men. Jill had guessed that some of the women were raped. I thought about that: *Were the men raped too?* Certainly, they were threatened, and I suspected some of the younger ones were targets.

After their release, the family remained under MOI control. They could not travel outside Saudi and were under constant surveillance. When they heard nothing more about Hussain after his arrest in Dubai, they assumed that the Emiratis did what the Saudis do, and had executed Hussain. The family was overjoyed when they learned he was in Guantanamo and had been in American custody for four years.

His mother told Jill that, "When I heard the US had him, I knew nothing bad had happened to him. I mean, it's the United States."

When Jill told her that Hussain had been tortured by the US, she and the other women began crying.

"This is not the United States we know."

The evening before our departure, the leader of the MOI team quietly said, "Mr. Connor, we know you and Miss Jill are special friends. It is okay." And it seemed like he winked at me.

I told Jill about the message, and her response was.

"Well, that settles the question of whether we were watched in London. Do you suppose it was the Americans or the Saudis?"

We sat in silence. Finally, Jill said, "I wonder who's behind this?"

"In the fullness of time, all will be revealed."

CHAPTER 19

I received a call from Samantha Brooks. "I'm in DC for a couple of days. I'm looking for stories. Wanna have a drink? I'll buy. Or really, the paper will buy."

We met at the bar of the Hotel Monaco across from the National Portrait Gallery. Maker's Mark on the rocks for me. A Cosmo for Brooks.

"So, how can I help you?"

"I need your help understanding some of this stuff."

She continued that she could not distill the arguments over jurisdiction and discovery of information pertaining to the CIA's torture program.

"The discovery arguments are pretty straightforward. The defense is entitled to all the discovery concerning the torture program. The prosecution still has not provided the information."

I took a breath and explained that this is a death penalty case and anything that might make one juror conclude that death is not an appropriate penalty is mitigating. And because the torture is mitigating, it is discoverable. Indeed anything that might lead to the discovery of mitigating evidence is discoverable, and not to put too fine a point on things, we want it all. We want names, places, methods, when, what, and why. When was Hussain subjected to techniques, who did it, what did he say, how did he react? Who was notified? What was their response? The list goes on and on and it is in the motion. We want it all. The defense is entitled to all the information.

"Why doesn't the prosecution just give it to you? It would speed things up."

"Yes, it would, and in a federal court, that is what would happen."

Brooks took a sip of her drink. She noted that the prosecution had provided summaries of information.

"Samantha, the stuff they have given us is rubbish. If the truth is that In April, Connor Mendelson went to DC for two weeks, worked in his office eight to twelve hours a day, stayed at the Monaco, went to the Diplomat for dinner a couple of times, and on April 15 met with Samantha Brooks, the summary would say that in the first quarter of 2012, Connor Mendelson went from his home to another city for two weeks."

"That bad?'

I explained that the process can't be fair or move forward until they provide the actual material.

I then told Brooks that the lead torturer was a woman with the code name Hermione.

"We're working to identify her."

"And the jurisdictional Issue."

I explained that jurisdiction is what allows a particular court to hear a particular case. The jurisdiction in Guantanamo is limited to war crimes committed in the context of hostilities subject to the law of war. The question is: Was the Kuwait attack committed while the US was at war? The attack happened before 9/11. So there is the question that since the US was not at war when the Kuwait attack occurred, persons involved in that attack must be prosecuted in Federal Court rather than Guantanamo."

I observed that before 9/11, no one, not Congress, the President, the military, and certainly not the public, thought the US was at war. The law is that if the US was not at war, there can be no war crime, and the case must go to Federal Court, not Guantanamo. She looked around.

"Government says we've been at war since 1996. How do you respond to that?"

"Get real. A war no one knew about? Really?"

I explained that going to war has lots of consequences. For the military and for civilian life. You can't have a war where no one knows it. I continued, "But in this trial, since being at war is critical to the case judge says it's a jury question. And a handful of military officers will decide, years after the fact, whether the US was or was not at war. So the prosecution is betting that these officers will understand how they are supposed to rule."

"And suppose the jury says we weren't at war, or later the appeals court says we weren't at war. Then we have wasted years and will realistically preclude any effort by both sides to obtain justice."

A waiter came by, "Another?"

We both nodded yes. I asked to make mine a double.

"So tell me something interesting about yourself. Any good war stories. I need background."

Searching my memory bank, I recounted how I'd been a member of the bar for five months and a public defender for about two or three months. I was assigned to defend a guy. John Wilson. John was a forty-five-year-old, six foot, thin white hillbilly with a wide, broken nose and a bunch of prison tattoos. Some were crudely done, and others were pretty good. His left hand had the word LOVE with a letter on each finger, and his right hand had HATE. I described John as "a piece of work."

Drinks came, I took a slug, and she took a sip.

I told her that John's profession was breaking into drug stores. When he got caught, he would say, "Well, prison is a cost of doing business, and it's only two to five. I'll be out in eighteen months."

In our second meeting, John realized he had more court time and more court experience than me and told me we were going to trial. But John had no defense – he'd triggered the alarm and, coming out of the store, had literally walked into the arms of the waiting police – When I pointed it out to him, he just shrugged.

"Look, I'm getting two to five either way. You may as well lose your trial virginity. And lawyers always remember their first trial, so at least you'll remember me." This always stayed with me. John got quiet and said, "In fact, kid, you may be the only one who remembers me after I'm gone."

"I found that really sad. Still do."

Another slug, I continue to recount. So we're in court, the jury is coming in for opening statements, John turns to me and says, 'Christ. I never thought it would come to this.' I almost lost my shit. I had to try so hard to keep from laughing. But, as I said, Wilson had more court time than me, So he coached me through the trial, nudging me when to object. At recess, he would tell me what I did well or badly—graded my paper. Well, the jury was out two hours, which put us well into moral victory territory. Between the evidence and the fact that I had no clue what I was doing, I was expecting a ten-minute verdict.

After the verdict – guilty, of course, as John was being led back to the cells, he said, "Kid, stay with it. You'll be okay."

"You know it's weird. That gave me a lot of pride. And confidence. I often wonder what became of John. And if I am the only one who remembers him?"

We chatted some more. We shared some appetizers, and with a handshake, she went to wherever she was staying, and I took a walk around the block before heading to my room. During my meeting with Brooks, I had noticed a petite dark woman in the bar. I thought little of it when she was in the lobby when I returned from my walk.

CHAPTER 20

I wandered into Mann's office, "Question, Do you think you could identify Hermione?"

She scratched her cheek, "I'd need some help. The computer would only take me so far. Someone would have to do some on-the-ground investigation."

We agreed on what she needed and that Reyes could do the necessary investigation. Mann explained to Reyes what we needed.

And his response was a smile and, "We'll find her."

Six weeks later, the three of us met again in Mann's office. Mann had a big smile. She explained that she had determined who Hermione was by looking at the CIA's purchase of airline tickets. She found that the same woman would take commercial flights to airports near the black sites where al-Yemeni was tortured. I was sure when the same woman who went commercial was on GTMO flight manifests when al-Yemeni was in GTMO. And she stayed in base housing for several months. She only left after al-Yemeni was moved.

"So I am certain that Hermione is Victoria Hancock."

Mann continued to explain that Hancock is the assistant to the DDO, the Deputy Director of Operations, which oversees the clandestine operations. Based on tax records, she lives in Maryland. Silver Spring. Appears to be unmarried. Keeps a low profile.

The following week Reyes came in, eyes blazing with excitement. Took me to Mann's office.

"It's Hancock. A former CIA guy confirms it. Says her reputation during that time was that she was really getting off on the torture."

Reyes' contact told him that Hancock was an Army brat. Her father did a lot of special ops. Father retired after thirty years in the Army and died a few years later. The mother died when Hancock was young. She raised her brothers and sisters when her dad was deployed. She went to the University of Kentucky and joined the agency a couple of years later. Always on the clandestine side. He says she got promoted mainly on merit, although she was known to be willing to sleep with targets or her superiors.

"My guy describes her as cold, his words, 'snake blood cold.'"

"Did you happen to ask about the cable about the endgame? Killing the detainees?"

"It was a big subject of gossip for a time. Finally, Hancock met with Tenant, which was unusual for someone in her position. She recommended they take all the detainees the CIA had been holding in the black sites and kill them. Apparently, she told Tenant that they couldn't be prosecuted and couldn't be released, and it made no sense to keep housing and feeding them. She was quite blunt. Supposedly Tenant rejected the notion out of hand. There must be a memo somewhere in the bowels of the CIA describing the meeting."

I turned to Mann.

"Anyway, to get her file?"

She smiled.

"Not without risking prison."

We decided that Reyes would try to take a photograph of Hancock so we could show it to al-Yemeni. And then we would confront her.

"Just to see what happens."

CHAPTER 21

Tax records told us that Victoria Hancock lived on tree-lined Featherwood Street in Silver Springs. Reyes told us the home was a well-maintained white house with many trees on a small lot. Lights indicated that someone was home the evening he drove by. We decided that the best time to confront her was Saturday morning.

Fredricks, in uniform, and Reyes and I, in slacks and polo shirts, drove in Reyes' Toyota SUV to Silver Spring. Before the doorbell had stopped ringing, the door was opened by a middle-aged, trim, pale white woman dressed in black slacks, running shoes, and a golf shirt that said Army-Navy Club. She had short dark hair and, to my mind, empty soulless eyes.

"Yes?"

"Hi Hermione, We are investigators and lawyers for Hussain al-Yemeni. Could we speak with you?"

Her eyes widened big as saucers, and she tried to close the door, but Reyes had his foot placed to keep it from shutting.

"Don't know what or who you are talking about. Please leave."

Reyes shook his head.

"Ma'am, we know you work for the CIA; we've followed you to Langley. We know you were at the black sites. Witnesses have confirmed that. We know you had the code name, Hermione."

"Ms. Hancock," I interjected. "Please give us a half hour of your time. We know who you are. We know what you did. We just want your side of all this so we can assess whether you'll be a witness when the case goes to trial."

She did not budge and continued to push on the door. After a few seconds, she said, "You are going to have to leave. If you do not leave, I will call the police. As of right now, you are trespassing. You have to leave now." Not shouted, firm.

"Okay," and to be an asshole, I said, "Thanks for confirming that you are Hermione. I'm sure we'll see each other. Would you like our cards?"

"Please leave."

When I arrived at the office on Monday, there was an email from General Lawson.

> You have threatened to expose the identity of a CIA operative. There are penalties under Federal law for exposing CIA identities. There will be criminal prosecution if you continue investigating any personnel presently or formerly associated with your client's lawful interrogation by the CIA without first notifying the prosecution and obtaining the prosecutor's permission.

A copy had been sent to General Ward.

Ward called Fredricks and me to his office. As Lopez ushered us in, Ward shook his head.

"You guys screwed the pooch here."

He looked at Fredricks, "I would have thought you were smarter than this. I'd expect this kind of stuff from a civilian but not from a Marine JAG."

Fredricks bristled, "I'm sorry, sir, but we did nothing wrong. We have a right to investigate, and we did not threaten to expose her, although we did suggest she might be a witness, which is both true and hardly a threat to expose."

He looked at both of us.

"Lawson is not bluffing, and if you get prosecuted, you'll get no support from this command. Understood?"

"General, are you saying we can't do a lawful investigation? If that is what you're telling me, I'd appreciate it if you would put that in writing." Ward rocked back at the challenge, looked at me hard, and paused. He closed his eyes, thinking.

"Investigate all you want, but the line is different here, and if you cross it, you're on your own."

He stood.

"I trust I've been clear."

Later that day, I got an email from Sanders' private account.

"Hear, you've been a bad boy. If you can meet, I'm game for a drink."

Two days later, things got really complicated.

CHAPTER 22

Ty phone buzzed. The screen told me the number was from area code 812. Bloomington, Indiana, where my daughter Emily was in college, is in the 812 area code. I was not going to answer; probably some spam. But then I got queasy.

"Hello."

"Is this Mr. Connor Mendelson?"

"Yes."

"Mr. Mendelson, don't panic, but this is Sargent Helen Nelson of the Spencer, Indiana Police Department. Your daughter is here. She is not in custody. She is safe now. But she is very upset and wants to speak with you." *What the fuck.* I began sweating. My heart was racing as I heard my daughter say,

"Dad,"

Through tears and ragged breathing, she told me that as she was walking to class, two men grabbed her, and before she could react, she was face down in their car. They held her down, put a hood over her head, and taped her ankles and wrists with duct tape.

"Dad, it was so fast."

They drove a distance out into the country, pushed her out of the car, and while she was on the ground in the leaves, one of them put what felt like a gun to her head and said, "Emily, it would be this easy to kill you."

"Daddy," And she began sobbing again. "I was so scared." The hood still on, they shoved her back in the car. While driving, one of the guys said, "Tell your father if he does not back off the next time, we'll leave you, your sister, or your mother in the woods for the critters. Make sure you tell him all this. He has to stand down. Back off. Leave Hermione alone."

Those motherfucking bastards. I stood, phone in hand. Sweat was soaking my shirt. My chest constricted, and my stomach roiled.

Emily told me they drove for a while after loading her back in the car. They finally cut the tape, removed the blindfold, and put her out of the car. She found she was on the courthouse square in Spencer, Indiana, thirty-five miles from Bloomington. Muddy, still startled and unable to see because of the sudden brightness, Emily brushed the leaves out of her hair and scanned the square. Finally, she asked a friendly woman with a baby stroller how to find the police station.

"It's a block this way, she said, pointing, "Honey. Are you okay?"

"Yes. Thanks."

And she walked in and told them what had happened. They assigned Sgt. Nelson to the case. She helped Emily clean up; and calm down just a bit.

When Emily had finished telling me all this, she was still crying, but it was much softer. Her breathing was more normal. Mine was ragged. Like I'd run a race. I had to sit.

"Let me talk to Sgt. Nelson."

"Sargent Nelson, Thanks so much for your help. Can you get her back to Bloomington, or do I need to arrange some transportation?"

"Sir, we offered. She has called a friend who is bringing her some clean clothes and will drive her back to Bloomington. We have notified the university police department and Bloomington PD. IU says they will check with her later.

She continued, "Sir, I don't know what your daughter is into, but she needs to have different friends. Probably some kind of drug thing. She's lucky. I've seen too much violence from the meth heads around here. You may want to talk to her. Get her some help."

"Thanks, Sargent. I appreciate your help. Truth is, I think it is about me. About me and a law case I'm working on."

Then anger overwhelmed me, and I blurted out, "It was probably the fucking CIA."

Nelson said, "The CIA. Really?" with a tone that conveyed *you're as fucked up as your kid*. I took a breath. I stood again and began to pace. "Let me speak with her again."

Before Emily could speak, I said, "I think you need to go home. We have to consider your safety. We have to talk to your mother. She is going to want you to come home. I do too."

"Dad, right now, I just want to get to my apartment. I have friends who will stay with me. But can we talk this evening? I'll have to call you since I have no idea where my purse is." I stayed on the line, speaking with her for ten more minutes. Then, "Dad, Julie is here. Love you. I love you so much."

"Emily, call me as soon as you are home. Promise."

"Dad, I'll call tonight."

I called Molly and interrupted her during a psychotherapy session with one of her patients. I explained what had happened.

"Damn it, Connor. I asked you not to do this case."

"I'm concerned about her safety too. I told her she should come home. But she didn't want to. I'll see about a bodyguard. I know a couple of retired cops who maybe can pull some strings or help out."

Molly's voice was shaking and unnaturally loud.

"You need to quit this stupid case. This has gone too far. We can't live like this."

I said, "I'll do whatever is necessary to keep all of you safe." I was thinking, *Hancock, I'm not gonna quit. I'll kill you if I have to, Or you can kill me, but I'm not gonna be run off.* "Let me make some arrangements. I'll call you back at seven. We'll speak with Emily then too."

After we hung up, I called Mathot. Right after she said hello, I shouted, "Tell your friends at the agency that they have crossed a line. I'm not backing down. They can come after me and take their best shot. But if anything happens to any of my family,"... I drew breath.

Mathot interrupted, "Connor, I have no idea what you are talking about."

"Just deliver the fucking message." And I ended the call, turned, and vomited into the wastebasket.

CHAPTER 23

I sat, trying to collect myself. I had to tell the rest of the team what happened to Emily. We met in the conference room. Sun was streaming in the room, and dust motes were visibly floating. I felt like I carried the smell of puke and fear. I told them about the threat to Emily and my family. As I told them, I was overwhelmed. My voice broke. I wiped my eyes with my sleeve.

"Sorry."

There was silence.

Then Fredricks said, "The Marines train that the best course in combat is to attack the source of the action. You don't run from an ambush; you attack one side or the other. That may apply here."

"I have to keep my family safe. I want to continue. My wife wants me to quit. Maybe I should."

Carter looked at me, "Conner, you need to do whatever is necessary. I don't know how you'll do that. Full-time protection? Have her drop out of school? You leaving the case? You need to do what you can so your family is safe. We get that."

Fredricks took over.

"But we can't back off. Clearly, they don't want Hancock to have to testify. So we have to keep pushing. No choice." She paused. "You know, and this is easy for me to say, this is really pretty desperate. Threatening your family. If they scare you off, then what? Go after Carter's kids? My dog? You leave; they see weakness. They'll come after us. So we have no choice but to keep pushing."

Reyes turned, "If it helps, I can take some leave and go out there. Be her bodyguard for a couple of weeks."

"Would you do that, really?"

"Sure. My wife would understand. If you want that, I'll do it. If you think about it, college is pretty easy. If she keeps people around, she is never alone. It's pretty hard to get to her once people are paying attention. And I'm sure there are lots of guys who'd be happy to guard her at night." Said with a grin. "Your wife and other daughter more difficult."

"I'll talk to Molly tonight, and we'll see what makes sense. But I'm not sure what's the right thing to do."

Carter straightened up.

"Fredricks is right. No matter what you decide, we have to forge ahead and continue to try to get them to admit Hancock is Hermione and force her to testify."

That night when Emily, Molly, and I spoke, I told them I was considering quitting and conveyed Reyes' offer.

Emily said, "My purse was in my mailbox. I wonder if they put it there to let me know they know where I live." A long silence as we contemplated the obvious. "I'm going to live with a friend for a bit. I think my friends can keep me surrounded and safe. I know I don't want to come home. I can't just sit in your house or mom's. No safer there."

Molly chimed in.

"You know, I agree. The mother in me wants you home and hiding. The psychologist in me says that is the wrong thing to do. So long as you are not alone, you are relatively safe. I'll drive Anabel to and from school. I'll be careful. Connor, it's not like you to back down from a challenge. I don't think you should quit."

"Not what you said earlier. The client is difficult, the case is a mess, and now this. No case is worth this kind of shit."

Molly breathed into the phone.

"I've been thinking about what I said. I think that was wrong. I think if you quit, you'll regret it. And I fear that you'll see yourself as weak or blame me or both. I don't want that for you, and selfishly I don't want that for me," and a long pause, "for us."

This is different—way, way different. I don't think you get how evil these people can be.

"I appreciate what you are saying, but I'm not sure. I'm just not sure."

Anabel, our younger daughter, said, "Dad, When you convinced me not to quit soccer. You said I'd regret it. Same thing."

Not even close to the same thing. After we talked, I poured some Maker's over ice and sat in a darkened room. I could smell food from the room down the hall and the bourbon. I could hear the traffic from outside. But all I could see was my daughter or wife in the woods, "left for the critters."

For the next several weeks, We made sure that Emily would call Molly or me every couple of hours. She stayed with friends, locked in their apartments at night. Molly and Anabel were cautious. I spoke with Molly every night. I took her through her day to see if anything suspicious had happened. Questioned Emily about suspicious things. On the surface, we seemed safe. But the threat remained like a black cloud. Always in the back of my mind.

CHAPTER 24

Reyes had taken photos of Hancock with a long zoom lens, and we had them enlarged. We found some earlier pictures, including some from her time at the University of Kentucky. On our next trip to Guantanamo, we took both old and current photos into our meeting.

"Hussain, I need to show you a picture. Do you recognize this person?"

Fredricks set the photos down in front of him. He looked at them, eyes darting. I noticed a sheen of sweat on his forehead. He licked his lips. He then stood and shouted, "Get out, leave. How can you make me look at this? You are animals."

Fredricks grabbed the photos, and we remained seated. Hussain stood over us.

I looked up.

"That's her, isn't it?".

He was shaking. His whole body vibrated.

Then softly, "Hussain, what can you tell us?"

He shook his head and screamed, "She is an animal, and you are animals for making me look at her. She is a whore. She grabbed my qadib, and she would make fun of me. Had her men," and he just went silent. His face twisted, "and she threatened my mother."

Louder.

"She said they were going to rape my mother."

He collapsed into the small chair, put his face in his hands, and said, "She told me they were going to rape my mother."

Then he stood and wheeled. Screamed. Clearly, Arabic invective in which the only word I understood was Jew. Mohammed did not translate.

"Leave. Leave now. He looked at me. You are responsible for this. You do not need to come back. When we are next in court, I am telling the judge I want nothing more to do with you." And he rubbed his hand together and flung them apart—a classic Middle Eastern gesture. I wash my hands of you.

He sat. Did not look at me.

"I wanted never to see those eyes again."

He wiped his eyes and looked at the others.

"If you come back tomorrow. I will try to tell you what I remember about her and what she did to me." He looked at me. "I do not want to see you again."

That night, in my room, we discussed how best to diffuse his anger. Carter suggested that, "Perhaps you should skip the next meeting. Absence makes the heart grow fonder. That sort of stuff."

Mohammed stood. "Perhaps I should not say this. I am just the interpreter. But Mr. Connor should go back tomorrow. Act as though nothing happened. He is afraid. Avoiding him will not solve anything."

"What if I don't want to go back? What if I am sick up to here with him, with the case?" And I held my hand flat over my head.

"I am just tired of all this."

Moretti turned and looked at me. Grinned.

"Ohhh, was someone mean to Connor? Are his fee-fees hurt?"

She then turned serious.

"Mohammed is right. We go back as if nothing happened. We all go back. If he starts on the religious stuff, the rest of us will tell him he's wrong, and when he insults you, he insults us. But we all go back."

Hussain's eyes widened when I walked into the meeting room. He recoiled when I sat down across from him at the round white table.

"I told you not to come back."

Carter cleared his throat.

"We insisted that Connor come. He is your lawyer. We are your lawyers. We need him here. You need him here. We need to keep working. So we need to talk about the woman and the things that were done to you."

There was some resistance. Some shouting. I said nothing. But when the others stood firm, he calmed down and began to tell us what he remembered about Hermione. What he told us was far worse than we imagined.

CHAPTER 25

Back in DC a few weeks later, I arranged to meet with Sanders at Oyamel, an upscale Mexican restaurant and bar on 7th Street, near the Hotel Monaco where I was staying. We exchanged pleasantries and ordered drinks.

She looked at me.

"If I tell you something, can you keep the source secret?"

"Depends. We both have obligations. Don't know; I can promise that."

She gracefully scratched her face with her knuckles and put her chin in her hand.

"Ahhh. I shouldn't do this, but I can confirm that Hancock is Hermione. They will try to hide that from you. Claim that's not the case. But she is Hermione."

She took a sip.

"When you guys confronted Hancock, she was beside herself. She was all over Lawson, which is why he attacked you."

"I'm betting she didn't tell Lawson about what they did to my daughter?"

Sanders looked blank, and I explained the assault on Emily and the threat to my family.

"Jesus, that's just outrageous."

I took a sip of my margarita and a couple of chips and salsa.

"We're committed. We won't back down. We're going to try to get her on the stand. Expose what she did. I'm a pretty hard guy but what she did to al-Yemeni is just shocking. And, of course, the threat to my family."

"I know." She continued, "reading the cables keeps me up at night. "Her eyes went down.

"What a mess."

After an hour, another drink, and a long hug, Jennifer went home to "hang with the hubby." I sat quietly and asked myself again. *Mendelson, what are you doing?*

Five days later. I received a voicemail from Sanders.

"I think there is a chance you are being followed; perhaps we both are. Weird shit going on. Lawson knows we had drinks at Oyamel. Confronted me about it. I wanted to let you know."

I began acting like a character in every bad spy novel I'd ever read. I would leave my hotel early and take random Metro rides to random stops, and return looking to see if I saw the same faces. I'd stroll aimlessly, stopping in front of store windows looking for reflections. I'd walk and do an about-face, trying to see who reacted. After a couple of days, it all seemed pretty silly.

I was thinking, '*The hell with it,*' and about to go back to a normal way of being in the city, until one evening, I kept seeing the same young woman. Black hair, seemed like I'd seen her before. She was trim and wore good running shoes, loose fitting black slacks, and a tee shirt with the logo of some band I'd never heard of. Attractive. I saw her first in the hotel lobby, *no big deal*; then, as I walked to dinner, I saw her again. *Okay, that could be a coincidence,* but later, when I left the restaurant, I saw her loitering across the street. When I began to walk back toward the hotel, she followed.

I had two reactions. At first, I was pissed; then I broke out in a big, shirt-soaking sweat. When I returned to the hotel, I went to a corner of the lobby bar to see if she followed. Sure enough, a few minutes later, she came in, looked around, and stood surveying the lobby. I decided, *Fuck it* and approached her. She saw me coming and seemed paralyzed. As I got closer, I said quietly, "Joan, how good to see you. Please, let's have a drink. I'd like to talk to you about our friend Victoria."

She turned and quickly disappeared across the street.

Back in my room, I paced aimlessly for a bit, sat on the bed, stood, sat, paced, sat at the desk, checked email, stood, paced, sat on the bed again, looked out the window, back to the desk, paced in circles around the room, laid on the bed, and then grabbed my computer and went to the bar. I positioned myself to see into the lobby. I ordered a double Maker's Mark with one big ice cube. Drank it slowly.

Meeting with Fredricks, Reyes, Moretti, and Carter the next day, I told them about my meeting with Sanders, her call, and my confrontation with the woman who had been following me.

"Wondering if our phones are tapped?" Fredricks asked.

We batted things around and concluded all we could do was do our jobs. But, Moretti asked, "What is the deal with you and Sanders?"

"Nothing, just friends, keeping lines of communication open."

Moretti responded with a wink and, "Interesting way to put it."

CHAPTER 26

We were preparing for a hearing that addressed the prosecution's efforts to shield the identity of Hermione. The goal was to get the prosecution to formally admit that Victoria Hancock was Hermione. With this admission, we could begin taking steps to subpoena her. We did not seek public identification of Hancock, just a finding under seal.

Carter, Fredricks, Moretti, Reyes, Mohammed, and I were meeting with Hussain and sharing our approach with him. Fredricks, who was going to make this argument, was practicing and preparing Hussain for what he would hear.

"Judge, this is pretty simple. Our client tells us that he was repeatedly tortured by a female interrogator whose code name was Hermione. We know from our investigation that Hermione led the torture team. We know Hermione's real name, although the person we've identified denies that she is Hermione. Our client has confirmed her identity. We will challenge the admissibility of any statements Hussain made to the CIA and the FBI. If they are admitted into evidence, we will challenge their voluntariness and accuracy before the jury. So the evidence presented by Hussain's torturer is obviously relevant."

Fredricks stopped her practice. She said, "I have a question, do we tell the judge and the prosecution that Hussain was sexually assaulted, or do we keep that secret?"

"What makes you think they don't know?" I asked.

"Nothing in the records and sexual abuse was prohibited under the guidelines. I mean, that is against the law. So I can't imagine telling them about that stuff unless she were certain nothing would come of it."

Carter looked at me, then Hussain.

"My vote," he said, "is we keep that secret. That is something they can fix if they know we know that. Change the records, and have her lie if we get to her. Best to spring that if we get her on the stand. And why embarrass Hussain?" Hussain nodded after the translation.

"What about the thing with his mother?"

Carter said, "The same. We keep that under our hat."

Hussain nodded again.

The prosecution occupied three tables on the right side of the court, facing the judge. Besides the lawyers, there were paralegals, FBI agents, translators, and other unidentified people. Probably CIA.

The defense was on the left. Carter, Fredricks, Moretti, me, Mohammed-the translator, and Hussain.

The judge took the bench and said, "We'll now consider AE 137 a motion to identify the female interrogator. Who is for the defense? "

Fredricks stood.

"Major Fredricks, approach the podium."

Before Fredricks took a step, Lawson was on his feet, "Your honor, I need to advise the Commission and the defense of something that greatly impacts this motion."

"Okay. Major Fredricks stand in place. General?"

Lawson went to the podium, looked at the judge, and looked at us and said, "We have reason to believe the defense thinks the female interrogator committed crimes while questioning the defendant. We are investigating that and are advised that if this person exists, which we do not concede, she will assert a Fifth Amendment privilege. Since she will assert a privilege, the defense is not entitled to her information and accordingly not her name."

Fredricks looked at Carter and me. Her face was a mixture of shock and anger.

"Your honor, may we have a moment?"

"Why, Maj. Fredricks? This seems straightforward. Whoever this person is has a Fifth Amendment privilege unless you can assure the

Commission that you do not allege that they did anything illegal. Can you make that representation to the court in good faith?"

I stood.

"Sit down, Mr. Mendelson. The question was to Major Fredricks. Major, please answer my question?"

"No," she stammered, "We cannot tell the Commission that we do not think that crimes were committed. On the contrary, we are certain that crimes were committed during the torture of Hussain."

"Well then, that settles it, doesn't it? AE 137 is denied. The witness' right to protection under the Fifth Amendment trumps the defense's right to this classified discovery. If the person is not going to testify, you do not need their name."

I looked over at the prosecution. Lawson was sitting looking straight ahead. Willis was looking at him, staring, actually. Sanders sat mouth open, slowly, almost shamefully, shaking her head back and forth.

At the recess, we wandered into the courtyard. Fredricks was steaming, "How did those fuckers know? That was our secret. We never discussed it outside of the office except with Hussain. We have a mole. We have to find the mole and get rid of him Motherfucker."

Carter came up a minute later. He looked at me with accusing eyes and said, "Dude, pillow talk?"

Fredricks looked at him, looked at me, and said, "I'll be fucked," and walked off.

Carter and I stood silently. Moretti approached, sensed a problem, and turned and walked over to Fredricks, and they huddled, Fredricks, talking rapidly and looking at me. I looked at Carter dead on.

"Jack, that's bullshit and unfair. But this is not the place. We'll talk later."

The rest of the day was a series of motions, which we only half-heartedly argued. There was no energy. The internal distrust sapped all our passion. Hussain noticed. He called me over, "Mr. Connor, is something wrong? You have no fight."

"It's okay,"

I said, "Everyone is just tired."

He looked at me questioningly and said, "I hope that is it."

Later we met in Carter's room. It was identical to my room. Yellow walls, brown couch, chair, tan carpet. The smell of stale food, sweat, and humidity.

Carter started, "Let's air it out. Connor, you're," air quotes, "friends with Sanders. You sure you didn't let things slip?"

Fredricks said, "You said it was lines of communication. That is fucking special. Jesus Christ, on a crutch. What a goat rope."

"Look," I said, "I've told you. Sanders and I are friends. We've had drinks a few times. Nothing more."

Fredricks asked, "You've never slept with her?"

"No. She's married. Not how she rolls."

"And this wasn't a play to get her to change her mind? Tell her some secrets?"

I looked around the room.

"Harriet, I did not tell her anything. If you don't believe me, tell me. If you," and here I looked around "if any of you don't trust me, say so. I'll quit right now."

Silence. Fredricks stood to leave. I raised my hand.

"No, Harriet, please don't leave. We need to resolve this now. All of us, as a team. I'm telling you, I certainly did not, would not betray Hussain. So, you tell me, how do you want to proceed? Want me to quit? Your call."

They looked at each other. Fredricks said, "If it turns out you're lying, I will gut you."

Carter looked at her, then at me.

"I can live with that."

I shrugged, "So can I."

CHAPTER 27

I wandered the aisles of the NEX, the combination supermarket and dry goods store that is the main, really the only shopping venue at Guantanamo. My cart had several frozen dinners, some Newman's Own coffee pods for the Keurig in the room, a six-pack of diet coke, two bags of Fritos, and a bottle of Maker's Mark. As I wandered down the aisle toward the ice cream, I saw the Deckers who were with their escort. They were from my hometown, and I'd known them very casually. Their son was killed in Kuwait. I'd noticed they were part of the victim contingent that came to this set of hearings. At Andrews, they both seemed to try to catch my eye and glare, but there was no contact. I tried to turn my cart in the aisle and make an ungraceful retreat, but Ben Decker saw me, turned, and started toward me.

"Mendelson, I don't know how you can do this; how can you represent the man who killed our son?" He was glaring. His wife, Carla, and the escort came to his side. The escort looked at Ben and appeared poised to grab him if he lunged.

"Ben, I'll be happy to speak with you, but not here. This is not the right place. If you want to talk, I'll meet you outside at one of the tables in, say, twenty minutes?" I looked at the escort, whose look and nod was of both thanks and approval.

"No, Goddamnit, I want to talk now."

I looked at the escort, who said, "Mr. Mendelson is right, this is not the place, and I don't want anything to happen that will revoke your right to remain on the base. Let him finish his shopping, and you can speak with him outside."

He swiveled between the escort and me.

"This chickenshit won't show up."

"Ben, give me twenty minutes. I'll see you outside."

Immediately in front of the entrance to the NEX is a covered courtyard. To the right is a Subway sandwich shop, and to the left is a store selling Guantanamo gifts and tchotchkes. Shot glasses with the Joint Task Force logos, that sort of thing. Several dark metal red square tables with attached benches dot the courtyard. A group of muscular men and women in uniform sat at one table, eating sandwiches. Under their table, an Iguana, maybe four feet long, lazed, taking full advantage of its protected status, perhaps waiting for crumbs but otherwise indifferent to the eight booted feet surrounding him.

Couples or groups in civilian clothes occupied some of the other tables. In the middle of the courtyard, only partially shaded, a table was available, and I parked there. I opened one of the diet cokes I'd bought and poured it over some ice I swiped from the Subway drink dispenser.

Ben and Carla approached; there were no smiles. Carla was a petite short-haired blond. Ben was much bigger, muscle gone to fat. Ben's jaw was set. Both glared. The escort was lanky and smooth-faced; his camouflage uniform had the three strips of a Sargent. I could smell Carla's perfume, the baking Subway bread, and their anger.

"Please, sit."

They looked at each other and wedged into the bench to my right. The escort looked at me questioningly.

"Sargent, please sit. It's okay.

He nodded and sat across from me and close to Ben.

I turned, "Before we begin, I just want you to know that I cannot possibly know the pain and anger you must feel. I cannot imagine losing a child, even in war. So I just need to say that."

Both looked a little shocked. Perhaps surprised I'd not flinched from their son's memory. I sat silent.

"How can you defend the man who killed our son? Killed over sixty Americans? We know each other. Darryl went to the same school as your kids." He shook his head and straightened and said more forcefully,

"You motherfucker, how can you do that to us."

Carla was softly dabbing her eyes.

"I'm happy to answer that question and any others you have. Anything else you want to say."

I wanted to allow them to vent.

Ben snarled, "I'll bet you're doing it for the money. You fucking lawyers, all you think about is money. I don't know how you can sleep at night. You are a traitor and should be shot for treason, defending a terrorist who kills Americans. And your client doesn't even like you. I heard he doesn't like Jews. Serves you right."

They sat.

"I'm going to say something that will sound defensive. You can believe it or not. When I was contacted about this, I did not make the connection that Darryl had been killed in Kuwait. Perhaps my fault. Had I made the connection; maybe I would have turned this down. Don't know. But I'm here."

"But here's the thing. If we believe in what the US supposedly stands for, someone has to defend Hussain. If not, then it's all a joke. Perhaps I'm doing the right thing, perhaps not. But as painful as this moment is for all of us. I am not going to apologize. As I said, I can't imagine your pain. I suspect if I were in your shoes, I'd feel the same way you guys feel.

"I will, however, promise you that when there is a trial. I will try to honor Darryl with the truth. The truth of his life and his courage to be sure. But also the truth of the attack and investigation. But I'd ask you guys to consider that we also honor him by exposing the truth of the torture the US inflicted on Hussain. And if the trial is fair, something I am skeptical about, we can all honor Darryl by respecting the results."

"If you think your bullshit convinces me of anything. You're mistaken. You're an asshole. And a lying one at that. This is all bullshit."

"Ben," as I said, "I accept your feelings. Not gonna argue."

I sat and looked at them. The escort nodded. Looked at his watch. Touched Ben's arm.

"I think we should be getting back to the housing. Join the others."

Carla's head swiveled between the two of us. Then she said.

"Honey, we best follow Jimmy's advice and go back."

Apparently, the escort was Jimmy. She stood. Nodded.

"Thank you for meeting with us."

Ben stood. Glared.

"If you think this is over, if you think you can just placate us with this bullshit, you are wrong. Better watch your back."

The escort looked at them.

"Sir," he said forcefully, "That will be enough."

"It's okay, Sargent." I nodded.

He steered Ben and Carla toward the parking lot and, as they were in motion, said, "I'll meet you at the van. Give me thirty seconds."

He turned, straightened, looked at me, and nodded.

"Thank you, sir. Thanks for diffusing all that."

I nodded.

"No problem Sargent. I'm glad you were there."

I exhaled. Felt the tension leaving my body. Felt a low from the adrenalin dissipating coming on.

"Sir." And he nodded. "Pretty classy. Thanks again, sir."

He could not see my legs shaking or know how fast my heart had been beating.

CHAPTER 28

Evening in DC, Sanders called my cell.

"Hi. How are you? To what do I owe this pleasure, or are you just calling to deliver some new personal or prosecutorial indignity?"

"Look, I can only talk for a second. Your conversations with your client are not confidential. There are listening devices where you meet with him."

"Sorry?"

"Your conversations with your client are not secret. Someone, probably the CIA, is listening and recording. I saw a transcript in Lawson's office. You did not learn this from me. I'm not the only one upset on our team, but I'm the only one with the guts to act. You have to keep this a secret that you got this from me. I gotta go."

She hung up.

The following day I told Carter about the phone call.

"Well, that explains what happened on the motion about Hancock."

He called Fredricks and Moretti into his office. They had been distant since the hearing over Hermione's identity blew up. Didn't chat, kept a noticeable distance, chilly. I told them what Sanders had told me. They seemed to relax, first smiles in a while. We discussed what to file. Carter thought a bit and said, "Nothing. We file nothing. We do nothing until we go back, and then we see what we can find. Start taking things apart. Their reaction will tell us what we need to know. Until then, silence is critical."

"We have to protect Sanders," I said.

Carter looked at me.

"We can try—no need to out her now. But really, think about it. If we pursue this, someone will say, 'What's your basis for making this accusation?' How do we respond without looking like idiots or giving her up?"

"She told me in confidence. She's taking a huge risk. We've got to respect that."

Fredricks jumped in, "Connor, you can respect all you want, but it will come out. Her career versus Hussain's life. At some point, we will have to choose, and we all know there is no real choice here."

I shook my head.

"No need to say anything about Sanders now. We can claim we just had a bright idea."

Carter smiled.

"And as you say, I want a fucking pony. Connor, it's going to come out."

A pause. Then, "I'm asking again. Anything you need to tell us?"

"Jesus, we've been over this and over this. We're friends and have a few drinks in DC or GTMO. We talk. That's it."

Sanders and I met at Ruth's Chris in Crystal City a few days later. We were seated at a table for two in the ornate bar; the Washington Monument and the Capitol Dome were visible in the distance. The smell and feel were of power, money, broiled steak, and alcohol. Drinks ordered, preliminaries complete. I looked down, mentally shrugged, and asked, "What can you tell me?"

She pursed her lips and ran her index finger around the rim of her drink.

"Is this between us, or will it end up in a pleading?"

"I'm going to be under a lot of pressure from the others. I've told them I want to keep you out of it, but," I shook my head, "They say eventually it will come out."

She sighed. To my eye, she was contemplating a big decision—another sigh.

"A few months ago, we were in Guantanamo getting ready for one of the hearings. Lawson was in full craziness. He had us in the courtroom practicing. Willis mis-cited some rule, and Lawson went nuts. He sent me to get the book from his office so he could continue to ream Willis. I saw this transcript on his desk. It was of one of your meetings with your client."

"You sure it wasn't a court transcript? You're absolutely sure."

"Yes. Completely different, and your client has not said ten words in court since the arraignment. This was you, Fredricks, and Carter with the translator. A few days later, I confronted Lawson. It was horrible. He told me I was wrong, told me I had seen nothing. He was very clear, without saying anything, that I was to keep my mouth shut. I talked to my husband. He said I have to be able to look at myself in the mirror. I hoped that this was just a one-shot deal; maybe I hoped that I was somehow wrong. So I kept silent."

She looked down at her untouched drink.

"What changed?"

"That last hearing. He knew your strategy, knew your secrets. No way should he have known that you thought Hancock committed crimes. I could tell from your reactions that he had completely undermined your case. There's another thing. I was supposed to argue the motion about Hancock. A couple of days before, Lawson emailed me and said he would do that argument. He did not even want my notes, did not want me to brief him on the argument. Lawson is rigid. He never changes things at the last minute. It felt strange. Things were moving so fast that I didn't think about it until I saw how your guys were reacting. And I could tell Fredricks was upset. Connor, someone is listening to you guys. No other possibility."

The waiter came by and saw my empty drink.

"Another?"

"Hell, yes."

He looked at Jennifer's glass, "I guess you are good?"

She nodded.

I looked at her.

"You know, we have to do something, file something. We can't just sit."

"I know. I've thought about it. I see this blowing up. I should have kept quiet. Telling you is the right thing, but," and she shook her head, "there are others who are upset as well. But no one else is willing to take any risks. I'm actually sitting here with very mixed feelings. Part of me is glad to have this out; part of me is already regretting telling you."

I nodded and said, "I'll take the heat. You told me I couldn't tell where this information came from. In my mind, I promised you I'd agree to that, and I'll keep my promise."

She grimaced.

"No, that won't happen, can't happen. Carter, Moretti, and Fredricks will not sit still for that. I wouldn't if I were them. You wouldn't if it were someone else on your team in this position."

We looked at each other. *Fuck, she's right. They're right. It's going to come out.*

I said quietly, "You took a risk and trusted me. I'm going to honor that. Otherwise, you are going to face a complete shitstorm. Lawson will go after you; the CIA or whoever is behind this will too. So I see no choice but to leave you out of this."

She looked at her glass. I thought she looked very sad.

"Of course, I'd prefer that; It's just got to come out."

She picked up her drink. Took a serious pull.

"I made my choice; I gotta be a big girl and live with it. You have to do what you have to do."

My forehead rested on my palm as I thought it through. *She's right. Carter and Fredricks are right. In the end, there was going to be no option. She will be identified as the person who gave up the secret.* But I said, "Let's see how it unfolds, but I'm not betraying your confidence without your permission. That's my decision."

We finished our drinks in relative silence—only polite chatter, avoiding the obvious. There was just not much to say. She stood.

"I gotta go."

"It'll be okay," I whispered.

We hugged tightly, our cheeks together, and without any thought or prelude, I slid my lips over her bottom lip. She did not pull back.

Oh, sweet Jesus. I should have shaved. This is not supposed to happen.

But, oh god, she feels nice, Just too complicated. Mmmm….She tastes like strawberries and whiskey.

We both pulled away. She looked at me and whispered, "No more of that."

A pause.

"It's going to be bad. Goodnight, Conner."

She walked away, and I continued thinking — *I hope no one saw us kissing. This is going to be so bad. Kissing can't help…Mmmm, strawberries.*

I sat back down and ordered a very large drink. And as I tried to guess the future, I could only conclude that the die was cast. *Jennifer was right. It was going to be bad, very bad for her.*

I was half right.

CHAPTER 29

Our motion seeking to examine the place where we met with Hussain for listening devices was a legal Hail Mary. We knew what was true. That someone was listening to our conversations, but the only evidence was Sanders' brief statement to me, and I'd promised to protect her.

The motion asked that we be allowed to immediately examine the room where we met with Hussain, remove as necessary any ceiling tiles that were not cemented, any removable wall plates, and make small holes in the walls in up to six different locations. We also asked to search the two drains in the room. The prosecution's response was surprising. There was no denial. But they took the position that we had demonstrated no justification for the search. The prosecution advised that "as officers of the court, they could assure the court there were no listening devices."

The court agreed to an emergency hearing to be held the next day.

Moretti argued for our side, "The prosecution says there is no problem. We say, take them at their word. Let us do this search. If there is no problem, we'll find nothing. And that will be the end of it."

When Willis stood, the judge asked, "So if there are no issues, why not allow them to waste a few hours and search?"

"Because it will be a waste of time, and it is insulting to the prosecution that we must endure these attacks."

Pierce smiled, "I'm sure you'll endure worse as things go on. You probably should get used to it. I'll take this under advisement. I'll have an order promptly."

And he did. That evening, shortly before we left the Guantanamo office for the day, we got an email with a signed order attached. Moretti opened her email before any of the rest of us. She exclaimed, "Holy shit, look at this."

We stood over her, reading on her screen. Smiles, shock. Carter turned to me, "We've got to move now."

We looked at each other and nodded.

"Fredricks, you and Reyes need to go to the visiting facility immediately. Don't take no for an answer. Document everything. Take lots of pictures."

"What if the prosecution is there?"

"As long as they don't interfere, so what."

As they headed out the door, Moretti shouted.

"Work your magic."

Three hours later, Reyes and Fredricks came into the office. I was on the computer reading Twitter, a half-eaten sandwich on the desk next to me. Carter and Moretti had been sitting around the central table, chatting about nothing and waiting. Reyes and Fredricks were smiling, beaming, chattering excitedly, and laughing.

Carter looked up.

"Well, anything?"

Reyes was literally vibrating; he was so excited.

"We've got them. We've got them. Those stupid mother-fuckers. We got them. We found microphones in the meeting room."

Silence. Then Moretti.

"You're kidding."

"No, we found one in the ceiling behind the vent—one in the wall and one in the drain on the floor. Wires were attached to something. Couldn't follow where they went." Reyes was just giddy as he said this.

"You took pictures, right," I asked.

He shook his head at my stupid question, "Yes, of course, boss."

"Were the prosecutors there?"

"No."

Reyes was beaming.

"Fredricks was spectacular. We get to the facility. In the foyer of the facility, we showed the guards the order. She told them we wanted to search now.

"Now the supervisor is a corporal. He nearly shits himself."

"Ahh, Ma'am, I need to speak with the Staff Judge Advocate. He's in charge of this facility or the prosecution about this. I've been told to contact him when anything unexpected arises."

Reyes continued, "Fredricks put on her best Marine face and voice." He imitated her. 'Corporal. You are free to call the SJA or anyone else after you let us in. This is an order from the judge, and I don't think you want to disobey it. Poor kid was quaking. When he said he didn't want to get into trouble, Fredricks told him, 'I'll protect you. I'll put it in writing that you are ordered to let us in before notifying anyone.' After she wrote out her order, he let us in. Didn't bother us. No one from the prosecution showed up."

"Probably caught a big break there. Good work, guys."

"How do we proceed? Call Brooks, and alert her. Create publicity?"

Carter held up his hand.

"Slow down, big boy. Let's be smart here."

We looked at each other.

I said, "Microphones in the room where lawyers meet with a client. Here with the CIA hovering, knowing the prosecutor has transcripts, we could break this nonsense wide open."

Moretti spoke first.

"We need to memorialize this right away. I'd suggest Reyes and Fredricks make statements about what they saw and found. Detailed. Notarized. That makes them admissible here if something weird happens and they're somehow unavailable. Then we start filing."

Fredricks looked at Moretti and smiled warmly.

"That is a good idea. I think she's right. I think King and I should go now and make declarations while stuff is still fresh."

The next day, we filed motions seeking additional evidence about the microphones that Fredricks and Moretti found. We wanted the who, when, how, and why of the microphones. We also wanted to know who shared in the product that came from the microphones. Who was told what we said? We filed the declarations as an exhibit to our motions. Kind of a legal – I told you so. Shortly after we filed, I received a call from Willis.

"Mendelson, we saw the motion and declarations you filed. I'm calling to tell you that an agency has determined that everything pertaining to this issue is classified. Therefore, this is not to be discussed publicly. The declarations and your motion are being transferred to the classified docket."

"I'm going to put you on speaker so that everyone can hear this."

Carter, Moretti, and Fredricks looked up.

Willis repeated his admonition.

Carter said, "Major Willis, we have to tell our client."

Over the phone, a forceful, "This is classified. I trust you understand the implications. You can't tell anyone who does not have a clearance and a need to know. Obviously, that includes your client. End of discussion."

"Thank you, Major Willis. We'll be in touch."

We hung up. We sat staring at each other. Fredricks smiled, "First thing, we file a motion seeking to tell Hussain. Surely they won't oppose that. That would be really stupid. Places us in an impossible position. We can't meet with him if we think someone is listening, at least without his consent, and to get his consent, we need to tell him what we know. Surely the prosecution will see that."

We explained in the motion that we were ethically obligated to tell him so that he could decide whether to continue meeting with us, as our conversations had lost the protection of the attorney-client privilege if we knew someone else was listening. A few days later, the prosecution opposed our request that we are allowed to tell Hussain about the microphones.

We then filed a motion to dismiss the entire case due to governmental misconduct. The motion to dismiss alleged that the government, writ large, acted improperly by listening to our attorney-client conversations. The motion also alleged that the prosecutor was complicit in this and, "on information and belief," had been provided transcripts of our attorney-client conversations. We filed a motion for discovery at the same time, requesting that the prosecution produce all transcripts of our conversations with Hussain in its possession.

The prosecution responded to the accusation that there were transcripts by claiming that we had not demonstrated that we had any "good faith basis" to make this accusation and that absent that, the prosecution was not obligated to respond. This was far different from the outraged denial we expected.

Moretti said, "This is fucking clever. Their position is: we don't have to respond to your accusation until you tell us what you base the accusation on. They are trying to find out what we have."

"Which, for the moment, we can't provide. I promised Sanders."

Carter sighed, "Ahh, Mendelson. Can I have an 'I told you so'?"

"So, how do we answer?" Carter asked. "We've gotta have an explanation. Can't say we made it up."

Moretti smiled, "I have an idea. How about we call her a whistleblower and demand her identity be kept secret and that she have all the protections the law grants to governmental whistleblowers? If people follow the law, she should have a fair amount of protection."

"I like it," Fredricks and Moretti asked almost in unison.

"Will she sign an affidavit?"

Back in DC, I emailed Sanders at her private email account.

"Can I buy you a drink?"

She responded that evening.

"I figured you'd be reaching out. Ruth's Chris, tomorrow at 6?"

Over a double Woodford Reserve, I explained to Sanders what was happening. She was aware of the prosecution's response to our allegation and sighed,

"I told you this was going to happen. But the whistleblower idea probably gives me the best protection I can hope for."

She looked off into the distance, shook her head, and looked back.

I asked, "So will you sign an affidavit?"

"Don't see I have much choice."

"Yes, you do. I can't force you. If I say you told us and you deny it, Pierce will accept your word over mine. I don't know about Lawson. But once you admit you told us there will be hell to pay."

She shook her head.

"And if I do nothing, or, worse, if I lie, they get away with absolutely unethical, illegal behavior. I can't do that and stay a part of this. I'd have to quit."

She sighed and took a pull of her drink.

"But if I quit, people will ask why and I have to tell more lies. If I lie and deny that I told you about the transcripts, if I stay with the prosecution and allow this to continue, I'm as sleazy as Lawson. Coming forward is the only honorable thing."

"If you are identified, if somehow Lawson finds out, you know you're gonna get attacked? They will fuck up your career, maybe your husband's career. It will be bad. You know how these people are."

She smiled ruefully.

"I'll speak with Steve again. But, honestly, if this is what it means to be an Army lawyer or a lawyer at all, I'd rather sell shoes."

The drinks were finished with brief snippets of conversation and long periods of silence as we contemplated the havoc that was about to unfold. There were hugs and a slightly longer kiss when we parted.

A week later, Sanders gave me a declaration invoking whistleblower protection and setting out what she'd seen and done. That was filed under seal; only the judge could see it. The filing under seal and invocation of whistleblower protections under Federal law was to keep her disclosure secret from the prosecution.

That worked. For five days.

CHAPTER 30

Sanders called my cell. "Lawson knows."

Ruth's Chris was pretty empty when I arrived. Jennifer was not there yet. I got a booth in the bar and ordered the usual Makers. She came in, still in uniform. Her hair was disheveled. Eyes red and puffy. Cheeks mottled.

She sat and held her head in both hands and looked up.

"What a mess. I'm reassigned permanently to Guantanamo. I did not see that coming. I'm guessing the judge or one of the judge's staff told him. Doesn't make a difference. Fuck, they're sending me to Guantanamo permanently; just hoping I'll resign. If I complain, they can say it was an operational necessity, not punishment. She dropped her head and wiped her eyes.

"Next, they'll go after Steve." She paused. "He's upset, upset for me, upset for himself. It's a mess."

"You want something to drink?"

"Yes, a Double Booker's. Might as well get drunk."

"Tell me what you can."

"Well, I got to the office, and Lawson called me in, all officious; you know how he is. Willis was there. Lawson got in my face. I mean six inches from me. He said, 'We know you and Mendelson are involved; we suspect you told him about the microphones. We suspect you lied to him and claimed that we had transcripts of his conversations. I told you there were no transcripts. Yet he claims there are. So you have to be the source; you have to be the whistleblower. We know you met with him both here and in Guantanamo. We assume you were romantically involved, which is a military crime.'"

Here she began to cry softly.

"He fucking advised me of my rights and asked if I wanted to say anything. I told him you and I are friends, not romantic and that I would not respond further until I consulted with counsel."

She continued, "Lawson told me, 'Your choice. I am transferring you to Guantanamo. I want you there in ten days. You will manage our office there. Your rating will obviously be impacted. I am very disappointed in you, Jennifer. You should have known better than to betray our confidence.' That was it. I'm to report to Guantanamo and stay there until the case is over, or I resign my commission, whichever is first."

"What'd Steve say?"

"He's upset. Like I said, he fears his career is fucked. I knew, we knew something would happen, but it feels worse than we thought it would. And I'm not sure he completely believes there is nothing romantic between us. Just a feeling I get."

"Anything I can do to help, to smooth it over? Make things right with your husband."

"Nothing."

She smiled.

"Unless you can show Steve you don't have a dick. Otherwise, he's just going to have to believe me, and if he can't get past the allegation … well then …" and she trailed off, and more tears welled. Dabbing her eyes.

"Sorry."

After a time, I said, "Look, I'll do anything I can to help you."

She smiled.

"I know."

"What now?" she asked.

"Your call. Happy to stay in contact. As I said, I'll speak with Steve if that will help."

I paused.

"You did the right thing. The honorable thing. In time, that will come out, and you'll be vindicated. May not save your military career, but it was the right thing."

She smiled weakly.

"If I can save my marriage, I'm good with that. But if not…" Her voice trailed, and there were more tears.

We looked at each other. There was a lot to say, and there was nothing to say. We went with nothing.

We hugged tightly for a long time. Then a kiss that lasted longer than it should have. Both felt kind of like a farewell.

Then we went our separate ways.

CHAPTER 31

I walked down the hall to General Ward's office. Sgt. Lopez was sitting outside.

"Yes, can I help you?"

"Sure, if General Ward is available, I need to brief him about a development that he needs to be aware of in the al-Yemeni case."

"I'll check."

When she came back, "He asked if you could come back in fifteen? He said I should tell you he's on the phone with General Lawson."

Silently, '*Oh, shit.*' Aloud, "Okay."

I wandered back to my office and moved papers for a bit before returning to Ward's office. When I arrived, Lopez looked sad, "He'll see you now."

I walked in, and Ward was sitting behind his desk, framed by his Indianapolis Colts memorabilia. The Peyton Manning jersey. A signed picture of the owner holding the Vince Lombardi Trophy. A new photo of Ward with some running back. His uniform jacket was off, and he rocked back with his hands over his belly—a weird smile.

"So you and your split tail got caught?"

"Sir?"

"Lawson told me that he thinks you and Sanders have been doing the nasty, and he believes there was some improper pillow talk. She's being transferred to Guantanamo, and he wants me to fire you. Says you have privileged information and can no longer ethically serve as defense counsel. You got a response?"

"Sir, first, Sanders and I were not romantic. We're friends. We talked a lot, but there was nothing to it."

He raised an eyebrow with a look that said, bullshit.

"You can believe that or not; I don't really care. The only thing she told me that Lawson could possibly complain about is the microphones and the fact that he gets transcripts of our conversations. So if Lawson thinks that his illegal, unethical behavior is protected, we can certainly litigate that."

Ward rocked forward.

"Or your successor can litigate it."

"Look, sir, I don't know why this is adversarial. I thought your mission was to support us?"

Ward frowned.

"I have a responsibility to have ethical lawyers under my command."

"Sure you do." Which came out as sarcastically as I thought it would.

Ward said, "Mendelson."

"General, I need to be clear with you. I have an attorney-client relationship. If you want to try to fire me, take your shot, but I suspect Pierce will say it's up to him to approve, and I don't think he wants a lot of delays while my successor gets up to speed. And really, do you want a delay? I thought you wanted a quick trial. Fire me; then, there is no chance of a trial for a long, long time."

Ward's lips moved without words. Then, "I want a sworn full accounting of your involvement with Sanders. I want it by the end of the day tomorrow. Then I'll decide how to proceed."

I began to say something, "You're dismissed, Mendelson."

I spent the rest of the day going through my calendar and email, trying to recreate the times I spent with Jennifer. Most troubling were the evening visits when we were in Cuba. I showed the timeline to Carter, who read it and sat quietly. Turning, he smiled, "Man, you spent this amount of time with her and didn't sleep with her. You are a fucking saint. I believe you, but I'm the only one who will. No way Lawson or Ward will believe there was no sex involved."

I shrugged, "Why does everyone focus on sex? The question is, did she tell me any privileged stuff? If not, the rest is no big deal."

Carter raised an eyebrow.

"You can't be serious. She's a married military prosecutor. You're a defense lawyer. You can be friends, maybe, but not lovers. For her, adultery is a military crime.

"Lawson would try to replace you just to hurt the defense. Ward is not a big fan. They'll use this to try to get you. So grab your ass 'cause they're coming. But," he continued, "You do have them in a box. They fire you; we have a big delay getting a new death penalty lawyer. If we can find someone stupid enough to get into this mess."

A few days later, I was called back into Ward's office.

"So you spent about twenty-eight hours over sixteen meetings with this woman, and the only important, privileged things she told you were about the transcripts and the microphones?" Ward looked incredulous.

"Yes, sir. That's correct. And criminal activity is not privileged. She's a whistleblower. Although her rights have been destroyed."

Ward stood, hunched, both palms on the desk.

"That's bullshit."

He sat back down.

"I've got to let you go."

I pretended indifference.

"Fine, okay, but you know that'll cause a big delay while my replacement gets up to speed."

I shook my head.

"I'll notify the Commission. I'd like to tell Hussain. Shall we agree that my last contact with the case will be in three weeks? After the next client visit. That fair?"

Ward pursed his lips, frowned put his right palm over his mouth.

"Will you help find a replacement? You know who the players are."

"Nope. If I'm fired, then; I'm fired. You find a replacement. I'll help them get up to speed. I'm obligated to do that. But, I'm not gonna help you replace me. I did nothing wrong; Jennifer did nothing wrong. Lawson wants to fuck with me; that's on him; you do his bidding, that's on you. But I'm not gonna help you."

We stared at each other. Hard.

"Get the fuck out of my office."

"Ok, I'll prepare the notice. I'm leaving the case."

"You prepare nothing till I tell you. I want to give this some more thought. Now get the fuck out of here."

I heard nothing for the next few days and tried to put all the drama aside. Then Ward called me into his office again.

"I just got off the phone with Lawson. He wanted to give me a heads-up that he is moving to disqualify you. Gonna ask for a hearing."

"You were going to fire me a few days ago. If you fire me, there won't be a hearing. So what's it going to be?"

Ward smiled.

"You quit, there won't be a hearing, Won't be bad publicity. So, what's it going to be?"

We looked at each other, expecting the other to speak first. Finally, I broke.

"I'll make this simple. I'm not quitting. If you want to fire me, that is your choice. Lawson wants to say bad things about me and have a hearing; that is his choice. All that will come from a hearing is that Sanders and I will say the same thing, and there will be more evidence of his misconduct. Worst case, the judge disqualifies me and continues the case. No downside for Hussain."

"Is there a downside for you? Lawson is going to claim you and Sanders are involved."

Ward smiled at the prospect.

"None for me. If I'm disqualified, I get my life back."

"Bad press," he observed.

"If people think I was messing with Sanders, that's their issue, not mine. I know the truth."

Ward sat still. I could almost see the calculations, the weighing of pros and cons through his eyes. He straightened.

"I think I'm Switzerland here. I won't fire you, though I could, but I'm not supporting you. You are on your own."

I shrugged.

"Fair enough. But if the judge does not disqualify me, I don't want to hear any more of this firing nonsense. So if I stay on the case, I want your interference to end."

He glared.

"Mendelson, I'm a general in the US Army. I don't take orders from my subordinates; I give them." He stood.

"This meeting is over."

I gave him a look I hoped was a non-verbal 'Fuck you' and left. I briefed Carter, Fredricks, and Moretti, E-mailed Jill and Grace, and then called Molly.

"So why are you calling in the middle of the day?"

"Ah, there's gonna be some bad press. The prosecutor is moving to disqualify me from the case. He's going to claim I was in a relationship with one of his lawyers Jennifer Sanders and that I got confidential information from her. Neither is true, but I wanted you to hear it from me. I'll call Emily next."

Silence and disapproval were transmitted telephonically.

"I guess you're a free agent. You can see who you want, not for me to say." Clearly, she did not mean this.

"Look, Molly, you know I still want to get back together. Nothing happened between Sanders and me. But I wanted you to hear this from me, not read about it on the Internet or get blindsided by some reporter."

Silence.

"Well. Thanks for telling me."

Then nothing.

"Are you still there?"

"Yes, but I need to go back to work. Call Emily. I'll speak with Anabel. And, for what it's worth, I'm trying to believe you."

The call to Emily was more troubling. There was a lot of, "Oh, Dad. How could you do this?"

Ultimately there was half-hearted acceptance and even less certain promises of support and love. It really hurt when she said, "I know you are still concerned about the CIA, but I'd rather just mom calls me for a while. I'll call you if there is an emergency."

By this time, I had an email from Sanders, "Lawson is moving to disqualify you. His staff wants to interview me. I'm getting a lawyer, and we should not communicate until this is over. My lawyer will be in touch if need be. Jennifer."

My response to her was simple: Hold your head high.

But I spent most of the night staring at the ceiling, wondering if I'd dealt the final blow to my marriage and my family.

CHAPTER 32

Because it was classified, the press and al-Yemeni were not allowed to attend the hearing on our motion to dismiss the case due to the discovery of the listening devices, which was coupled with a motion for production of the transcripts of our conversations with Hussain. These motions were, in turn, joined with the prosecution's motion to disqualify me.

Pierce began by acknowledging ample evidence that there had been microphones in the meeting room. Additionally he held that based upon a confidential affidavit the defense filed under seal, the defense had a good faith basis to believe that the prosecution or other federal agents were improperly listening to attorney-client conversations and that transcripts of those conversations had been provided to the prosecution. Pierce noted that General Lawson, under oath, claimed the prosecution had never had any transcripts.

Pierce turned to Carter, who was arguing for the defense, and asked, "Any chance the person who provided the affidavit was wrong?"

Carter responded, "No, your honor. I am advised that the person is clear about what they saw, and there is no chance they are wrong. The prosecution had transcripts of defense meetings with Mr. al-Yemeni."

Pierce fiddled with his pen.

"Counsel, it seems we're at an impasse. One side says yes and provides an affidavit, which on the face of it, I have no reason to doubt. On the other hand, General Lawson is adamant that no transcripts exist. And while he does not explicitly say he never had any transcripts, I will assume that is the case. General Lawson also alleges improper contact between Mr. Mendelson and one of his staff, Major Sanders. General Lawson would not make this accusation without some basis. The defense and Mr. Mendelson acknowledge that Sanders and Mendelson are friends but specifically deny the accusation that Sanders improperly revealed prosecutorial information.

"The only solution I see is to hear the evidence from everyone and air this out. This means Mendelson and Sanders testify on the motion to disqualify Mendelson. The whistleblower will also have to testify on the motion to dismiss and the motion for production of transcripts. I understand the whistleblower's reluctance. So I will affirm right now that he or she is entitled to protection as a whistleblower. The whistleblower will testify in closed session. From this point on, no person in the government can impact his or her assignment or employment outside the ordinary course of his or her duties. The hearing will be tomorrow. We're adjourned for the day."

Probably the best we could have hoped for. But this will be bad for Jennifer. And I hope to hell no one saw us kissing. Fuck, what a mess.

CHAPTER 33

That night, Carter came to my room. He was beaming.

"You will not believe what was sitting at my door when I got back from dinner."

He held out a box wrapped in shiny brown paper. A white, computer-printed address label said: 'Lawyers for Hussain al-Yemeni.'

Carter opened the already unsealed box. It contained six transcripts of meetings with Hussain. There was a note generated on a computer. "Not all prosecutors are unethical. We support Sanders." No signature.

The team met at the office before the start of the hearing. Carter showed them the transcripts.

"Should we tell the prosecution we have them?"

Fredricks was adamant.

"No. Let's just let Lawson lie. And crush him with this."

As she said this, there was a rare smile.

Jennifer was the first witness. Her testimony was in closed session as she was allegedly protected, But there was no protection from the culture that hated snitches. And she was a snitch. An honorable one, to be sure, but the military hates snitches. So an air of hostility emanating from the prosecution's side of the room was palpable.

She was in her Green Army class A uniform. Green skirt, Jacket, ribbons. Hair pulled back.

I sat thinking how strange this was, how courageous she was, and how bad this was likely to be.

Willis swore her in and asked her, State your name and your present duty location.

"Jennifer Sanders, Guantanamo Bay, Cuba. Major, United States Army."

Carter did the questioning, bringing out her history as a lawyer and her past with the prosecution. Then, he took her through her discovery of the transcript and her confrontation with Lawson. When she was asked to tell the judge what Lawson had said. Willis objected.

"That's hearsay, your honor."

Almost simultaneously, Carter and the judge said, "Reliable hearsay is admissible here."

Willis responded, "Yes, but it has to be reliable."

Carter asked, "Are you suggesting a general in the US Army, your boss, is not reliable, or that a US Army major is not reliable?"

Willis answered, "Only this major."

Pierce frowned and replied, "I'll hear what she has to say."

Jennifer told about Lawson's denial and his directive not to reveal information about the transcript.

"Well, this raises the question, Why did you tell Mr. Mendelson?"

Jennifer tilted her head.

"In the hearing on the discovery about the female interrogator, it was clear to me that the prosecution had gained an advantage. We had information we should not have had, and it was used unfairly. At that point, I knew that if I had any fidelity to my oath as a lawyer and any personal integrity, I had to tell someone. Frankly," and here she paused, perhaps knowing the impact of what she was about to say, "I did not, and do not trust, Gen. Lawson. I could not look at myself in the mirror if I did not tell about the transcripts. At the time, I thought someone had to act, so I told the defense."

Carter then pulled out a blue notebook.

"Maj. Sanders, the notebook in front of you has some exhibits. Would you open it?"

She complied.

"Look, please, at Exhibit AE 177-1. Have you seen it before?"

Jennifer looked at the notebook. She looked up Carter, shook her head as if to clear it, and looked down again. She looked up and said, "It appears to be a copy of the transcript I saw in General Lawson's office."

Carter turned, walked across the room, and handed Willis a copy of the exhibit. And said, "Now that the witness has identified it, the defense offers Exhibit 177-1."

Willis was purple with rage. He stood. Lawson had paled, but he sat impassively. Like he was trying to absorb or process terrible news.

Willis asked, "Your honor, what is this, and where did the defense get it?"

Pierce held out his hand, "Counsel, give me the exhibit."

Carter walked past the bench. I could sense his smile as he handed the notebook of exhibits we had prepared to the judge.

Pierce read the exhibit and looked ahead to the next two. He turned.

"Maj. Sanders, do you recognize the next exhibits in the notebook?"

Jennifer was paging through the book and looked up.

"Your honor, based on the contents, these appear to be additional transcripts of defense meetings with their client. I've not specifically seen these before today, but they are so similar to the one I have seen that I'm confident they are additional transcripts of conversations between the defendant, Hussain al-Yemeni, and his defense team."

Pierce asked, "Can you tell us if these were in the prosecutor's possession?"

"No, your honor. I've only seen exhibit dash one in the prosecutor's office."

Willis was quivering. His face was tomato red.

"Your honor," he nearly screamed, "we need a hearing outside the presence of the witness so that we can learn the origin of these exhibits."

Pierce looked at Carter, "Major?"

Carter stood, "Sure, your honor. But I can simplify things. These were delivered anonymously to me last night."

Willis snorted.

"That's a lie."

"Major Willis, calm down."

Turning to Carter, "Can you be more forthcoming?"

Carter shrugged.

"Yesterday, you ordered this hearing to proceed today. Last evening a box containing these exhibits was delivered to my room." Here he pulled out the now empty box and the note that was in the box.

"We confirmed their accuracy from our notes. To the best of our knowledge, these are transcripts of meetings we had with our client."

Pierce sighed.

"Can you say these were in the prosecutor's possession?"

"No, judge. I can't say that, although the note that came with this certainly seems to indicate that they were in the prosecutor's possession. Maj. Sanders has identified dash 1. Our position is that these are admissible. Any dispute goes to the weight you want to give the exhibits."

Sweat glistened on Willis' face. His hands were clenched. Knuckles were white. Voice shaking.

"This is not admissible. There is just no evidence of where they came from. For all we know, the defense created them."

Pierce looked at Carter.

"Did you do that? "

"Of course not."

The judge sighed.

"Major Willis, I'm admitting them for now. I'm not sure what weight they carry. Maj. Carter, you can resume questioning the witness."

Willis, "Your honor, please."

Pierce held up his right hand, palm out.

"Maj. Willis, I've ruled. You will have a chance to cross-examine the witness, and given how this is combined with the request to disqualify Mr. Mendelson, I'll be liberal as to the scope." A clear message that he could go after Jennifer with everything he could think of.

Carter asked her more questions about why she thought Exhibit Dash-one was what she's seen on the prosecutor's desk. Then, "You and Mr. Mendelson are friends?"

"Yes, that is true."

"And you told Mr. Mendelson about the transcripts? "

An affirmative nod.

"Did you have any form of sexual or improper relationship with Mr. Mendelson?"

Forcefully, "No, I did not. We're friends. That's it. I'm married."

"No further questions."

Willis stood, rapidly approached the podium, and turned it to face Sanders directly.

"Maj. Sanders, you admit you and Mr. Mendelson are friends."

"Yes. Of course, I've admitted that. I consider you a friend as well."

"Close personal friends?"

"I wouldn't describe it like that. We're friends."

"Friends with benefits?"

"If you mean sexual, absolutely not."

"You've hugged Mr. Mendelson?"

"Yes, I have."

"Kissed him."

She paused. Glanced at me. *Here it comes*

"Yes, but it was a friend kiss."

There were sniggers from the prosecutor's table, and Pierce barked at the prosecutors. "Gentlemen, please."

"What is a friend's kiss, tongue or no tongue?" Willis sneered.

Jennifer scowled, "Major Willis, it's a kiss. Kind of similar to the one you gave me when I was promoted."

Willis rocked back from the verbal punch Jennifer had delivered. "You've spent time in bars with Mendelson?"

"Yes. I have. Just like I've spent time in bars with you."

Wow, Willis, the hits just keep on coming.

"You've been to his hotel?"

"No."

"That's your story, right?"

"Major Willis. That's the truth."

"You went to his room in Guantanamo on several occasions."

"We have talked in his room at the BOQ on, I believe, three or four, perhaps a few more occasions."

"For several hours?"

"I don't know how long. We talked. Nothing more."

"And you deny you had sex with Mendelson?"

Jennifer straightened up.

"Major. Willis, I would not, did not, sleep with or have sex with Mr. Mendelson. I know you want to make this dirty but," and here she turned, so she was directly facing the judge. "We behaved properly and ethically. We did not discuss the case. We've become friends, good friends, but that had nothing to do with my decision to tell him about the transcripts. I told him because I did not trust, do not trust General Lawson. We did nothing improper. And other than about the transcripts and the listening devices, I've told him no secrets."

Willis stopped, stared, and threw up his hands.

"No further questions."

Carter had nothing more, and the judge said, "Thank you, Major Sanders. You may return to your duties."

Jennifer stood and looked around the room as though she wanted a last memory of a place she might never see again. Looked at me. Looked at Lawson and Willis. She shook her head slightly, turned, and left out the door behind the witness chair.

Pierce turned to me.

"Mr. Mendelson, how did you come by these transcripts?"

"As Major Carter said, they were delivered to his room last night. Major Carter found them."

"What did you do to verify these transcripts?"

"Checked the dates against our notes of meetings on those dates. The subjects lined up perfectly. Our notes follow the same order as in the transcript. Also, we recalled bits and pieces of the conversations."

"You have any evidence the prosecutor saw these or that they were in his possession?"

"Other than the note, No. As Major Sanders said, only dash one, your honor."

"Major Willis or General Lawson, do you care to add anything?"

Willis and Lawson looked at each other. Lawson stood.

"The accusation is so scurrilous that I will not respond to it. We are military JAG officers, and we play by the rules."

Pierce looked at Lawson, "Is that a denial? You've never seen these transcripts? You have no transcripts? Never had any transcripts?" the judge asked.

Lawson paused. Longer than expected drew breath and said softly, "Yes, that is a denial."

Carter stood.

"Your honor. General Lawson should be under oath, so we will know how to proceed when his denial is proven to be false. And to be clear, Mr. Mendelson is available to testify. His testimony will mirror Maj. Sanders."

Pierce said, "No, that will not be necessary. I want to adjourn so my staff and I can do some research."

After Pierce left the bench, Lawson walked over and crowded Carter.

"Major, you just called me a liar. Majors don't call generals liars without consequence."

"General," Carter straightened, puffed out his chest, and looked him in the eye.

"You know you had the transcripts. You know you lied to the judge, and I know you lied to him. I'm sorry if you don't like what

I said. But that does not concern me because what I said was true."
And he loudly, forcefully added, "Sir."

As Lawson scuttled away, Carter looked at me and smiled.

"That probably wasn't the smartest move, but it was fun."

All I could do was smile at his courage.

"Let's go change, figure out what's next.

CHAPTER 34

Fredricks stared at the Marine Corps Times. On the third page, she had circled an article in black ink.

NEW COMMANDER APPOINTED AT GUANTANAMO BAY

Today the Department of Defense advised that Lt. Col. James Lukemeyer has been assigned to command Joint Task Force-Guantanamo Bay. As a result of this assignment, Colonel Lukemeyer will become the custodian of all detainees at Guantanamo, including Camp Seven, where the so-called High-Value Detainees, such as Khalid Sheik Mohammed, are held while awaiting their death penalty trials in Guantanamo.

Colonel Lukemeyer is considered one of the Marine Corp "rising stars." After graduating from Annapolis, he served on embassy duty in Turkey. He has also served at Camp Lejeune. He was decorated for his service in Afghanistan, where he was a battalion commander. After serving in Afghanistan, he was assigned to the Pentagon, where he was on the staff of the Commandant of the Marine Corps.

Col. Lukemeyer will assume his command at Guantanamo on July 1.

After four days and three sleepless nights, Fredricks decided she had to confront the Lukemeyer situation. She was standing, almost at attention, in my office.

"Connor, Sir, I'm going to request a transfer, and I need your approval before I ask General Ward."

I'm sure I was slack-jawed in surprise.

"Why? Why do you want to leave? Did Carter do something? Or me? We're getting close to important hearings, close to trial; leaving will hurt the team. Hurt Hussain."

"Sir, I have good reasons that I'd rather not get into. But I need to leave this assignment."

I idly picked up a pen and tapped it on the desk. *There is no good response. I hurt the team or her feelings.*

"Harriet. I'm sorry, but unless I know why you want to leave, I will not agree." I could see her slump slightly in response. I continued, "You may think this is unreasonable. Probably is. But before I can disrupt things, I need to know the problem. Hell, maybe we can fix it."

Softly she said, "This can't be fixed."

I gestured for her to sit, and she did. We looked at each other. Her eyes seemed to be begging.

"Please, Sir. Trust me. I need to leave." I shook my head back and forth. She got the message.

"I'm going to ask the General to approve my transfer whether you do or not." She stood.

"Harriet. Ward will want a reason. And you know he's a bigger asshole than I'll ever be. You've got to tell someone. Tell me. Or if you don't trust me, tell Carter or Moretti. If whatever it is can't be fixed, I'll support you. But I know enough to know you'll have to tough things out, or we can try to sort this out. But to do that, we've got to know your reason."

Lamely she suggested that she'd realized she was not qualified to do this serious a case. Connor smiled.

"Nice try. But first, no one is truly qualified for this shit show, and I think there is something else."

"Connor, Please Help me."

We looked at each other. *Now I just want to know what's bothering her.*

"Harriet. I want to help, but I need to know the problem."

She stood. Looked around the office as though searching for help. "Thank you, sir." And left.

***

Fredricks was sitting at her desk staring blankly at the computer when Moretti came in and sat down. The article about Lukemeyer assuming the command at Guantanamo sat to Fredricks' right in the middle of the desk.

"What do you want?"

"Connor asked me to talk with you. Says you're requesting a transfer but won't tell him the reason. He thinks maybe you'll tell me. Sisterhood shit."

She smiled.

"Men are so fucking stupid."

Fredricks turned.

"I just can't." Moretti shrugged.

"Okay. Not going to pressure you. I'll tell Connor you wouldn't tell me either." She stood to leave.

"Wait. I have a question. Do you know anyone who has been assaulted?" Moretti frowned.

"Better question, do I know any woman who hasn't been groped, grabbed, date raped, the whole nine yards?"

"You?" Moretti's eyes went to another place another time.

"Yes. The worst was when I was a senior in high school. I was dating a sophomore in college. He got me drunk. I woke up—skirt over my head and pants off. Part of me figured I'd asked for it by drinking. Part of me wanted to fuck him."

She paused. "But not that way." She paused again. "Truth is, I was pretty slutty in those days. Hell," She smiled. "I was slutty till the whole judge thing blew up. So I've kind of chalked it up to experience. Made peace with it."

They looked at each other.

"Harriet, you'll feel better if you talk about whatever it is. It helped me to talk to people. Helps me tell you about my wanton youth."

She smiled. Fredricks glanced at the Lukemeyer article. Moretti picked it up.

"Who is this guy? Is this why you are upset? Former boyfriend"?

Fredricks shook her head back and forth. Then Moretti walked around the desk behind

Fredricks, and turned the chair to look her in the face from a couple of feet away.

"Whatever it is, you can tell me."

"I'm good. It's okay."

Moretti stood and went behind her. Bent down and held her. Fredricks stiffened. She relaxed when Moretti whispered, "You are not good. You are hurting. I see that. You can tell me. It's okay." Fredricks took a breath. Then another, almost a sob. Then softly.

"You'll keep it between us."

"Of course."

"In Afghanistan." He raped me." Then louder. "That motherfucker raped me."

Fredricks described how Colonel Lukemeyer was her battalion commander. How he kept hitting on her, becoming increasingly aggressive and suggestive. And how one day, after he returned from a four-day mission where the unit had been in two firefights, he came to her tent and told her, "you know we both want to do this."

He'd left her naked on her cot, tee shirt cradled in her arms. Her legs were bruised, and her ass was bleeding from a second assault. She'd wiped herself off with the tee shirt, taken photos with her cell phone, and taken what passed for a shower in their encampment. Moretti asked softly,

"Did you report it?"

"I did. But they didn't do much."

She then told her how NCIS said that her photos were not proof because she took them herself and that the investigators wouldn't take her tee shirt.

Then bitterly.

"It has his shit on it from where it spit it out. It has his shit from my butt, and they wouldn't even take it." And she began softly crying.

"The next thing I knew, I had orders to go on leave, and while I was home, I got orders here."

Moretti said, "You have photos on your cell, right?" Fredricks nodded.

"Could I see them?"

Fredricks found her phone and scrolled to the pictures. Moretti thumbed through them.

"That fucking bastard. Oh, Harriet. I am so sorry."

They sat silently.

"I'll tell Connor you have good reason to transfer if you want."

"Thanks. Do you think that's what I should do?" Moretti looked at Fredricks.

"I never saw you as a quitter. I know what I'd do. But I'm not you. You have to answer this yourself. Probably good not to see Lukemeyer, but then maybe seeing him, maybe fucking him up, would be good revenge. You have to figure that out."

***

"Conner, I'm sworn to secrecy, but I can tell you Fredricks has a good reason for wanting to transfer."

"Can you give me a hint?" Moretti shrugged.

"Has nothing to do with the team or the work. But in her shoes, I'd probably consider leaving as well. All I'm going to say."

I hate secrets. I've kept a few from Molly over the years. But now, I'd clearly put myself in a position where I had no choice but to respect what Kristina told me.

Three weeks later, Fredricks and I were preparing to meet with General Ward to discuss the transfer. I had approved Fredrick's request, but Ward made it clear in e-mails he was skeptical. His view was that this was Fredricks' assignment and without a really compelling reason demonstrating severe personal hardship, he was unlikely to approve it.

"Harriet, when Ward presses, as he will, what will you tell him?" Fredricks sat considering the question. Her eyes clearly reflected that she did not know what she would tell Ward.

"Conner, I don't really want to get into my shit with the General. Would it be possible for me to stay here and not go to Guantanamo?"

"Harriet, the human in me wants to say yes, but without knowing the backstory, how do I make an exception for you and not others? No one really likes to go to GTMO."

Fredricks then briefly told me what had happened in Afghanistan. Then, to drive home the point, she showed me the pictures on her phone. *Fuck, I don't know who is worse. Lukemeyer or the Marines who let him get away with what he did.*

"If you want to leave Ward out of it. I'll try to find a way to keep you here. But honestly, I can't promise." Fredricks shook her head.

"You know, I think you should go see Ward without me. I don't want him to know my business. Do the best you can to sell it. Don't tell Ward what happened. I just don't trust him. If he denies the transfer and I have to go to GTMO, I'll suck it up." She stood quietly for several seconds. "I'm so tired of thinking about this."

I told Ward that Fredricks had a good reason for a transfer. I told him it was a huge mistake and cruel to deny her request. Ward was adamant.

"Mendelson, that's not good enough. Tell Fredricks she can either come see me within twenty-four hours and tell me face to face why she needs a transfer, or her request is denied with prejudice and will not be revisited. I see no reason to change the composition of your team to accommodate someone who gets the vapors over going to trial."

When I protested that this was not fair and that there was much more to her request, Ward became even more inflexible.

"She can tell me tomorrow. Or the issue is closed."

Hearing the ultimatum, Fredricks frowned.

"What I figured. Fuck him. Fuck the Marines. Fuck Lukemeyer. I'll deal with it."

CHAPTER 35

We received the following order:

Order on Motions AE 177 and 164

Before the Commission is AE 177 in which the defense seeks relief from what it alleges is improper prosecutorial behavior. The defense alleges that some unidentified agency is listening to conversations between the accused and his lawyers. In support, the defense presented the testimony of a prosecutor who identified a transcript of what appears to be a privileged conversation between the accused and his counsel. Similar transcripts were admitted. This prosecutor has whistleblower protections, and the name is withheld.

The prosecution denies that these are transcripts of attorney-client conversations. However, even if they are, the prosecution denies that it has or had possession of them.

The commission does not need to resolve this dispute.

The commission finds that his conversations may have intelligence value because the accused is an alleged al Qaeda terrorist. It is expected that Intelligence agencies will continue to seek intelligence through lawful means. The court assumes that any listening that may have occurred was part of the intelligence function and, therefore, lawful. The prosecution is a part of the intelligence community and, as such, would be allowed to review information as part of its intelligence function.

The defense, by agreeing to represent the accused in this forum, implicitly agreed to be subject to monitoring by the intelligence community and no privilege of any kind, including an attorney-client privilege, attaches to communications with an alleged al-Qaeda terrorist under these unique circumstances.

Accordingly, the defense's motion is denied. Under Rules of the Commission, the defense has no right of appeal.

The prosecution has accused the defense, specifically Mr. Connor Mendelson, who is lead counsel, of having access to improper information due to a "friendship" between the lead counsel, Mr. Mendelson, and a third chair prosecutor Major Sanders. The prosecutor and Mr. Mendelson admit they are friends but deny any improper relationship or that improper information was obtained by the defense.

The Commission declines to disqualify Mr. Mendelson. As learned counsel, his presence is necessary, and it would take years for his successor to be ready to proceed to trial. The commission does not need to resolve the nature of his relationship with Major Sanders. Any information Major Sanders provided to Mr. Mendelson is not privileged and, in light of the commission's decision regarding the transcripts, is of no consequence.

This order is classified TS/SCI and is not for public comment or dissemination.

So Ordered.

Col. James Pierce

Judge US

Military Commission

CHAPTER 36

Carter was in his Army fatigues; his face was flushed. He held some papers.

"Have you seen this shit? This is the order that Pierce issued on the transcripts and microphones. This is ridiculous."

When I read the order, all I could do was let out a sarcastic laugh.

The judge had effectively said, who gives a fuck if the prosecution is listening to your conversations with your client? You should have expected it. Deal with it. Worse, now, because they classified everything, Lawson is protected. The public can't know how bad this is.

He is saying that we implicitly agreed to the prosecution and intelligence communities listening to our conversations with our client. We didn't. We wouldn't have. It was outrageous and legally unprecedented and unsupportable. Lawyers are trained, literally from the first day in law school, that client communications and secrets must be carefully guarded. The judge said that this client and his lawyers had no privacy at Guantanamo. The government could know everything we told him and everything he told us. I collapsed into my chair, queasy from the implications of the ruling.

When Moretti came in, Carter handed her the order. She read it standing and shook her head.

"Wow, this is seriously fucked up." She sighed. "We gotta do something. What are your thoughts?"

I said, "They win."

Carter and the others all looked at me.

"I don't know what to do. We can't appeal."

Moretti glared.

"Are you kidding me? This says we have to either talk to Hussain knowing the prosecution is listening or not see him. That's impossible either way. I'm maybe out of line, but doing nothing is just not an option."

I looked up.

"Any ideas? Because I am out of gas here. This is the last straw. This is so outrageous, and honestly, I'm just not sure I'm the right guy for this anymore. I mean, I should be angry. This is ridiculous. But in reality, I'm just tired. In the beginning, I would have been insane with anger; now, I'm just numb. So I think I should step back, let you guys take the lead. I'll continue to be here but more as an advisor."

Fredricks muttered, "Figured as much."

I looked at her, "Civilians, you guys are all alike. Things get tough. You guys bail. I asked you about that at the beginning, and you assured me you weren't like that."

She shook her head.

Coming from her, this really hurt.

"I don't think that's fair. I'm being honest. It's not about toughness. I'm not getting it done."

Moretti coughed.

"Connor, when I started, you told me how hard this case was. Told me we had no tools and little support. Said that's what made it challenging. I remember you telling me that there would be good and bad days but that the commitment to the client and the truth were what saw you through. Remember saying that? What have you done with that, Connor?"

She continued, "Before we knew for certain they were listening, did you think they were listening?"

"Yes, of course, that was always a possibility."

"So the only thing that has changed is this asshole says it's okay."

TORTURED JUSTICE: GUANTANAMO BAY

"No, what's changed is the certainty that this process will not be fair. That I've believed my own bullshit that somehow fairness would seep into this."

Moretti smiled.

"Believing our own bullshit is how we survive. You are this hot-shot death penalty lawyer, and you're getting the vapors over a bad ruling. You, of all people, should know that bad rulings are good rulings because bad rulings can save our client's life. You've preached that."

She paused.

"And while I'm on a roll, you promised Hussain's father you'd treat him like you'd want your daughter treated. If your daughter was arrested and her lawyer said, 'I need to walk away; this is too hard,' how would you feel? Connor, you told me, told all of us, told this team, we were about the truth. The truth of the crime, the truth of the investigation, the truth about the torture, and the truth about the system. Why would you walk away from the fight for the truth? Becoming an advisor is just walking away."

She looked directly at me and shrugged—a non-verbal challenge.

I looked around. *Unfortunately, they were right—time to man up.*

"Anyone else got anything? Anyone else want to pile on?"

Carter looked around and smiled.

"No. I think Fredricks and Moretti about covered everything. I got nothing to add." And then whispered, "Fucking Wimp."

Everyone laughed, including me. I looked up.

"Message received. Thanks. I hate it when you're all right."

Fredricks looked at Moretti and nodded.

"Do we call him Wimpy, or have you got another name?"

Moretti, "I can live with Wimpy."

"That will be Mr. Wimpy to you, Miss Moretti."

Fredricks asked, "Now that we've finished giving Wimpy therapy, can we figure out what to do? "

Moretti said, "I have an idea. Let's see if we can get an ethics opinion. See what a lawyer would be expected to do?"

Carter and I looked at each other and looked at Kristina.

"Any suggestions?"

"Sure. Do any of you guys happen to know Tony Peaks?"

I said, "Yes, I've met him a couple of times."

So I sent an email to Peaks. I gave him a hypothetical that generally resembled our situation and a simple question: What do you make of this?

A couple of hours later, Peaks called me.

"This is insane." He was nearly sputtering. "This undermines any pretense of regularity."

Peaks explained what we knew and how important it was that lawyers and clients be able to speak confidentially. He was in full law professor mode, explaining in his law professor drone, "The American system is accusatory. The prosecution has the burden of proof. The defense has no obligation to prove innocence; rather, the prosecution must prove guilt. This may seem counterintuitive, but, Imagine you committed a crime. You're not required to plead guilty. Instead, the prosecution has to prove it. So you tell your lawyer. Hey, I did it, but they can't prove it because I hid the evidence. Here is where I hid the evidence. If the prosecution heard that, it would give them a huge advantage. So under these circumstances, there is no way a lawyer can encourage a client to tell him the truth. Indeed, there is no way for a lawyer to ethically represent a client under these circumstances."

"Can I quote you on that?"

"Sure, look, this is not controversial," Peaks said. "If this stands, you guys are obligated to quit."

CHAPTER 37

We told Hussain the next time we met with him that we did not believe our conversations were truly private and that we would have to find a way to communicate that relied less on speaking.

He said, "What if I bring you a list of written questions, you write out the answer, and Mohammad writes the answers in Arabic? I read them and so on."

I shrugged, "Seems complicated, but I honestly have no better idea."

So the next day, we tried that. Sat in the room for about eight hours, and not more than a few hundred words were spoken. That night we got a memo reflecting that the prison had a new policy. Prisoners would not be allowed to have pens in their cells, and lawyers were prohibited from loaning pens or pencils to them. If the lawyer permitted a prisoner to write, his visiting privileges would be suspended.

When we got the email informing us of the new policy, I lost my composure. Really, I had a complete screaming crazy fit. I was threatening to call Lawson when Carter took the phone from my hand and said, "Let's just settle down, big guy. Let's file a motion setting all this out and ask for a hearing. Offer the judge the alternative of we quit, or he has a real hearing into who is behind all this."

"He's not gonna have a hearing, and then, what?"

"We quit,"

Carter said. Calmly, matter of fact.

"How do we quit? Will … no. Pierce will say no."

"We just refuse to come. Citizens can't be forced to come to Guantanamo."

"You prepared to be arrested? Really?"

"Arrested for what? This is not ideal, but what choice do we have? We're choosing between two unpalatable alternatives?"

I sat in silence. The audacity of what Carter was proposing was breathtaking.

"Lawyers can't just quit," I said. "Besides, couldn't you be court-martialed? Disobeying an order?"

"I suppose, but then a neutral judge and jury would decide."

"Suppose they decide you're guilty; you could lose your rank, pension, all that stuff. Hell, you could be sent to jail."

Carter looked directly at me, "Your point? Connor, You said it earlier. Ethically we're in an impossible position. We have no recourse. We either enable a system that is grotesquely unfair, or we don't. The rubber is meeting the road. Here and now. Sure, I can be court-martialed, and everything you described can happen. So could Fredricks. You and Kristina, I assume, could face bar disciplinary charges. I suppose you could be disbarred."

I interrupted, "That is unlikely, but I suppose. Look, I have to give this some thought. This has way too many ramifications. I don't like the idea of you throwing away your pension. And frankly, I'm not sure it's best for Hussain. They'd find another JAG to take your place. I suspect they could find someone to take mine. So he is still fucked and possibly has worse lawyers."

Carter looked at me.

"Hadn't thought of that. You're right. They could replace me in a nano-second. I don't know if the ACLU could find someone to replace you. I'm sure the ACLU would support you."

I nodded, "I suspect they would, but there are dozens of lawyers who would do this for the publicity. Or DOD steps in and finds a hack who would be happy to preside over a lynching. We quit; we don't help Hussain. Look, Sanders' career is in the dumpster, and for what? Nothing. We exposed this crap, and nothing happened. No point in you or Fredricks or any of us doing the same. If it would change anything, perhaps. But it won't."

We looked at each other. He sighed.

"Unfortunately, you're right. So where do we go from here?"

"Got no idea. I guess we dot our i's and cross our t's. File a motion to withdraw and when Pierce denies it, forge ahead."

CHAPTER 38

After I made my daily call to Molly and Emily to make sure they were okay, I called Brooks. We met at a bar in the Monaco. She came in dripping from a persistent rain that had plagued DC for a couple of days—shaking off the water.

"I need to towel off in the lady's room. Order me a Vodka martini, extra dry, Tito's up."

When she came back, she smelled of the remnants of her conditioner and damp.

Sitting down, she looked at the transparent glass, picked it up, and looked at me.

"Salud. So, what do you have for me?"

"Look, this is off the record."

She nodded in agreement. And I explained about Jennifer, the microphones, our ethical dilemma, and the judge's indifference. I told her about the assault on Emily and the threat to my family. I told her I was being followed.

She shook her head.

"This is incredible. This needs to get out. Can I try to find out about it from other sources and write it? "

"Of course, that's why I'm telling you. But not the threat to my family or what they did to my daughter. That stays out of any story. Is that fair?"

Another nod of agreement.

She thought, looked around, caught the waiter's eye, and signaled for another round by circling her finger. She didn't even ask, though both our drinks were half full.

"What is your suspicion?"

"Again, off the record?"

She nodded.

"I'm guessing the CIA is concerned we are getting too close to making the torturer appear in court, which is true. We have identified the woman who led Hussain's torture, and I suspect she or someone else in the CIA is behind the threats. Right now, the only thing you can write, if you think there is a story, is that we continue to seek to confirm the identities of the people who tortured Hussain. And present their testimony."

"What have you seen about the torture?"

"Can't tell you details but it's really, really bad.

She smiled, "Can you give an example? Off the record."

"Let me answer it this way. Suppose you were held naked, forced to sit in your own piss and shit for several days. Would that qualify as torture in your mind?"

"Jesus. This is the United States. We don't do that? Will it come out in trial?"

"It should," I explained how at a minimum, this was mitigation, and as long as the prosecution sought to kill Hussain, it should be admissible because it might make the jury less likely to impose death. But with Pierce, it's unpredictable.

CHAPTER 39

Iggy's, also known as the Gold Hill Galley, sits atop a hill just above Sherman Avenue, the main road that runs through the Windward Side of Guantanamo Naval Air Station. When one enters the main door of the Galley, there is a desk to pay the modest charges for meals. Breakfast is $2.90, lunch is $5.40, and dinner is $4.60. All you can eat. Breakfast is the best.

At lunch and dinner, there are two lines, one serving large hot meals, the other hamburgers, tacos, that sort of thing. It's filling; sometimes the food is tasty, sometimes not.

After getting drinks from the dispensers, there are two sides to sit on. No real difference, except on one side, the ever-playing Fox News is more oppressive. A portion of that side is reserved for senior officers.

Reyes, Fredricks, Jill, Carter, Moretti, and I were sitting near the area reserved for senior officers. We'd been at GTMO a few days, seeing Hussain. The following day we would return to DC.

Fredricks startled, "Oh shit," and appeared to pale.

Behind me, I heard, "Major Fredricks, I heard you were on a defense team; good to see you."

I turned to see a Marine uniform—a Lt. Colonel. The man was tan, solid, and appeared strong, with a big watch on his left wrist and a big class ring on his right hand. Over his pocket, Lukemeyer. Wavy brown hair, cut very short on the sides.

He stood behind me across from Fredricks.

"You doing okay? Glad you got this job. It's a good fit for you. I gave you a good Efficiency Report from your time in Afghanistan. And you earned it. You did a good job."

Fredricks nodded and mumbled, "Thank you, sir." Then, "Excuse me, sir, I'm not feeling too well."

She stood, nodded, and walked rapidly toward the restroom. Jill and Moretti followed her.

I turned and said, "I'm Connor Mendelson. I've heard a lot about you."

"I suspect it's all good."

"One can always hope. I'm sure we'll see each other again."

He ambled off with his tray to the reserved section, and Reyes, Carter, and I went to the parking lot. Reyes shook his head.

"What was that about?"

"Can't talk about it now. We'll talk later."

A few minutes later, Moretti came out.

"Harriet wants us to go to the client visit without her. Jill and I are going to stay with her. You guys go ahead. We will see you later."

In the car, Reyes asked again, "What's the problem?"

"Look, I can't tell you. We'll all meet tonight."

The visit would have been short without the drama. Under the circumstances, all we wanted to do was stay a polite time and leave.

Hussain asked, "Where are the women?"

"Harriet has a problem; she wasn't feeling well. The others stayed with her."

"If you need to go, I understand."

An hour later, we said goodbye, telling him we'd see him before court in three weeks.

Driving back, I called Jill.

"Where are you guys?"

"At Harriet's."

"Okay, come to my place when you can."

Reyes, Carter, and I were sitting in my living room when the three women came in. We looked at each other in silence.

Finally, Harriet said, "Here's the deal. When I was in Afghanistan, I worked for Lukemeyer. He raped me. The NCIS is not doing any investigation. I didn't know what to do. I told Connor and Moretti a few months ago, and they promised to keep it secret." She paused. "I tried to transfer, but Ward wouldn't agree. I thought I could tough it out. But seeing him, I'm not so sure. I think I should stay in DC."

We sat, looking at one another.

"Harriet, it's your call. I'd like you to continue here and in DC, but there will be no pressure."

Reyes said, "Do you have any evidence, or is it your word against his?"

Harriet smiled wanly, "Soiled underwear with his jizz on it and photos."

Reyes asked, "How good are the photos?"

Fredricks pulled out her phone, punched and swiped, and silently held the phone out for Reyes. Jill walked over and took Harriett's hand as she began quietly crying. Moretti embraced her, and they stood protecting her as Carter and Reyes looked.

Reyes held one up, "What's this?"

Moretti quietly said, "Blood on her legs from her butt."

"And NCIS did nothing with these?"

Through tears, "They would not even look at them. Said since I took them, they were useless." More silence. Reyes and Moretti looked at each other and nodded.

"Great minds think alike. If we can get some of his DNA from a shirt, comb, or somewhere and find someone to make a comparison, we can link him to the underwear. It's like the blue dress in Clinton's case."

Reyes looked at Fredricks.

"If you want, we can seriously fuck with him. Can't promise we'll get him, but we can make a run at it."

Harriet sat up. Wiped her eyes.

"I need to think. Thank you all."

Looking at Moretti and then the rest of us, she said, "Your support means more than I can tell you." She stood. Softly said, "Fuck, I don't know; I just don't know what to do."

CHAPTER 40

After returning to DC from Guantanamo, Carter and I met with General Ward. His office looked exactly as it had when I'd been there months earlier. I wondered if he'd actually done any work there. To my eye, the same papers were in the same places on his desk. He sat, behind the desk, leaning back in his chair. He listened as Carter and I explained that the consensus of the ethics experts we'd consulted was that we could not continue to represent Hussain ethically.

"Why not?"

"Because in light of the judge's rulings and the prison change in policy, there is no way to have a privileged conversation. How can you ethically represent someone in a criminal case, especially a death penalty case, when you can't talk confidentially? It's impossible. And given that it's classified," and I used finger quotes here, "we can't even get a waiver. It's an untenable situation."

"So, what do you want from me?" he asked. Saying, without saying,

"Why are you bothering me with this shit?"

"Because we need you to excuse us. That's what the rule provides. So you have to do it."

He pursed his lips and looked like he was sucking a sour lemon, "And if I don't?"

"Either way, we'll have to ask the judge, but the starting point is you. If you approve, then we can go to the judge. We are thinking of simply resigning from the case, but that is the nuclear option. We don't want to go there. We want you to recognize our ethical obligations. We want your approval for us to leave the case."

Ward sat silently, his jaw tightening and loosening as if chewing on this decision. Then said, "Can you give me anything from the ethics experts?" "Sure," and I pulled out three letters from experts,

"Tony Peaks from Columbia, Nancy Sparks from the University of Texas, and Stephen Mazur from Indiana Maurer School of Law."

"I'll study these and get back to you. But how do you walk away from a client you've been representing for some time?"

I shrugged.

"Look, this is not easy; this is not something we've come to lightly. Pierce's ruling is crazy wrong. We figured he'd say there was no evidence or some other bullshit to avoid this. But he told the truth about what is going on."

And here I held up my arms, palms outstretched, "But the fact is, legally, he's put us in an impossible position."

Ward shook his head.

"I'll take a look at things and let you know. I have to do my own due diligence. No promises."

Minutes later, in Carter's office, the door shut; Carter sat, and I paced.

"What do you think?"

"He didn't throw us out," Carter said. "He was more receptive than I expected. What do we do if he says no?"

"Go to the press. Air it out. Tell the world what is going on and what a goat rope this all is."

Carter said, "Ahh, but remember it's classified. We have to be careful with the press."

"I can resign from the bar. Or seek a bar opinion."

"That's like when I said I'd just refuse to go. It would be dramatic, But I don't know that it would change much. And as you pointed out, we can be replaced. A bar opinion is no different than what you have now. It's like you said earlier. Unless Ward and Pierce support us, we're hosed."

"Well, let's see what Ward says."

Two weeks later, we got his response.

Mr. Mendelson:

I cannot support your request for excusal. While I acknowledge that the judge's ruling places you in a difficult position, your obligation to your client, in my view, trumps the legalism of the attorney-client privilege. You both have a long history with the client, and the judge's ruling would apply to any lawyer who replaces you. Releasing you would only delay the case. I find that the need to keep the case moving is paramount. The victims, the public, and indeed your client have an interest in a resolution of this matter. So your request to be excused is denied.

Moreover, there is no reason to believe the judge would grant this request, so even if I had approved it, which I do not, you would still be obligated to continue your representation.

If you decide to file a request with the judge, I will file a more thorough explanation for my decision.

As I read this memo, I thought - *"You spineless motherfucker."*

CHAPTER 41

My law firm holds periodic meetings to discuss management issues. I sat in my office, looking out at the clear, bright blue sky. This office now felt foreign. Like visiting a home, I used to live in— full of memories. I was rarely there physically and even less present emotionally. I'd admitted to myself, and occasionally others in the firm, that "I don't focus on or care about much besides Guantanamo."

I was pretty sure this meeting was to discuss my role in the firm and knowing lawyers, the focus would be on the money.

Jake, who I hired out of law school, and mentored as he grew into a really solid lawyer, cleared his throat, "Connor, I want to give you a heads up. We think your share of the firm's income should be smaller."

I smiled.

"That's not surprising. It's not like two hundred an hour I get from the ACLU is big money, and I'm not doing anything else."

"You okay with it?"

Jake looked intense. We both knew this was a turning point in the life of the firm. And, for me, it felt like a personal crossroad.

"Yes," I said. "I understand. I'd feel the same way if our positions were reversed."

At the meeting, sitting around the large conference room, surrounded by shelves of books that were largely unused because computers had replaced law libraries, I started by saying, "Jake explained that you all feel my share is too high."

There were worried looks and a couple of glares at Jake, but I continued, "I'm glad he came to me and raised the issue. I agree. It is too high. Here is what I think is fair. I'll keep the Guantanamo money and twenty percent of what I happen to bring in or work on. All I want in return is to keep my office and have the flexibility to decide to stay or leave when Guantanamo is over. I suspect I'll need time to figure out what I'm doing next. But I'd like to be able to make my own decision, not have it pushed on me."

There were nods and murmurs of assent.

"But there is one other thing I want from the firm. I want the firm to spend ten thousand on some DNA testing."

There were some quizzical looks, and I explained what had happened to Fredricks and our plan to match a known sample of Lukemeyer's DNA with that on Harriett's underwear.

Paula Beckett, a junior partner, asked, "Just out of curiosity, how did you get the," and here she did air quotes, "known sample."

I smiled.

"One of the women on the team, Kristina Moretti, has the balls of two burglars. She met the rapist at the Officer's Club bar one night, returned with selfies of the two of them in the bar, and a comb and a toothbrush from his apartment. She also had a handkerchief of his jizz. All she would say was, "I learned, working here, that soldiers sometimes throw themselves on a grenade for their buddies. The least I could do was take one for my girl Harriet."

I paused and smiled.

"She won't say more than that. And honestly, I don't want to know."

The group readily agreed to spend the money on DNA testing.

The meeting with the firm had me in a reflective mood. I called Molly.

"Can we have dinner? I need to talk."

She drew a breath.

"Not tonight. I have plans. Tomorrow?"

"What, you have a date? Jeez"

A silence which Molly broke with, "If you want to talk, come by tomorrow at 7:00. Bring wine." She said a polite goodbye and hung up—that hurt.

I was looking at the TV but not really watching, nursing a Maker's, and I tried to think of a way forward. Pierce would deny a motion to excuse us. No appeal allowed. I contemplated resigning from the bar, but I concluded I would just throw Carter and the others under the bus, not help Hussain. As I took a big gulp, the warmth began to kick in, and I began to relax. I recalled what an early mentor once said: "Mendelson, sometimes in this game, you are just fucked. When that happens, relax, bend over and enjoy the moment because being angry and bitching will not change anything." Unfortunately, this seemed like one of those times.

Later that night, well into the bourbon, I booked a flight back to DC for early the next day. I called and left a message for Molly that I would see her in a few weeks. As I tried to sleep, the thought I could not shake was, *Mendelson, you have pretty much fucked up everything. Your ego has written checks neither your heart nor the law can cash.*

It was a bad, bad night.

CHAPTER 42

Carter and I met Brooks for drinks at the bar at the Monaco in DC, across from the National Portrait Gallery on F Street. Not too crowded at five-thirty. The Congressional staffers would not begin to show up till later—a good place for a quiet talk.

We ordered drinks, two Woodford Reserves and one dirty martini, very dry.

"So, is this trial going to happen?" Brooks asks.

Carter shrugged, "Yes, Lawson and Pierce are thick and want this to happen. And with Lawson pushing, It's going to happen."

"Are you ready?"

"No, not even close to what we should be."

"Can you get it delayed?"

I laugh.

"Let me tell you a story from my young lawyer days. There was this legendary lawyer, a character, Sam Goodman. Guys like Sam just don't exist anymore. Anyway, Goodman wanted a continuance. The judge said 'No,' and told the bailiff to 'Go get the jury. The trial will begin in a half hour.'; Goodman winked at me and said, 'Kid, watch and learn.' A few minutes later, we were in the hallway, and there was a loud noise from the courtroom. People came running out. 'Oh God, Mr. Goodman is having a heart attack.' Medics were called, and a few minutes later, Goodman was wheeled out of the court on a gurney. As he went by, he looked at me and winked again. I could swear he said, 'told you I'd get a continuance.' However, that might be my imagination. So Carter and I are fighting over who has the heart attack."

Carter chimed in, "Yes, but the problem is to have any success here, it has to be fatal."

Laughter all around.

"What does the jury selection look like."

I explain how death penalty jury selection, voir dire is what lawyers call it, works.

"The law is that people who can't consider the death penalty can't serve. Also, people who can't consider mitigation, reasons weighing against death, can't serve. Both are unable to follow the law. The judge and prosecutor will try to get jurors to commit in the abstract to being fair without a focus on this case. Our position is they have to be able to consider life or a sentence of less than life in this case."

Brooks shakes her head, "That's gonna be hard for military jurors to do. Lots of dead US military."

"Of course. That's a big issue. And in our view, we get to ask what I call the ultimate question: It goes like this:

"I want you to assume that after you hear the evidence, you are convinced beyond all reasonable doubt of the following, all of which is alleged in the charge sheet:

That Hussain al-Yemeni was a disciple of Osama bin Laden.

That he swore allegiance to bin Laden.

That he was the mastermind of the Kuwaiti attack.

That he planned the attack for maximum casualties.

That he recruited the suicide bombers.

That he obtained the explosives.

That he orchestrated things so that the greatest possible damage was inflicted on the air base.

That he has no remorse and is only sorry that more were not killed.

Assume all those facts are true beyond a reasonable doubt. Could a sentence other than death be full and fair justice for this guilty terrorist, killer of over sixty of your brothers and sisters in arms?"

Brooks takes a sip of her drink.

"When you put it that way, I'm not sure how I'd answer that question. And if someone says no, I'm not wedded to death, what do you say?"

Carter answered that one, "We ask, tell me why? The why is the critical part of the answer. Some will say why? Because I'm not sure he's guilty or you're jumping the gun. Then we say yes, but we have to look ahead, so supposing you think he's guilty beyond all reasonable doubt, what then? Others will say he's crazy, and if we say he's not crazy, we're telling you he's not. They'll come back to death."

Carter continued, "Then we follow up with questions about the torture. Would the fact he was tortured change your mind? Would the fact that the United States tortured the guilty terrorist killer weigh against a death sentence? Would a bad childhood weigh against a death sentence? We've tried to vet these questions as best we can. Military folks are used to death, sending people to their deaths. They are mixed on the issue of the torture."

Brooks sipped, "So, It seems like it's going to take some time to get a jury."

I took a swig of bourbon, rattling the ice against the glass.

"Should take quite a while. I've had trials where it took a month or more to pick a jury. This is harder since military folks are more comfortable with the notion of people dying. I mean, commanders send people on missions knowing some will get killed."

"And when you get a jury, what is your defense?"

Carter shrugged, "S O D D I T."

"Huh?" Brooks questioned.

He smiled, "Some Other Dude Did It. S O D D IT."

"So, who can you blame this on?"

I laughed, "Samantha, it's not bullshit. First, al-Yemeni was not the mastermind. Walid Quatini was the mastermind. He probably was second to the real mastermind. But also, the Government of Kuwait was up to its eyes in this. It couldn't happen without the Government of Kuwait."

"Really?"

"Yes, No way this happens without Kuwait. We've got lots of

circumstantial evidence of Kuwaiti involvement. Many important pieces to the attack could not have occurred without Kuwaiti assistance. Where does he get two tons of military-grade explosives? How do they get onto the base? How do they know when the mess hall is full? Where are the fuel tanks? Inside job, and that can't happen without Kuwaiti support. And the Kuwaitis really hampered the investigation. The truth is, the FBI couldn't interview many Kuwaiti officials, and those officials the FBI were allowed to interview told them to look for Hussain. He's a patsy. No way is he the mastermind."

"So, is the US covering for Kuwait?"

Carter interjects, "Hard to say. The FBI did its best, but the agents were up against a lot of opposition from the Kuwaitis."

"Does Lawson know this?"

Carter snorted, "Samantha, Robert E. Lee Lawson is so far up his own ass that it's hard to tell what he knows. It's there."

"He speaks highly of you, too. "

Brooks took another sip, "Seriously. Do you think he does not recognize this evidence? "

Carter and I looked at each other.

"I learned a long time ago not to try to read the mind of another lawyer. We can all get tunnel vision. See what we want to see."

"When can I write this? This is a good story. Our ally behind the huge terror attack."

"Not that unusual. Saudi had a role in 9/11 that got buried, Yemen a role in the Cole that's been kept off the radar; no surprise the US would protect Kuwait too."

The waitress came, and we looked at each other quizzically and nodded in agreement—one more round. The waitress smiled warmly and walked off to get more drinks.

"So, how long do you think the trial will take?"

I smile, "Depends on recesses, if there are no breaks, other than weekends, six, seven months. If the judge takes breaks so people can leave the island somewhat longer. I'm kind of expecting eight to ten months."

"Do you want breaks?" She asked.

"Of course. If not that, conjugal visits."

I was laughing at my own joke.

"But really, the jurors can't leave. If we're really interested in a fair trial, there is no way jurors can go home. Too much possibility they could hear improper stuff. Knowing Guantanamo. This will be nuts. The over/under on someone going crazy is five weeks. Something will happen. Someone is sleeping with someone else, or someone breaking down. Some kind of weird shit. It's too close, too much pressure. I predict craziness."

CHAPTER 43

CELLMARK LABORATORIES

Cellmark Laboratories was asked to compare several samples of material containing DNA from a known subject, James Lukemeyer, and underwear containing material from an unidentified subject.

Among the items submitted was a comb (KS1) containing hair, some of which were adequate for the recovery and testing of genetic material. Also, a toothbrush (KS2) that contained material adequate for the recovery and testing of genetic material. Finally, Cellmark was provided with a handkerchief,(KS3) which contained material that was adequate for the recovery and testing of genetic material. All the foregoing are samples obtained from James Lukemeyer.

Also provided was a buccal swab (KS4) containing genetic material from a subject identified as Harriett Fredricks.

These items were tested against each other as well as against an unknown sample contained in olive green women's military-issue underwear. (KS5)

Conclusion:

Genetic material from the (KS 1 2 AND 3) are from the same individual: James Lukemeyer. The possibility of the genetic material on these items being from another individual is 1/15,000,000,000,000.

The olive green underwear contains genetic material from two subjects. This material was compared with both (KS4), the buccal swab from Harriett Fredricks and (KS 1,2, and 3) the samples from James Lukemeyer. A portion of the genetic material on the olive green underwear is identical to (KS4) the buccal swab from Harriet Fredricks. The other genetic material on the olive green underwear is sufficiently similar to (KS 1, 2, and 3) that Cellmark can say with confidence that this material is from James Lukemeyer. The possibility that this genetic material on the green underwear belongs to a person other than James Lukemeyer is 1/10,000,000,000.

Respectfully Submitted

Dianne Tollman

Forensic Analyst Cell Mark Laboratories.

CHAPTER 44

I was in my room at the Hotel Monaco. I'd had a drink and was trying to figure out dinner when there was a knock on the door. I was surprised to see Connie Mathot, who silently bustled in. She didn't shake hands or say hello before pulling out the desk chair, turning it around, and sitting down. She looked completely different. She looked so ordinary that I would not have noticed her had I seen her in the lobby or on the street.

"Been a while since I had to do this spy stuff. Out of practice. Could I have some water?" Water fetched and drank; she looked up, her cheeks flushed.

"I spoke to Hermione, who, as you know, is Victoria Hancock. I've decided to help you."

She paused and continued. "I told you I would not keep secrets. I'm pretty sure that your visit to me provoked them to follow you. But when I spoke to Hancock, she bragged to me how they are hiding the torture from you, how they've been shadowing you, interfering with you. She laughed about the threat to your daughter, which is unforgivable. I told you at the beginning that when I left the agency, I would no longer lie. But I'm just not being honest by remaining silent after what she told me." And here she went into a fake western drawl, "Buckle up, pardner."

"Where do we begin?"

Mathot said that from what she knew of the torture and Hancock, there was probably a sexual component to the torture. She reminded me that Hancock was more comfortable with the sexual stuff than she'd been and suggested that Hancock probably enjoyed the sexual humiliation.

"So here is what you need to ask for."

And she then described what she called a tranche of four hundred cables and memos that would have had a special code word designation. The code word for these cables was WIZARD. These would have been different from the material provided to the prosecution.

She was clear, "Good chance the prosecution does not know about this body of material. When you request the Wizard files, the shit is really, really going to hit the fan because this is the material they want to keep hidden from the world. Connor, the CIA will keep this material secret from everyone.

"When I worked there, I saw some of the reports. I was sickened, and I don't get rattled easily.

"And you need to know that very little you are doing is secret. You are being followed; your phones are tapped, and your computers are monitored. The judge is probably compromised."

She smiled.

"Do you mind ordering room service? I'm hungry. I'd like to go out, but if they see me with you, there will be hell to pay."

"How did you get here? "

Mathot gave me a little grin, "Secretly. Using tradecraft the CIA taught me."

Over room-service dinner with mini-bar wine and liquor, we formulated a tentative plan. Well after midnight, I left the room and went for a walk to get any "tails" to follow me, and she left and, if she was to be believed, began her drive back to Iowa the next day. But she had promised to be a resource. She also promised that after we fought over the WIZARD cables, she would help if needed.

The next day I briefed Carter, Fredricks, and Moretti about what had occurred. Fredricks asked the first, most obvious question.

"Do you trust her?"

"I don't know. I think I do, but this seems too easy. Just get the WIZARD files. While we were skeptical and even concerned this was some kind of setup, we concluded that there was little harm in asking for the WIZARD file—worst case. The government says there is no such thing."

Within hours of filing the motion requesting the WIZARD files, we were notified that all mention of WIZARD was immediately consigned to the most highly classified system. Two days later, I was summoned to General Ward's office. To my surprise, General Lawson was there.

Ward got right to the point.

"General Lawson wanted to speak with you and asked me to be a witness.

"I'd like to get Major Carter here as well." A suggestion I did not trust Ward or Lawson.

Ward looked at Lawson, who nodded. Carter was summoned. A few minutes later, Lawson looked at Carter and me,

"Gentlemen, I owe you an apology. We have told you that you have all discovery as ordered by the judge. This was apparently incorrect. We were unaware of the WIZARD files."

"Okay, So when can we get them?"

"You can't. The agency has determined that neither we nor you need to know the information in the files, and they will not release them to us."

"I'm going to ask you to drop this. This is a matter of national security, and if you have any loyalty to the United States, you will do the right thing and move on. Let the case proceed as though this information never existed."

I shook my head.

"Oh, so the government can hide information and then kill Hussain, and we're supposed to stand idly by?"

Lawson looked directly at me.

"Mendelson, your client will almost certainly be sentenced to death. He will die in Guantanamo. No reason to harm national security getting there. Time to get with the program. Do the right thing. You're putting up a good fight, nothing to be ashamed of. But some things are more important than your client or your feelings. You need to look at the big picture. Sometimes sacrifices have to be made in the interests of national security."

I looked at Carter, who shook his head.

"I'm sorry, I disagree, and I am not, we are not, going to pretend these files do not exist. I would still be obligated to proceed if I believed this was necessary. But I am sure there is nothing in these files that pertains to crimes committed by Hancock, by the CIA, and for all I know, the military that could possibly implicate national security. So with all due respect, Generals, Go fuck yourselves. And unless there is something else, I'm leaving."

Ward stood.

"Mendelson, I can fire you."

"Ahh, General, you guys tried that already and got your asses handed to you. But take your best shot. We can describe this goat fuck of a meeting on the record, and if Pierce kicks me off the case, I guarantee you will not like the press conference that will follow. Or the appeal, or the delay, while you try to get this fraud of a process back on track. So do what you gotta do."

Lawson angrily said, "There won't be any press conference. Classification guidelines still bind you."

I turned.

"You don't want to take the risk on the press conference thing. I just might not care about this bullshit classification. And while I'm at it. Tell Victoria Hancock the truth about what she did is coming out". I paused, then, "Sirs."

And I walked out. Carter followed.

When Carter and I were back in his office, he was serious.

"I am guessing neither of those guys has been told to fuck themselves in several years, if ever. Content is a ten-point zero. Delivery, nine point nine. I'm deducting a tenth for the last 'sirs.' Too much respect. But I have another question. In what country are you planning to live the rest of your life?"

And then he laughed and said, "That was wonderful. Telling not one but two generals to fuck themselves. You, my friend, are a god. A fucked god, to be sure, but a god. Let's tell Fredricks and Moretti so they can begin saving to buy flowers for your funeral or tickets to visit you."

And he laughed again and slapped me on the shoulder.

"That was just great. Just great."

I did not see the humor. I saw a corrupt system and leaders and lawyers who had no interest in fairness.

After a week of unanticipated silence, without any request to fire me, we filed two classified motions. The first requested dismissal of both the case and the death penalty request. We argued that if the WIZARD information was not provided that the government could no longer seek the death penalty, but more appropriately, the case should be dismissed.

The second motion identified Hermione as Victoria Hancock, currently the assistant to the Deputy Director of Operations of the CIA, and a request that she be ordered to testify at trial.

The prosecution's responses were both predictable and unexpected. Willis and Lawson argued that the judge had no authority to order the CIA to produce the WIZARD files as they were classified, and the CIA said we had no need to know the information in those files. That decision, the prosecution said, could not be challenged. However, the prosecution agreed that Hancock should be a witness so the case could go forward. They said she would testify one time during the penalty phase of the trial if Hussain was convicted and that her testimony would be in secret session. Only the judge, counsel, jury, and court personnel could be present. Hussain, too would be excluded. The record of her testimony would be sealed.

Within hours after the Prosecution's filing, Pierce issued an order denying our access to the WIZARD files but confirming Hancock as a witness.

When we met, Moretti was railing, "Clearly the fix was in."

"Yes, but look on the bright side. We get Victoria Hancock as a witness."

"She'll lie."

Moretti countered.

"Christ, you are so naive."

"Of course, she'll lie. But we can get some portion of the truth, which is fuck all more than we had before. So let's meet with Mann, and we can begin preparing."

Later, I bought a cheap cell phone, got a new number, and called Mathot on her burner phone.

"We need to meet."

A pause.

"I knew you'd be calling. Hancock is beside herself. She can't believe she will be a witness. She says she's been hung out by her own people, which is probably true. For her enemies in the agency, this is a good way to marginalize her and maybe get her out. But what do you want with me?"

"Connie, it's decision time. You know the questions we need to ask. You know more of the truth than I do. You know what is in the WIZARD files. We need your help. If you are committed to the truth, we need your help to prepare to question Hancock. That's as clear as I can make it."

Mathot agreed to meet in Chicago. She gave us instructions on how to shake any followers, get to Chicago, and meet with minimal risk of discovery. This involved burner phones, cash, and driving Fredrick's car but stealing license plates to use on the trip. We met at a cheap hotel in downtown Chicago for three days.

Driving back to DC, Fredricks observed, "When Hancock testifies, she is going to have a couple of very, very bad days."

CHAPTER 45

Shortly before the commencement of the trial, Brooks wrote a preview article that provided thumbnail resumes of the major players. The article also focused on what was at stake for both the prosecution and al-Yemeni in the trial. This part was the easiest to present to the reader. The stakes were life and death. Hussain al-Yemeni, the alleged al-Qaeda terrorist, faced the death penalty if convicted. The jury, all military officers, could decide on a sentence of life imprisonment or some lesser penalty. Still, the prosecution's goal was to persuade the jury to impose a death sentence. The trial would consist of three phases: the first phase is jury selection. Then the guilt /innocence phase, in which the prosecution would try to prove al-Yemeni's guilt beyond a reasonable doubt. Al-Yemeni's lawyers, the article suggested, would ask the jury to find that the United States was not at war when the Kuwait attack occurred. The defense was also going to try to persuade the jury that the evidence was insufficient and that al-Yemeni should be found not guilty. Should al-Yemeni be convicted, the court would hold a penalty phase. During this third trial phase, the prosecution could present aggravation, matters which would justify a sentence of death. This includes what the law refers to as victim-impact evidence. The defense's focus in the trial's penalty phase was to present mitigation, evidence weighing against a sentence of death to persuade the jury that al-Yemeni's life should be spared. The article continued:

> While this may look like a regular trial, the rules and procedures are, according to legal experts, much different. First, hearsay, what one person said to another, is admissible if it is deemed by the military judge, James Pierce, to be

reliable. This is significant because much of the evidence of al-Yemeni's involvement comes from statements taken by the FBI in 2001.

Also significant is the role the US torture program plays in the case. Al Yemeni was in CIA black sites where according to his lawyers, he was tortured by the CIA. The defense contends his statements, taken by the FBI after he came to Guantanamo, were the product of torture. Pierce has rejected that claim, has ruled the statements will be heard by the jury, and also ruled that the defense can, to a limited degree, question witnesses about the circumstances under which they were made. Should the case get to a penalty phase, Pierce will allow the defense to question a CIA operative who led the torture. This operative has never been publically identified, but sources have told the Times that the operative is Victoria Hancock, who is now one of the top career officials in the CIA.

The jury pool is filled with officers selected from all the services by the Convening Authority, a bureaucrat who oversees the Military Commissions. The defense has challenged this pool of jurors. The defense argues that they were hand-picked by the Government official responsible for overseeing the Military Commissions and not randomly selected. This, the defense argues, stacks the deck solidly in favor of the prosecution. Judge Pierce has rejected that challenge.

CHAPTER 46

Jury selection proceeded as expected. Slowly. The jurors were flown to the island in groups of thirty. They were housed in a facility on the island's leeward side, close to the airstrip, so they could be kept segregated from the hubbub surrounding the trial. They were brought to the court in groups of five to be questioned individually. First, the judge would question the jurors getting their basic information, present and former assignments, history, attitude about the case and terrorism, and did they feel they could be fair. Many candidly said they could not and were excused on the spot. Others were more equivocal. Then Lawson or Willis would question the juror, focusing on their ability to sit in a capital trial and their attitude about the death penalty. Finally, when the prosecution had completed its questioning, one of us would begin questioning, focusing on their feelings about terrorism and Islam.

We would then turn to their knowledge of the Kuwait, Cole, and 9/11 attacks and whether they had lost friends or comrades in those attacks. Finally, we would inquire about their ability to consider mitigation evidence and ask the ultimate question we had outlined for Brooks. Most frankly said, they would impose death and, having staked out that position, wedded themselves to it to the point where they would be excluded. A few felt they could consider a sentence other than death, so they were provisionally seated. The judge ruled that we would later exercise our limited challenges where we could excuse any juror for any reason other than their race.

Two months into the process, Judge Pierce announced that the process was moving too slowly and that he would do all the questioning rather than counsel. Lawson readily agreed to this procedure, knowing that leading questions from the judge would teach prospective jurors the correct answers. We objected to this change, but Pierce was adamant. The process sped up as Pierce's superficial questioning led jurors to state that they could be fair.

For example, Marine Colonel Quick, who was "very much a supporter of the death penalty for terrorists," was provisionally seated because "I would not let my support for the death penalty override my duty to follow the Court's instructions." When we pointed out that the Court's instructions would leave the life/death decision to each juror, Pierce responded, "He said he can be fair, he is a Colonel, I take him at his word, he will be provisionally seated."

Despite the rushed and one-sided nature of Pierce's questions, it took three additional weeks to seat a total of twenty-two jurors provisionally. Each side exercised their three peremptory strikes, and, over our objections, a jury of twelve and four alternates was seated. Three men were senior Army officers, Colonels, and Lt. Colonels. Two men were Air Force Colonels. There was one Marine Lt. Colonel. There were four women, an Air Force Captain, a Navy Commander, a Lt. Commander, and a Major in the Army. There were four alternate jurors. Three men and one woman. All Majors and Colonels.

CHAPTER 47

Leonardo DiSilva, the court watcher who taught me so much in law school, believed that opening statements were the most critical part of the trial after jury selection. In his view, after opening statements, the case was ninety percent over.

"Think about it, kid," he'd said. "You pick a jury. If the people you select can accept your view of the evidence, you are halfway home. The jury hears both sides back to back in the opening, and if they are thinking, I think the defense's version is more believable. So you are ninety percent there. But if they think the prosecution has the strongest case, the prosecution probably wins. There should be no surprises in the evidence, so that initial judgment generally hardens into a final decision. Common sense."

Years of trials led me to conclude that Joe was right.

The atmosphere in the courtroom was electric as both sides fidgeted through final preparations before court began. Papers were nervously shuffled, and there were brief muttered conversations. On the left side of the room, our team occupied the better part of two tables. Hussain was at the far left, closest to the guards, who were sitting about ten feet away. The guards wore splotchy green and gray fatigues. Hussain was in white prison garb. This was our choice. We wanted the jury to understand how long he had been in custody. Mohammed sat next to him, and I was next to Mohammed, trying to project a calm that I did not feel. I'd sit, look at my notebook, then talk briefly to Hussain through Mohammed. Carter sat next to me, then Harriet and Kristina, who was closest to the podium, which was turned to face the, for now, empty jury box. Behind us sat the three paralegals and Reyes. Behind the paralegals, General Ward sat by himself. I guess he was the Chief Defense Counsel and was showing support. But we'd hardly spoken in months, and it was hard to hide the disdain the team had for him. He'd become 'that fucking Ward' after the meeting with him and Lawson. And he had done nothing to persuade us that the moniker was unfair.

Across the aisle, Willis was closest to the podium, then Lawson. No one had replaced Jennifer. She was forced to sit in the small gallery, still nominally part of the prosecution but exiled to the back because of her honesty.

A day or two earlier, over coffee, Jennifer told Carter and me that Lawson tried to force her to return to Washington, but her status as a whistleblower allowed her to stay, and Lawson relented. She told us that her husband was not thrilled she was still here during the trial. In a resigned and disappointed tone, she continued, "I don't know if we'll make it. I hope we do, but who knows? My being here and unwillingness to leave until this is over has not helped."

Carter asked, "Why are you staying?"

She looked at the two of us.

"I just need to be a witness. It makes no sense, I know it makes no sense, but somehow I feel like if I leave, Lawson won."

Carter shrugged and said nothing.

"Yes, that's Steve's reaction too. But that's how I feel."

At the back, behind the glass wall, the small viewing room was packed. Survivors of the bombing and family members of some of those killed sat on the right of the room facing the bench. To their left were the members of the press and representatives of organizations such as the American Bar Association and the American Civil Liberties Union. Samantha Brooks sat in the front row. She was by far the most senior press person there. There were a couple of TV reporters from national networks. Familiar faces with no understanding of the mess they were about to see.

The jury of sixteen filed in. There were some pretty impressive chests of medals. By tradition, Col. John Mortenson, the most senior officer on the panel, sat closest to the judge.

After the initial crescendo of anticipation, the courtroom grew silent as Pierce took the bench, wearing what appeared to be a new jet-black robe with gold bands around the cuffs. After welcoming everyone and remarking on the historic nature of the proceedings, he began to read the panel the preliminary instructions. The instructions included definitions of such legal terms as the presumption of innocence and proof beyond a reasonable doubt and provided a general outline of the jury's responsibilities. As he read, the instructions were displayed on screens throughout the courtroom. After completing the reading of the instructions, the judge sat taller and asked, "Does the prosecution wish to make an opening statement?"

Lawson stood. He was wearing his Army dress dark blue uniform with gold stripes around the sleeves. The Combat Infantry Man's Badge topped the rows of ribbons signifying all his awards over his left breast. This badge, a silver rifle on a blue background surrounded by a silver wreath, signified he'd been in combat. I considered this to be improbable, as lawyers were not exactly warriors. But my dislike for Lawson was certainly impacting my judgment.

"Yes, your Honor." He stood. Smiled at the jurors.

"And with the Commission's permission, I'd like to use the screen to display a Powerpoint."

Lawson stood, began to walk, and before he arrived at the podium, he began speaking. More experienced lawyers would have milked the moment. But as he walked, he said, "Members of the panel, I am Brigadier General Robert E. Lee Lawson, and I, along with Major Thomas Willis," and here he swept his arm to direct the jury to his entire team, "and our paralegals and agents, represent the United States of America. I am the Chief Prosecutor here in Guantanamo Bay. In this trial, we will prove beyond a reasonable doubt that the defendant, Hussain al-Yemeni, was the leader, organizer, and the mastermind of the cowardly attack on the Ali al-Salem Air Force Base. Over sixty brothers and sisters in arms were killed, scores injured, and millions, if not billions, worth of equipment was destroyed. The manner of this attack—surprise, stealth, perfidy made it a war crime punishable by this Commission. Make no mistake. After the defendant is convicted, and I say this because I am confident in our proof, we will have a separate hearing in which we will ask you to impose the death penalty.

"Let me now describe for you the prosecution's evidence. Before I do that, you need to know one thing. In this Commission, reliable hearsay,' and he emphasized reliable, 'is admissible. Much of our evidence consists of FBI statements taken in Kuwait after the attack. These statements that the judge has concluded are reliable will be presented to you either by the agents who took the statements or other agents. You will learn about the defendant's confession. You will learn he gave this confession freely and voluntarily. Indeed he bragged about his role in the attack. Combined, this proof is overwhelming."

My inner voice said, *If he quits here, we've got problems. This was good.* But he was wedded to Powerpoint, so I was confident that Lawson would go on for at least an hour. And he did.

Lawson displayed and read slides, dense with information, to the jury. After fifteen minutes, jurors began to look bored; after forty minutes, there was a lot of shifting and looking at watches. Everyone except Lawson was ready to pee or poke their eyes out in an hour. Finally, he closed.

"As we told you in jury selection, this trial will take a long, long time. Our proof is extensive, and we will be methodical and thorough. However long justice takes, in this case, we will ask you to find the defendant guilty of the crimes and specifications in the charge sheet. And then, after the second hearing, we will ask you to order that he be put to death. Thank you"

He left the podium, and Willis gave him a nod of approval.

Pierce turned, "Does the defense wish to make an opening statement?"

I stood, "Yes, your honor. But first, may I ask for a comfort break? I've had too much coffee, and the jurors may be in the same boat."

And I looked at the jury. Some of the jurors nodded yes. Some also smiled, perhaps sensing the battle for power that was going on.

Pierce glared and said, "Can it wait until you have finished your statement?"

I looked at the jury, who shook their heads no. Pierce knew he had no choice. He'd wanted them bored, distracted, and restless, but with the 'comfort break,' they would be restored and hopefully attentive.

Court breaks at Guantanamo always last at least a half hour. Lots of people need to use limited toilet facilities. There was a lot of milling around in the black cement courtyard. The victims and families, the press, and representatives of the NGOs huddled in the shade of a tent next to the court's entrance. I caught Jennifer's eye. She nodded. I winked, appearing more confident than I felt. I actually felt like throwing up. Again. I had thrown up at about 3.30 that morning. Nerves overcoming experience as the magnitude of the day truly hit me.

After everyone returned to their places in court and silence followed, Pierce asked,

"Does the defense wish to make an opening statement?"

"Yes, Your honor."

I stood and came behind Hussain. I touched his shoulder, bent down, and whispered, "I will tell your story with truth, and I hope with passion."

He looked at me and nodded. I blinked back a tear as I slowly approached the podium, stood to the side of it, and put my hands together as if in prayer. I wanted all attention on me, but more importantly, I needed to compose myself and to breathe—a few beats, and I began,

"There is no question that al-Qaeda suicide bombers attacked the Kuwaiti airfield. There is no doubt that the attack killed over sixty airmen. Many more were wounded. There is no question that the attack destroyed a billion or more dollars of equipment. There is no question that this was a black eye for the US.

"But, there is a big question. Did Hussain al-Yemeni have a major role in the attack? It is, you will learn, impossible that he was the mastermind in the attack. The mastermind of the attack was Walid al-Qatari, who planned and carried out the attack with the assistance of officials of the Government of Kuwait.

"While the prosecution's focus is on the alleged guilt of Mr. al-Yemeni, before you reach that question, you will be required to resolve two questions the prosecution did not mention."

As I spoke, our Powerpoint displayed the questions the jury would have to answer.

"In February of 2001, was the United States at War?

"If the US was at war in February 2001, was the attack, an attack by stealth and deception, a war crime? Put more bluntly, if, in 2001, the United States was at war, did the other side of the war have a right to fight back?"

I slowly walked to the other side of the podium to allow the moment to sink in.

"Let me be as clear as I can be. If, as the prosecution contends, the US was at war with al-Qaeda, then you, as men and women of the military, know al-Qaeda gets to fight back. That is war. And you know war allows surprise, even sneak attacks. So if you find that the US was at war in 2001, then Hussain is not guilty because this attack was legal and proper under the law of war.

"If, however, you find that the United States was not at war in early 2001, then there will be additional proceedings that will address what happens to Hussain."

Here, I was being less than forthright. If the jury found the US was not at war, the case was over as there would have been no jurisdiction in Guantanamo, and the entire proceeding and the years leading up to it a waste of time. I moved a few steps left, and the jury followed me with their eyes.

"As I told you, there is no dispute about the attack. However, there are serious disputes about the evidence connecting Hussain to this attack. The sad truth, the FBI investigation into the attack was hopelessly compromised. It was compromised by interference with the investigation by the Government of Kuwait. Make no mistake; the FBI did not fail. Instead, the FBI investigation was improperly hindered, hindered by the Government of Kuwait. This interference undermines the reliability of the investigation and of the hearsay statements you will hear. To be blunt, the evidence you will receive is not trustworthy. These are hard words, so let me tell you why I say them and provide you with a preview of the evidence that supports them."

For the next several minutes, I outlined the problems with the investigation, the interference by the Kuwaitis, and the FBI's frustration.

"So why would the Kuwaitis interfere? The only way this attack could have occurred was with the direct assistance of Kuwaiti officials. Let me be more direct, The Government of Kuwait was a major player in this attack. That involvement made it necessary for the Kuwaitis to deflect the investigation. The Kuwaitis needed to deflect the investigation away from those in their government and military who approved and assisted the attack. The Kuwaitis needed to blame others. Among those blamed by the Kuwaitis was Hussain al-Yemeni. His name was first given to the US by Kuwaiti officials. Kuwaiti officials first expressed the notion he was the mastermind. The sad fact is that officials in the government of Kuwait, which was central to this attack, focused the FBI on Hussain not because that was true but to protect Kuwaiti officials and the al-Qaeda members working with them.

"But beyond the misdirection by the Kuwaitis, there are other reasons why the evidence you will hear is unreliable. The statements linking Hussain to the crime are what we lawyers call hearsay. What John tells Fred is hearsay. Hearsay is not trusted in most courts.

"The Kuwaiti witnesses whose statements you will hear, and often their families, wives, parents, and children, were held for months in Kuwaiti jails before being allowed to speak with the FBI. They were questioned by the FBI, at the jail, in the presence of the Kuwaiti secret police. They were effectively hostages. You will learn they knew that telling the FBI what the Kuwaiti government wanted them to say was critical. Only if they kept to the story could they and their families be released. These statements would not be admitted in a real court or a court martial. Yet you are asked to uncritically accept these statements as true because the judge has ruled they are admissible. We trust you will not do that and that you will bring your collective wisdom to bear and reject these statements."

For the next several minutes, I outlined some of the inconsistencies in the many statements using Powerpoint. The jurors were not

shifting. They followed my movements. A few took notes from the slides.

"The second thing that compromised this case and makes the evidence unreliable is the extensive, brutal, and ongoing torture inflicted on Hussain by the Central Intelligence Agency. This torture was so profound that it impacts and undermines the reliability of what he said to what is called the FBI Clean Team. The so-called clean team statement, the so-called confession, was theater because Hussain knew what he was supposed to say to avoid additional torture." Here, I looked at Hussain, hoping the jury would follow. They did.

"From 2002 to 2006, the CIA tortured Hussain. Hung him up, waterboarded him, stuffed him in a coffin for days. Other times they crammed him into a much smaller box. A box the size of a small floor safe. They beat him and raped him. After four years of abuse, Hussain was trained to say whatever they wanted to hear to avoid further abuse. For reasons I am not allowed to tell you, what you will hear about the torture is truncated. You will not be allowed to hear the whole truth of the torture that led to the so-called confession. But if you focus on the little we will be allowed to present to you; you will conclude that Hussain's statement to the FBI is, like much of the prosecution's case, unreliable and not trustworthy enough to support a conviction, much less an execution.

"Beyond its unreliability, should you convict Hussain, you are approving torture. Should you do so, you put future generations of the US military at risk of torture by our enemies. How can we complain about your brother and sister military being tortured if our enemies only do what we've done?"

This provoked an objection that "this was argumentative." This objection was completely correct. We'd been hoping for an objection about the torture.

When the judge hesitated, I said, "Your honor, is the government opposed to calling torture, torture? Or is the government opposed to telling the jury the full weight of the responsibility that the jurors bear? They bear the responsibility for the truth. They bear the responsibility for Hussain's life. And they bear the responsibility for the lives of future US military. Which part does the prosecution want to hide?"

Pierce shot me THE look. The look judges have when they want you to shut up. He then sustained the prosecution's objection. Having made my speech, I responded, "Fine, your honor." And I returned to the jury.

"In several months, one of the four of us will speak with you again, and we will discuss what we have told you. We'll tell you why what I've told you today is confirmed by the evidence, and we'll ask you to do four things:

"To say aloud what you all know – in 2001, the US was not at war. Or, if we were at war, then this attack, brutal as it was, was allowed under the law of war.

"To say torture is wrong.

"To show the world that American justice is even-handed.

"To find Hussain al-Yemini not guilty."

CHAPTER 48

After the opening statements, Pierce said, "Call your first witness."

Typically the prosecution calls an emotional witness first. The goal is to get the jury angry early in the case. Here the prosecution had a stable of witnesses with tragic testimony. Senior Airman William Dale was selected to be the prosecution's lead witness.

Dale came into the courtroom through a side door. He was pale white with a shock of black hair. Dale appeared to be about 6 feet tall, but it was hard to tell because he sat in a black wheelchair. He used a chrome circular attachment to turn the silver and black wheels. His upper body looked strong and wide. His lower body was obviously damaged.

He rolled himself across the room and looked at the judge.

"Your honor, may I testify from my chair? I can get up the steps, but it's pretty awkward."

Pierce asked if either side had any objections. He may have thought we would be stupid enough to oppose this request.

Willis gave Dale the oath.

"State your name and place of residence."

"William Dale, Reston Virginia."

Dale described his fourteen-year career in the Air Force. He was an airframe specialist. He'd been assigned to Kuwait from Minot, North Dakota, only two months before the attack. He and three others from his unit were in the dining facility when the truck came through the wall. He thought he was hit by the truck and thrown across the room. But "it could have been the blast." He survived. Staff

Sergeant Paul Bagley, Senior Airman Susan Marshall, and Airman First Class Valerie Palmer, sitting with Dale, died.

Dale told the jury how he woke up in the hospital in Germany. He described his despair at learning that his friends had been killed. He told about realizing he was paralyzed from the waist down. Dale, we learned, was medically separated from the Air Force with a pension after his treatment was completed.

Dale spoke about his life before and after the attack. He was surprisingly matter-of-fact about the obvious issues of incontinence and the need to wear a bag. He described the inability to have sex and the effect on his relationship with his wife. He was now divorced. He now has a job with Leidos, a government contractor. He liked the job but missed the service. When he told the jury of his love of golf and how he could no longer play, sadness and anger radiated from his whole being.

With that, Willis, who had been questioning Dale, passed the witness to us for questioning. We'd known Dale was coming and knew from discovery and interviews what he would say. His anger and sadness, while not unexpected, were quite moving, and more emotional than we'd expected. Perhaps it was because I, too, love golf and could barely imagine life without it that I was touched by Dale's loss.

We'd agreed Carter would question Dale. The first few minutes would be critical. To show Dale and the jury our humanity and to defuse their anger.

"Sgt. Dale, can you accept that we cannot imagine your pain and anger? I want you to know that. Okay?"

Dale nodded.

"Thank you, sir."

"The jury knows how horrible this attack was."

"Yes, it was."

"I'll bet you think of it every day."

"Yes."

"If only?"

"Yes. If only I'd not had that meal."

"And if only you and the others had picked another table?"

Dale looked down softly, "I chose it."

"I sense you feel guilty?"

"Yes, I do."

"And I'll bet your therapist has told you countless times. 'There is no rhyme or reason to who gets killed in war and who doesn't?' But I'll bet you still feel guilty."

Dale nodded. But said nothing.

Willis broke the moment by saying, "Mr. Dale. You have to answer verbally."

Dale glared at Willis.

He said aloud what we all knew, what did not need to be said.

"Yes, I feel guilty." And he added, "I also wish I'd been killed, and they lived."

And he looked back at Carter, who Dale seemed to know, had maybe a glimmer of understanding of his pain.

Carter continued softly.

"Do you mind if I ask some questions about before the attack?"

Dale said, "It's okay. I'm good."

Carter nodded, "When you got to Kuwait, did they tell you that you were entering a theater of war?"

Dale looked at Carter, "Sir, I don't understand your question."

Carter nodded, "I'll be more precise. Did they tell you that the air base was part of a war footing?"

Dale looked up, "No one ever said anything about war" He was emphatic.

Carter continued, "No one briefed you on war-time rules of engagement?"

Dale looked puzzled.

"No. We were told that we were assisting the Kuwaitis and providing support for law-enforcement operations in Yemen associated with the Cole bombing."

A gift there, I thought.

Carter brought out how Dale had not received a Purple Heart or other wartime-based awards such as increased insurance benefits.

Carter then had Dale describe from his point of view how the government of Kuwait controlled the base. This line of questioning brought a lot of objections, "Speculative, your honor."

Dale seemed frustrated that the prosecution's objection was sustained.

Carter asked, "Are you speculating, or is this what you know? What you saw?"

Dale sat up taller.

"I saw it. I heard it. You could not do shit," here he turned to the judge, "Sorry, Your Honor."

Turning back to the jury, he continued, "Because of the Kuwaitis. They were into everything."

"Tell the jury how the Kuwaitis kept you from doing stuff? How were they into everything?"

Willis again objected. Dale glared at him, and Pierce sided with Dale, overruling the objection. Dale began a monologue about how the Kuwaitis impacted the base and its operations. No alcohol, reduced staff on Fridays, and constant questions about the loyalty of the civilians who were employed on the base. The Kuwaitis wanted some of their civilians to work on the planes, supposedly for training.

"But the truth? We didn't trust them. We never let them work alone. Too easy to sabotage. It was just a cluster."

"No further questions."

Carter sat down next to me, and I whispered, "That was great."

Willis had no redirect. Dale wheeled himself out of the court, and the second witness, Colonel James Winston, was giving his name and place of residence.

The following weeks were spent hearing from military men and women who witnessed the attack. Some carried obvious evidence of their injuries. For others, the damage was less outwardly physical and more emotional. The prosecution's evidence painted an accurate picture of an attack that resulted in chaos. Death, destruction, and heroism were described carefully and completely. The physical injuries were addressed in clinical detail—charts showing who was where when the attacks occurred were all over the courtroom. Hundreds of photographs allowed no doubt about the amount of destruction and loss. There were surveillance videos from the multiple cameras recording events on the base.

What was initially horrifying became numbing. The first time we saw the truck plow into the dining facility was frightening. By the fifth time, the jury could focus on details. We did not object. The truth is we did what we could to encourage this prosecutorial overkill. We wanted, needed, the horror to become commonplace, to let the anger dissipate so that the facts could be objectively considered. And the truth was that as horrific as all this evidence was, it said nothing about whether or not Hussain was guilty.

Carter, Moretti, Fredricks, and I split the crosses. Generally, we acknowledged the witness's pain and their heroism. We focused on Kuwaiti interference with the running of the base, distrust of the Kuwaitis, or the lack of a wartime footing before the attack. Occasionally we would ask no questions, trying to alter the rhythm of the case. We tried not to be the ones boring the jury, although we speculated that it was all quite repetitive for the jury.

The judge tried to keep to a 9:30 to 4:30 schedule, and things moved slowly. Some days, court would be delayed because "difficulties" transporting Hussain would leave him sick to his stomach. He told us, "Some days, it seems like the guards go out of the way to make it hard for me." Complaints to the judge about Hussain's transportation were brusquely batted away.

The schedule gave us little release or respite. After court, the team would meet and plan for the next day. Sometimes we'd eat together, and sometimes just go to our separate rooms and work or try to unwind. But there was no way to really take a mental break.

A trip to the only store, the NEX, was likely to result in an awkward encounter with a prosecutor, a witness, a family member of someone killed in the attack, or a member of the press. Sometimes these encounters were polite, a nod, a greeting. Except with the press, more often than not, there was an attitude of keep your distance. Unspoken but palpable.

Occasionally, I would run into Sanders at the dining facility, Kelly's, the NEX, or just in passing. We would chat briefly. We'd talk about the quagmire of the trial, the difficulty of separation, and her continued exile. She was stuck in Guantanamo, although this was her choice. No hugs.

The stress, and the time away from family, created ample opportunities for mischief. Rumors about who was supposedly sleeping with whom were rampant and progressively absurd. Brooks was supposedly involved with Lawson or me. Carter was linked to Moretti or a prosecution paralegal. Ward was said to be close with one of the court reporters. It was all just gossip. Carter snorted,

"This shit is out of control. Next, they'll have Connor fucking Lawson."

"Hey, It's love. It is true love."

Kelly's, the faux Irish pub at Guantanamo, was the focal point of what passed for a social life during the trial. By unspoken agreement, Kelly's, the Dench Gym, and the few other recreational places at GTMO were neutral zones. Places where opponents could have brief conversations. Like the Christmas truce during WWI, only early in the mornings at the gym and weekends at the bar.

Many of the trial participants were at Kelly's on a Friday, a few weeks into the trial. The prosecutors were in the back room. A group of victims was sitting on the veranda outside. We were in the main room in a booth across from the ornate wooden bar, which fronted an array of different liquors and beer taps. A gaggle of press sat a few booths down from us. Some contact between the groups relied on an unspoken agreement, "What happened at Kelly's stayed at Kelly's, and what happened on Friday or Saturday night was forgotten by Sunday afternoon."

There were continued rumors of some random couplings.

This night, Kristina, Jill, Carter, and I were sitting, nursing the last drink of the evening. The prosecutors had left. Brooks came up to us and asked if the remnants of the press table could join us.

"Sure," I replied, "so long as we agree everything, and I mean everything, is not only off the record but 'didn't happen.' We're drunk or getting there and generally have no boundaries."

Nods all around.

A reporter from Fox, Mary Ligouri, said, "No boundaries; I like that in my men." She forced a chair taken from their table between Carter and me. Jill on my left, and now, Ligouri my right. The conversation quickly drifted away from legal stuff.

Ligouri asked, "So I'm unclear; where do you guys live while you're here."

Jill answered, "The defense is in the BOQ, the large building up the hill. The prosecution is in another section of the BOQ. Prevents murders that way."

Ligouri smiled, "I can't stand the tents they make the press stay in. It's like going back to Girl Scout camp."

Looking at me she said, "I'd love to have a private and truly hot shower."

Jill said, with a smile, "You're welcome to use mine." Then, unspoken, 'Stay away bitch.'

A frown from Ligouri.

"Thanks, that's generous."

Carter smiled.

"Shots fired."

The manager came up, "I'm closing soon. Anything else?"

Brooks said, "One more round, I'll buy."

As we finished our last drinks, Ligouri leaned over and put her hand on my leg, and whispered, "I was serious about that shower."

I whispered back, "Sorry, it's just too complicated."

The press had a bus that took them to their tents near the court.

Our group walked the half-mile up the hill together back to the BOQ. It was a brilliant warm night. Stars were bright and beautiful, the Milky Way was visible, and there was little distortion from man-made lights. Jill was walking next to me. Quietly she said, "I guess you dodged that bullet."

"Ahhh, yes," I replied, "I'm committed to you."

She looked serious, "No, you are committed to Molly."

"Yes," And at that moment, walking under the stars, I missed Molly terribly.

CHAPTER 49

After the witnesses to the attack, the prosecution began presenting the necessary evidence that the people killed were dead and that they died in the attack. In addition, they had to prove that the cause of death was the result of the blast and not cancer or some natural cause. We'd repeatedly offered to stipulate these facts. Still, they insisted on presenting the evidence in great detail to show the jury how devastating the attack was and to shock the jurors with the horrible injuries that were inflicted.

One military pathologist, Robert Agular, had done the largest number of the autopsies. His direct questioning lasted about two trial weeks as he went through each autopsy. The judge had offered to let us cross-examine after each autopsy was described, but we declined, figuring that the jury would become bored as the descriptions descended into a stew of blood and gore. With each victim, Agular would describe the injuries and then display photos of the fatal wounds. In some cases, the victims were literally in pieces, and Agular would show a picture of the person reassembled on the examining table. In other cases, the injuries were less pronounced, and the photos were of the victim during the autopsy. It was all quite gruesome, and it was boring and unnecessary after the first day.

After the third day, Willis came and asked if we would now stipulate. Fredricks looked at me and subtly shook her head back and forth, looked at Willis, and said,

"If you acknowledge to the jury that we offered to stipulate this stuff months ago, we'll discuss it. But you must acknowledge that we made the offer and the prosecution refused."

He shook his head.

"I can't imagine Lawson agreeing to that."

I laughed, "Neither can I, so you guys can continue to bore the jury."

Two weeks later, Agular finished the description of the wounds that caused the death of Tech Sgt. Roberta Rodriquez, and Lawson, who had been doing this examination, passed the witness for cross-examination. This cross was my responsibility.

"Dr. Agular, I think we can all agree that this attack inflicted horrible injuries."

"Yes, that's obviously correct."

"And I'm not seeking to minimize this when I ask; you've done other autopsies from war zones, isn't that right?"

"Yes."

"Warfare generally produce horrible injuries, true?"

"Yes, of course."

"And modern warfare produces truly horrific injuries."

"Yes, it does."

"Indeed, much of the science of warfare has been about how combatants can kill each other with more certainty."

"I guess that is true."

"As a military physician, you've learned that the military wants weapons that are more accurate? That can kill with precision? And from a greater distance?"

Agular nodded agreement and added, "With more lethality."

"While these injuries were horrific, aren't they pretty common wartime combat injuries?"

"Unfortunately, that is true."

At this, Lawson stood.

"Your honor. While this was a wartime attack, The prosecution insists that this was an unlawful attack. It was a suicide stealth unlawful attack and punishable under the law of war. We object."

Pierce, "Response?"

I couldn't believe this gift. Lawson, if I could, I would kiss you.

"Judge, if the US was at war with al-Qaeda in 2001, as the prosecution has alleged, the air base is certainly a lawful target. Assaults in which the attacker is likely to be killed are a part of combat. Suicide attacks are part of warfare. For example, Pickett's charge at Gettysburg was described by many as a suicide attack. Whole companies were lost in the first wave at Omaha beach. US men and women in combat often knowingly sacrifice their lives in wartime attacks. Here, as regrettable as it was, Al-Qaeda fighters did the same."

Pierce's eyes darted to Lawson's, silently imploring him to interrupt. When Lawson did not get the hint, Pierce raised his hand, palm facing me, "Counsel, I get your point." Then, he turned to the jury, "Whether the US was at war and whether this was an unlawful attack are issues you will have to address in due course."

He then turned back to me.

"Counsel, I'm going to insist you keep the editorial comments to a minimum."

"Fine, Your honor, but I'm unclear. Is the objection overruled or sustained?"

I wanted him to commit.

"Counsel, I've ruled."

Fuck you. And I turned and asked the same question,

"While these injuries were horrific, they were not unusual for wartime combat injuries?"

Lawson said nothing, Pierce glared, and Agular said, "As I said before, unfortunately, that is correct."

"I want to turn now to another subject. The materials you've shown the jury are horrific." And here, I turned, looked away from the witness to the jury, and said,

"The jury has to try to remain objective in the face of this horror. How do you remain objective when you see horror, day after day after day?"

Dr. Agular sat back.

"You know, I've never been asked that. And it is a good question."

I interrupted, "Thank you. And your response?"

"As a doctor, I am a scientist. I have to remain objective. If I get emotional or angry, I may miss something important. If I allow myself to focus on these kids, I get emotional. Death in war is so wasteful. Of course, premature death is sad. But it is kids who are in the military and kids who die. As a scientist, I have to work to focus on being objective. Because objectivity is what is necessary."

While he was saying this, I was looking at the jury. Trying to see if they got it. That they had to remain objective despite the horror, and unable to contain myself, I said, "You do what the judge instructs the jury to do. Remain objective in the face of complicated evidence?"

"I hope so."

"As does everyone here," I said, looking at the jury.

"Nothing else, judge."

After two weeks of direct, Lawson expected a cross that lasted more than an hour. He was clearly caught off guard. He and Willis looked at each other. Lawson said, "Nothing further."

"Call your next witness."

Lawson said, "Judge, we expected a longer cross. Our next witness won't arrive for two days. He's on the next flight."

Pierce glared.

"You got anyone here? I don't want to waste two days."

"No, your honor. We have an order, and we want to keep it."

Pierce excused the jury. When they were out of the room, he turned on Lawson. Pointing and shaking his right index finger as though disciplining a child, Piece forcefully said,

"General, you WILL have a witness standing by. I don't want to lose two days. We already lost all this time because you would not stipulate to the medical information."

Lawson stood. His palm faced the judge as though to ward off his words, "Colonel Pierce," clearly pulling rank. "We're doing the best we can. But we have a plan, and we WILL stick with the plan. Just as the defense may have a plan. And I'd expect them to stick with it."

Judge Pierce continued to wag his finger, "Do not push me, General. I've told you what I expect."

A grudging, "Understood."

So we waited two days for the next pathologist, who testified for five days. More gore, more photos. More boredom.

The cross-exam continued to emphasize the need for objectivity in the face of horror. We hoped jurors were hearing it, if not repeating it in their sleep.

CHAPTER 50

The first law-enforcement witness was the lead FBI investigator. Charles Keenan. Keenan's testimony was broken into three sections.

First is an overall description of the investigation and identifying specific physical evidence and photographs. He would be cross-examined about those topics. Then he would offer the many statements of Kuwaiti witnesses that the judge had said were admissible. The judge ruled that what weight to give the statements was the jury's responsibility.

We would then question Keenan about the circumstance of the statements.

Then Keenan could testify about his questioning of Hussain at Guantanamo, what the prosecution called the clean team statement, the statement taken from Hussain after he was brought back to Guantanamo.

During the first portion of his testimony, Keenan described his arrival in Kuwait, gave an overview of the investigation in Kuwait, and identified numerous exhibits and photographs. He told the jury that his mission was to identify and capture the persons responsible for the attack, arrest them, and bring them to trial.

Lawson asked, "Have you completed your mission?"

We could have objected. We remained silent.

"Yes, with Mr. al-Yemeni's arrest, we felt our mission was complete."

Lawson turned to the details of the investigation and, for the rest of the day and into the following week, did an overview of the investigation.

Throughout his testimony, Keenan alluded to interference from the Kuwaitis but told the jury,

"It was not too big a deal."

Carter was going to do this cross and was scribbling furiously, drawing big stars on subjects he wanted to highlight.

Finally, Lawson said, "Your witness."

Carter stood at the podium, fixed his gaze on Keenan, turned, and looked at the jury. He continued to look at the jury as he questioned Keenan, turning only occasionally to look at Keenan.

"Agent Keenan, the FBI was not the first agency that held Hussain, isn't that true?"

Keenan agreed that he did not "arrest" Hussain until 2006 when he encountered Hussain in Guantanamo. Carter also forced Keenan to acknowledge that he knew Hussain was in torture centers called black sites and that on two occasions, he had gone to black sites and had seen al-Yemeni being "subjected to so-called enhanced interrogations."

All of Carter's questions were short, designed to elicit the answer, Yes, and Keenan dutifully complied.

"The CIA questioned Hussain?"

"The CIA used methods you could not use?"

Keenan shrugged.

"That is true."

The jury began to sit up and pay closer attention.

"The CIA used waterboarding?"

"So I read in the newspaper."

"Stuffing Hussain in a box the size of a coffin?"

Here Lawson objected, "Outside the scope of direct."

Carter said, "They brought up the mission being completed with Hussain's arrest. But it was the CIA that arrested Hussain. The prosecution opened this door. And your honor, the jury needs to know what was done to Hussain before the FBI questioned him."

Pierce sustained the objection but told the jury this topic might be covered later in Keenan's testimony.

Carter returned to the FBI agent, "I'm confused, and perhaps the jury is as well. You say the Kuwaiti interference was not a big deal? Of little significance?"

"That's my testimony." His tone was matter-of-fact.

Keenan acknowledged that the Kuwaitis had surrounded the plane that brought the American investigators and tried to convince them to allow the Kuwaitis to do the investigation alone. As this information was elicited, Keenan's answers were quieter. He seemed to be sweating despite the frigid air conditioning in the courtroom. Carter also forced Keenan to admit that the Kuwaitis controlled who the FBI could interview.

"And in doing so, you could not use your judgment about what was and was not important?"

"We respected their opinions."

"And only interviewed the witnesses they allowed you to interview?"

Keenan would not budge.

"Counsel, we respected their opinions."

"The Kuwaitis did searches without your knowledge and participation?"

"Yes."

"Including major locations?"

"Yes."

"The Kuwaitis collected evidence? Did not document how or where it was found?"

"True."

Keenan was now clearly uncomfortable. He was picking at imaginary lint on his suit.

"You have no idea if their actions were real or not."

"I trust them."

"It was the Kuwaitis that found evidence that significantly helped the case? Right? Not the FBI?"

"Yes, that is correct."

"And you trust them? Despite the fact they held you at gunpoint and would not let you interview some witnesses?"

A soft, "Yes."

Carter said, "I've got a bridge I'd like to sell you. Do you trust me?"

Willis objected with a whining, "Your honor."

Carter smiled at the jury. Some smiled back. He turned to the judge, "Withdrawn, sorry, your honor."

A mock lowering of his head to escape incoming wrath.

Carter spent the next two days taking Keenan through the inconsistencies. The notion that the Kuwaiti interference was not that bad when examined in detail it was nonsense. The Kuwaitis impacted every aspect of the investigation. Carter exposed them all. It was detailed, thorough, and exacting.

Finally, he got to the end.

"Agent Keenan, You've done countless investigations in the United States?"

"True, that is correct."

"And worked with other law enforcement agencies?

"Yes."

"None of them held you at gunpoint, right?"

"That is true."

"None of them said you could not interview witnesses?"

"Yes."

"Or told you they found evidence without telling you where it was found or how it was found."

"Yes."

"All this must have seemed strange, surreal?"

"Surreal is a good word. Yes," Keenan said.

CHAPTER 51

On a Friday, after court, as we were preparing to unwind, Fredricks came to me, "I need to speak with you and the others. Can we meet this evening?"

We met in her room. It was identical to mine, Carter's and Kristina's. Same brownish gold furniture, the same layout, only different stains on the carpets and the walls. We all had drinks.

"The Pentagon wants me to approve an agreement to resolve Lukemeyer raping me. He'll be publically relieved of his command here at Guantanamo. A couple of weeks later, he'll resign his Commission and leave the Marines with an honorable discharge. He will not be prosecuted. But I will not be able to make any statements to the press. There will be no mention of what he did to me. It will be hidden."

Reyes asked, "If you say no?"

"He'll be charged, and presumably, there will be a trial. A court-martial. They tell me he claims the sex was consensual. That I like rough sex. But here's the thing. If I turn this down, they will take me away from the team and the trial because his trial could be in the next few months. So I'd have to be available to the prosecutors and, of course, testify."

She looked down.

"So even now, they are protecting him." Kristina took her hand. "What do you want to do? "

"I don't want to leave the case. Not now." Fredricks looked at me. "Connor, what do you think?"

I took a sip and shook my head.

"Not sure I'm the best person to ask. The warrior in me wants you to fight. The case against him is strong. But I'm not the person who would be attacked. The father in me wants you completely vindicated, and the bastard in me wants that fucker exposed. But the lead counsel in me wants you here. I think we could give Brooks the material we gave the Pentagon, and perhaps she'd write a story. That would expose him. But that's not the same."

I shook my head. "I support whatever you decide."

Moretti said, "I know what I don't want. I don't want you being attacked. It's selfish, but I do not want to think of them saying you wanted to be butt raped. And if he is acquitted…if they stack the jury with guys who protect him…"

Carter looked at Fredricks and shook his head.

"I'm with Kristina on this. Trials sound good, but this is the military. You win, you lose, he wins, you lose. I'd vote to try to get Brooks to write something after he is relieved of command but before he leaves the Corps. Honestly, probably the best you can do." Reyes looked up.

"Connor, how would you feel about asking Brooks before Harriet decides?"

"I'm happy to ask her right now if that's okay with you, Harriet?"

A nod.

I called Brooks' cell. "Samantha, it's Connor. I know it's Friday, and you are busy unwinding, but we have something we need to share with you. Can you meet with Moretti and me?"

Settling into one of the wood-benched banquettes at Kelly's Pub, drinks and fried pickles ordered, off the record assurances given, we explained how Fredricks had been raped, the military's attempted cover-up and how we put together a packet to try to force the Pentagon's hand. I explained how I told the Marine's top lawyer that if they didn't act, I would send the packet to the two female Senators who were most critical of the military's indifference to sexual assault. We then explained how the Marines were still trying to protect Lukemeyer with the settlement.

"So, if we give you the material, would you write the story after he is relieved of command? And, can you leave Harriet out of it?"

"Of course, I'll write it. I don't know if it will be published. Best I can do."

We nursed our drinks. Brooks looked around the room, "Everything that happens here is just so nuts. Why would they protect this guy? Why do they hide the torture? It's like there is no integrity here. I'll do what I can. I promise. I'll do what I can."

"All we can ask." "We went back and told Fredricks.

She looked at me, "What do you think?"

"The more I think about it, the more I think Kristina and Carter are right. Suppose he's convicted. Okay, maybe he goes to jail or gets a dishonorable discharge. That's the only way he is truly hurt, and let's be honest, that doesn't change your life any. But you've had to go through the trial with all the lies he'd tell. And, if he is acquitted, he stays in the Marines and is completely vindicated. None of us want that. It's a bad deal either way. Being relieved of command is a big deal. But in the end, the price he pays is pretty small. So how bad do you want him in jail, and are you willing to risk all the attacks to get that?"

Fredricks sat silently, her eyes searching each of us. Moretti took her hand.

"I'm not leaving the team for that piece of garbage. If this is what the Marines want, if this is who the Marines are, let them have their way. At least the motherfucker will be out of the Marines. I want to sleep on it, but I think that's where I am on this. And we've got to focus on saving Hussain's life. That is way more important than Lukemeyer."

She smiled and let out a big sigh. Nodded silently.

"Yes, I think that's the way to go."

CHAPTER 52

The next phase of Keenan's testimony was the reading of the statements taken by the FBI in Kuwait. Keenan was present when the majority of the statements were taken. Through him, the prosecution introduced the statements. Several of the Kuwaiti witnesses had identified Hussain by photographs shown to them first by the Kuwaitis and then by the FBI.

We had argued that this process was unfairly suggestive and the identifications should be suppressed. Pierce predictably ruled that the jury could decide what weight to give this evidence. This crystallized the unfairness of this process. The jury would decide whether an identification supposedly made by a Kuwaiti years earlier was reliable based not on what the witness told the jury but an FBI agent's description of the identification. Our objections that this was both hearsay and unreliable hearsay were rejected. Pierce impatiently heard our arguments and, with a dismissive wave of his hand, ruled, "These are all questions the jury will have to answer."

During this phase of his testimony, Keenan described how he interviewed the Kuwaitis at a Kuwaiti police office located at the central prison in Kuwait City. He acknowledged that the "witnesses" had been in Kuwaiti custody. He admitted he did not know how long they'd been in custody or the conditions of their custody. He acknowledged that in "some cases," the Kuwaitis had also taken the witnesses' families into custody. But in response to the prosecutor's questioning, he said that "in his professional opinion, the witnesses were reliable and doing their best to be truthful."

We'd agreed that Fredricks would do the first cross.

She stood at the podium, and I could see the light sheen of sweat glistening on her forehead. Then, in a shaky voice, she asked, "The Kuwaitis had arrested these folks?"

Keenan, sensing her struggle, said condescendingly and with a snarky grin, "Yes, I said that."

"And their families in some cases?"

"Yes, I said that as well."

"And you don't know the conditions under which they were held?"

"Yes, counsel," waving his hand, "I've admitted that."

"You'd agree, I hope, that for the jury to evaluate these statements, they need all the facts?"

"Yes, and they have them." And Keenan looked at the jury.

We'd expected all this, and as things were going to plan, Fredricks gained some confidence her voice became firmer.

"Well, let's examine that, shall we?"

"Is that a question?" Fredricks had had enough. She took a breath, stood a little taller, looked at the jury, then looked at Keenan and forcefully asked, "An effective investigation needs to be thorough, Right?"

"Of course, and this was," Keenan retorted.

"Accurate?"

"Yes."

"And complete, isn't that true?"

"Of course, we are as thorough and complete as possible given the circumstances."

"But in this situation, there is a lot you don't know that might be important to the jury?"

"Nothing significant, Counsel."

Fredricks smiled. She looked at the jury and said, "The conditions in which the Kuwaiti witnesses were held are not significant to you?"

"You're putting words in my mouth."

"Or if they were abused, that is not significant. Is that what you are telling this jury?"

"I don't think they were. No one complained."

"Can you make room for the possibility they did not complain because their captors were sitting in the room with them?"

Keenan shook his head and said, "You can say that, but we used our best judgment."

"Agent Kennan, do you have a family?"

"Yes."

"If they were in arbitrary custody, would you do everything in your power to get them released?"

Keenan admitted the obvious.

"Of course."

"Fight for their release?"

"Yes."

"Pull strings for their release?"

"Of course."

"Lie for their release?"

Keenan sensed the trap and said, "I'd only lie if it could be hidden. If I got caught, it would be worse."

"So you need to be a good liar to save your family?"

"Yes, I suppose you could say that. But I don't think I'd take the chance."

"You'll agree others might see it differently?"

A long pause, then, "Yes."

"And if you knew your family's captors wanted you to tell a particular lie would you do it?"

A pause, "No, I would not."

Fredricks looked at the jury, "You would not lie to save your wife, your kids?"

"That's correct, counsel."

Fredricks turned to the jury and said.

"Wow, I'm glad I'm not married to you." Jurors smiled. One Navy Commander laughed out loud.

Fredricks turned back to Keenan.

"Do you think others may be more willing to save their wives and children than you?" Keenan stared,

"How do you want me to answer that?"

Fredricks looked at the jury, turned back to Keenan, and said, "You might consider the truth." She paused.

Keenan frowned. Willis whined. Fredricks continued.

"The fact is, you made no effort to find out the conditions under which the witnesses were being held. Isn't that the truth?"

Keenan sat for a moment.

"We used our best judgment."

"And if they were being held in dungeons, full of vermin, under oppressive conditions, your best judgment was not to learn that fact. Right?"

"I don't think that is the case." Then lamely, "We never saw any rats."

"You never went to the cells, did you? Never saw the conditions, never saw the food. So your best judgment was to not know, isn't that about it?"

There was no answer.

Her closing question,

"Rats as big as small dogs could have been crawling over some of the witnesses or their wives or their children, and the FBI does not know that? True?"

"No one complained," was all he could say.

Then, "Now you were not in charge of the decision to hold or release the witnesses? That was up to the Kuwaiti authorities, isn't that true?"

"Right."

"As the supposed witnesses were being questioned, the Kuwaiti authorities were watching."

"Yes."

"The witnesses could believe they had to say what the Kuwaitis wanted?"

"Counselor, I don't know what the witnesses were thinking."

Fredricks smiled and turned to the jury. "Exactly." And she looked back at Keenan, "You never asked them, did you?"

Keenan recoiled. Paused.

"No, I guess I didn't."

Fredricks looked at the jury and us. She smiled again.

"I have nothing further."

Pierce shuffled some papers. 'It's four o'clock. Let's adjourn for the day."

CHAPTER 53

Moretti nearly shouted.

"You have got to read this!"

Mann had sent us a document that was a report of an interrogation conducted at Black Site Green by an agent whose code name was Draco. The report described how the CIA had captured Mohammed Assad. He was thought to be mid-level al-Qaeda. The report, a cable to CIA headquarters, said, AFTER THREE HOURS IN THE LARGE BOX ASSAD WAS QUESTIONED ABOUT ANY KNOWLEDGE HE HAD ABOUT THE KUWAITI ATTACK. WHILE HE DENIED KNOWLEDGE, INTERROGATORS DID NOT BELIEVE HIM AND TOLD HIM THEY THOUGHT HE WAS LYING. HE WAS THEN PUT IN THE SMALL BOX FOR TWENTY MINUTES. UPON REMOVAL FROM THE SMALL BOX, ASSAD CONFESSED THAT HE, ALONG WITH WALID, WERE THE LEADERS OF THE KUWAITI ATTACK. WHEN ASKED ABOUT HUSSAIN AL-YEMENI, ASSAD LAUGHED. HE WAS A HELPER. HE RAN ERRANDS.

My first reaction was shock.

"I can't believe the prosecution withheld this. It is clearly exculpatory. Shows he is not the mastermind. They were obligated to produce this."

Carter shook his head.

"I told you Lawson would cheat. We need to present this to the jury."

Motions were prepared and filed. We asked that the next day of the trial be postponed so the judge could hold an emergency hearing. We further requested that Draco be produced as a witness and that the prosecution disclose when Assad was released or where he presently was located if he was still in US custody.

That evening we received a message that the court would hold the hearing the following day. There would be no spectators or press. Hussain was also excluded.

The prosecution team was already in their seats when we filed past the guard, whose job was to punch in the combination to the court multiple times per day. After setting my notebook down, I looked over at Lawson.

"General, You've known that Hussain is not the mastermind of the attack. You know he is a bit player at most, yet you are still trying to kill him. You are lying to the jury, to the press. Do you have any sense of fairness or shame?"

Lawson just sat, looking ahead. Then, louder, I said, "Do you have a fucking conscience?"

He turned, "We'll discuss this with the judge."

He turned away.

Pierce was brusque when he took the bench. His concern radiated.

"General Lawson, can you explain why this was not produced to the defense?"

Lawson stood.

"It was our judgment that since this statement is not admissible, it has no value, and we were not obligated to produce it. This statement is clearly derived from torture and, as such, is not admissible. If we were wrong in our assessment, I apologize."

Pierce's anger subsided.

"Where is Assad now?"

"He is here at Guantanamo Bay. In Camp 6. He has been in US custody since his capture. He is cleared for release and may be shortly released."

Pierce turned.

"Defense, how would you like to proceed?"

Carter made some comments accusing the prosecution of dishonesty before concluding.

"We think that Mr. Assad should be brought to court so we can question him." Pierce nodded and thought that seemed reasonable.

Lawson shrugged, "Sure, but Assad has civilian counsel. The defense needs to work through him."

"Who is his lawyer?"

Lawson looked at us, then the judge.

"Your honor, his lawyer is James Zahn of the New York bar."

"Counsel, if Mr. Zahn is Assad's lawyer, you need to go through him. Since I've called the jury off, contact Mr. Zahn, and we'll reconvene at fifteen hundred."

Back in our office, a quick internet search revealed that Zahn had once been assistant deputy counsel for the CIA.

When we called Zahn, he was clear that Assad would not agree to be interviewed. He will assert his fifth amendment privilege, and he now claims that what he told the agents was false. That he would have said anything to avoid more torture.

"Have you actually met with him?"

"No," he paused. "After the prosecutor asked me to be his lawyer, they arranged a phone conference with him. I've never actually met him."

Are you kidding me? The prosecution gets this guy a lawyer, and he is now cleared for release. They are hiding this guy to protect their case.

"So, how do you know you were actually talking to Assad?"

Silence then, "I just have to trust the prosecution."

We met in the courtroom that afternoon. After explaining what Zahn had said, we advised the judge that we still wanted to interview Assad and that Zahn should be brought to Guantanamo, actually meet with using air quotes, "his client," to facilitate that interview. We also wanted all of Assad's statements to either the CIA or the prosecution. I continued,

"Honestly, judge, in light of this, how can this case go forward as a death penalty case? There is reason to believe that the prosecution's entire theory is based on a premise they now know is false. If we have any fidelity to the truth, at least the request for the death penalty should be stricken."

Lawson stood.

"The prosecution sees no reason that the court should strike the request for the death penalty. We think the statements given under torture were false. Assad has never spoken with the prosecution or any agents other than the CIA. The CIA has advised us that his other statements are highly classified and that the defense had no *need to know* things Assad said that do not pertain to the Kuwaiti bombing. So the defense cannot have his other statements. He opened both arms. I think we are done with this issue."

Pierce looked at me, "It would seem General Lawson is correct."

I was nearly spitting with rage.

"Another man has confessed to being the mastermind of the Kuwaiti attack, and you intend to withhold that information from the jury. Do you intend to allow the prosecution to continue to lie to the jury? Is that where we are?"

Pierce shook his head.

"Assad confessed under torture. That is clear. Your client's statements under torture are not admissible; why should this be different?"

"Because it's defense evidence and fundamental fairness says it should be presented to the jury. If they choose to reject it, so be it. But they need to know someone else confessed to the same thing al-Yemeni is charged with. It's evidence of innocence. A juror could easily decide to acquit Hussain or to not sentence our client to death if they know this evidence."

"Counsel, the rule prohibiting evidence derived from torture does not distinguish between defense and prosecution evidence."

Pierce raised his voice.

"Evidence derived from torture is not admissible. That's the rule, and I am obligated to follow the rule.

"His lawyer tells you Assad says what he told the CIA is false. And that Assad will not consent to an interview. That seems like a reasonable position. My hands are tied. This evidence is not admissible. You are not to mention it to the jury. End of discussion."

"Your hands are not tied, and honestly, if you do nothing and allow this to proceed without the jury hearing about Assad's confession, your hands and General Lawson's hands have blood on them."

Pierce and I glared at each other.

"We are adjourned. The Commission will reconvene at 0900 tomorrow."

He walked off the bench.

We sat in silence. Moretti looked at me and shook her head. Fredricks's lips were a thin line, barely visible. Carter held his head in his hands.

When I questioned Pierce at the beginning, he said he just followed the rules, and if it was not fair, that's how it goes. He didn't lie, that's for sure. Hussain, you are so, so fucked.

We picked up our papers, stalked out of the courtroom, and after an hour of angry venting, concluded that we had no options until we could appeal after the trial was over. We collectively accepted reality and sadly began preparing for the next day.

CHAPTER 54

Walking toward the courtroom the next day, we encountered the prosecution team. Willis looked at us and said, "Good morning."

This usually would provoke a similar greeting. Not today.

Carter barked, "You should be ashamed. You guys are a disgrace."

Both sides glared at each other, and we sat in angry silence until Pierce took the bench. After greeting the jury and advising them, he said, "Yesterday, there was an emergency legal matter we had to address. We were not wasting time but were working through it all day. We appreciate your understanding."

I began to stand, and Pierce waved me down.

"The matter is closed. Prosecution recall Agent Keenan."

Lawson directed Keenan's attention to the individual statements given by Kuwaitis to the FBI. Keenan would identify the statement and show a photo, if they had one, of the person who provided the statement. Read the statement to the jury. Then the cross-examination. Split between Carter, Moretti, Fredricks, and me.

The cross-exams were functionally identical. We elicited that the FBI did not know if the witness was in Kuwaiti custody, if his family was in custody, what the conditions of confinement were, and what the Kuwaiti authorities had said to the witness before they met with the FBI. Obviously, once we established they had no information, we could raise all manner of possible scenarios. Threats of torture or rape. Threats to children or wives.

By the end, the jury could have repeated the cross-examinations in their sleep. This process took a week.

Lawson then questioned Keenan about Hussain's statement to the FBI a few months after arriving at Guantanamo.

Keenan described how, after Hussain had been brought to Guantanamo, a decision had been made to question him "free of any claims of abuse." Keenan recounted the circumstances of the statement and outlined Hussain's confession, which he read to the jury. This description and the reading of the statement took most of a day.

I stood to cross on this topic. Everyone knew this was central to our case, and the courtroom was unusually silent. I could hear the hum of the air conditioner. I fixed my eyes on Keenan and pulled out a large white notebook that contained the outline of my cross and supporting exhibits. Keenan preparing for the assault pulled out a handkerchief and wiped his brow and upper lip.

"Agent Keenan, let's talk about what you knew about Hussain's whereabouts before he arrived in Guantanamo."

Keenan nodded.

"You knew he had been in CIA custody, right?"

Keenan again nodded.

"Agent Keenan, you knew Hussain was tortured prior to being questioned by you?"

Keenan shrugged, "I know he was subjected to Enhanced Interrogation."

"You knew that Enhanced Interrogation meant being hung by his arms, naked for days?"

"I don't know that."

"Deprived of sleep?"

"I think I read that."

"Put in a coffin which was filled with bugs?"

"I heard that."

"You were at site green, weren't you?"

Keenan shifted in his chair.

"Perhaps." I confronted him with documents demonstrating he'd been at several torture sites, including green. He reluctantly admitted that was correct.

I then took him through his knowledge of the large box, the small box, face slaps, walling, and other forms of abuse that al-Yemeni endured.

"You knew he was anally raped?"

"I know he was force-fed anally."

"Do you know if that provides nutrition?"

"I don't know."

"You knew he was waterboarded?"

"Yes."

Referring to the document we'd discovered earlier, "Agent Keenan, did you know that after he arrived at Guantanamo, Hussain was put on a psychotropic medication by the medical staff?"

Keenan waved his hand as if to bat away an invisible insect or an ugly thought.

"Ahh, no, I did not know that."

I showed him the document.

"Do you know why a person would be put on this kind of medicine?

"No."

"Do you know the effect of this medication? What it does to memory?"

"No, of course not. But I presume it was not significant. He seemed fine."

"Just as he seemed not to be impacted by torture."

Keenan sat silently.

"But he was clearly impacted by torture because he'd been placed on psychotropic medication after his arrival."

"Could have been for other reasons."

"But you don't know, do you?"

"No, I guess I don't."

"Now you were instructed to put anything he said about abuse, EITs, whatever you want to call them, in a separate classified document. Do you have that with you?"

I showed him our copy of the report detailing what Hussain had told the FBI about the torture.

"As Hussain gave his statement, he talked throughout the statement about the things that were done to him. Isn't that true?"

"Yes."

"And you separated those portions of his statement into a separate document. Isn't that true?"

Keenan shrugged, "Yes. That is what we were told to do."

"AE 2620, is six pages describing abuse?"

I paused and looked at the jury again.

"Now, can you meld this with what you read to the jury?"

"I don't know what you mean."

"Would you agree that the statement, 'I led the Kuwaiti attack,' is a lot different than a statement that says, 'When they were beating the crap out of me, I told them, I lead the Kuwaiti attack to make the beating stop?'"

Keenan began to answer but stopped and sat silently.

Lawson stood to object, but Willis pulled him down.

I took Keenan through each time Hussain complained about abuse. Keenan finally admitted that there was no way to accurately reconstruct what Hussain told the FBI during the interviews.

The looks of sadness and perhaps sympathy told me that the jury seemed to understand that Hussain tried to tell Keenan he said those things to stop the torture.

Then Judge Pierce turned to the jury.

"Members of the panel, I have heard extensive evidence about how Mr. al-Yemeni was treated prior to his statement to the FBI. I have heard all the evidence you have heard and more. The commission has ruled that Mr. al-Yemeni's statement to Agent Keenan is admissible and has ruled that it is presumptively reliable. While you can consider all the evidence, and the final decision is yours, I instruct you that there is a presumption that the statement the accused made to the FBI is both reliable and," he paused for emphasis, "true."

Pierce had dropped a bomb. We all stood, shouting "Objection!"

and seeking to make a record of how improper his statement was. Pierce waived us down and dismissed the jury. Our objections were quickly batted away, and he broke for the week.

Sitting in my room an hour later, lights out, three fingers of Makers over ice in my glass, I was pondering the probable impact of the judge's improper, unfair, and unwarranted ruling. *We are so fucked.*

Carter knocked and opened the door.

"You okay?"

"Numb. This is just so unfair."

"If you're interested, Brooks is looking for a comment."

I called Samantha.

"I understand you want an on-the-record comment. So here it is: I've never, ever seen a judge work so hard for a conviction. I've never, ever seen a judge so blatantly put his hand on the scales of justice."

We chatted for a few more seconds and hung up.

Carter was quiet. Then, "What if she prints that."

"So, what can he do, shoot me?"

"He might."

My quote was published on Saturday. The following Monday, Pierce came into the courtroom. Glared at me. But said nothing.

CHAPTER 55

We decided that Fredricks would make the guilt/innocence phase final argument. I wanted someone in uniform to do the argument, as I knew I'd be doing the penalty phase arguments. Carter pushed for Fredricks to argue.

"A black woman, a Marine, makes a more compelling picture than another middle-aged, white guy, even if I am an Army lawyer."

Fredricks looked troubled.

"This is way, way beyond my experience. I'm not sure I'm up to this."

Carter turned to her, "You have time to prepare. Just speak from the heart."

Willis's final argument for the prosecution was brief. "My fellow brothers and sisters in arms. Over sixty of our comrades were killed by a plot conceived and planned by Hussain al-Yemeni. We have proved that beyond a reasonable doubt. You have seen and heard witness after witness paint a clear picture of a well-planned plot to kill Americans. You have heard what the Kuwaitis told the FBI. You have seen their identifications of al-Yemeni. The defense throws accusations because they have no evidence. They throw accusations about the Kuwaiti government, the FBI, and the CIA because they have no evidence.

"Okay, he was beaten up months before he confessed. So what? Some of you have taken a whipping or two. Perhaps even some of you have been beaten up when you were young. Would you confess to something you did not do? It's common sense."

Turning to the defense, "You heard his confession. He proudly said he was the mastermind of the Kuwaiti attack. A confession the judge has told you is presumptively reliable and true. So here it is. The witnesses say he is guilty, and he told the FBI he was guilty. So we ask you to find him guilty. And have no doubt, as General Lawson told you in his opening statement. After you find him guilty, we will ask you to sentence him to death."

Pierce turned to us.

"Would the defense like to make a final argument?"

"Yes," said Maj. Fredricks. Dressed in Marine dress blues. Her battle ribbons gleamed. She stood before the jury.

"I am a young lawyer, and I will confess that I am more nervous than I was before combat in Afghanistan. There, I was afraid I might die. But I was trained for that kind of combat. There is no real training for this.

"Today, now I am afraid, no, terrified, that I do not have the words, the skill, to help you see why you should not convict Hussain, why, when the evidence is considered objectively, he is not guilty.

"When the Kuwaiti airfield was attacked, was the United States at war? The evidence is clear; the answer is no. No one, not the President, not the Congress, not our military leadership, was suggesting to airmen and women or indeed," and here she looked hard at the jury, "Any of us, because we were all in the military then, that we were at war. The judge will tell you that you may consider your experience in reaching your decision so ask yourself the same question I have asked myself. In 2001, before 9/11, did my commanders tell me I was at war? Did I think I was at war?

"There were none of the precautions at the airbase that a war footing demands. There were peacetime rules of engagement. No purple hearts, no combat after-action reports, and nothing indicating that the military treated this as an act of war. So we ask you to find that the US was not at war in early 2001.

"And if we were at war as the prosecution claims, what about this attack violated the law of war? Sneak attacks are encouraged. Suicide attacks are allowed. History has examples from Pickett's charge to Omaha Beach to Viet Nam of the honor we accord men who attacked, knowing full well they would die for their cause. But the prosecution wants the victor's justice. In their view of the world, the other side does not get to attack."

Now, she turned and looked at Willis and then the jury.

"The prosecutor tells you there was no evidence of Kuwaiti involvement. You heard from airmen how the Kuwaitis controlled access to the base. You heard from witnesses how this could not have occurred without the direct complicity of the Kuwaiti government. You heard that it was the Kuwaiti police who first mentioned Hussain to the FBI. You know that the Kuwaitis had held the witnesses, who supposedly identified Hussain for months. Their families had also been held as a form of insurance that they would tell the FBI what the Kuwaiti government wanted them to say. The fact is, there is no evidence not influenced by the Kuwaitis linking Hussain to this bombing.

"Ahhh, you say, and you should say this: The confession."

She paused. Looked down.

"Interrogators from the Air Force, from NCIS, told you that once you torture someone, nothing that person says is reliable. And make no mistake, Hussain was tortured. Hussain told Keenan about the torture as best as he could. The experts told you, and common sense tells us, that people lie to end the pain of torture. Doctors testified that taking someone off psychotropic medication would disorient them and make what they said less reliable."

After discussing the instructions the judge would give, Harriet was reaching the end.

"Each of us has, multiple times, taken an oath to preserve and protect the Constitution of the United States. When we took that oath, each of us swore to protect the judicial system, not this made-up system but a real system where witnesses appear and are questioned.

"But I say this to you in all humility; each of us knows that what drives us is loyalty to our country and, even more directly, loyalty to each other. If we tolerate torture inflicted on our enemies, can we complain when our enemies inflict torture on us? You not only hold Hussain's future in your hands, but you also hold the future of your brothers and sisters in arms. Make no mistake, the world has been watching this court and found it wanting. The world is watching me and may find me wanting. And soon, the world will be watching you. To see if you can put aside your natural inclination toward reflexive anger and look at the evidence coldly and objectively.

"I must sit down, and when I do, I give you – Mr. Mendelson, Major Carter, and Ms. Moretti, as well as our assistants and I – we give you this decision. We trust you will follow the law and weigh the evidence coldly and fairly. When you do that, you will return a verdict of not guilty."

Willis jumped up, nearly snarling,

"I have the right to rebut what she says because we have the burden of proof. There is no proof of torture; there is no question the US was at war; there is no question that this was an illegal attack; there is no question he confessed, and there is no question he is guilty. He has, for the past how many months, received fairness. Now is the time to dispense justice. Convict him."

We expected Willis' rebuttal. But hearing him, and seeing his anger, just made me sad. And all I could do was slowly shake my head.

Judge Pierce then read and displayed the instructions, which emphasized the presumptive truthfulness of Hussain's statement to the FBI. When he had completed the reading, he smiled, thanked them for their patience, and, with a wave, sent them to begin their deliberations.

CHAPTER 56

The hardest part of being a trial lawyer is waiting on a verdict. The initial relief, "Thank God, it's over," quickly moves to self-doubt. The initial reaction is, "I would not have done anything differently. I left it all on the courtroom floor."

That soon gives way to, "What should I have done to make it better?"

This, at least in my case, turns to self-abuse. *I am a failure and a fraud; my failures will lead to Hussain's death.*

While I was fretting, pacing, waiting, feeling ill, and trying to keep my own and everyone else's spirit up, the jurors were working.

They would report to the courtroom at 9:30. We would all be there. The judge would take the bench and say, "You may resume your deliberations."

We would be searching their faces for some clue of their thinking. At 16:30, we would reassemble, the judge would inquire, "Do you have a decision?" The senior officer, Colonel Mortenson, would say "No."

The judge would then say, "You must now cease deliberations. You will be escorted back to your quarters. Deliberations will resume at 0930 tomorrow."

After the third day of deliberations, there was an email from Molly.

YOU NEED TO WATCH THE NEWS. YOU WILL GO INSANE. STAY STRONG. — MOLLY

I turned on the TV in my apartment. I saw what she was referring to, and she was right; my anger was nuclear. In a Rose Garden news conference, the President responded to a question posed by a reporter from Fox News about the length of the Guantanamo jury deliberation.

The President said, "We are paying close attention to the jury deliberating in Guantanamo."

He continued, "We are hopeful those officers will understand that proper support for their comrades would mean a conviction and a sentence of death. Indeed, I would question the judgment of any officer who ruled otherwise."

I called the team together. Carter was pale, and Fredricks was literally shaking with rage. I began with, "This is bad."

Fredricks said, "No! It is beyond bad. This ensures a conviction and death sentence. He is the Commander in Chief. He can obtain the jurors' identities in thirty seconds and destroy their careers in a minute more. Remember the Navy Seal the President ordered exonerated. He ordered Medals withdrawn from the JAGS who prosecuted him. This is how much power he has as Commander in Chief. As soon as the jurors see this, they will understand that they have no choice if they want to finish their careers. Jesus, I am sick."

The following day we moved for a mistrial arguing that this was unlawful command influence of the worst kind, explicitly designed to influence the jury. The argument was that any senior officer would understand that with this President, failure to convict and impose death would be a career-ender.

The prosecution argued the jury was sequestered, that there was no reason to think they knew about the President's remarks, and further that no officer would betray his oath as a juror.

We asked that the jurors be questioned individually and kept away from all news coverage.

Pierce denied these requests as well as our motion for mistrial.

Seven days of deliberations later, The jury announced they had a verdict.

We had some hope that we had a chance with the length of deliberations, but when they filed in, we could tell. Like a spouse admitting to infidelity, to betrayal, they would not look at us. They looked everywhere but at us. They seemed resolute in their collective shame.

The jury found that the US was at war in February 2001, that the surprise attack violated the law of war and that Hussain was guilty of all counts, including premeditated murder in violation of the law of war.

I knew when they came in and would not look at us. And I felt a mix of emotions: anger, disgust, and a sense of frustrated failure. But I had to be strong. To look calm even though my heart was beating fast and my breath was shallow. And until I heard the word Guilty, I clung to a slender hope for a miracle.

Pierce thanked them and reminded them that they would soon be hearing evidence regarding the penalty they could impose. Death, life without parole, or some lesser term of years.

While the jury was deliberating, we discussed with Pierce how quickly to begin the penalty phase after the verdict. The prosecution wanted a delay, and we argued that it would be best to start the penalty phase as soon as practical. In our view, the penalty phase would begin five days from the day of the verdict. The judge had rejected our suggestion, deciding instead that there would be three weeks between the verdict and the beginning of the penalty phase so that everyone could return to their home for, as he put it, "a break." We argued that a break of several weeks ensured that the President's comments would be known to the jurors and that this made a death sentence a certainty.

Pierce said, "Perhaps that is true, perhaps not. We'll deal with that when it comes, if it comes. Trial will resume in 21 days,"

He paused, and seemed to think. Looked at the jurors. Smiled.

"No, I've changed my mind; thirty days from the date we leave the island. Adjourned."

Mother fucker is just going out of his way to fuck us.

CHAPTER 57

I returned to my room after we left Kelly's. The Maker's had had no impact. And the sting of the jury's verdict was still sharp. I couldn't sleep, couldn't turn my mind off. I wandered to Jill's room. I knocked softly. No answer and I began to walk away when the door opened. She was in running shorts and a red Wisconsin tee shirt with "Fuck'em Bucky." Bucky was holding a football.

"Come on back. I was just trying to sleep. You need to talk?"

"No, I just need to sit, but I don't want to be alone. This was not unexpected, but it really hurts. I guess I thought after ten days of deliberation, seven after the fucking President commanded a verdict, that we had a chance."

Then tears began flowing. Jill silently gave me a towel, and I buried my face in it, feeling the prickle of cheap cloth. I don't know how long I cried. I finally said, "I just can't tell you how defeated I feel. I am just gutted. Fuck, what a wimp."

She said, "You know, we knew once the President weighed in, we had little shot. You said it yourself. We might save his life, but we had no real chance. Jesus, they were out for ten days. The President told the jury to convict. They had to have learned what the President said. They were out seven days after that. That could count for something. Try to get some sleep. You can stay here if you want. We'll try to figure out what makes sense tomorrow."

I laid down on the bed, on top of the covers, clothes still on. Eyes open, nose still runny from the tears.

Jill hovered.

"Come on, get under the covers. We'll just be. Don't worry. You helped me in London, held me, my turn."

"I just feel so lost."

"I know," she replied. "We'll have to try to find a way back tomorrow. But the good thing is we have a month; a lot can happen."

I turned over, and I felt her rubbing my back. The next thing I knew, it was morning.

Later that day, the team met. We discussed how and where to prepare for the penalty phase. Carter, Hendricks, and Moretti said they'd prefer to go home but would do whatever was necessary.

Jill was clear, "I need to go home. I need to coordinate documents with Grace, get her ready to come down here, and organize Hussain's family to testify if that will be allowed."

I told the others I was uncertain what I would do.

"For me, it's as easy to work here as it is there."

Jill cleared her throat, "You need to get out of here. This place is toxic. We'll all go to see Hussain tomorrow and take the flight to Andrews. You need a break. See your kids. See Molly. We've done the work. We can meet in DC if we need to. We've got this as much under control as possible."

I sighed, "I suppose you're right, but, fuck, I just feel like if I'm not thinking about this, something will slide." *And the whole Molly thing is a blur. I'm not sure where we are. Maybe still the same. And I don't know if I can handle that.*

Moretti said, "I agree with Jill. We all need to get out of here."

CHAPTER 58

As always, when we visited Hussain, we sat around the white table. This visit, there was a dank smell I couldn't place. I realized that despite the air conditioner's cold, Hussain was sweating profusely. He smelled of fear.

"So, will they kill me? Mohammed translated.

"The brothers in the camp think they will kill me. They tell me their lawyers have said there is no way this judge and prosecutor allow the jury not to kill me. What do you think? Tell me honestly."

Softly I answered, "Hussain, I don't know. That could be the case. This has been very unfair. And the President. What he did makes things much, much more difficult. All I can tell you is we will continue to fight as hard as possible. The judge has made many mistakes, so whatever happens will take years to sort out. That is the most honest thing I can tell you."

Jill looked across the table and took Hussain's hands.

"Hussain, when things resume, we will have the penalty phase. The prosecution will present what is called victim impact. That will be very hard—lots of grief, pain, and anger. The survivors will testify about their loss. It will be very emotional. We want to present your family. We're trying to get them here, or we'll try to present them by video link. Or the videos we did. That too will be emotional."

I interjected, "We don't know what the judge will allow and what roadblocks they'll put up."

"Then," Jill said, "if necessary, I can tell your story, and then Victoria Hancock."

"Who is she?"

"The woman who tortured you. That may be classified. You may not be able to see that," Carter said.

Hussain looked at all of us.

"I think that is best. I'm not sure I could bear to be in the room with her.

Reyes smiled, laughed, looked at the ceiling, and in a loud voice said, "For you fuckers who are listening. Did you hear Hussain does not want to be in the room with Hancock?"

To us, Reyes smiled and said, "I'll bet twenty-five bucks that he gets to be there. Now that they know he doesn't want to be there."

Moretti, "I'll take that."

Reyes responded.

"Book it."

We all laughed. Even Hussain laughed when he heard Mohammed's translation.

Then, I looked at him.

"Hussain, you have the right to speak to the jury. Don't know if you should or not, but if you did, what would you say?"

He sat still. Seemed like minutes, and then, "I have to think about that. It is complicated."

As the meeting broke up, we told him we were going back to the US for a time and would be back a few days before things resumed.

Hussain looked at all of us. He had tears brimming in his eyes.

"I want to thank you all. That is all I can say. I want to thank you all. I think they will kill me, but I know how hard you have fought, and I am grateful."

Hugs all around. And I noticed Moretti and Fredricks had tears. I, too, was wiping my eyes. *Dust is what I told myself.*

CHAPTER 59

My home felt spacious after months in the BOQ. There was no food in the refrigerator, no noise, and I felt very alone. I didn't want to eat. I tried to watch TV but couldn't sit still or concentrate. I called Molly and planned dinners with her and the girls. But I felt disconnected. My life was in Cuba, in the trial. The mild Midwestern late summer felt strange. Familiar and foreign at the same time

The office was worse. When I came in, Beverly, the receptionist, was happy to see me. My partners wanted war stories. But I had nothing to do. Beverly explained, "Clients know you're gone, so they call the others. Or don't call. We've got stuff under control. I mean, you haven't really been here for over a year."

One of my partners, Josh, was more direct.

"When this is over, we'll need to have a serious conversation about the future. You built this firm, but with you gone, it's a different place. The question we have is, do you really want the day-to-day practice of law again? If not, we understand; but if you do want that, you'll have to be all in. No more big but badly paying cases."

And a perfunctory, "Hate to lay this on you now, but you have some decisions to make, and honestly so do we." *No surprise. Hell, I wish I knew what I wanted to do.* A few days later, my family gathered for dinner. Emily came home from college. While she still checked in frequently, the drama from the kidnapping seemed distant.

Anabel was there, sort of; her cell phone was heavy competition for the gathering. We were at our favorite restaurant. Malbec for Molly, Maker's for me – Emily asked if she could have a beer. When we pointed out she wasn't twenty-one, she rolled her eyes and said, "I drink every weekend at school. What nonsense."

Over platters of fried fish, hush puppies, and fries –she told of college adventures, living with different friends in response to the attack. A vague reference to some guy named Jorge who acted as "her bodyguard" after the CIA threat. While unclear, the bodyguard seemed to sleep over several times a week.

With this, Molly looked at me as if to say, "*Say or do something.*" I shook my head slightly. And said with a smile.

"Tell your mother this is all just platonic."

Emily smiled. She took a drink of her mother's wine, "Both of you need to grow up. Little Emily is a big girl now."

Anabel talked about the colleges she was thinking about.

"Dad, I think small. What's that college where Jill lives?"

"Ripon College."

"Yes, someplace like that."

Molly interjected, "Make sure it is very, very expensive. We would not want to have to slow down."

We all laughed. Then Emily asked, with tears welling, "What will happen to Hussain?"

"Honey, I don't know. The judge is bad, very bad, and very much wants death. The jury is pro-death. It's hard to be optimistic. And there have been lots of errors. It wasn't fair. So he has a good chance on appeal. I can't imagine he will actually be killed. This seems like theater."

"Oh, dad. What will you do if they give him death?"

"I'll be crushed, but that comes with the territory. I'll second-guess every decision. But when I started doing these cases, I was told you must be prepared to hear a death verdict. So it comes with the territory."

Molly laughed,

"You second guess every decision, even when you win."

"Yes, but this will be worse. And I'll cry again."

"What?" They all stared at me.

"After the conviction, after I had a chance to sit and absorb a bit, I cried. I could not stop crying. I was a mess. I cried myself to sleep."

Emily said, "Who are you, and what have you done with my father? My father never cries."

"Yes. Yes, he does. Now."

The night before I returned to DC, I had dinner with Molly at our house, well, her house now. Anabel was staying at a friend's house. Emily was back at school. We sat over wine. I looked at her.

"Just so you know, when this is over, I'm going to quit."

"No, you won't."

"Yes. The firm is pretty clear they want to go in a different direction. I'm not going to do drug cases or some white-collar bullshit. There is nothing for me there. And I don't want to make you crazy, but if we don't get back together, there is nothing for me here."

She frowned, then her adorable grin, "Blackmail? Guilt? Well played."

"No, not how I meant it. Just being honest. It's like being in a foreign place being here. If you and the kids weren't here, there is nothing. When I leave the firm, or they throw me out, there'll be no reason to stay here, except for the kids, and they're almost gone, and of course you. But I accept that might not happen."

She tilted her head to the side, looked at me.

"Have you really thought this through?"

"No. Not completely, but I know that I can't do the law like I've always done anymore. I have no idea what I'll do next. Or where I'll be."

"You'd leave? Really? Where would you go?"

"I don't know. Hilton Head area, Savannah, Mexico? We liked Merida. Or Oaxaca. I know that a change of scene may be necessary."

Molly sat quietly, sipping her wine, "Wow. I was not expecting this."

"I'm not trying to ruin the mood, but I wanted you to know what I was thinking. Besides working on this mess of a case, all I've done for the past few weeks is think about the future. Where I live is open, but I'm clear I need to do something different."

There was a long silence.

"You have a ride to the airport tomorrow?"

"I was just going to Uber."

"Why don't I drive you?"

"Okay, pick me up at 7."

"Better idea, you can stay here"—a smile.

I gave her an intense look.

"Same question. Have you really thought this out?"

"No," and then, "But, no promises."

Molly smiled the smile I love again and said, "At least one of us has some clarity. Better than it has been."

We looked at each other and smiled. I stayed.

CHAPTER 60

Sitting in the courtroom before the beginning of the penalty phase, I was fidgeting, shuffling papers, and talking softly to the others and to Hussain, who sat quietly, eyes down and glazed, no smiles. I would periodically scribble something in the notebook or get up and pace back and forth across the courtroom, hands clasped behind me. Then I'd stop and quietly speak with one of the other lawyers, Reyes or paralegals, and resume pacing. *I hope I don't throw up again or pee myself. Is my zipper up? God, I hope I don't fuck this up.*

Lawson was sitting at the prosecution table, staring at the insignia of the five branches of the military on the wall behind the judge's chair, three feet higher than the rest of the room.

I suppose it is like going into battle. It really is life and death. But not kinetic, Everything is in slow motion. So there is no release. And it is not my life that's at risk.

When Judge Pierce took the bench, I asked him to question the jurors about what publicity or other influences they had been exposed to during the break. And I raised the President's comments again. We wanted the questioning done individually. Pierce refused individual questioning, suggesting it would "take too long." When the jurors came in, he asked, "During the break, did any of you have any conversations or see anything that makes you question whether you can be fair to both sides during this phase of the trial in which you will be asked to determine the penalty that will be imposed on the defendant?"

Two jurors raised their hands. Captain Mitchell and Colonel Natale. The others were excused and the two jurors were questioned.

Mitchell saw an article about the torture the CIA did to Hussain and said that could impact his judgment. Pierce asked no questions and prohibited either side from asking follow-up questions. Colonel Natale had talked to his wife, who strongly supported the death penalty. He'd also learned from her about what the President had said. Claimed he didn't know how that would impact him. Pierce said, "If I order you to put that aside, will you follow my order?"

Natale said, "I'll try, Your Honor."

"Okay, I'm going to excuse Captain Mitchell, and keep Colonel Natale. We still have fifteen jurors."

We stood to object. I thought Carter was going to have to be restrained. Pierce listened for a bit and then waved his hand and looked at the clock.

"I've ruled; you've made your record. We'll proceed."

Lawson opened for the prosecution. He told the jury that they would hear weeks of victim impact, and then the defense would present their case.

"Their case, he said, "would be more of the same. Smoke, whining claims of torture. But, in the end, it will amount to nothing that should deter you from your duty, your sworn duty to order the execution of this cold-blooded killer."

More objections. Pierce was stoic and quick with his decisions overruling and ordering the defense to move on.

I approached the podium, looked at the jurors, stood quietly, and in a soft voice, said, "With your verdict, you have ensured that Hussain will spend the rest of his life in prison. You could sentence him to a term of years, but we honestly would not expect that. The question is, does justice require that you kill him?"

I then proceeded to talk about the victim's pain and anger and how decisions made in anger were often emotional and wrong. I described how Hussain had left Saudi Arabia due to the preaching of the Saudi government and how he had grown and matured. I told the jury about Victoria Hancock, the torture they would hear about, and how that should impact their decision.

"My guess is you all know that the President wants you to kill Hussain. Some, maybe most, of the victims want you to kill Hussain.

Some, perhaps much, of the public wants you to kill Hussain. The easy thing to do will be to order his death. You can, if you choose, disregard the evidence you've heard and that we will present and order him killed. It is your responsibility to make a reasoned moral judgment based on the evidence and the law to arrive at your individual decisions. If you follow the evidence, you will see that death is not appropriate. But, we cannot and will not be able to look into your hearts, and perhaps some of you will believe that your personal interests require you to kill Hussain. I can only say this, for over two hundred years, members of the military have put their personal interests aside to protect their comrades and their country. From Valley Forge, Gettysburg, Omaha Beach, the I Drang Valley, and Fallujah, men and women have had the courage to do their duty. Military men and women have often sacrificed their lives, not to mention their careers, because they did the right thing and stood up for what is right.

"Here, the evidence will require no sacrifice, but the expectations of others might.

"Each of you has to decide this on your own. The law says this is an individual, moral decision. Each of you has the power to save Hussain's life. Only if you all decide that death is appropriate can you kill Hussain. This is an awesome responsibility. It is more awesome because," and here I looked right at Pierce, "there are powerful forces at work that will push you toward killing. But you, I believe, I hope, are men and women of dedication, dedication to service and the nation and the law. And we are hopeful you will have the strength and courage to resist the demand for death."

CHAPTER 61

The prosecution opened its case for the death penalty with the victim impact evidence. This evidence, authorized by the Supreme Court, allows the survivors to tell how the attack and the loss of their loved ones impacted their lives. The theory is that the victim's pain and anguish should affect the life/death calculus. The witness is not supposed to tell the juror how to vote, but it is often apparent the survivor wants the defendant dead. And if they don't want the defendant executed, the prosecutor is not required to tell the jury or call them as witnesses. It is brutal in any case, and here, given the magnitude of the destruction, it was numbingly horrific.

The first witness was Carla Decker. The several months since our meeting outside the NEX had changed her. She'd gained weight; her hair and eyes were dull. Her mouth had an angry scowl.

Willis took her through the basics. Her son's history, his enlistment, and her reaction to his death. His final questions, "Where did your son go to high school?" "Did Mr. Mendelson's children go to the same school?" "Did you know Mr. Mendelson before this case?" "What did you think of him then?" "What do you think of him now?"

These questions were objectionable on a host of grounds. The team had discussed the pros and cons of objecting if the prosecution went in this direction. Our conclusion, it would show weakness to object, and the Decker's anger might be used to our advantage.

Her answer, "He knows us, knew us." "We were friends." "He values the life of this terrorist more than friendship." "Perhaps more than ethics. I have no use for him."

"Your witness."

We'd agreed that I would cross-examine both her and Ben if he testified. I stood, walked to the podium, put my white notebook down, Took a breath, and looked at her.

"Good morning."

"Is that a question?"

"No, ma'am, it was a greeting."

She just stared.

"Mrs. Decker. We do know each other. As you told the jury. No question about that."

She nodded.

"But let's talk about how well we knew each other. Did our families socialize?"

"No."

"Eat meals together?"

"No."

"Have I been to your home?"

"No, thank God."

"Our children went to the same schools. But not in the same grades."

"That's true."

"We did belong to the same golf club."

She nodded.

"And your husband and I never played in the same foursome together."

A nod again.

"I've never represented you or any of your family?"

"That's true."

Roseborough, the paralegal, had suggested the final question of this segment.

"So, can you make room for the possibility that your anger at me for agreeing to defend Hussain is more about your anger at your son's death?"

She looked at me.

"I don't know how to answer that."

"Let's move on because I want to talk about anger. Is that okay? You and your husband and I spoke once here in Guantanamo. Outside the NEX. It was you, your husband, your escort, and me?"

She nodded again.

"I told you then, and I will say to you now. That I, that none of us can know the depth of your pain or your anger. Can you accept that from me, from my team, and perhaps from the jury?"

"You've said that. I find it patronizing."

"I'm truly sorry you feel that way. Whether you believe it or not, I mean that."

She stared at me. The room was silent. I looked back at her. Finally, she nodded.

"But there is more about your son I'd like to discuss and let me be clear, these are good things."

She looked hesitant. Sat back. Her white blouse contrasting against the black witness chair.

"You've told the jury what a good athlete your son Darryl was. But he was more than good. He was a star. What is your favorite memory of his athletic achievement?"

She looked hesitant and began to sniffle. Began to talk, got to the game against Catholic High, and began crying.

I did not ask for a recess. The goal was to let the tears flow and let the grief drain to get to the next section.

She composed herself and described a game-saving tackle.

"You were proud of that tackle and proud of Darryl?"

"Yes, of course."

"And proud when he enlisted? Proud when he completed Airman's training?"

"Of course."

"Proud when he got promoted and proud when he reenlisted."

"Obviously."

"Proud when he went to war?"

"No one told us about any wars."

"I don't want to argue with you, but you understood, I hope there were risks to military service. You accepted those risks because Darryl accepted those risks?"

"Yes, we had no choice."

"Now the prosecution describes Darryl and the others as victims. But would you agree with me that they are heroes who deserve our praise?"

She sat taller.

"I'd not thought of it that way, but yes. My son was a hero. But he was killed by your client."

"He died in the service of his country?"

She nodded.

"And when he completed training, were you there when he swore to defend the constitution?"

"Yes."

"Would it surprise you to know that everyone in this room, the judge, the jury, the defense, me, have sworn to defend the Constitution?"

"No, I would assume that that is the case."

"Mrs. Decker. I hope you find peace in the knowledge your son is a hero, and I hope you accept someday, if not today, that our defense of the constitution and our defense of Hussain means no disrespect to you, your husband, or your son."

She nodded.

I sat down. I felt relieved. I had, I hoped, defused her anger and also had begun to establish our theme. The men and women killed in the attack were heroes, not victims.

For the next three weeks, witness after witness described how the death of their loved one had impacted their families, their lives, their children, and their parents. There were photos and letters. Every day was a day of tears and grief.

The worst was an older man, Leo Lennington. He reminded me of my father. He spoke of how his daughter's death had literally killed his wife. How, with his wife's death, his remaining family broke apart, and now he was alone. The prosecutor asked him.

"What penalty do you want the jury to impose?"

All of us jumped up and objected. There was a conference, and Moretti explained that "under Payne v. Tennessee. This is improper. Under the Constitution, the witnesses are not allowed to tell the jury what penalty they want."

Pierce said, "The Constitution, at least the Eighth Amendment, does not apply in a Military Commission. Motion denied."

The witness was asked again, "What penalty do you want the jury to impose?" The old man looked at Hussain, fixed him with a stare of hatred, looked at the jury, and said almost with a shriek, "I want him dead. He killed my daughter, killed my wife, killed my family. I can't heal; I'll never heal. But I can get even, and I want him dead, and if his family suffers, well, they are suffering like I am, like my family did. So that is fair."

I looked at Hussain. He was nodding, perhaps in understanding or agreement, and tears were softly rolling down his cheeks.

CHAPTER 62

My eyes had trouble adjusting to the bright sunshine after three hours under the fluorescent lights of the courtroom. The team had spent the morning cross-examining the attack survivors who had testified about their losses and pain. For the most part, our crosses were short.

"You must miss your husband, or son, or daughter, or wife very much."

"Of course"

"We want you to know that no one in this room can know the depth of your pain."

Our goal was to take the sting of the horror out of the moment without being too callous. My guess - we were failing. Miserably. I felt that the jury was just being overwhelmed by all the grief that permeated the courtroom like a plague. We couldn't see it, but we could feel it, and it had a force, corrupting, infecting all of us.

As we walked out, there was a large group of survivors under the tent outside the courtroom door. They huddled at picnic tables, drinking bottled water drawn from cases that sat on pallets. Another group was standing, lined up outside the doors of the toilet trailer. This line was in the sun, and some were fanning themselves as they chatted. Our team was huddled off to the side, talking, comparing notes, and trying to soak up some warmth. The courtroom had been so cold that my hands were stiff.

I sensed, rather than heard, a commotion.

Then, "Hey, Stop. Halt"

Ben Decker came out of the courtroom. In his right hand, he held a gun. He stood for a moment, saw us, and came toward us, the gun in his right hand pointed straight out, a cold set to his jaw.

A woman screamed, "Ben, For God's sake, no."

In seconds he was a few feet away from us.

"Mendelson, you goddamn traitor. I told you, you should be shot."

I could see he was holding a light grey semi-automatic Glock, the same kind of pistol the guards carried. *This is fucked up.* Then, his head pitched backward as his legs were driven out from under him. One of the guards, a woman, had run up behind him, lowered from the waist and knees, then slammed into the back of his lower legs. Ben fell backward as his feet were driven out from under him. His back and head hit the ground with a loud "Oomph." His right arm hit the ground, and the gun went off. The noise was louder than I expected and reverberated throughout the compound. At the same time, a woman screamed. Ben's legs were on top of the guard, but as he began to try to get up, two male guards jumped on him, pinning his body. The hand holding the gun was still exposed. Fredricks pushed by me, stepped on Decker's arm, bent down, grabbed the gun, and twisted it while bending Ben's wrist backward until his fingers lost purchase and the gun came loose. She threw the weapon about ten yards across the courtyard. Another two guards jumped on Decker, pinned him, and tied his hands and ankles with plastic cuffs.

In the tent, an older man was on the ground, moaning. Others surrounded him, and a gray-haired woman was comforting him. Blood was staining the back of his blue shirt. Screams by both men and women of,

"Get the ambulance." "Help!" "Man down!" "Medic!"

Two guards ran up to the man and began to administer first aid.

I heard, "Stay with us, Goddammit, Stay with us."

A gurney arrived, and the man in the blue shirt was taken away. The woman who had been comforting him was still holding his hand. As they rolled the gurney toward the ambulance, he was surrounded by men and women in uniform and medical equipment. Then someone with a portable loudspeaker shouted,

"All victims and family members follow me. Now."

The group slowly moved away from the tent to the far corner of the compound. Then Carter shouted, "Defense over here." Pointing to a different corner. Willis chimed in with, "Prosecutors, assemble on me." In a minute or two, the three distinct groups huddled in the baking sun, standing in shock and disbelief. There was a low hum of distraught conversation.

Willis wandered over.

"You guys okay?"

"Yes, kind of shaken, but we're not hurt. How is the guy who was shot?"

"Don't know."

Willis shook his head.

"I don't think we can proceed for a day or two. Give things time to calm down. Jesus." And he shook his head.

Carter and I looked at each other. Nodded in agreement.

"NCIS will be taking statements. After we get done with the judge, will you guys stay in your office until they finish the interviews?"

Pierce called us into his chambers, a small twelve by twelve room dominated by a faux wood desk covered with papers. No windows, fluorescent lights. He was sitting on a corner of the desk, robe and uniform jacket put to the side. His close-cropped hair seemed shiny with sweat.

Both teams filed in. Stood in a semi-circle around the desk.

Pierce looked up. Shook his head.

"I've been briefed. What a fucking mess." He then looked at Fredricks and Moretti. "Sorry."

"I think we should adjourn for the week. Give NCIS time to do their work, although it seems clear what happened. Guy grabbed a guard's gun from his holster and went after the defense. Do we know who he is?"

I took a baby step forward.

"Yes, it's Ben Decker. His wife was the blond who testified at the beginning of the penalty phase."

"The guy you know?"

"Yes."

He looked at me with accusing eyes and shook his head.

"How do the parties want to proceed with the jury?"

Willis and I looked at each other. Willis took a step forward,

"Bring them in, and tell them there has been an emergency and that the trial will resume Monday. Try to keep things from them in the sequester."

I nodded.

"Yes. That seems about right. We'll need to make a record. We'll probably ask for a mistrial, but we can do that Monday or in motions as you prefer."

Pierce nodded.

"I'd prefer motions and then argue it Monday morning." He smiled. "You know I'm unlikely to grant a mistrial."

"Yes, judge. We know." I smiled. "I'm not completely stupid. But gotta make a record."

He nodded.

I continued, "Your honor, what did you hear? Because that is probably what the jurors heard."

"Really nothing. A noise that I associate now as a gunshot but didn't at the time. Then the chief of the guard force came in and told me what happened."

Later, the NCIS investigators came into our office, took us one by one into another room, and interviewed us. I was last.

"We understand you know the shooter?"

"Yes, casually, I know him from my hometown. Not well, not socially, just nodding."

"And he'd previously threatened you?"

"Yes, but neither the escort nor I took it seriously. Anger is part of this. And honestly, given the security here, threats seemed pretty far-fetched. But yes, he did say I should be shot. And that this was not over."

He nodded. As we were winding up, I asked.

"How is the guy who was shot?"

"Hurt bad, but don't know how bad. It's also a problem that they don't really have the best medical facilities here."

That evening Jill and Fredricks came by my room. I'd skipped dinner. I'd just finished speaking with Molly and the girls.

Jill smiled.

"At dinner, we were told by one of the guards that the guy who was shot has been airlifted to Miami. He's okay but maybe facing a long recovery."

CHAPTER 63

After all the victims and family members had testified, after weeks of grief, the prosecution rested, and the penalty phase turned to the defense. But we were hampered by the judge and other branches of government. Every time we scored points, Pierce would sustain some objection, excluding some evidence. We arranged travel so that Hussain's family could testify in person. The State Department refused to issue them visas. Pierce declined to intervene, ruling that he had no authority over the Department of State. For good measure, the Base Commander for Guantanamo ruled that he would not allow them onto the base. We then requested to have them testify by video link. Pierce decided that he would not accommodate the time difference between Guantanamo and Saudi Arabia to allow this testimony. We argued that the government's interference in preventing family testimony risked conveying to the jury the false notion that Hussain's family did not care. As Fredricks argued, "And if your family doesn't care if you live or die, why should we save you?"

Pierce was rigid and implacable.

So we sought to present videos we'd made with Hussain's family during our trip to Saudi Arabia. At the prosecution's insistence, Pierce limited what could be shown to the jury. Finally, after three days of fighting out of the presence of the jury, fifteen hours of video became four hours that could be shown to the jury.

One day after court, I went to Brooks, "The team would like to meet with you." The meeting resulted in an article.

Lawyers Attack Military Commissions System

In an extraordinary press conference today, the lawyers for accused terrorist bomber, Hussain al Yemeni, lashed out at the judge presiding over his trial, the prosecution, and the entire process. Connor Mendelson and his defense team allege that the trial is "essentially fixed." Mendelson said, "with the exclusion of important defense evidence from the trial, the use of classification to hide information from the public, the trial is reduced to a show trial where the result is foreordained."

Mendelson and his team criticized the judge during jury selection, alleging jurors who had clearly prejudged the situation had been seated over defense objections. The judge, Mendelson said, "has put not his thumb on the scales of justice, but his whole hand."

When asked what he and his team intended to do to counter the situation, Mendelson said that "he and the team had sought to withdraw over a classified situation, but that the Chief Defense Counsel would not approve their course of action, and the judge also rejected it. When asked further, Mendelson said, "The situation we are confronted with places us in an ethically impossible situation. The indifference of the Chief Defense Counsel General Charles Ward and the judge, James Pierce, to their ethical obligations has forced the defense team to proceed even though doing so is legally improper."

Finally, Mendelson labeled the Chief Prosecutor, General Robert E. Lee Lawson, dishonest and "a cheater." When asked for an explanation, Mendelson threw up his hands and said, "It's classified."

CHAPTER 64

After I saw and vetted the article, Brooks and I chatted briefly.

"Pierce will not like this kind of challenge."

I shrugged.

"I suppose, but frankly, what can they do? They can file bar charges against my license, but who cares. I'm just sick of this shit. The public needs to know how unfair this is. I mean, it is a joke."

Brooks' article appeared on Sunday. On Monday, when Pierce took the bench, he announced that he had postponed the jury coming to court until 13:00. He then held up the article and said,

"The Commission has read the article written by Ms. Samantha Brooks. Mr. Mendelson, do you or any of your team members have any response?"

I stood.

"Yes, your honor. While the team was present, I did the majority of the talking, so they are blameless. But everything I said, Colonel Pierce, is quoted accurately. And let me be clear there are things I said, complaints I made about you and General Lawson that Ms. Brooks left out. I'll be happy to repeat them here if you'd like."

Pierce glared.

"Do whatever you think is appropriate."

"This is like nothing I have ever encountered. You know what occurred; the classified thing is clear evidence of prosecutorial misconduct and corruption. You know this trial is premised on a lie. You know what a real judge who was interested in real justice and fairness would do, but you sit silently. Worse, you justify this misconduct and corruption. My sense and I'll admit I have no evidence of this, is that you, all of you, you, Lawson, maybe even General Ward, have been given orders as to how this should turn out, and you are not even trying to have a pretext of fairness. That's what she didn't write."

Lawson stood and said, "Judge, I must protest this accusation."

Pierce waved him down.

"Mendelson, I can't hold you in contempt; the law as written does not give me that power. I could file bar charges, and I may, but there is no rush. What I am going to do is admonish you in the presence of the jury. I won't dignify your statements by addressing them. But you have no authority to attack the system publicly, and the jury will be informed of your and your team's lack of respect."

I shook my head.

"Two things judge. First, I absolutely do have the responsibility to attack this system. If I remain silent, if this team remains silent, we are complicit in this" I paused, "judicial fraud. After you admonish the jury, will I be allowed to respond?"

Pierce glared. I thought he would respond to the judicial fraud comment, but he said only, "No, you will sit quietly, or I'll have you excluded."

"Fine, exclude me, exclude the whole team; we're just window dressing in this show. I'll leave now; we'll all leave if you want."

I walked to the table and began to pick up my materials as if to leave.

"Mendelson, Sit down. You are ordered to return at 1300. We're adjourned."

When the jury came back that afternoon, Pierce said to them,

"There was an issue that I had to address this morning. Mr. Mendelson gave an interview that was published in The Los Angeles Times. In that interview, he falsely attacked this process, me, the prosecutor, and in a way, he attacked you. I have told him his statements were improper and, in my view, false, and I want you to know that going forward, you should weigh what he and his team say carefully as this article suggests a willingness to lie."

I stood and shouted as loudly as possible, "Everything I said was true. This is all a hoax, a show trial, a joke."

Pierce looked at the jury and said, "See what we have to contend with."

He looked at Lawson and said, "Call your next witness."

CHAPTER 65

The interview with Brooks had been Moretti's idea. We had discussed it at length. Everyone agreed that telling the world the truth was necessary.

I'd told Fredricks, "This is a career wrecker for you. It could be for all of us, but for you, this is a no-win deal. Do you really want to do this?"

Fredricks smiled, "Yes. I'm getting out anyway. If we are about the truth, then we have to tell the truth. Fuck Pierce."

Carter shook his head, "I'm out after this either way. Who gives a shit what they think. The right thing to do."

After it was all over, after the jury had been told we were liars, we sat in the office.

Fredricks spoke first, "Well," she laughed sardonically, "In hindsight, I'm not sure that was such a good idea."

Moretti nodded.

Carter smiled.

"But it was fun, wasn't it? Wasn't telling the truth fun?"

Moretti said, "But we hurt Hussain's case. I mean, we really hurt his case."

Carter shook his head, "Let's be honest, Hussain is fucked. These guys are not going to let us get close to winning. Connor is right. We are window dressing. So at least we've told the truth. Hell, we're the only ones telling the truth." He turned to me. "You're quiet."

I shook my head, "I'm numb. It's like running in goo. We're working our guts out. I don't know what's right anymore. I got nothing."

Brook's story got lots of re-publications and went viral online. There was a predictable outcry from both sides. Guantanamo is good, and the defense is doing bad defense stuff on one side. Guantanamo is bad; the trial is a hoax, on the other.

To me, it was all noise. I had no fight left. But, going through the hundreds of emails I received, I found two that helped.

To: Connor Mendelson

From: Jennifer Sanders

As that wise man, Col. Nathan Jessup, said: "They can't handle the truth."

Hang in there.

Jennifer

The Few Good Men reference made me smile.

The other email that helped:

To: Connor Mendelson

From: Molly

"Illegitimi non carborundum" Don't let the bastards grind you down.

We're proud of you.

Molly, Emily, and Anabel.

Later an announcement went out that Ben Decker had been flown to Miami, where he was charged in Federal Court with various offenses. Carla had already been transported home.

CHAPTER 66

We did what we could, what the judge would allow. Grace was called to identify the documents she had obtained. She explained to the jury how she searched for documents and had gone to various places to find them. The jury seemed intrigued as she described how she had obtained documents in Saudi Arabia and Kuwait.

She explained why she could not obtain documents in Mecca, Yemen, or Chechnya. How others had to do that in the case of Mecca and Yemen or that it was just too dangerous in Chechnya. She explained what she had sought there and why she believed they existed and what she speculated the documents would show. Surprisingly Pierce allowed this part of her testimony over the prosecutor's objection. At a recess after his ruling, we concluded that perhaps the article wasn't such a bad idea.

Willis's cross-examination was largely screaming at her for close to a day. About what it was not clear. The jury seemed confused.

In the absence of Hussain's family, Jill had to testify about his life based on her meetings with Hussain, our work in Saudi Arabia, the meetings with the Saudi historians, his family, and her investigation.

Jill described, from US government documents, why it was clear that he was not a leader of the Kuwaiti attack and again stressed how the Kuwaiti government had assisted the attack.

She spoke about the impact his execution would have on his family and how the rest of the world had little confidence in the fairness of the process in Guantanamo. She extrapolated that ordering Hussain's execution would be considered barbaric in much of the world and could significantly negatively impact the United States and its military.

Willis's cross-examination focused on her anti-death penalty views.

At one point, Willis went too far.

"You acknowledge you are opposed to the death penalty."

"Yes, that is obvious."

"You'll agree there is nothing your client could have done that, in your mind, would warrant death?"

"That is true. I don't see how killing people who kill people proves that killing people is wrong."

"So you'd prefer to let him out to kill innocent people again."

"Sir, first, he is unlikely to get out. The jury has many sentencing options, including, 'Life without parole.'"

She continued, "The people who were killed were warriors in what the jury has found was a combat zone. I regret their deaths. I really do. I regret that in war, people get killed. But that is the nature of war. So in that sense, the people who were killed were not innocent. Make no mistake. They were heroes. Just as the sailors killed at Pearl Harbor were heroes."

She paused and looked at the jury. Then, "In my professional opinion, you are far more likely to kill an innocent person than Hussain.

"Indeed, my research indicates you, Major Willis, did just that in Missouri when you convicted and obtained the execution of John Muller, who was executed several years ago."

Here she turned to the jury.

"I learned that Major Willis resisted allowing DNA tests when he was a civilian prosecutor while Mr. Muller was alive. After Muller's execution, DNA testing was done. This testing proved Muller's innocence." She turned back to Willis. "So let's not get all high and mighty about killing innocent people."

Willis began screaming that the Missouri reference was improper and hearsay. I stood up and held up a file of documents.

"Here is the Muller file. If Maj. Willis would like to review it to refresh his memory. And, your honor, we'd like to offer it as evidence 'to eliminate the hearsay issue.'"

Pierce glared as he told the jury to disregard Jill's and my comments. He also admonished me…again.

CHAPTER 67

When the prosecution agreed to make Victoria Hancock available as a witness, it was with the caveat that she would only testify during the penalty phase if there was one and then only in a session with only the judge, the jury, and the lawyers present. Hussain and all spectators were excluded.

Pierce entered with the all rise and the other look-at-me-I'm-the-judge nonsense, and he turned to the defense table.

"I understand Ms. Hancock is present, so let's begin."

Carter stood, "Your honor, Mr. Mendelson is going to question the witness, but we want to renew our motion that our client be allowed to be present for this testimony. The witness tortured Mr. al-Yemeni, and he can assist us during her testimony by telling us if she is telling the truth. Also, it is hard to fathom excluding a man from the trial that might result in his death."

At this, General Lawson stood and objected, "This witness did not torture the defendant. She used legal, enhanced interrogation techniques that the United States Department of Justice has ruled are not torture."

Pierce looked at Carter.

"Major, we've had this fight over and over, both about the word torture and your client's presence. The court has determined that it will be for the jury to decide if what was done to your client impacts whether or not he should be put to death. What you call it, what the prosecutor calls it, is unimportant. Can we just dispense with the histrionics?"

Carter stood taller.

"It's not histrionics to call torture, torture, your honor, and we just don't want to be accused of waiving our objection to the fact that the defendant is not allowed to be here during this important, critical phase of the case. He could help us with the questioning."

Pierce tapped his pen and said, "Do you want a recess to speak with your client? We can proceed, and I'll arrange for you to see him this afternoon."

Carter looked at me. I gave him a shrug, a non-verbal, "Sure, why not."

Carter turned back and said, "Will we be allowed to tell Hussain about the details of her testimony?"

Pierce looked to the prosecutor's table where Lawson stood and said, "No, this is classified testimony, and they can't share anything about it with their client."

Pierce pivoted back to the defense.

Carter stood, looked at the judge, and said, "Well, then, what is the point? This demonstrates why this is so unfair. You've conceded that we should consult with Hussain to get his help. Yet, we can't get his help because," finger quotes above his head, 'it's classified.'" Hands down, eyes blazing.

Pierce shrugged.

"I don't make the rules here. If the CIA says it's classified, It's classified. We've been through this as well. Do you want a recess early to speak with your client or not?"

Carter stood, waited a couple of beats, and said, "What are we supposed to talk to him about? How the Cubs lost last night? Really, judge, this is just ridiculous."

"Shall I take that as a no?"

"Your honor, take it however you want to take it."

Pierce glared. Carter looked directly at him.

Pierce glared back and said, "Bring in the jury."

"Defense, call your next witness."

"Defense calls Victoria Hancock."

Hancock entered the courtroom from the door behind the witness stand. She was dressed in a tan sleeveless blouse with a pointed collar and black buttons, a black skirt, not tight. She carried a white sweater. Her skin was pale, as though the sun had never touched it. Her dark hair had a sheen of grey. Her eyes were hard—cold hard.

My legs were rapidly moving back and forth as I sat in anticipation. *Stay calm. You've prepared your whole career for this moment.* I tried to slow my breathing.

Maj. Willis administered the oath and asked her name and place of residence.

"My name is Victoria Hancock. My permanent residence is in Kentucky, although I reside now in the National Capitol Region."

"Counsel, you may inquire."

I stood, carried my big notebook, a large heavy white binder with multiple colored tabs sticking out from the edge away from the spine, to the podium, set it down and said, "You may suspect I have a few questions for you."

And Pierce interrupted, "Your definition of a few is different from most folks."

Everyone, including me, laughed.

"You're right, your honor. We'll certainly be here for a while."

Turning to Hancock, I took her through her history with the CIA and addressed her time in the clandestine service. Then, "I'm not interested in the details of your clandestine assignments. But I am interested in the skills necessary for that assignment. You with me?"

"Sure."

"Clandestine service can be dangerous?"

"Yes."

"Discovery means risk, embarrassment, and possible physical harm, even death?"

"Yes. That's true."

"To avoid discovery, you need to be able to act the part? To be a convincing actor? To lie, if necessary?"

"Yes."

And here I turned to the jury and continued, "To be a convincing liar?"

She caught the drift and said, "Well, counsel, that's different than here."

"Ma'am, you were a skilled enough liar never to get caught? True?"

"Yes."

"You could look people in the eye, lie to them, and they would believe you?"

"Yes, I guess."

"You dealt with government officials and foreign military officers? And successfully lied to them?"

"Yes. Since I was never exposed, I guess you could say I successfully lied."

"We'll return to your admitted ability to lie later; let's talk about history."

"In your work for the agency, did you study history?"

A quizzical look.

"Not really," she said, "not with the agency. I studied a little history in college, and I suppose I picked up some history over time."

"In college, or over time, did you study the history of war crimes prosecutions?"

"No."

"Did you pick up the history of war crimes prosecution from any source."

"No."

"Well, more precisely, did you ever study the charges brought against the Japanese after World War II?"

"No."

"Are you aware, from any source, that Japanese officials were prosecuted as war criminals for waterboarding allied prisoners?"

She frowned, "No, I'm not sure I've heard that, and frankly, I doubt that is true."

I then confronted her with evidence showing that Japanese commanders were prosecuted in capital cases for waterboarding Allied prisoners.

I continued in the same vein to show that historically waterboarding has been a war crime.

"Are you aware Filipino leaders were prosecuted as war criminals for waterboarding US prisoners?"

"No."

Again she was confronted with evidence.

"Do you concede that waterboarding is a war crime?"

She glanced at the prosecutor, "Counsel, the Department of Justice allowed us to do what we did."

"If waterboarding is a war crime, then it is your position that the US Department of Justice authorized you to commit war crimes. Is that what you're telling us?"

"I don't see how it can be a war crime if DOJ approves."

I responded.

"Ahh, if Hitler approved it, it's not a war crime. Is that your testimony?"

"Hardly the same, counsel."

Changing subjects.

"Are you familiar with the Convention Against Torture?"

"Of course."

"You aware that if other countries consider behavior to be torture, they have the jurisdiction to prosecute war crimes?"

"Yes, I know that."

"So even if the Department of Justice approved your war crime, England or Germany may not, and you could be prosecuted there?"

Lawson jumped up, "Objection, your honor. This is a trick. The witness is not a lawyer and is not qualified to answer. Moreover, what France or whoever thinks is not relevant."

Pierce looked over his glasses, "Response Counsel?"

"Your honor, she holds a senior CIA position. She should know what a war crime is; if she does not, it goes to her credibility. Also, given her international exposure to prosecution, she may lie to minimize her risk of prosecution in other countries. She says this is all okay, but if it isn't, her judgment is perhaps suspect. Moreover, as the jury is being asked to kill Hussain, this impacts the jury's decision. The jury should know how other countries view torture."

"Sustained, let's move along. I take your point. And I suspect the jury does as well. Splitting the baby."

"Now, besides waterboarding, have you used other so-called Enhanced Interrogation Techniques on Hussain?"

"Yes."

"The goal was to break people? Bend them to your will?"

"Counsel, the goal was to get information. If to do that, we broke them, so what?"

"Among the devices, you used to break people are so-called stress positions?"

She nodded, "Yes."

"Tell us about stress positions?"

"You want me to describe them?" Hancock turned. "Your honor?"

"It's a closed session. Answer the question."

"Well, in one, we have the subject sit on his shins and put his head against the wall."

"And if he moves off the wall?"

"He was pushed back."

"For how long?"

"I don't know; it could be hours."

"Would you question the subject while he was in that position?"

"Yes, of course."

"And was that a position you used with Hussain?"

"Yes, many times."

"Your honor, could the witness step down? I'd like the witness to assume the position, so we can describe it more accurately for the record."

Pierce's eyes darted to Hancock, to the prosecution, to the unidentified men sitting at the back of the room. Probably from the CIA.

"Major Willis?" Pierce asked.

"The government objects. It's not necessary."

I turned, "Look, this is a closed session; we can't have our client here. If we can't do the questioning properly, what are we doing here?"

Turning to Hancock, Pierce asked, "Can you get in the position?"

"Sure, your honor, no problem." A silent 'Fuck you' was thrown with her eyes at me and the others on our side of the room.

She got up, adjusted her skirt and went to the front of the bench, and got on her knees, knees nearly touching the front of the judge's bench, and leaned her head forward, so the top of her head was on the wood panel.

I asked, "Your hands? Handcuffed behind you? So put them there."

I pulled out some plastic cuffs and moved toward the witness's wrists. She immediately pulled away, and Willis shouted, "Don't touch her."

I responded.

"I'm just putting cuffs on her like she did Hussain."

Pierce snarled, "No, you're not counsel. What kind of nonsense is this?"

"Just a search for the truth, your honor."

A couple of the jurors were smiling. Most were stoic.

Pierce said, "Ma'am put your hands behind your back. No one will cuff you."

I asked again, "For how long was he in that position?"

She started to stand, and I said, "Please, stay where you are."

Willis stood, "Your honor, the witness should be allowed to return to the stand."

Pierce, "Counsel, why are you doing this?" Implied, 'Why are you being an asshole?'

I looked at the jury when I spoke to the judge.

"Your honor, we intend to continue questioning the witness while she is in this position. If it does not impact truthfulness, it should make no difference to her testimony, and the jury can see the impact."

Shouted objections from the prosecution.

Judge Pierce said, "We're going into recess. I want to meet with counsel to discuss the scope of the examination. I'll excuse the jury for the rest of the day."

Shortly after, we were called into the judge's office.

Pierce, sitting in his easy chair, waved us in, and we stood in separate corners, teams of fighters, waiting for the bell.

"Where are we going here?" the judge asked.

I said, "Judge, for years, the CIA, this woman, has hidden the truth. If the stress positions don't inhibit the truth, let them show us. If waterboarding is like being dunked, or dunking for apples, let them show us. More importantly, let them show you. Let them show the jury."

"How far do you propose to go?"

"Well, we're not going to hang her naked and hooded from the ceiling like she did Hussain; we can't keep her up for days and days, but we do intend to show the jury members the large and small boxes. We intend to try to demonstrate what waterboarding is truly like, with a willing subject, of course."

"Why can't you film it and present the films?" Pierce asked.

"Remember when the prosecution said it had a plan, and you deferred to them? Our plan, our turn."

Turning to the prosecution, "Your position?"

Willis, channeling Lawson, who was seething, said, "Oral testimony is good enough."

I replied, "Judge, I'm happy to go out and tell the media that the prosecution and, candidly, you, your honor, want to hide the truth from the jury and the world. If you didn't like our last press conference, you really won't like the next one. If we can't do this the way we need to, the kangaroo-like nature of this farce becomes even more obvious."

When Pierce glared, I added a perfunctory, "Respectfully."

"How long is this going to take?"

"It takes, as long as it takes. You told the jury the confession was reliable. You gutted our case. But you said that we'd be allowed a thorough examination of her when she testified. We'd like you to keep that promise."

Lawson stood, puffed his chest of ribbons, and said, "There is no need to spend time focusing on sources and methods. The prosecution has offered to stipulate. You could order them to reach a stipulation about what she would say. Then, this could be public."

Pierce looked surprised.

"Do I really have that authority?"

Lawson paused and said, "You can order them to meet with us."

Turning to me, Pierce said, "How about that?"

"Judge, I can't imagine a world where we can reach a stipulation. Unless the prosecution is prepared to stipulate that Hancock is subject to prosecution throughout the world, and describe her crimes in detail, let's just proceed. I can't imagine the prosecution stipulating to the fact that the United States subjected Hussain to rape and anal sodomy, hung him naked on several occasions for over five days, and made him soil himself and sit in the filth till his skin debrided. If they are unwilling to agree to that, we would be wasting our time."

Pierce pivoted. "How 'bout that, General?

Lawson said, "Judge, I think it's worth the effort. Ms. Hancock is in a difficult position and I am concerned that the CIA may decide to preclude further testimony from her."

Carter muttered, "For fucks sake."

Pierce paused, then said, "I've sent the jury home for the day. I'm ordering the parties to meet this afternoon and see if you can reach an agreement. You are to meet here in the courtroom at 1300. Report to me at 1600 as to progress. Then we'll decide the way forward. It feels wrong to humiliate this witness, and I have reservations about where this is headed."

I stood, "Your honor. It is just wasting time."

Pierce glared, "Counsel, you are ordered to meet. I want you to try to reach an agreement about what her testimony would be. I don't know what objections the prosecution might have going forward but an agreement might be better than how I might rule. You never know."

CHAPTER 68

Carter, Moretti, Fredricks, and I entered the courtroom. Lawson and Willis were standing near the jury box, chatting.

We decided that making Lawson negotiate with a female major would insult him, so Fredricks was to take the lead.

She said, "Good afternoon. We're here as ordered. We both know we're not going to reach an agreement, so let's go tell the judge we met and not waste any more time with this."

Lawson looked at her, then at me.

"Did you bring a proposal?"

Fredricks laughed.

"General, we went to lunch. If you have a proposal? We'll read it. If you don't have a proposal, we're done with this shit." Fredricks had confessed she loved swearing in front of Lawson as she knew it made him visibly anxious.

Lawson grimaced at the language. "We have one. Let's go through it line by line."

Harriet laughed again.

"No, give it to us, and we'll review it and get back to you."

"I think I'd prefer to tell you my thoughts on each line or paragraph."

Fredricks interrupted, snorted really, "I'll bet you would, but it's not going to happen. Give it to us. We'll review it. I suspect then we'll tell you to shove it up your ass." She paused. "This is fucking stupid."

There were a few moments of silence. Fredrick's breach of military decorum hung like a really loud fart in church. Then, finally, Lawson held out some papers.

"Here is our proposal; after your review, we can discuss any changes and report back by sixteen hundred as the judge ordered."

Kristina took the document from Lawson and handed it to me. I nodded.

"We'll be back in an hour."

In our office, we sat around the small conference table. I read a page, gave it to Carter, who would pass it on to Fredricks and then Kristina. Occasionally one or the other would write something. Nearly an hour later, we were finished. We looked at each other.

Moretti said, "No way I'd sign any part of this." We nodded.

Lawson came back into the courtroom expectantly, like a child asking his parents for permission to do something, "What do you think?"

Fredricks smiling, relishing her ability to be snarky to a senior officer, said, "General, this is bullshit. There are no details. It does not meaningfully address the things this woman did. It is just ridiculous that you would waste our time with this."

"We'll let's go through it line by line and see if I can convince you that it is enough for your purposes. " Lawson's voice was begging.

"No."

I stood.

"We're done. I'm going back to the office and send the judge an email that we met as ordered and cannot reach an agreement."

Lawson's arms opened wide, pleading.

"Why do you need to have this witness? Can't you be reasonable? You are compromising national security."

Fredricks stood a bit taller, "This woman is a monster, a criminal, and her crimes need to be documented so that when this record is released, as it will be someday, the world knows what a fucking," hesitating, "I don't even have the word for her, and what sham this proceeding is." She then looked at me.

I nodded.

"We're done here. I'll tell the judge we met. You tell Hancock she's going back up on the stand."

CHAPTER 69

The next morning Hancock looked tired. Bags under her eyes. She moved slowly. Awaiting the judge, she stood at a distance from the prosecution and stared at the wall. The tension between her and Lawson was palpable.

Resuming, I took her back to the stress position, but she refused to leave the stand.

"Unless ordered to step down, I respectfully refuse. I'm here to answer questions but not to be a dummy or a mannequin.'"

This went on through some of the other so-called EIT's – hanging by the arms and sleep deprivation. When we got to the music that was played to keep Hussain awake. *The Real Slim Shady* by Eminem. We played it at full volume. It was painful. After ten seconds, Pierce ordered it turned off.

I turned to Hancock.

"Hussain had no judge to turn that off?"

Her reply, "That's obvious."

"You played it that loud for days, true?"

"Yes, that was part of what the DOJ allowed."

"The goal was to keep him awake.?"

"Yes."

"And you kept him awake with that song and others for up to ninety-six hours."

"Yes"

I brought out the large box. A black box the size of a coffin.

"Is this identical to what you told Hussain would be his second home?"

She nodded.

"Are you afraid to get into it?"

Hancock paused. Looked at the judge.

"No."

"So, will you get in?"

Silence.

"I'll get in it."

After she lay down in the coffin, I put a pencil through the hasp so it could not open. And I continued to ask questions.

Quickly, her voice became raspy, and she said, "It's difficult to talk. Are you going to let me out?"

"Why should I? You didn't let Hussain out."

The prosecutor shouted, "Judge. Objection."

Looking at the jury, I said, "She's been in there two or three minutes. Hussain was in there for three days. So rather than let her out, I move to adjourn, and we come back Wednesday. But of course, the witness would stay where she is. Ms. Hancock, are you okay with that?"

There was no response.

"Your honor," from Willis. "Could we have a comfort break?"

"Of course."

"Your honor, to make this realistic, she should just have to soil herself; that's what she made Hussain do."

Pierce shook his head, "Counsel, get real, unlock that, and help her out."

I removed the pencil and opened the coffin, and extended a hand, but she did not take it. Instead, she climbed out using the sides of the coffin as support. And glared, giving me a scorching look with blazing eyes. A look that said, 'I would kill you if I could.'

We brought out the small box. I asked her to get into it. She refused. I posed a series of questions while sitting on the box. The final one was.

You left Hussain in this box sixteen hours once; isn't that true?

She softly said, "Yes, it was an error. But we did that."

I then changed the subject to the waterboard. I asked Hancock to describe it. She responded, "It's just a table with some straps. Not all that dramatic."

"Well, were the ones you used at Black Site Green slanted? "

"Yes."

"And Hussain was subjected to being waterboarded on the slanted table? And you have stated that waterboarding is not that bad, true?"

"Yes?"

"You've said it's like bobbing for apples at Halloween. Right?"

"Yes."

"And you've been waterboarded?"

"Yes, a couple of times. As part of my training."

I turned and nodded to the paralegal, who pulled a slanted table out from under our counsel table. She and Carter brought it out. I smiled, "We offer defense exhibit AE 468 AAA, your honor. It is a waterboard identical to the one used at Black Site Green, and we intend to have the witness confirm that and put it in evidence."

Pierce looked to Lawson, "General, your position?"

"I'll defer to your discretion, your honor." The message being, 'Help me, judge.'

Pierce paused for a minute and said, "It's admitted."

Silence. Then, the next question. I looked at Hancock.

"Waterboarding is 'not that bad.'"

"True."

"Dunking for apples?"

"That is how I have described it."

"So a brave CIA operative like you, a former spy, should not be scared of that, true? You claim you've been waterboarded. So you're not afraid, are you? You're not scared of dunking for apples are you?"

"No, I'm not afraid of the process, only of you. I don't trust you, counsel."

Looking at the jury, I asked, "Surely you trust the judge and General Lawson to protect you?"

She paused a beat, "I guess."

"So you're willing to be waterboarded? Or are you really afraid?"

"No, I'll do it."

There was a rustle as the magnitude of what was going to happen became obvious.

I asked her to step down from the witness chair and lie on the board. I then tightened the straps. I put a cloth over her nose and mouth and took a gallon jug of water, and slowly poured it onto the cloth. Hancock's back arched, and she strained against the straps. I kept pouring as Lawson and Pierce yelled, "Stop."

The jurors sat forward. A couple had their hands to their mouths.

When I stopped and pulled the cloth off Hancock, she moaned. And coughed. As she lay there, I reached down, grabbed the hem of her skirt and pulled it up as far as it would go, exposing her sheer white lace bikini underwear. She tried to clamp her legs together, but the straps kept her legs in place. In the ensuing uproar, she couldn't do anything because her hands were strapped down.

"What was that about?' Lawson yelled.

Pierce yelled at the same time, "Counselor, you are way, way out of order."

"With respect, your Honor, this is how she treated Hussain to induce a sense of learned helplessness."

Pierce glowered.

When she was unstrapped, Hancock sat up and quickly pulled her skirt down. Glaring, she stood and then bent over to gain some stability. She walked unsteadily back to the stand.

We looked at each other.

"Still like dunking for apples?"

Silence.

"When you were lying with your skirt above your waist, and we were all looking at your underwear, was that humiliating?"

"Yes."

"Degrading, upsetting?"

"Yes."

"Would it have been worse if I'd pulled your underwear off?"

"Of course."

"By the way, you waterboarded Hussain several times, true? And what you just endured was physically similar to what Hussain endured?"

"Yes, I guess."

"But you had a judge here and the prosecutor to protect you?"

"I suppose you could say that."

"You knew they would not let me kill you, right?"

"Of course, I hoped they'd stop you."

"But Hussain had no judge, no protection? He just had your willingness not to kill him?"

She nodded silently.

"I want to talk now about how you sexually abused Hussain. You follow me."

"We did not sexually abuse him." Her eyes looked away from me, away from the jury.

"Hussain was naked when he was waterboarded, wasn't he?"

Softly, "Yes."

"And it's true you abused him while he was strapped down?"

She did not answer.

"Did you touch his penis while he was strapped down?"

She sat still a second, the wheels turning, looked at Lawson, and looked back at me. Softly said, "No."

"With your fingers?"

She glanced at the prosecutor and hesitated.

I said, "He can't answer the question for you. Did you touch his penis with your fingers? Fondle it to humiliate him??"

Again softly, really a whisper, "No."

I looked at her and said, "You are lying. You know you did that. It's in the WIZARD files. So tell the jury the truth."

She said nothing.

Pierce said, "Counsel ask questions, no arguing with the witness."

"You talked about how he would never use his penis again?"

Silence.

"Told him you were going to cut it off and feed it to the fish?"

"Counsel, we said all kinds of things."

"Yes, one of the things you told him was that you would have your people rape his mother? Your exact words were 'front, back, and mouth until she fucking dies.' Isn't that what you told him?"

"We needed information."

"And when you threatened to kill him or to have his mother raped, front, back, and mouth, you wanted to be believed, right?"

"Of course."

"If he didn't fear you, there was no reason to give information."

"So just like you lied successfully to protect yourself when you were a spy, you used the same skills to convince Hussain you would kill him?"

"Or cut his penis off?

"Or kill his family?

"Or rape his mother, front, back, and mouth.

"So, how many additional times do you admit to waterboarding Hussain?"

"I don't know specifically; the records say three."

"Could it have been more?"

"Counsel, I don't know. I'll defer to the record. We wanted information."

I looked hard at her. Looked at the jury and looked back.

"You are lying; you waterboarded him eight times. Isn't that true?"

"The record says three; it is my testimony that the record is correct."

I pointed at the waterboard, "Want to do it again?"

A shake of the head. "No."

"Why not?

Pierce interrupted, "Counsel, you made your point."

"One final point, Ms. Hancock, Sexual humiliation was part of your approach, right?"

"We wanted information. We did what was necessary?"

"Again, not answering the question. And you raped him. Isn't that true?"

She glared at me, red-faced. Glanced at the prosecution. Shook her head no.

"You forced yourself onto his penis? Had sex with him against his will to embarrass him? And maybe you enjoyed it a bit yourself."

Hancock would not look at me, would not look at the jurors. She just sat stone-faced.

"And you had men rape him."

Silence. She just glared and shook her head.

It was time to end the examination. A series of questions to which the only answer she could give was "Yes."

"You admit you did things to him to degrade him, humiliate him, right?"

"Yes."

"Hung him from his arms? For days? Loud music? *The Real Slim Shady.* Blindfolded in complete silence and threatened to kill his mother? Rape her? Front, Back, and Mouth? The big box? The small box? Waterboarding? Your men anally raped him?"

"We force-fed him."

"By shoving an unlubricated tube up his rectum? Without a doctor present? And shoved ground up hummus and rice into him?"

"Yes."

No hesitation. Said with pride

"Do you know if feeding someone that way provides nutrition?"

"I'm not a doctor."

"If I asked you to get off the stand, so I could shove a tube of hummus and rice up your butt, would you agree to do it?"

"Of course not."

"Would you feel abused if the judge ordered it?"

"Of course."

"At risk of harm if I was doing it?"

"Of course."

"And to be clear, you raped him?"

"I deny that."

She said without conviction.

"Whatever. You are lying about that as well. But to be clear, you would lie to avoid these things, wouldn't you?"

"Counsel, I don't know."

"Yes, you do," I replied. "Because you have lied to this jury, to this judge, to the public, and probably you have lied to yourself."

And then, "Judge, I have no more questions."

The judge looked at Lawson. "How long is your re-cross?"

"Three Questions: Did you do what you did to get information?

"Did you believe you were acting within the law based on the guidance you'd received?

"Would you do it again under the same circumstances?"

She answered "Yes," to all three questions.

The judge said, "Ms. Hancock, thank you for coming here. You may be excused. Let's take a break."

After the jury left the room, Hancock stood and walked toward me. She took the time to look directly at me as she walked up to the defense table, stood over me, glared, bent down, and whispered, "Enjoy this moment, but payback will be a real bitch. And remember, we know where your wife and children are."

I glared straight back. "Anything happens to my family…"

"You'll do shit."

She turned away. And walked out of the courtroom.

CHAPTER 70

For the next several days, a series of experts testified that the torture inflicted on Hussain was outside the norm for the United States and the civilized world. It was a war crime. Other experts testified that the torture exceeded the most liberal reading of the Department of Justice opinions allowing torture.

After we rested our case, the prosecution presented witnesses who opined that torture was not torture. Moretti's cross-examination focused on Post Traumatic Stress Disorder as a permanent injury and nearly drowning as threatening death, all in an effort to show that even under the DOJ guidelines, the CIA's behavior was torture. Then the prosecution announced it had no further witnesses. The only questions that remained; would Hussain speak to the jury and would the jury vote to kill him.

Hussain decided he wanted to speak to the jury. He prepared with Jill and Kristina, whose message was simple. Speak from the heart.

He stood, and with short steps because of his shackles, he walked to the podium, looked at the judge, looked at the jury, turned, and looked at the spectators behind the glass. Mohammed stood next to him to translate. Hussain was sweaty and short of breath. The room was silent.

"I want you to know that the Koran does not preach violence. But for a time, I saw violence as a solution. That was wrong, and for that, I am sorry. I know sorry is not enough, but that is all I can offer. He turned and looked at the back of the room, where the victims were sitting.

"Seeing your pain, seeing the harm that you have suffered, I accept your hatred and your bitterness. There is so much hatred. I do tell you from my heart that what al-Qaeda did, what I did, was wrong, just as what a few Americans did to me was wrong. There is perhaps fault on both sides."

He took a breath and seemed to breathe more easily.

"It is not my place to ask for mercy or for forgiveness. The Koran teaches that mercy or forgiveness are granted, not requested."

Here he turned to the jury.

"But I do want to say to you that I forgive the woman, Hancock, and those who helped her for what was done to me."

He continued to look at the jury.

"So many people believe their lives will be better if I am dead. Many of the survivors believe that. Your President says he believes I should die. I don't know what to say. I hope your hearts are open. Being a martyr seemed like a good choice when I was young."

He paused, and seemed to be thinking. Then he said forcefully,

"I want to live. I want to live." Like he had just reached that decision. He gestured to the back of the room.

"If in your hearts, you believe that killing me will promote healing, will heal the pain and anger of those who were harmed, I will accept your decision. But, whatever you decide, there will be no anger; there has been too much anger, too much bitterness. Thank you for listening."

Hussain paused, looked over at us. Jill and Moretti were crying softly. I gave a small nod. He came over and as he sat down, his hand gently touched my shoulder. Sitting, he put his face in his hands.

CHAPTER 71

I had a day to prepare the final argument. Really it had been done for weeks, but I needed to break through what Jill called the callous on my heart. I was worn out and numb. I found a picture of Hussain's father. I looked at it and recalled his promise to make a place for me in heaven. My bond with his father was in my heart. So I printed the picture of his father that we had taken during one of the times we had been in Saudi Arabia. He was wearing a white robe and a white head scarf, his beard henna'd a dull orange, his weathered face. Looking at this picture, I recalled how he had looked at me, eyes glistening, holding back tears, imploring, begging really.

"Save my son. Treat my son like you would want your child treated. Because Hussain is now your child."

On the notebook holding the outline of my argument, I wrote. *Hussain is your child*. When I looked at that, tears welled. I was ready.

I walked to the podium. Stood in silence.

"How do I ask you to spare the life of somebody you have found responsible for killing so many of your fellow warriors? How do I ask you to find that he should have at least telephone contact with his parents and family when so many families have been shattered? How do I ask you to reach a decision that will appear to many to disregard the pain of the victims? How do I ask you to disregard the illegal demands of your Commander in Chief?

"The truth is I do not have the words or the ability to convince you to do this if mercy, forgiveness, or compassion are not already in your hearts. And if your hearts have mercy, forgiveness, or compassion, my words should not be necessary. So I will be brief.

"All I can ask is for you to simply follow the evidence, the law, and your hearts. Because if you follow the evidence, the law, and your hearts, I believe you will conclude that Hussain should not be sentenced to death.

"We know from the evidence that Hussain's government encouraged Jihad, which led to this attack. Our government encouraged torture, which led to the excesses to which Victoria Hancock admitted. The forces and excesses of his government overwhelmed Hussain. Just as perhaps they overwhelmed Ms. Hancock."

I turned now and looked at the judge, turned to the jury, and then looked back to the judge.

"For reasons I do not understand, a lot of evidence was kept from you. Before anyone could object, I waved them down, but you know Hussain has parents he loves. You saw how the threat to his mother, a threat he knows now was false, still affects him. This is who they want you to kill—a man who loves his mother and has come to understand love.

"Hussain told you, and you know from the evidence, that when he went to Jihad, he did not believe that love is better than hate. But that angry Hussain has been killed already. Perhaps the angry Hussain was killed by Victoria Hancock as she waterboarded, boxed, and raped him. Perhaps the angry Hussain was changed by the growth that we hopefully all have as we age. I don't know. I do know that the Hussain before you knows, as we all know, that there has been too much killing. And I ask you to consider whether, in the face of so much pain and death, will more pain, more death change the world for the better. If so, perhaps killing Hussain would make sense, but if not, then why?

"I read a story somewhere that may be appropriate here. During the invasion of Normandy, a group of German prisoners was killed by an angry US soldier who gunned them down as he was escorting them to a POW compound. It was war. People shrugged. That soldier, the story goes, survived the war and was haunted until his death by the faces of the prisoners he killed. His life was forever marred by what he did in anger.

"Hussain, too, is a prisoner of war, But we are far removed from the energy and anger of combat. Yet the decision is the same. Each of you has the power to spare Hussain. Only together can you kill him."

I continued, "I ask you to consider four things: It took you ten days to reach a guilty verdict. Clearly, there were things in the evidence that bothered some of you. The judge will tell you that residual doubt is a factor on which any of you can decide to vote for life; if you continue to be troubled by the evidence, you can, under the law, vote for life.

"I ask you to consider that we don't know much about what Hussain was like before the CIA got him. But the CIA destroyed that guy. You are being asked to kill the body of the guy the CIA tortured. That body houses a far different man than existed in 2001. That body houses the man who spoke to you several days ago. Is it really necessary to kill the man who spoke of love and who grants forgiveness but asks for none?

"Will killing a prisoner of war keep us safe? Hussain will almost certainly be in prison for the rest of his life if you spare him. But if you vote to kill him, the evidence you heard tells you what you know to be true. That you put future men and women at arms at risk of torture and death sentences? Make no mistake. If you vote for death, our enemies will use your verdict as justification to torture and kill."

Lawson objected, but Pierce said, "It's final argument, and it's a fair comment."

I turned back to the jury.

"If you vote to kill Hussain, you have to be prepared to read at some point that they are preparing for his execution. Like that soldier at Normandy, if you have doubts or regrets, you will not be able to do anything because once you are dismissed, you cannot change your mind. So all doubts and reservations must be resolved in favor of life, not for Hussain, but for each of you. None of you should have to live haunted by the memory of unnecessary killing.

"Some time ago, we met with Hussain's family. His father, whose photo you have seen," And here I displayed it again, "told me, Mr. Connor, please treat my son as if he were your own child. I hope I have done that. So it is difficult for me to give you the responsibility for this child's life. To give you the responsibility Major Carter, Major Fredricks, Ms. Moretti, and I have carried for the past many months.

"But I do that." Here, my voice broke. "I give, we give you, this child's life to hold in your hands. I give, we give you, the decision to preserve his life or to kill him. I give, we give you, the life of Hussain al-Yemeni and ask that you treat his life and your own with dignity and respect as you decide whether he lives or dies."

I sat down, put my head in my hands, and softly, silently, and unashamedly cried.

Several days later, we went into the meeting room and Hussain was sitting holding back tears, legs shaking, eyes darting. He looked up and asked, "When are they going to kill me?"

Carter shook his head and said.

"You are a long, long way from being dead."

Hussain looked at him numbly.

"I don't understand."

The end, when it came, had come with jarring suddenness. The jury had been deliberating for five days. The staff told us they heard occasional shouts, some laughter, and a lot of silence through the jury room door.

After three days, the jury sent out a note saying they were deadlocked. This would have meant a sentence of life imprisonment or less as a vote for death had to be unanimous. The judge brought the jury in and told them,

"If you cannot reach a unanimous decision, the defendant will be sentenced to life without the possibility of release or perhaps less. You will have to decide. The law and the Court prefer that you reach a unanimous decision, and I encourage you to work hard to reach such a decision."

Carter's apoplectic objection,

"Your Honor, we assume that the majority of the jury is in favor of death; you are telling the minority to surrender and that if they did not do so, the entire panel would be stuck longer in Guantanamo. This is as close to ordering a death sentence as possible."

When nothing happened for the next two days, we had our hopes up that the judge had failed to force a death verdict. We could do little but sit, chat, and pace. Every time the phone rang, hearts would jump, and the office would go completely silent. When the jury went back to their quarters after deliberations ended for the day, it felt as if a truck was lifted off my back. Only then did I feel I could breathe and try to eat.

Mid-afternoon of the sixth day of deliberations, the phone rang, "Mr. Mendelson, Connor. They have a decision." I had a physical sense of a wall going up that would shield me and keep me ready to do whatever I needed to do to get through the next couple of hours. After the call, Carter, Jill, Grace, Moretti, Fredricks, and I looked at each other and gripped each other for strength.

Reyes sat in a corner, head bowed, lips moving. He looked up, crossed himself, looked to the ceiling, and crossed himself again.

I gathered the entire team. I said, "Working with you has been the highlight of my career. I don't know how this will turn out. It doesn't look good, but we did not fail. We were fighting forces more powerful than us. Each of you has done all you could do." Here, I choked up. "and I am so, so grateful to have worked with you and to have fought the battle with you. Whatever happens, please hold your heads high. No matter what the verdict is, I love you all."

There were hugs all around, and we walked in collective numbness through the two gates, across the cement courtyard, and into the courtroom.

We went back to tell Hussain there was a decision.

He said, "I think they will kill me."

I held his hands, "Look at me; this is the first of many steps. If they vote for death, you are still years, years away from anything bad happening to you. After it is over, we will figure out what is next, but this is just a step in the process."

After everyone was there, spectators, the press, and the judge; Hussain was brought into the court, then the jury, who did not look at him, or us. One juror, a male Marine Colonel, was crying silently, tears running down dripping. No effort to hide them. All this signaled that the verdict was not going to be good.

The verdict was read:

WE THE JURY FIND BEYOND A REASONABLE DOUBT THAT THE AGGRAVATION OUTWEIGHS THE MITIGATION. WE THE JURY FURTHER FIND THAT THE ACCUSED SHOULD BE SENTENCED TO DEATH.

There was an audible gasp, a few cheers, and a loud "thank God" from the spectator section. A couple of quiet fist bumps among the prosecutor's support staff. Willis stood, arms in triumph. Lawson and I both sat quietly, shoulders slumped but for different reasons. Jill, Fredricks, and Moretti hugged each other, crying silently. Carter sat shaking his head. Before I realized what was happening, the guards escorted Hussain from the courtroom. I stood and spoke to a guard.

"We need to go back and speak with Hussain." There were quizzical looks, and one of the guards said, "He's gone; we immediately took him back to Camp Seven."

I was stunned. Shock turned to rage.

"Look, we need to talk to him; He's just been sentenced to death, for God's sake. Can you get him back here?" The judge looked at the guards. The chief guard said, "It would be difficult."

My voice was shaking.

"Well, we need to see him. Can you order a visit for tonight?" Again a look between the judge and the guards.

Again, the Chief Guard spoke, "We're not really organized for a visit tonight."

The judge looked up.

"When can you organize a visit?"

"Couple of days, your honor."

"Not acceptable. I'm going to order you to organize a visit for 0900 tomorrow. Mr. Mendelson, that's the best I can do. You can write your client a note, and I'll make sure it gets to him."

The press was insufferable but necessary. My message was delivered in a voice more positive than I was feeling, "This is a step in the process. We'll appeal. The judge made huge errors. There is no risk Hussain al-Yemeni will actually be executed, given the judge's errors. He will almost certainly outlive me."

Brooks was the only one who seemed to understand the magnitude of our feelings. She asked, "You said weeks ago that you felt the way the judge was ruling was one-sided and that this was expected. Given that, can you explain why you are all so upset?"

"I can only explain it this way. A surgeon may have a very risky operation and still be upset if he loses a patient. We like Hussain. We care for his family. In the same way, the surgeon may know he did his best, but he still feels he failed if the patient dies. So that is similar to how we feel. There were huge obstacles. This was not a fair trial. But we still feel like we failed. That is the best explanation I can give."

I called Molly and Anabel, then Emily. Anabel and Molly were subdued, Emily sobbing. They'd lived this case, through me. It has had a significant impact on their lives. The girls had seen my worry about Hussain; they had endured the threats, Emily the abduction. Hussain was a part of their lives. Emily said, "It's like I know him. And now they want to kill him," and she began crying harder.

I got an email from Sanders.

Sorry how things turned out. Hope you are okay. If I had to do it again, I don't know. I think I'd do the same thing, but I'm not sure.

I'm selfishly glad this is over. Now I can get out of here, get back, and try to figure out my life. You, I suspect, will do the same. Hope we both come out okay.

Be well.

J.

The team called Hussain's family. The call was on speaker so the whole team could hear and participate. As Mohammed, our interpreter, and I spoke with his father and brothers, trying to explain the process, we could hear his mother crying loudly in the background. Finally, his father said, "I know you fought for my son. I think you kept your promise to treat my son as you would want your child treated. Allah will bless you. He will bless you all. Shukran. Thank you." As we hung up, tears flowed freely.

Mathot left a voice message: "I heard what happened. I sense you did all you could do. I know Hancock was really upset about something that came out during her testimony. Apparently, you went into things she felt she had to lie about. Don't know the details. If you get to Grinnell, I would love to have you visit."

Sitting in the office, we sat in silence. Then Moretti stood.

"I need to be alone. I'm going for a run." We all stood, and without saying much, we went in different directions. I sat in my room. Thinking, replaying the whole trial in my mind, yet trying not to think. I alternated between anger at Pierce and the President. Self-blame and pity. I sat in the dark, trying to come to terms with the fact the trial and very significant milestone in my life was over. I was both relieved and sad, despairing that it was finished.

Later, with no planning, the entire team ended up at my place. Sitting in my living room, each with a beverage of choice, there were tears, lots of tears, some laughter, and hugs. It was as though only a human touch could ease some of the pain we were collectively and individually feeling. Around midnight, the court reporters came by to offer their thoughts, which lightened the mood. Their consensus was,

"You are great lawyers who were fucked."

One of the reporters, a crusty guy, who'd been a court reporter in criminal trials for over twenty years, said, "When this started, I wanted your client to get death. But, when he spoke to the jury, it was all I could do not to cry. I was so moved. I would not have given him death."

It was a sad celebration full of despair, anger, laughter, and joy. The source of joy, we would all get to go home soon.

Things wound down around 4:00 a.m.

Up at seven, with sour stomachs and throbbing heads, Carter, Fredricks, Jill, Grace, Reyes, and I met for breakfast of eggs, grits, and coffee. Lots of grits to absorb the alcohol. Lots of coffee. We planned to visit Hussain, to sit with him, to share his pain, and try to help him gain courage and strength. Or perhaps to get some courage and strength from him. When we sat down and heard Hussain ask about being killed, Carter said, "Hussain, we're a long way from being killed. And we are going to fight every step of the way."

There was silence. Then a quiet smile.

"Shukran, thank you. What happens next?"

I shrugged and said, "There is a process called an appeal. It will take years. We predict that at least your sentence will be set aside. This trial was very unfair."

"So I'm still here waiting, waiting to die here whether they kill me or not. I will die here. Is that true?"

"Perhaps," I shrugged again.

"Really, nothing will change, at least for several years. I'm sorry, but that's the way it is."

Hussain began an angry rant.

"You don't care. You are like all Americans. You are like the woman. You can do nothing. You did nothing. You are animals. And he looked at me. I suspect that you are secretly happy, Jew."

Carter interrupted Hussain, "I think we are all tired. We'll come back tomorrow. Perhaps then we will all feel less anxious."

"Don't bother."

"No, we'll come back."

There were no hugs as we left, only insults. Driving away, Carter said, "That was fucking special. We work our guts out for that."

I replied, "We're upset. For all the bluster, he's upset. Twelve people just told him they wanted him dead—heavy shit."

The next day Hussain greeted us with embarrassed apologies.

"Mr. Connor, I am so sorry I insulted you. I am ashamed, and I beg you to forgive me."

I nodded. Smiled. Gave him a long hug.

"Hussain, of course, I forgive you. This is a difficult time for all of us. You know, when we first met, you wanted us to leave. And the truth is we would have been happy to leave. But now, when we must leave at least for a time. I am sad. And I will miss sitting here in this dreadful place with you. But we will see each other again, and I look forward to that."

We explained that appellate lawyers would take over representing him but that we were still his lawyers and his friends and would be both until the end of his life or ours, whichever came first. I told him that his father had promised me a place in heaven and that I expected to get to heaven before him and would greet him there.

He looked at me.

"Ah, Mr. Connor, Perhaps I will greet you. You never know."

As we parted, we hugged, and he said, "Thank you, Mr. Connor. Thank you all. I know I was a difficult client, but you fought hard. I thank you. You showed courage. You all showed courage. I am grateful."

Then he said, "Ahbak." Softly. Then louder 'ahbak."

Mohammed translated. He says, "I love you."

I said to him, "Ahbak."

And we hugged again.

CHAPTER 72

The flight back to Andrews was almost unbearable. Judge, prosecution, Kuwait survivors, and families all happy or relieved.

The defense huddled morosely at the back of the plane. Few people approached. Fear or embarrassment kept them away from the losers.

Brooks sat down next to me.

"You okay?"

"Yes, no, fuck, I don't know. There is a part of me that's glad it's over, a part that is heavy into self-abuse, and a part that is very angry. This was such a fucking joke. Pierce is such a pig. I'm glad I'm done with this. Maybe done with the law."

She frowned, "You gonna take some time?"

"I honestly don't know what I'm going to do. I'm a mess. Just tired."

We talked a bit more, but she left when I put on my earbuds, pretended to be watching the film, and then closed my eyes.

As we got off the plane at Andrews, Lawson was waiting at the bottom of the steps.

"Can we speak a moment, Mr. Mendelson?"

My inner voice said, *Fuck you, go die.* But aloud, I said, "Sure."

"Look," he said, "I know this is a difficult situation, but you were a fierce opponent, and you have my respect." His hand was outstretched.

I took it and said, "Thanks. I need time to have perspective. You cheated."

He began to protest, and I raised my hand, "Sanders and the transcripts proved you guys cheated, and I have a huge problem with that. And the trial was a joke. So I'm not feeling too gracious now."

I paused, "But I appreciate the thought and this gesture."

A bus from the plane to the terminal, the wait for the ridiculous 'customs check,' and then I was outside, waiting for my luggage and a trip to the Marriott at Reagan, where I would try to sleep as I replayed every decision in a loop of "if onlys." The flight home was booked for 6 am the next day.

I heard a familiar voice,

"Sailor, you new in town? Need a ride?"

I stared, not sure what I had heard. Molly?

"What are you doing here?"

She shrugged.

"I just felt like I should be here. To see if you wanted a ride home. Canceled all my appointments. No rush to get home."

Over her shoulder, I saw Jill, Grace, and Sanders chatting. They all looked at me and smiled. Sanders nodded approvingly, and Jill gave a thumbs up.

I looked back at Molly.

"You sure?"

She gave me the look I loved so much.

"No, but…"

Then she reached out and gave me a hug big enough, long enough, tight enough to hold all my pain, anger, and darkness. And through my tears, for the first time in forever, I smiled.

CHAPTER 73

It took Molly and me eight days to complete the fourteen-hour drive home.

Leaving Andrews, we stopped at the McDonald's immediately across from the main gate, got some coffee, and, sitting in a red Formica booth, confronted the fact that we'd only spent one night together in over three years.

"Where do you want to go? Or do you want just to head straight back?"

She nursed her coffee.

"Got time, no rush. Beach, lake, mountains, resort, your preference."

She looked to her right and paused,

"Let's go south. See what feels right."

I laughed, "You've apparently forgotten that I need a plan. Life without a plan makes me break out in hives."

"Well, cowboy, you better be prepared to itch. Let's go south."

An hour out of DC, driving south on I-95, she said, "Williamsburg. Let's go to Williamsburg." Before I could give an opinion, she was on her phone tapping and reading, then tapping some more. She pulled out her purse and a credit card—more tapping, then an announcement.

"We're going to the Fife and Drum Inn. We'll take it from there."

The next few days, we were a couple spending their first weekend together, exploring attitudes, preferences, and bodies. But we already knew all that stuff, so the discoveries were subtle. How had she changed? How was I? How was I going to go forward? Were we going to go forward—together or not?

The third full day in Williamsburg, we stopped for a drink at the Hound's Tale. Sitting in the faux colonial lounge, Maker's for me, Malbec for Molly, we looked everywhere but at each other.

Finally, "Thanks for coming; it means a lot. But I'm confused and feeling at sea here. I mean, where are we going?"

"You mean the drive?"

A smile because she knew that was not what I meant.

"Obviously not," I tapped my glass nervously, "I mean, are we back together? Do I keep my place? What is going on?"

"Conner, you are just going to have to manage some uncertainty. I know that's not comfortable for you, but that is how it will have to be. I love you, but I'm still not sure if I want to live with you, but," she smiled, "I'm not sure I don't. So you're going to have to be patient."

On what ended up being the last day of our journey to normalcy, we were in a diner in Central Ohio. We were going to be home either that day or the next.

The phone buzzed, and Fredricks' name was on the screen. Pushing the slide button to the right to accept.

"Hi."

The response was breathless, choking.

"Hussain's dead. Those fuckers killed him."

"What?"

"Hussain is dead. SJA sent me a note early this morning that they found him dead. They claim he committed suicide. He supposedly hung himself. That is bullshit. No fucking way did he kill himself."

It was like a thick invisible shield descended. I could feel it. I could sense it. The shield that allowed me to function, but not feel the pain. Or be conscious of my heart breaking.

I vaguely heard Molly say, "Are you okay?"

I continued with Fredricks, "Is Carter there?"

"Not yet. He and Moretti will be here shortly."

"Can you do some things?"

"Of course."

"Tell the SJA we want an autopsy. Demand that he prohibits any destruction or modification of the scene. Reach out to NCIS and ask for an investigation. Put it all in writing." A pause.

"Then, when Mohammad comes in, we need to call his parents. Let Carter and Moretti know. We'll conference at eleven."

Disconnecting the call, I sat with my forehead resting between my thumbs, hands intertwined like a child's bridge. My mind was both blank and racing.

Molly interrupted my despair. I told her what had happened.

"Oh, Connor. What can I do?"

I snarled, "Not a Goddamn thing," as I got up from the table and walked outside the diner. I could mentally list tasks I would need to do, but they had no form. Call Brooks, Call Mathot, Call Jill, were just random thoughts.

Then tears, just a few, then a few more, then a torrent as the sadness, a dark sadness, washed over me. I'd had clients die before. Even a couple of suicides as the prospect of prison or shame overwhelmed them. But this was different. Murdered. Sudden, raw, unexpected, unlikely. Molly came outside and held me. And we just stood close in the parking lot.

And as we stood there, I had the sickening realization that perhaps my predictions that he would never be executed convinced Hancock or whoever to ensure that he died. Was my hubris somehow responsible for his murder?

Carter, Moretti, and I spoke, and their reactions were the same.

"No. Fucking. way."

A blank space of time later, Mohammad called. It was mid-afternoon in Saudi Arabia.

The phone call to his family was brutal. Part matter of fact: There is no easy way to say "your son is dead" other than just to say it. And we could not provide answers because what we knew we did not believe.

At the end, his father said, "Mr. Connor, I forgive you. I forgive you for failing to protect my son. I know you did your best, but in the end, you could not protect him, and they killed him. I hope our paths cross again in heaven so I can bless you. Shoukran, Thank you."

I then called Mathot. She answered with, "Connor, I really can't talk to you."

"Connie, what is going on? Did the CIA kill Hussain?"

"Connor, I am sorry, I just cannot talk to you. Good luck."

The phone went silent.

A few minutes later. The cell phone screen said BLOCKED NUMBER.

"Yes, this is Connor Mendelson."

"Mr. Mendelson, this is David Richardson. I am a lawyer with the Department of Justice. This call is being recorded. I have to tell you that. I have been tasked to remind you of the provisions of 50 USC section 421, which states that it is a crime to release the name or identifying information of present or former CIA agents. This crime carries up to ten years in prison. Do you understand what I am telling you?"

"I don't know who you are or why you are calling me but fuck you."

"Mr. Mendelson, do you hear and understand what I have told you? I want to be clear that you are aware of your obligations and understand them."

"Message received, motherfucker." I hung up.

Throughout all of this, as she drove. Molly wisely said little.

Brooks called.

"I know you've heard. Any comment?"

"He was murdered."

"Connor, on or off the record?"

"On the record. Look, I spent a lot of time with this guy. I know him. No way, none, did he commit suicide."

"Lawson says the realization that he would not get out drove him to suicide."

"That's bullshit. And when the autopsy is done, we'll know it was bullshit. There will be defensive injuries or drugs. No way did he hang himself. He was murdered, and the autopsy will prove that."

There was a pause. A much longer than normal pause.

"They didn't tell you? His body has been cremated. There will be no autopsy. According to the press release, let me find it here, ahh, here it is. According to Muslim custom, the body was disposed of in twenty-four hours. Following US policy, the body was cremated, and his remains will be returned to his family in due course. Connor, when were you told this happened?"

"Learned of it this morning. Why?"

"The press release said this all happened three days ago."

I sat back; I guess the phone was still at my ear, "Connor, are you there? Connor, Connor."

"Say that again. This all happened three days ago? They waited to tell us?"

"So it would seem."

I could feel a burden of emotion as clearly as an ocean swimmer feels a wave. It just buried me. But it has no real name. Grief? Sadness? Despair? Whatever it was clouded my vision, leaving me feeling there was no light or joy in the world. I had no words.

"Samantha, I gotta go. I just can't think right now. I'll call you back."

I tried to explain to Molly what the last hour had revealed but I was too angry and felt it was not right to burden her with my grief. I could feel my wall that had been crumbling beginning to rebuild. But I had no way and no words or thoughts to halt the construction.

CHAPTER 74

The stages of grief are denial, anger, bargaining, depression, and acceptance.

I couldn't progress to acceptance. I only had three: This cannot be, followed by sadness, followed by, – those motherfuckers killed him. Then over and over and over again. Each part interchangeable. Intellectually I knew I had to accept that Hussain was dead and his murder was successfully covered up. I paced aimlessly, wandering from room to room and touching a desk or chair, straightening a slightly crooked picture, opening then closing the refrigerator taking food out and either eating mindlessly or not eating it but setting it on the counter and putting it back minutes later.

The phone buzzed periodically, Reyes, Carter, Moretti. We had the same conversation over and over. "No way. They killed him." Anger, tempered by the certainty that, in the end, there was nothing we could do to counter the government's narrative.

And we were right. My statement that Hussain was murdered was discounted "as the ramblings of an upset lawyer who could simply not accept reality. The US would not murder his client. Hussain al-Yemeni committed suicide. It happens. End of story."

CHAPTER 75

Brooks called.

"I tried your firm's number and was told you resigned. What's the deal?"

"It was just not possible to go back to the usual. I just need a break, a long break. Probably time to do something else. Right now, I'm playing a lot of golf, relaxing, and trying to find perspective. I'm still pretty fucked up and bitter about all this. I'm kind of back with Molly. Hoping it will work out. We're still living apart but together. Sort of. Life is uncertain these days."

As the conversation wound down, Brooks said, "I found that client of yours, John Wilson."

"Really? He's still alive? I'm surprised."

"Yes. I tracked him through his parole. Got out of prison and went to Somerset, Kentucky. Seemed to straighten his life out. He lives with his daughter in Jebez, Kentucky. Not too many Wilsons there, so I was able to find him by calling the local police. They knew him as a pretty good guy. I've spoken with his daughter several times. She told me that at some point, he decided prison was no life. Learned to weld and worked until he couldn't work anymore. Got married. Had three kids. She said he was a good dad. He was ashamed of his life before he met his wife, her mother.

"He remembers you. Melissa, the daughter, told me that when the al-Yemeni case was on TV, he'd say, 'That guy was my lawyer.'" She laughed. "Apparently, no one believed him."

I was silent for a bit.

"Wow. That's good to know," Another pause. In a thick voice, "Hey. Thanks for finding him. Means more than I thought it would."

CHAPTER 76

A month after we learned of Hussain's death, I received a call from Sargent Lopez, "General Ward would like to meet with you and your team. You have been booked on a flight Thursday morning and a return flight Friday. You'll be staying at the Ritz Carleton in Pentagon City."

"What if that is not convenient?"

Lopez was almost laughing. "Really, Connor, get serious. This is not really optional. See you Thursday."

When I arrived, I found Jill, Moretti, and Reyes with Fredricks and Carter in Carter's office. Styrofoam cups of coffee in hands. The conversation drifted between anger and acceptance. Hussain was dead, murdered. And there was fuck all we could do about it. Gallows humor masked our collective pain. In a way, we were sitting Shiva, but it was only for an hour.

Lopez knocked and announced us into Ward's office.

We took chairs. He looked at each of us.

"Of course, you understand this team is being disbanded. You all need to be read off the various programs, and your clearances pertaining to this case are being suspended. You have a meeting at three this afternoon at the Pentagon. You'll be required to sign documents acknowledging your obligations to continue protecting classified information, including information about the torture, al-Yemeni's death, and the identities of any CIA agents. Also, the transcript of Hancock's testimony will remain classified for the next twenty years."

He paused and looked at me.

"No press conferences, no interviews, No more speculation about what happened. Silence is part of your obligation. Your contract with the office ends Saturday. What the ACLU does is up to them. Ms. Moretti and Ms. Hanson, your employment ends Saturday as well, but of course, your obligation to secrecy continues. Major Carter, You will be receiving orders for Fort Sill. This will be your terminal assignment; not sure how much time you have left, but I suspect it will be mainly for out processing and final leave. Mr. Reyes, if you want to stay with the office, you'll be transferred to another team. Let me know in a week what you want. Major Fredricks. I've recommended that you do victim advocate work at Quantico. I understand you have eighteen months left on this tour; perhaps you'll stay in, perhaps not, but I think this is a good position for you."

Harriet nodded.

"Thank you, sir."

"A bit of advice, which I think will make you angry, but I need to say it. I don't know if your client committed suicide or was killed. It could be either. I gather there was a lot of panic when his body was discovered, which might explain how quickly the body was disposed of but who knows? But let's assume he was murdered."

Ward paused.

"One of the realities of the military is that people die in service of a greater good. We can argue if attacking this hill or this town is the best approach, but when the decision is made, the military accepts that often people will die in furtherance of that decision. I hope, in time, you will see how that applies here." I snarled, "Death in combat is different than being murdered."

Ward looked at me.

"Is it really so different? Dead is dead. I may disagree with the objective of secrecy, hiding the torture. I know you disagree. But a decision may have been made, and like many military decisions, death follows. Good commanders learn to live with the consequences of their decisions. Subordinates learn to accept that some things are out of their control. I don't know if this helps, but I'll ask you to think about it."

He paused again.

"I know you think I'm an asshole. I know this has not been a great relationship. But I really do respect the work you do, the work you did. I make no excuse when I say there are, were, multiple pressures. I did the best I could. I know you think it wasn't much. Maybe you're right."

He stood.

"You are expected at the Pentagon at three. Boxes will be available so you can clean out your office. I wish you all good luck, and I hope our paths cross under less complicated circumstances."

As Ward advised, we were required to sign documents acknowledging our continued obligation to secrecy and silence at the Pentagon. Arriving back at the Ritz Carleton, where Jill, Moretti, and I were to spend the night, before heading to our homes the following day, we all retired to the bar.

Jill voiced the obvious, "Was Ward in on it? Do you think he knew what the deal was? Do you think he knew it was all theatre?"

Carter shrugged, "I just don't know. It really doesn't make any difference. It is what it is. Hussain is dead. We're muzzled. Hancock's testimony will be secret. They certainly made that clear. And, the truth is no one cares about a murdered terrorist."

CHAPTER 77

Dinner was a wake and a celebration. Over mounds of hummus and baba ganoush, roast lamb and chicken with lots of wine, we laughed and cried as moments of joy and sorrow were re-lived. Promises of undying love and respect were made. Futures discussed. Jill had two new cases. One in Detroit and one in Texas. Moretti thought she was no longer toxic and hoped to return to Brooklyn. Carter said he "was "gonna coast for awhile. Live off the pension and see what feels right." Fredricks thought that she would try to be a capital defender.

"I think the Marines will let me out early if I push. They owe me that."

Reyes thought he'd "just move to another team, see how it goes."

"And you, Connor?"

"All I know for sure is I'm done with the law. Beyond that, I have no idea."

At one a.m. in the lobby, indifferent to other people returning from wherever they had been, we hugged and said our goodbyes. We whispered how much we meant to and loved one another. Then as we parted, we all began the long journey to the rest of our lives.

CHAPTER 78

In the lobby of the CIA Headquarters, there is a white wall with bronze stars. The stars recognize the memory of CIA agents killed in service to the country. Victoria Hancock's retirement ceremony took place in the lobby, attended by many of her present and former peers. But this was different because the President was also attending.

After the President read the various letters of congratulations, he continued, "Ms. Hancock. I have one other duty here today before we conclude. The director and I have decided that you should receive an additional honor. The Distinguished Career Intelligence Medal. The highest award available to a CIA agent."

There were cheers and hearty applause before and after the proclamations were read to the audience. The proclamation about her career referred to Hancock's clandestine service, her anti-terrorist activities, and her leadership role at the CIA. In addition, it referred obliquely to the creation and implementation of interrogation protocols used to great effect in the war on terror.

"Ms. Hancock's work both inside the United States and overseas, and her implementation of those protocols were at great personal hardship." The proclamation concluded, "Victoria Hancock's dedication to service was exemplified by her secret testimony against Hussain al-Yemeni, which was instrumental in securing a conviction and death sentence."

A reception followed the President's departure. Among the well-wishers was Connie Mathot, who had flown to DC for the ceremony. Mathot touched her glass of single malt Scotch to Hancock's red wine.

"The recognition is well deserved. You must be very proud. What's next? R and R?"

"For a bit. I will probably go to Hawaii for a while. But I have offers from Raytheon and Core Civic for pretty good money. I suspect I'll take one of those."

They chatted for a bit as well-wishers lined up behind Mathot.

As Mathot began to walk away, Hancock reached out, pulled her close, and said, "Thanks for your help, my friend. I appreciate it."

"You're welcome. Too bad about the suicide."

"Yes, a fucking tragedy. Would have loved to see the look on Mendelson's face when he heard,"

For a few seconds, the retired agents made eye contact and smiled knowingly. Then Mathot turned and walked toward the buffet table, and Hancock pivoted to receive more compliments.

Epilogue

My drive from the West Texas Detention Center had not calmed me down. Sitting alone at the overly cold bar at three-thirty in the afternoon, an unfinished double barely dented my anger.

The ACLU had called again. This time they asked me to go to West Texas to tour the detention facility and "see if there was anything a lawyer could do."

When I'd asked, "Why me?"

The response was, "We need someone familiar with concentration camps, and after Guantanamo, you are the first guy that came to mind."

When I suggested I was retired, "done with that shit, trying to get some perspective. Trying to figure out my life and my future," they said the magic words, "Can you really sit by and do nothing? Just make the trip. Please. We need your perspective."

So I flew from middle America to El Paso. I fought with some officious Department of Homeland Security lawyers for a couple of days and finally was told, "You can look around. You can stay for an hour or so if you can stand it. And then after that, we'll discuss if you can go back. If you want to."

When I walked into the facility, it was hard to tell which was worse, the smell, the heat, or the noise. The smell was an invisible wall. It stopped me. I couldn't move forward, couldn't take a full breath without feeling like I might puke. I stood for several minutes, coming to terms with the stench. The mixture of sweat, piss, baby shit, fear, old food, and god knows what else resulted in a stink like nothing I'd ever encountered. When my senses finally dulled to indifference, I slowly ventured into the large brown tent. It was about fifty yards long from the entrance and twenty-five feet high to the top of the sharply slanted ceiling. The smell and the South Texas heat made me sweat. Sweat that ran in visible streams down my face, soaking my shirt and turning it dark blue.

The din was a babel of babies crying, men, women, and children shouting, shrieking, or sobbing quietly. They were talking in several languages, mainly Spanish. But also Mexican Indian dialects, unintelligible. Several kids wore snot strings that spiderwebbed from their noses to their knees. Some children sat motionless while others involuntarily rocked back and forth, left and right. Others, some wrapped in thin, shiny metallic blankets, looked around frantically for a glimpse of parents who were not there and who they would probably never see again. Women sang or cooed to children they held and comforted. I would learn that these children often were not their own. Some sat completely still, eyes dead, hope gone, quietly defeated. Others keened a frantic wail. Collectively they held a grief known only to parents whose children had been taken from them by men with guns. And laws.

I walked with my escort, a stocky black man dressed like all the guards in a green uniform. A small boy, about five or six, with lots of black hair, skin the shade of light toffee, and black eyes, stood in front of me.

"Senor, senor." He held his arms up. "Senor, Me ayudarás a encontrar a mis padres?" Will you help me find my parents?

Instinctively I picked the boy up, so his butt was riding on my arm. His arms went around my neck. I could feel his heart beating rapidly, and my memory flashed on my daughters, Anabel and Emily, and the times I'd held them to shield them from the monsters under their beds or in their dreams.

"Gracias, senor. Me ayudarás a encontrar a mis padres?" As I was about to say something to comfort the boy, the escort grabbed him around the waist and yanked him away from me. He then literally pushed the boy away, who now looked wide-eyed with betrayal

"Alejate de el." Get away from him. "Vete." Go away. The boy just stood and looked at the escort and me and dropped to his knees. Staring with wounded eyes.

"Why did you do that?"

"You are not allowed to have contact with the detainees. You were told that."

"Christ, he was a little boy."

"Sir, you were told the rules. I could end the visit now."

The escort looked at me, eyes fixed on mine, silently begging. Slowly shook his head in small movements, side-to-side. A silent plea – 'Man, I gotta follow the rules. Please understand.'

Touring the facility, I became sad, sad deep into my bones.

'It has come to this,' I thought, *'What the fuck has gone wrong with the United States?'*

Then I thought I saw a phantom across the room - could it be her? I discretely changed directions to get a better view of the pasty-faced, middle-aged woman wearing the same green uniform as my escort. Wandering a few steps to my left, looking across the sea of defeated men, troubled women, and distraught children, I got a clear view. Seeing her again, seeing that half smile, those icy eyes, I somehow prevented myself from pointing and shouting. I just stared. Perhaps sensing my glare, she looked up. Our eyes locked in a moment of mutual disgust. She turned and gave a direct shake of her head, then pulled a microphone off her shoulder and spoke into it. I knew that my visit was going to be over. I heard my escort's radio crackle, and then, "Sir, we've got a situation, and we need to cut your visit short."

I protested and was still protesting as I was gently but clearly hustled out the door. A liaison officer met me a minute later, full of apologies.

"I'm so sorry, Mr. Mendelson. Unfortunately, we've got a situation. This is for your safety."

"Bullshit," I was nearly spitting. "That monster works here, and she wanted me out of here."

"I don't know what you're talking about, sir."

"Tell me that wasn't Victoria Hancock."

"Sir, I'm not allowed to discuss individual names. Especially leadership."

"Ah! So she's leadership, and her name is secret? That fucking figures."

"Sir, calm down. If you call me tomorrow, we can discuss future visits."

"Fuck, calm. How can you people employ that woman?" My voice was trembling. Then breathing deeply, silently counting to regain my composure, I said, "Okay. I'll call tomorrow."

But I knew I didn't need to call to know I'd never be allowed back in that camp. Not while she worked there. There was no way she was going to let me back in there.

I walked through the gravel parking lot, scorched to an eye-watering white brilliance. As I walked, my anger returned, and as I tried to find the button on the key to unlock the car, my hands shook. Driving back to the El Paso hotel, I had to stop to calm down. Sitting by that South Texas road, breathing hard, sweating, and silently cursing, trying not to vomit from rage or shame, my thoughts returned to Hussain al-Yemeni, my client and my friend. I flashed back to the first time I'd heard of Hermione, Victoria Hancock. A torturer. Now she was warehousing and destroying Mexican families. An even worse version of Guantanamo had moved north and west.

Back in my room, the internet revealed that Hancock had been hired by CoreCivic, which ran the chain of detention centers. She was being paid two hundred and forty thousand a year, plus stock options in addition to her CIA pension of over one hundred thousand dollars per year. I also saw an article that suggested that if there was a new administration in Washington, she might resurface in a senior CIA leadership position. Possibly even as Director.

I knew that Pierce had become the TJAG of the Air Force, the head of the Air Force Lawyers. General Ward retired and was an immigration judge double dipping at the government trough, pension, and salary. Lawson, dubbed by the media as "The Hero of Guantanamo Bay," was teaching law at Pepperdine University. Fredricks is out of the Marines in Savannah, Georgia, letting her hair grow out and working with the Georgia Capital Defenders and doing an excellent job. Moretti is back in Brooklyn, restored to the good graces of the public defender's office. Reyes ultimately left the Defense organization and works as an investigator for a capital defender office in Alabama. Carter, as he predicted, "is blissfully coasting."

And here I am, sitting in a hotel room in El Paso, wondering for the first time in a year if I should get back into this shit. Rethinking all the promises I'd made to myself. There had to be some way to attack the atrocities happening at that detention center and all the other concentration camps that the US was now running on the Southern border. A thought began to percolate, "They said they needed a lawyer's help?"

I called Molly. To see what she thinks.

Disclaimer

This is a work of fiction and any similarities to people, living or dead is both unintentional and coincidental. That is true.

But it is a work of fiction set in a real place where real people who I know and dealt with are actually working so I must say a bit more.

Connor Mendelson's good qualities are derived from the many wonderful defense lawyers who I worked with over my career. Whatever negative qualities he has are a figment of my imagination. While some may think I tried to model Connor after myself, he is thinner, smarter and shrewder than I would ever hope to be.

Similarly, Mendelson's team of lawyers Moretti, Carter and Fredricks are composites of men and women I dealt with over my many years as a criminal defense lawyer. While they have the good qualities of the men and women I worked with during my time at Guantanamo, their flaws are entirely fictional.

The several chief defense counsels with whom I worked were nothing like General Ward. The real chief defense counsels were always completely supportive of the defense mission. Three, Dwight Sullivan, Steven David and John Baker are, in my view, undiscovered American heroes. But the others I worked with also strongly believed in the obligation to provide truly effective representation to those incarcerated in Guantanamo.

While I routinely disagreed with the prosecutor's I dealt with during my GTMO years I have no question about their patriotism and their belief they were "doing the right thing."

I practiced in front of two military judges in my time at Guantanamo. Col. James Pohl who is nothing like Judge Pierce and is someone I would have loved to have gotten to know better.

I also practiced before Col. Vance Spath. For those who care, Col. Spath has been clearly and in my opinion accurately described by the DC Circuit Court of Appeals in US v. Nashiri (No. 18-1279).

Samantha Brooks takes her wisdom and other good qualities from my friend Carol Rosenberg of the NY Times who has been described as a "national treasure." Any negative qualities Brooks has, are my creation.

Finally, I acknowledge that the book was cleared for release by what ever agencies were charged with reviewing my submissions. While others have had problems with pre-publication review, I found the agencies to be reasonable and their redactions minimal. Perhaps that is because they finally understood that this is a work of fiction and that the characters and events portrayed here do not exist and did not actually occur.

Acknowledgements

As a first-time author I owe tremendous thanks to the many who supported me in this journey. I am reluctant to identify them by name because I will invariably omit someone who deserves recognition. But I am especially grateful to Maia Williams and my friends in the San Miguel de Allende Wild Muse Writer's group who encouraged me, criticized my work when appropriate, and were incredibly supportive in this journey.

Also important were my several beta readers, Craig Thomson, Peter Uhrig, Kari Siirala, Susan Boland, Michael Schmidt, Dorothy Wallstein, as well as Ray Auckerman. They provided valuable insight, guidance and support.

Special thanks to Molly Kathleen Robertson, an old friend who agreed to edit this work and provided invaluable contributions. Her support was critical and there are not enough words of appreciation to convey my gratitude.

Finally, thanks to my children, Amanda and Claire and my wife Linda who endured years of what they called my pretrial fugue states, were subjected to countless practice cross examinations and endured hours of practice opening statements and final arguments.

I could not have had my career or written this book without your love and support.

CPSIA information can be obtained
at www.ICGtesting.com
Printed in the USA
LVHW041537040323
740934LV00004B/132